Chinese
Folktales

Chinese
Folktales

Introduction by Xiulu Wang & Chuanji Hu

General Editor: Jake Jackson

FLAME TREE
PUBLISHING

This is a FLAME TREE Book

FLAME TREE PUBLISHING
6 Melbray Mews
Fulham, London SW6 3NS
United Kingdom
www.flametreepublishing.com

First published 2024
Copyright © 2024 Flame Tree Publishing Ltd

24 26 28 27 25
1 3 5 7 9 8 6 4 2

ISBN: 978-1-80417-782-2

The tales in this book are selected and edited from these original sources:
The Jade Story Book: Stories from the Orient by Penryhn W. Coussens, 1922 (New York:
Duffield & Company); *Edmund Dulac's Fairy-Book: Fairy Tales of the Allied Nations,*
1924 (New York: George H. Doran Company); *Some Chinese Ghosts* by Lafcadio Hearn,
1887 (Boston: Roberts Brothers); *Chinese Folklore Tales* by Rev. J. Macgowan, D.D., 1910
(London: Macmillan and Co. Limited, London); *A Chinese Wonder Book* by Norman
Hinsdale Pitman, 1919 (New York: E.P. Dutton & Co.); *Strange Stories from a Chinese Studio,
Vols I & II,* by Pu Songling, translated by Herbert A. Giles, 1880 (London: Thomas De La
Rue and Co.); *Entombed Alive and Other Songs, Ballads, etc. from the Chinese* by George
Carter Stent, 1878 (London: William H. Allen and Co.); *The Chinese Fairy Book*, Ed. Dr. R.
Wilhelm, Trans. Frederick H. Martens, 1921 (New York: Frederick A. Stokes Company).
The Ballad of Mulan is licensed by The Tsoi Dug Foundation, translation © 2007 Feng, Xin-ming.

Printed and bound in China

Contents

Series Foreword

STRETCHING BACK to the oral traditions of thousands of years ago, tales of heroes and disaster, creation and conquest have been told by many different civilizations in many different ways. Their impact sits deep within our culture even though the detail in the tales themselves are a loose mix of historical record, transformed narrative and the distortions of hundreds of storytellers.

Today the language of mythology lives with us: our mood is jovial, our countenance is saturnine, we are narcissistic and our modern life is hermetically sealed from others. The nuances of myths and legends form part of our daily routines and help us navigate the world around us, with its half truths and biased reported facts.

The nature of a myth is that its story is already known by most of those who hear it, or read it. Every generation brings a new emphasis, but the fundamentals remain the same: a desire to understand and describe the events and relationships of the world. Many of the great stories are archetypes that help us find our own place, equipping us with tools for self-understanding, both individually and as part of a broader culture.

For Western societies it is Greek mythology that speaks to us most clearly. It greatly influenced the mythological heritage of the ancient Roman civilization and is the lens through which we still see the Celts, the Norse and many of the other great peoples and religions. The Greeks themselves learned much from their neighbours, the Egyptians, an older culture that became weak with age and incestuous leadership.

It is important to understand that what we perceive now as mythology had its own origins in perceptions of the divine and the rituals of the sacred. The earliest civilizations, in the crucible of the Middle East, in the Sumer of the third millennium BCE, are the source to which many of the mythic archetypes can be traced. As humankind collected together in cities for the first time, developed writing and industrial scale agriculture, started to irrigate the rivers and attempted to control rather than be at the mercy of its environment, humanity began to write down its tentative explanations of natural events, of floods and plagues, of disease.

Early stories tell of Gods (or god-like animals in the case of tribal societies such as African, Native American or Aboriginal cultures) who are crafty and use their wits to survive, and it is reasonable to suggest that these were the first rulers of the gathering peoples of the earth, later elevated to god-like status with the distance of time. Such tales became more political as cities vied with each other for supremacy, creating new Gods, new hierarchies for their pantheons. The older Gods took on primordial roles and became the preserve of creation and destruction, leaving the new gods to deal with more current, everyday affairs. Empires rose and fell, with Babylon assuming the mantle from Sumeria in the 1800s BCE, then in turn to be swept away by the Assyrians of the 1200s BCE; then the Assyrians and the Egyptians were subjugated by the Greeks, the Greeks by the Romans and so on, leading to the spread and assimilation of common themes, ideas and stories throughout the world.

The survival of history is dependent on the telling of good tales, but each one must have the 'feeling' of truth, otherwise it will be ignored. Around the firesides, or embedded in a book or a computer, the myths and legends of the past are still the living materials of retold myth, not restricted to an exploration of origins. Now we have devices and global communications that give us unparalleled access to a diversity of traditions. We can find out about Native American, Indian, Chinese and tribal African mythology in a way that was denied to our ancestors, we can find connections, match the archaeology, religion and the mythologies of the world to build a comprehensive image of the human experience that is endlessly fascinating.

The stories in this book provide an introduction to the themes and concerns of the myths and legends of their respective cultures, with a short introduction to provide a linguistic, geographic and political context. This is where the myths have arrived today, but undoubtedly over the next millennia, they will transform again whilst retaining their essential truths and signs.

Jake Jackson
General Editor

Introduction to Chinese Folktales

HINESE CIVILIZATION is one of the most fascinating and enduring in the world. Over its vast history, it has cultivated a remarkably opulent tradition of folklore. Often infused with a hint of mystique, Chinese folktales are characterized by intriguing plots and extremely rich imagination, and for thousands of years, they have been a most vibrant source of inspiration for the Chinese literary tradition. At the same time, these stories contain a wealth of details and subtleties of Chinese culture, providing contemporary readers with a unique window into the intricacies of ancient Chinese wisdom, folk beliefs and ways of life.

Chinese Folktales: Echoes of Ancient Marvels

Among the earliest collections of Chinese folklore is the *Shan-hai Ching* 山海經, also known as *The Classic of Mountains and Seas*. With its origins possibly dating back to the fourth century BCE, this Chinese classic is a wondrous book of mythic geography and tales of fantastical creatures. It introduces us to awe-inspiring figures like *Pangu*, who cleaved open the earth and heavens with a mighty axe, and *Nüwa*, a goddess with a serpent body, credited as the creator of humanity.

Around 350 CE, the historian Gan Bao compiled a very influential book of Chinese folktales. This canonical work, titled *The Soushen ji* 搜神記 (variously translated as *In Search of the Sacred, In Search of the Supernatural* and *Anecdotes about Spirits and Immortals*), includes 464 stories about Chinese deities and supernatural phenomena. In Chinese literary history, it is recognized as a pioneering work within a literary genre known as 'Zhiguai Xiaoshuo' (志怪小說) or 'Marvel Tales'. This genre of writing focuses on extraordinary events and is characterized by the depiction of spirits, ghosts and supernatural occurrences.

Another noteworthy collection is *Liaozhai Zhiyi* 聊齋誌異, a compendium of classical Chinese marvel tales penned by the seventeenth-century literary maestro, Pu Songling. Initially rendered into English by Herbert Giles as *Strange Tales from a Chinese Studio* in 1880, this collection holds a prestigious status as the foremost repository of Chinese marvel tales, earning acclaim both within China and abroad. Samuel Wells Williams extolled it as 'a flawless work distinguished by its pure language and elegant style'. It is even listed as one of Jorge Luis Borges' favourite books.

During the eighteenth and nineteenth centuries, foreign readers started to show a keen interest in Chinese folktales. Among the pioneers in introducing Chinese folklore to the West were Lafcadio Hearn, a Japanese writer of Greek-Irish heritage, and German sinologist Richard Wilhelm. Hearn's *Some Chinese Ghosts* (1887) offers a retelling of six Chinese ghost stories, reflecting a deep fascination with the 'weird beauty' of Chinese folktales. Wilhelm's compilation, *The Chinese Fairy Book* (1921), contains 73 enthralling tales. As described in its preface, these fairy tales and legends exude an Oriental essence reminiscent of *The Thousand and One Nights*, and an exotic flavour that is distinctly Chinese. Both collections have remained widely read and appreciated to this day, and readers can discover some of the stories from these collections in the current book.

The Fusion of Oral and Written Traditions

Folktales are typically seen as integral to oral tradition, setting them apart from official historical records. Yet, when it comes to Chinese folklore, the situation is more intricate. From its inception, the Chinese folktale tradition has been a fusion of both oral and written traditions.

Unlike European folktales, which usually feature sailors as storytellers and draw inspiration from maritime adventures, Chinese folktales are largely rooted in the nation's agricultural heritage, celebrating the deep connection between the land and its people. In this collection of stories, you will find the legend of the Silkworm Lady, the guardian goddess of silk culture, and tales such as 'The Herd Boy and the Weaving Maiden', which eloquently expresses the desire of ordinary or impoverished labourers, such as cowherds or peasants, to marry and start a family.

While common folks such as peasants and weavers were important tellers of folktales, Chinese literati also played a crucial role in preserving and disseminating these narratives. In ancient China, the invention of written script occurred remarkably early, and the meticulous inscriptions found on oracle bones and gold scripts stand as tangible proof of this nascent written tradition. The penchant for written documentation extended to Chinese folktales, where written accounts became intertwined with oral traditions from an early stage. These tales were not just recorded; they also evolved into literary treasures in the hands of successive generations of Chinese literati. A case in point would be Pu Songling's *Strange Tales from a Chinese Studio*. According to accounts from friends and family, Pu Songling dedicated over two decades to gathering this treasure trove of tales. He would sit by the roadside, conversing with passers-by to collect stories, and would even venture into the countryside to seek out people who could share their tales. While Pu Songling did not originate these stories, his skilful penmanship and storytelling prowess elevated them to the status of classics. The unique interplay between oral and written records has therefore been instrumental in shaping Chinese folklore tradition.

The Kaleidoscope of Chinese Folktales

Folktales can be tricky to categorize precisely. In 1978, Nai-tung Ting, drawing from a rich source of approximately 7,000 stories, put together a collection of Chinese folktales. This comprehensive work, known as *A Type Index of Chinese Folktales*, follows the model of the Aarne-Thompson-Uther tale-type system (often referred to as ATU Index). Ting classifies Chinese folktales into primary types, including animal tales, ordinary tales, humorous tales and formula tales.

While the ATU Index is a useful tool in folklore studies, it has been criticized for its Eurocentric focus and limited inclusion of fairy tales from other cultures. In the case of Chinese folklore, many tales do not neatly fit into any single category. Instead of attempting to pigeonhole these stories into rigid classifications, it may be more appropriate to acknowledge their diverse and multifaceted nature. The world of Chinese folktales resembles a kaleidoscope – captivating, ever-changing, and even somewhat bewildering. One way of obtaining a more nuanced and comprehensive understanding of Chinese folktales is by delving into the intricate roles of characters and the overarching themes embedded within these tales.

Chinese folktales feature a diverse cast of characters, ranging from mythological figures with exceptional abilities to ordinary individuals struggling in their everyday lives. The characters in Chinese folktales generally include animals, mortals and supernatural beings. Animal characters, whether real (such as cows, magpies, carps or rabbits) or mythical (like dragons, phoenixes, the bird with nine heads, or the fox with nine tails), are often depicted as having certain human qualities and share a close connection with human life.

As for human characters, Chinese folktales feature individuals from all walks of life, encompassing roles like generals, judges, scholars, officials, landowners, peasants, cowherds, vagabonds, skilled craftsmen, magicians and apprentices. These stories explore the ethics and morals of mundane life, celebrate secular virtues, and record the marvels that ordinary people either experience or learn of in their daily lives.

The supernatural realm is the most intricate domain in Chinese folklore, populated by different kinds of gods, deities, spirits and ghosts. Among them, fox spirits and ghosts are the most prevalent and prominent figures. Some of these supernatural beings may bring blessings and good luck, while others evoke fear and retribution.

Then, there is also a distinctive group of characters who straddle the line between the mortal and the supernatural: the accomplished monks and the Taoist priests. Some of them are capable of immortality, while others are skilled in capturing demons and banishing ghosts. Most of them are gifted with the power to foretell the future, draw charms, or place spells on others. These enigmatic figures contribute to the complexities in

Chinese folklore by symbolizing an enduring link between the mystical and the everyday.

The Unifying Power of Tao in Chinese Folklore

Among the vast array of animals, mortals and supernatural beings depicted in Chinese folklore, there exists a deeper unifying belief in the 'Unity of Man and Heaven'. This profound concept emphasizes the interrelation of all beings and their bond with *Tao*.

Tao is a central pillar of Chinese philosophy and spirituality. It represents the origin of the universe and the fundamental principle that governs all existence. It encompasses the idea of living in harmony with nature, recognizing the interconnectedness of all things, and embracing balance and equilibrium. Tao is eternal, all-pervasive, absolute, and invisible to the human eye. It is embodied in people's virtuous deeds. Therefore, *Tao* and *Te* (or 'virtue') are one and the same. In Lao Tzu's *Tao Te Ching*, he closely links the two, suggesting that virtue is derived from *Tao*, and it is the quality of acting in accordance with the principles of *Tao*.

Within the context of Chinese folklore, the *Tao* serves as a potential guiding force that reinforces the significance of equilibrium, reverence for nature and the celebration of virtue. In the triad of animals, mortals and supernatural beings, none reigns as the absolute dominator. Instead, their interactions must be delicately balanced. Secular virtues such as empathy, courage, humility and love serve as guiding beacons across these three realms. Virtuous acts are met with rewards, while malevolent deeds are punished. In Chinese folktales, this moral compass extends its influence even into the afterlife, where the consequences of one's actions continue to hold significance and meaning.

The power of *Tao* applies universally, whether one is an emperor, a monk, a fox, or a ghost. Under the influence of the *Tao*, even the most seemingly frail women can wield formidable, god-like strength. The tale of Meng Jiangnu, which is included in this book, is a compelling example.

It revolves around a woman whose sorrowful wails for her husband had the power to crumble the Great Wall of China. There is also a tale in this book about Yen-Tchin-King, the Supreme Judge of the Tang Dynasty, who died heroically at the hands of rebels. The story takes an intriguing twist when his family brings his body back for an honourable burial. Despite the decaying coffin, Yen-Tchin-King remained rosy-cheeked. With the metaphor of an 'immortal body', the story extols the eternity of virtue. In other words, no matter what hardships or even deaths ordinary people may endure, as long as they consistently engage in virtuous actions, *Tao* always prevails.

Enchanting Tales of Ghosts and Foxes

Among the plethora of Chinese folktales, none have left a deeper resonance than the stories of ghosts and foxes. These stories, having been told, retold and evolved over generations, have become a most cherished part of China's rich folktale tradition. In ancient times, ghost and fox tales were veiled in taboos and fears, but they have gradually transformed into narratives more captivating than frightening. Readers are drawn into a world where supernatural beings coexist with mortals, and the boundary between reality and fantasy fades into obscurity.

In the modern era, the allure of ghost and fox stories has only grown stronger. Netflix's much-buzzed animated series *Love, Death & Robots* (2019) features a compelling episode titled 'Good Hunting'. The episode unfolds the enthralling tale of a profound bond between a young inventor and a fox spirit, resulting in a formidable alliance that instils fear in their oppressors. What makes this episode particularly intriguing is its seamless integration of the Chinese nine-tailed fox spirit with the futuristic steampunk genre. This fusion resonated strongly with both commentators and the audience, offering a compelling testament to the global appeal and far-reaching influence of Chinese supernatural tales.

There are many Chinese folktales about ghosts and foxes. In *Strange Tales from a Chinese Studio* alone, there are 258 such stories, constituting over 50 per cent of the entire volume. When the ghost and fox spirit appear together in one tale, the dynamic between the ghost and fox, and their respective associations with human beings, can make for complex and deeply stirring stories. One such exceptional work is 'Miss Lien-Hsiang', also known as 'The Fox Girl', which has received longstanding critical acclaim as Pu Songling's finest work. Readers can also explore this story within the pages of the current book.

Whispers from the Shadows

In China, death has been a sensitive and taboo topic. Even the revered Confucius, as recorded in the *Analects*, maintained a deliberate distance from conversations involving the supernatural: 'The Master did not discuss prodigies, feats of strength, disorderly conduct, or the supernatural' (*Analects*, 7.21). Out of respect for deceased ancestors and fear of death, most Chinese Confucian scholars were reluctant to speak of ghosts. For common folks, however, life and death have always been the most consequential events in their lives. Even the strictest taboos could not dispel their enduring curiosity about the world after death. This is why ghosts remain a prominent theme in Chinese folklore.

Chinese folklore is replete with diverse ghostly characters, each with its own unique traits. The lovelorn ghost stands out as a particularly intriguing type. These ghosts may be drawn into human affairs and, against all odds, fall deeply in love with mortals. Such tales often follow the enduring formula of scholar-beauty romance, a literary genre created by traditional Chinese literati to convey their yearning for genuine love. They fantasize about chance encounters with soulmates from vastly different backgrounds, and as fate would have it, they fall in love with each other.

This theme comes to life in 'The Story of Ming-Y', a delicately written, dreamy and idyllic tale. Here, a young scholar becomes enamoured with a mysterious beauty who resides in a forest hermitage. They share feasts during the day, recite ancient poems, and listen to harmonious musical melodies. They spend the night together, and this mesmerizing life continues until Ming-Y's father and teacher intervene. They insist on visiting his beloved's azure-tiled house, which turns out to be a deserted tombstone bearing the name of SIË-THAO, an eminent poetess from many dynasties ago. It is only then that Ming-Y realizes that he has unwittingly fallen in love with a ghost. Such human–ghost love stories indeed reflect the romantic fantasies of Chinese literati. Their ideal partners, much like SIË-THAO, are not only beautiful and charming, but also extraordinarily talented. The disappointment in seeking love in the real world drives them to contemplate and imagine the perfect relationship they might find with a ghostly companion.

Haunting Tales, Forbidden Desires

There are also malevolent ghosts lurking in the shadows, ready to wreak harm and havoc on the living. In 'The Ghost Who Was Foiled', you can read what is probably one of the scariest stories you will ever encounter. In Chinese folklore, 'the ghosts of those who have hung themselves are the worst'. They are the most spiteful ghosts and would keep victimizing people to suffer the same tragic fate. In this tale, a brave soldier steps in to prevent this vicious event from happening again, but it also infuriates the vengeful ghost. The descriptions of the evil ghost in the story are so ghastly that it is not recommended that one reads it alone at night.

Many ghost stories are not meant to scare for the sake of being scary; they serve a cautionary purpose by eliciting fear in the reader. In a famous tale entitled 'The Painted Skin', a young scholar named Mr Wang has a fateful encounter with a beautiful young girl, leading him into a passionate but perilous romance. Wang's wife discovers their affair and pleads with him to stop, but to no avail. One day, Wang encounters a Taoist monk who observes that he is haunted and his days are numbered. Since he is getting suspicious, Wang snoops into his study, only to witness a ghastly sight: a hideous, fanged and grim-faced ghost is painting on a human skin that is spread out on the bed. Upon completing the painting, the ghost dons the skin and transforms into a beautiful maiden. Many are familiar with the tale's grim ending, where the ghost cuts out Wang's heart and ends his life. However, with the intervention of the Taoist monk and Wang's wife, the malevolent ghost is entrapped in a gourd, while the monk resurrects Wang through his mystical incantations. This eerie and unsettling tale mirrors the common folk's convoluted mentality: on the one hand, they recognize the dangers of indulging their desires, and on the other, they are prepared to pay any cost to fulfil them. Ultimately, these ghost tales serve as a poignant reminder that actions, whether well-intentioned or malicious, are seldom without consequences.

Versatile and Endearing:
Fox Spirits in Chinese Folklore

In the repository of Chinese folklore, fox tales present a less foreboding realm of the supernatural than the often spine-chilling tales of ghosts. When confronted with ghosts, one must always remain vigilant because these spectres reside in shadows and can claim human lives in unfortunate encounters. For the romance between man and ghost to work, it must ultimately find its way back to the human world. Fox spirits, however, are rather different: not only do they possess unparalleled beauty and shapeshifting power, but, most importantly, they are inherently living beings. Tales of fox spirits unveil a distinct facet of the supernatural world, where the lines between humans and spirits are blurred. Humans and foxes can joke and playfully tease each other. Take 'The Talking Silver Foxes' for example; these foxes would play pranks on travellers passing by, inviting them to smoke a pipe and laughing when the timid ones fled in fear.

In Chinese folktales, the relationship between humans and foxes is marked by a 'love/hate' dynamic, echoing the emotions one might experience when gazing upon his or her own image in a mirror. It is a mixture of affection and frustration, as the mirror reflects both the beauty and the flaws of the person.

In Chinese folklore, fox spirits are portrayed in a variety of ways, including Loving Foxes, Virtuous Foxes, Heavenly Foxes, Literary Foxes, Bewitching Foxes and Ordinary Foxes. Among them, Loving Foxes are often regarded as the most captivating characters. They usually embody sincere emotions and noble virtues, demonstrating an unwavering commitment to love and an ability to make resolute choices even in challenging circumstances. For example, in 'Miss Lien-Hsiang', or 'The Fox Girl', from *Strange Tales from a Chinese Studio*, the protagonist is an endearing fox spirit, characterized by compassion, wisdom and deep love. She lives for the sake of love, willingly sacrificing herself and even undergoing a protracted process of rebirth, all in the name of love. In the first half of the story, she repeatedly contends with the ghost Li, both to protect her love and out of her genuine concern for her beloved man. In the second half of the story, her compassion extends to altruistic kindness; she even sympathizes with her rival Li, giving her guidance like an older sister to help her mend her ways. In her quest for love, Lianxiang also shows profound wisdom and resilience. Not only does she go through hardship to gather medicine to save the life of her beloved, but she also figures out a way to gain a chance at a new human life for herself, even if it necessitates her death followed by a lengthy period of reincarnation. Throughout this arduous journey, her devotion to her beloved remains steadfast. Miss Lianxiang's charm, compassion and tenacity are perfectly balanced, making her the epitome of the ideal feminine persona in traditional Chinese society.

It's worth noting that in contemporary interpretation, fox spirits are predominantly thought to be female vixens. In traditional Chinese folktales, however, foxes can be male, female, and even androgynous. There is an interesting tale of a fox spirit who decides to have some fun with a lecherous man. In the beginning, the cunning fox spirit assumed the guise of a beautiful woman, effortlessly luring the man into its trap. At an intimate moment, they start to kiss each other while the fox spirit suddenly sprouts its beard stubble, leaving the man's face riddled with small holes as though pricked by a hedgehog. This story, documented in *Zi Bu Yu* 子不語 (literally 'What the Master Does Not Speak Of'), a collection of allegedly true supernatural stories compiled by Qing Dynasty scholar and writer Yuan Mei 袁枚, is likely to entertain modern audiences as well.

Folktales as Social Satire

Chinese folktales draw inspiration from life, reflecting the essence of being while soaring beyond its confines. One of the especially commendable aspects of Chinese folklore is its ability to not only mirror but also cleverly satirize the prevailing social order of its time. In traditional Chinese society, there prevails a rigid hierarchical structure, which is also reflected in folktales. Emperors govern the earthly realm, the Jade Emperor presides over the heavens, and the Dragon King reigns over the East China Sea. The brilliance of folktales, however, lies in their capacity to acknowledge the existing hierarchy while simultaneously transcending the constraints of reality to envision a potential path toward a new and imagined order.

One noticeable example is the portrayal of female characters in Chinese folktales, which can be regarded as a satirical critique of the deeply ingrained patriarchal system in traditional Chinese society. In a culture where men are often deemed superior and wield control over women, folktales present an alternative perspective by spotlighting many female characters with distinctive personalities and a deep yearning for freedom. Consider, for instance, 'The Herd Boy and the Weaving Maiden', a tale that is often perceived today as a love story. In its original version, the Weaving Maiden is a daughter of the Ruler of the Gods who weds the Herd Boy only because he takes her clothes while she bathes. Nevertheless, after merely seven days of living together, the resolute Weaving Maiden returns to Heaven, and even takes a long needle to draw a line in the sky to create Silver River to thwart the Herd Boy's pursuit. Equally determined is Tschang O, who chooses to abandon her princely husband and fly off to the moon alone. She ultimately transforms into a solitary but contented moon goddess.

Folktales are often associated with female storytellers, and these depictions of independent women likely reflect the profound yearning for freedom that women had in Chinese history. Perhaps the sharing of these tales has indeed kindled a spark of hope among traditional Chinese women who grappled with patriarchal oppressions. Who can assert that this is not so?

The Universal Appeal of Folktales

Storytelling is one of the most ancient practices of human beings. Within this rich tradition, Chinese folklore occupies a rather unique place. Folktales have the power not only to bridge the chasm between the antiquated and the contemporary, but also to cultivate both understanding and harmony among diverse civilizations. These tales have a remarkable attribute: they transcend linguistic boundaries and thrive despite formidable translation challenges. To borrow the words of Roland Barthes, these stories are 'as existential, international, trans-historical, and trans-cultural as life itself'.

As long as people are willing to set aside their prejudices and remain curious about unfamiliar worlds and traditions, the opportunity to forge a deeper connection through shared narratives across time and space remains ever-present.

This book of Chinese folklore is an invitation to explore, to learn, and to uncover the mysteries of a rich and vibrant cultural tradition that spans millennia. Here, you will traverse through time to exchange greetings with the scholars of ancient China, stroll past the majestic thrones of dragon kings and emperors, and immerse yourself in the enchanting realm of ghosts, fox spirits, flower fairies and curious creatures.

In short, this is a world of wonder that awaits your discovery.

Xiulu Wang and Chuanji Hu (Introduction), both from Sun Yat-sen University in China, bring their rich expertise to this collaborative project. Professor Wang, an expert in translation and comparative cultural studies, offers insights into modern interpretations and translations of Chinese folktales. Professor Hu, a distinguished literary critic and historian, contributes knowledge of Chinese literature and intellectual history. Together, they enrich readers' comprehension of Chinese folklore, ensuring an engaging voyage through this invaluable cultural heritage.

Myths, Deities & Legendary Figures

GREAT MEN AND WOMEN make great stories – but they have to have humbler, human touches. This is even more true for gods and goddesses, of course. So it has certainly been in Chinese legend. Many of the greatest mythical narratives have formed around deities and legendary figures. By turns charming, stirring, heartwarming, humorous and downright awe-inspiring, the stories here have delighted audiences for generations.

In one form or another, the heroic tale of 'Meng Cheng's Journey to the Great Wall' to help her husband – pressed into labour there – has been told for over 2,500 years. Almost as old, and equally compelling, is the romance of 'The Herd Boy and the Weaving Maiden'. The Folklore Movement of the 1920s chose these as two of the Four Great Folktales. And rightly so: all human life is here. Then there's Mulan, who assumes a boy's apparel so she can take her elderly father's place in the army draft. She gains great glory and helps to save her homeland.

Lu-San, Daughter of Heaven

L U-SAN WENT TO BED without any supper, but her little heart was hungry for something more than food. She nestled up close beside her sleeping brothers, but even in their slumber they seemed to deny her that love which she craved. The gentle lapping of the water against the sides of the houseboat, music which had so often lulled her into dreamland, could not quiet her now. Scorned and treated badly by the entire family, her short life had been full of grief and shame.

Lu-san's father was a fisherman. His life had been one long fight against poverty. He was ignorant and wicked. He had no more feeling of love for his wife and five children than for the street dogs of his native city. Over and over he had threatened to drown them one and all, and had been prevented from doing so only by fear of the new mandarin. His wife did not try to stop her husband when he sometimes beat the children until they fell half dead upon the deck. In fact, she herself was cruel to them, and often gave the last blow to Lu-san, her only daughter. Not on one day in the little girl's memory had she escaped this daily whipping, not once had her parents pitied her.

On the night with which this story opens, not knowing that Lu-san was listening, her father and mother were planning how to get rid of her.

"The mandarin cares only about boys," said he roughly. "A man might kill a dozen girls and he wouldn't say a word."

"Lu-san's no good anyway," added the mother. "Our boat is small, and she's always in the wrong place."

"Yes, and it takes as much to feed her as if she were a boy. If you say so, I'll do it this very night."

"All right," she answered, "but you'd better wait till the moon has set."

"Very well, wife, we'll let the moon go down first, and then the girl."

No wonder Lu-san's little heart beat fast with terror, for there could be no doubt as to the meaning of her parents' words.

At last when she heard them snoring and knew they were both sound asleep, she got up silently, dressed herself, and climbed the ladder leading to the deck. Only one thought was in her heart, to save herself by instant flight. There were no extra clothes, not a bite of food to take with her. Besides the rags on her back there was only one thing she could call her own, a tiny soapstone image of the goddess Kwan-yin, which she had found one day while walking in the sand. This was the only treasure and plaything of her childhood, and if she had not watched carefully, her mother would have taken even this away from her. Oh, how she had nursed this idol, and how closely she had listened to the stories an old priest had told about Kwan-yin the Goddess of Mercy, the best friend of women and children, to whom they might always pray in time of trouble.

It was very dark when Lu-san raised the trapdoor leading to the outer air, and looked out into the night. The moon had just gone down, and frogs were croaking along the shore. Slowly and carefully she pushed against the door, for she was afraid that the wind coming in suddenly might awaken the sleepers or, worse still, cause her to let the trap fall with a bang. At last, however, she stood on the deck, alone and ready to go out into the big world. As she stepped to the side of the boat the black water did not make her feel afraid, and she went ashore without the slightest tremble.

Now she ran quickly along the bank, shrinking back into the shadows whenever she heard the noise of footsteps, and thus hiding from the passers-by. Only once did her heart quake, full of fear. A huge boat dog ran out at her barking furiously. The snarling beast, however, was not dangerous, and when he saw this trembling little girl of ten he sniffed in disgust at having noticed any one so small, and returned to watch his gate.

Lu-san had made no plans. She thought that if she could escape the death her parents had talked about, they would be delighted at her leaving them and would not look for her. It was not, then, her own people that she feared as she passed the rows of dark houses lining the shore. She had often heard her father tell of the dreadful deeds done in many of these houseboats. The darkest memory of her childhood was of the night when he had almost decided to sell her as a slave to the owner of a boat like these she was now passing. Her mother had suggested that they should wait until Lu-san was a little older, for she would then be worth more money. So her father had not sold her. Lately, perhaps, he had tried and failed.

That was why she hated the river dwellers and was eager to get past their houses. On and on she sped as fast as her little legs could carry her. She would flee far away from the dark water, for she loved the bright sunshine and the land.

As Lu-san ran past the last houseboat she breathed a sigh of relief and a minute later fell in a little heap upon the sand. Not until now had she noticed how lonely it was. Over there was the great city with its thousands of sleepers. Not one of them was her friend. She knew nothing of friendship, for she had had no playmates. Beyond lay the open fields, the sleeping villages, the unknown world. Ah, how tired she was! How far she had run! Soon, holding the precious image tightly in her little hand and whispering a childish prayer to Kwan-yin, she fell asleep.

When Lu-san awoke, a cold chill ran through her body, for bending over her stood a strange person. Soon she saw to her wonder that it was a woman dressed in beautiful clothes like those worn by a princess. The child had never seen such perfect features or so fair a face. At first, conscious of her own filthy rags, she shrank back fearfully, wondering what would happen if this beautiful being should chance to touch her and thus soil those slender white fingers. As the child lay there trembling on the ground, she felt as if she would like to spring into the fairy creature's arms and beg for mercy. Only the fear that the lovely one would vanish kept her from so doing. Finally, unable to hold back any longer, the little girl, bending forward, stretched out her hand to the woman, saying, "Oh, you are so beautiful! Take this, for it must be you who lost it in the sand."

The princess took the soapstone figure, eyed it curiously, and then with a start of surprise said, "And do you know, my little creature, to whom you are thus giving your treasure?"

"No," answered the child simply, "but it is the only thing I have in all the world, and you are so lovely that I know it belongs to you. I found it on the river bank."

Then a strange thing happened. The graceful, queenly woman bent over, and held out her arms to the ragged, dirty child. With a cry of joy the little one sprang forward; she had found the love for which she had been looking so long.

"My precious child, this little stone which you have kept so lovingly, and which without a thought of self you have given to me – do you know of whom it is the image?"

"Yes," answered Lu-san, the colour coming to her cheeks again as she snuggled up contentedly in her new friend's warm embrace, "it is the dear goddess Kwan-yin, she who makes the children happy."

"And has this gracious goddess brought sunshine into your life, my pretty one?" said the other, a slight flush covering her fair cheeks at the poor child's innocent words.

"Oh, yes indeed; if it had not been for her I should not have escaped tonight. My father would have killed me, but the good lady of heaven listened to my prayer and bade me stay awake. She told me to wait until he was sleeping, then to arise and leave the houseboat."

"And where are you going, Lu-san, now that you have left your father? Are you not afraid to be alone here at night on the bank of this great river?"

"No, oh no! for the blessed mother will shield me. She has heard my prayers, and I know she will show me where to go."

The lady clasped Lu-san still more tightly, and something glistened in her radiant eye. A tear-drop rolled down her cheek and fell upon the child's head, but Lu-san did not see it, for she had fallen fast asleep in her protector's arms.

When Lu-san awoke, she was lying all alone on her bed in the houseboat, but, strange to say, she was not frightened at finding herself once more near her parents. A ray of sunlight came in, lighting up the child's face and telling her that a new day had dawned. At last she heard the sound of low voices, but she did not know who were the speakers. Then as the tones grew louder she knew that her parents were talking. Their speech, however, seemed to be less harsh than usual, as if they were near the bed of some sleeper whom they did not wish to wake.

"Why," said her father, "when I bent over to lift her from the bed, there was a strange light about her face. I touched her on the arm, and at once my hand hung limp as if it had been shot. Then I heard a voice whispering in my ears, 'What! would you lay your wicked hands on one who made the tears of Kwan-yin flow? Do you not know that when she cries the gods themselves are weeping?'"

"I too heard that voice," said the mother, her voice trembling; "I heard it, and it seemed as if a hundred wicked imps pricked me with spears, at every prick repeating these terrible words, 'And would you kill a daughter of the gods?'"

"It is strange," he added, "to think how we had begun to hate this child, when all the time she belonged to another world than ours. How wicked we must be since we could not see her goodness."

"Yes, and no doubt for every time we have struck her, a thousand blows will be given us by Yama, for our insults to the gods."

Lu-san waited no longer, but rose to dress herself. Her heart was burning with love for everything around her. She would tell her parents that she forgave them, tell them how she loved them still in spite of all their wickedness. To her surprise the ragged clothes were nowhere to be seen. In place of them she found on one side of the bed the most beautiful garments. The softest of silks, bright with flowers – so lovely that she fancied they must have been taken from the garden of the gods – were ready to slip on her little body. As she dressed herself she saw with surprise that her fingers were shapely, that her skin was soft and smooth. Only the day before, her hands had been rough and cracked by hard work and the cold of winter. More and more amazed, she stooped to put on her shoes. Instead of the worn-out soiled shoes of yesterday, the prettiest little satin slippers were there all ready for her tiny feet.

Finally she climbed the rude ladder, and lo, everything she touched seemed to be changed as if by magic, like her gown. The narrow rounds of the ladder had become broad steps of polished wood, and it seemed as if she was mounting the polished stairway of some fairy-built pagoda. When she reached the deck everything was changed. The ragged patchwork which had served so long as a sail had become a beautiful sheet of canvas that rolled and floated proudly in the river breeze. Below were the dirty fishing smacks which Lu-san was used to, but here was a stately ship, larger and fairer than any she had ever dreamed of, a ship which had sprung into being as if at the touch of her feet.

After searching several minutes for her parents she found them trembling in a corner, with a look of great fear on their faces. They were clad in rags, as usual, and in no way changed except that their savage faces seemed to have become a trifle softened. Lu-san drew near the wretched group and bowed low before them.

Her mother tried to speak; her lips moved, but made no sound: she had been struck dumb with fear.

"A goddess, a goddess!" murmured the father, bending forward three times and knocking his head on the deck. As for the brothers, they hid their faces in their hands as if dazzled by a sudden burst of sunlight.

For a moment Lu-san paused. Then, stretching out her hand, she touched her father on the shoulder. "Do you not know me, father? It is Lu-san, your little daughter."

The man looked at her in wonder. His whole body shook, his lips trembled, his hard brutish face had on it a strange light. Suddenly he bent far over and touched his forehead to her feet. Mother and sons followed his example. Then all gazed at her as if waiting for her command.

"Speak, father," said Lu-san. "Tell me that you love me, say that you will not kill your child."

"Daughter of the gods, and not of mine," he mumbled, and then paused as if afraid to continue.

"What is it, father? Have no fear."

"First, tell me that you forgive me."

The child put her left hand upon her father's forehead and held the right above the heads of the others, "As the Goddess of Mercy has given me her favour, so I in her name bestow on you the love of heaven. Live in peace, my parents. Brothers, speak no angry words. Oh, my dear ones, let joy be yours for ever. When only love shall rule your lives, this ship is yours and all that is in it."

Thus did Lu-san change her loved ones. The miserable family which had lived in poverty now found itself enjoying peace and happiness. At first they did not know how to live as Lu-san had directed. The father sometimes lost his temper and the mother spoke spiteful words; but as they grew in wisdom and courage they soon began to see that only love must rule.

All this time the great boat was moving up and down the river. Its company of sailors obeyed Lu-san's slightest wish. When their nets were cast overboard they were always drawn back full of the largest, choicest fish. These fish were sold at the city markets, and soon people began to say that Lu-san was the richest person in the whole country.

One beautiful day during the Second Moon, the family had just returned from the temple. It was Kwan-yin's birthday, and, led by Lu-san, they had gone gladly to do the goddess honour. They had just mounted to the vessel's deck when Lu-san's father, who had been looking off towards the west, suddenly called the family to his side. "See!" he exclaimed. "What kind of bird is that yonder in the sky?"

As they looked, they saw that the strange object was coming nearer and nearer, and directly towards the ship. Everyone was excited except Lu-san. She was calm, as if waiting for something she had long expected.

"It is a flight of doves," cried the father in astonishment, "and they seem to be drawing something through the air."

At last, as the birds flew right over the vessel, the surprised onlookers saw that floating beneath their wings was a wonderful chair, all white and gold, more dazzling even than the one they had dreamed the Emperor himself sat in on the Dragon Throne. Around each snow-white neck was fastened a long streamer of pure gold, and these silken ribbons were tied to the chair in such a manner as to hold it floating wherever its light-winged coursers chose to fly.

Down, down, over the magic vessel came the empty chair, and as it descended, a shower of pure white lilies fell about the feet of Lu-san, until she, the queen of all the flowers, was almost buried. The doves hovered above her head for an instant, and then gently lowered their burden until it was just in front of her.

With a farewell wave to her father and mother, Lu-san stepped into the fairy car. As the birds began to rise, a voice from the clouds spoke in tones of softest music: "Thus Kwan-yin, Mother of Mercies, rewards Lu-san, daughter of the earth. Out of the dust spring the flowers; out of the soil comes goodness. Lu-san! that tear which you drew from Kwan-yin's eye fell upon the dry ground and softened it; it touched the hearts of those who loved you not. Daughter of earth no longer, rise into the Western Heaven, there to take your place among the fairies, there to be a star within the azure realms above."

As Lu-san's doves disappeared in the distant skies, a rosy light surrounded her flying car. It seemed to those who gazed in wonder that heaven's gates were opening to receive her. At last when she was gone beyond their sight, suddenly it grew dark upon the earth, and the eyes of all that looked were wet with tears.

Meng Cheng's Journey to the Great Wall

In tracing back time's ever flowing stream,
I will not sing of heroes, war or glory;
A simpler subject far shall form my theme,
A woman's love – Meng Cheng's pathetic story.

At once a wife, a widow, yet a maid,
No jade could be more pure, no snow be whiter;
The lustre of her name will never fade;
Ages have passed, it shines out clearer, brighter.

Couched in rude language though the tale may be,
To braver, nobler deeds you cannot listen;
Her journey to the Wall, ten thousand li,
Will cause the breast to swell, the eye to glisten.

My efforts will not altogether fail,
Should my rough verses but succeed in wringing
A tear or two from those who hear this tale,
Perhaps a sigh for those of whom I'm singing.

In Kuating city ages long ago,
There lived, as local chronicles still show,

A man named Meng-lung-te, who, with his wife,
Passed many years an uneventful life,
Tranquil and happy, for no other care
Disturbed their peace, save that they had no heir;
Had they a child on whom their love to pour,
Then were they blessed, they craved for nothing more.

At length their fondest hopes were gratified,
The dame, with rising glow of conscious pride,
Announced herself, thanks to kind destiny,
The way all married ladies wish to be;
Ere long a little stranger blessed their sight,
Though but a girl, they hailed it with delight.
This child, e'en as the tendrils of the vine
Help to support the props round which they twine.
Would to their green old age new vigour bring,
And, by her love, support as well as cling.
With joy, then, o'er this little pledge they hung,
And at the 'full moon' named the child Meng Cheng;
Nor was it ever changed, the name they gave,
She bore in life, and carried to her grave.

Years passed, the little Meng Cheng grew apace,
All hearts delighting by her childish grace,
Clever beyond her years, she passed her hours
In study, needlework, embroidering flowers.
In all accomplishments the girl excelled,
Charming her parents, who with pride beheld
Her industry, her kind and winning ways.
The neighbours too spoke loudly in her praise;
So beautiful, so skilful, yet so young,
Who was the equal of the fair Meng Cheng!
The time rolled on, the girl was now sixteen.
In all her life her thoughts had ever been
How by her fond devotion day by day,

She could her parents' kindness best repay.
Like to a rosebud 'neath a genial sun,
Her budding charms unfolded one by one,
Each day developing some lovelier grace,
Bounding her form, and dimpling her fair face,
The young girl blossomed into maidenhood,
Fair to the eyes, yet not more fair than good.

Her birthday dawned: the happy parents blessed
Their blushing daughter, whom they thus addressed:
"You're now sixteen, as each revolving year
Rolls on, still 'sweet sixteen' may you appear;
May your young life be one continual spring,
And every added year new pleasures bring.
But yet my child – 'tis written so by fate –
The time will come when we must separate;
We both are old, and time steals slowly on,
Our care then is for you when we are gone.
You will be rich, all that we have is yours;
But 'tis not wealth that always best insures
Content and happiness. We must provide
A fitting husband for so fair a bride;
Invite a son-in-law to assume our name,
This, for your sake, must be our highest aim;

Graft our child's husband on the parent tree,
Your children then we yet may live to see.
"What say you, child?" The blushing girl replied,
"Why should you wish to drive me from your side?
The thought of marriage only gives me pain,
Ah! rather let me ever thus remain,
To wait on both, and by increasing care,
Still, as of old, your fond affection share:
I'm but a child, then let me, I implore,
Stay as I am, what can I wish for more?"

I'll not sing of Kua-ting or of Meng Cheng now:
– That portion of my task's already done –
But of a couple living in Soochow,
On whom, in old age, heaven bestowed a son.

When three days old the child received his name,
'Twas Wan-Tisi-liang – 'tis in old records shown.
From then till death it still remained the same,
Never was he by any other known.

The child was beautiful beyond compare,
More like a fairy being who had played
With baby angels in the upper air,
And then unconsciously had earthward strayed.

His parents watched with love his rapid growth,
Each day developing some mental grace,
Which more endeared him to the hearts of both.
Than e'en the beauty of his fair young face.

When eight years old, he could repeat by rote
All the 'Four Books', and the 'Five Classics' too;
The sayings of the Sages he could quote:
Besides, he much of Ancient History knew.

When he had studied and had mastered those,
He next tried Essays. These he wrote so well,
In composition, poetry or prose,
But few could equal, none could him excel.

I'll leave the boy thus, and the scene will transport
To the capital city, the emperor's court; –
The frontiers long had been ravished by hordes
Of fierce mounted Tatars with spears and with swords.
The Emperor, thinking their inroads to check,

And fearing, perhaps, their wild troops to attack,
Called in to his aid many workmen well skilled,
And gave them directions a great wall to build;
The wall was to be the whole country in length,
With towers and gateways of suitable strength.
This wall would his subjects in safety enclose,
And be an effectual check to his foes.

The work advanced slowly, at ruinous cost,
For myriads of lives in its building were lost;
The dying and dead were enclosed in the wall,
No matter their rank, 'twas a vast tomb for all.

One night, on retiring, the Emperor dreamt,
In Soochow was a lad who from vice was exempt –
Who, whatever he did, or wherever he went,
Would a myriad of common-place men represent.
The Emperor woke, and, elated and pleased,
Sent to Soochow instanter to have the lad seized.
Soochow's six gates were immediately guarded,
And every available spot was placarded.
In every alley and lane of the city,
People assembled with looks full of pity;
Many a murmur and shake of the head
Were heard and seen as the placard was read.

It ran thus: – "If anyone dare to conceal
The lad Wan-hsi-liang, he shall certainly feel
The law's direst terrors for treason so great;
He shall suffer beheading, a murderer's fate;
The family shall also, of him who so dared,
Be cut off root and branch, not a soul shall be spared.
But, if, on the other hand, anyone know
Where Wan is concealed, and shall instantly go
And give such information as may at length lead

To his capture, he'll do a most praiseworthy deed.
And further, a handsome reward shall be paid
To the person or persons by whom it is laid;
And those through whose prowess the capture is made,
If official, shall each be promoted one grade."

When the father read this he was nearly distrait,
Tore his hair in despair, and cursed his sad fate;
"Why should he seek to rob me of my son?
Other fathers have many, while I have but one!
If my son is taken to build the Great Wall,
He will never return. Losing him, I lose all.
On whom, save my son, can I hope to depend
For comfort and help as I draw near my end?
In old age or sickness who but him can soothe
My last dying moments, the road to death smooth?"
Bewailing his fate thus with sad tears and moans,
He at once hastened home, and in heart-breaking tones,
Imparted the news to his agonized wife,
And tremblingly bade his son fly for his life.
The wondering lad both his parents obeyed,
First bathing, and then in clean robes was arrayed; –
Sacrificed, with his parents, to Heaven and Earth,
To the Gods, and to those who had given him birth; –
To their ancestors' tablet, their forefathers' tomb,
Praying their manes to avert such a doom
As the one that hung over themselves and their son –
To guard him and them. The sacrifice done,
The poor weeping youth bade his parents not grieve,
Cried he, "'Tis but for a short time I leave,
A few days or weeks and this crisis once o'er,
We'll all be united again as of yore."

Here the poor lad broke down, fondly looking at each
Through his tears, while deep sobs interrupted his speech.

"If I'm apprehended and die at the Wall,
On you both, in old age, this sorrow will fall.
Is't for this you both reared me? Oh! why was I born?
Oh! why must I leave you? Why from you be torn?"
With dreadful forebodings they'd never meet more,
Mid' sobbing and tears, the lad rushed from the door.

On he ran, with untiring feet,
On, through alley, and land and street;
Meeting many a face he knew,
But heedless of all he onward flew;
Turning neither to left nor right,
Till the gate of the city appeared in sight.
People to many a village belonging,
Coming and going to and fro,
In and out of the city were thronging.
Some seemed struck with his look of woe.
On through the gate of the city he sped,
And out through the open country fled,
For he knew that a price was set on his head.

Everyone on the road he met,
Eagerly asked, "Have they caught him yet?
Living or dead, he's sure to be found,
He cannot escape if he's above ground;
It wouldn't be pleasant to be in his shoes."
For everyone 'ere this had heard the news.
Over the dusty road he speeded,
Footsore and weary still he ran;
Towns and hamlets he passed unheeded,
He dreaded to go near the haunts of man.
Over the dusty road he sped,
With wearied limbs and feet that bled,
For he knew that a price was set on his head.

Over the hot and dusty road,
On, the weary fugitive strode;
Till, tired and faint, he suddenly spied
A garden wall close by the roadside;
Farther on, a temptingly open gate.
Seeing no one near, he made for it straight.
The garden looked so cool and shaded
"Ah! what a refuge 'twould be for me!
I'll venture!" – at once he its precincts invaded,
And threw himself down at the foot of a tree.

Here, he in safety might pass the night,
Base at the dawn and continue his flight,
With a body refreshed and a heart more light.

I'll leave the lad upon the greensward flung,
Weary and footsore, sad and sorrow-laden;
And tune my muse once more to fair Meng Cheng,
And sing of what befel the gentle maiden.

'Twas eventide, the sun was sinking fast,
And, as he sank down in his western bed,
His dying radiance o'er the landscape cast,
Tinging the foliage with a golden red.

Some remnants of his brightness still remained,
A filmy veil of glorious light and shade;
As if, though out of sight, he still refrained
From taking all the glory he had made.

The fair Meng Cheng, her daily task being done,
Tripped from the house and towards an arbour ran;
To watch from thence the slowly setting sun,
Her taper fingers toying with a fan.

The bower stood on a gentle eminence,
Some twenty feet above the garden raised;
She gained the summit, turning round from thence,
On sinking sun, and hill, and dale she gazed.

The scene enclosed within the garden wall –
The house, the bower, the lake so still and pure,
The flowers, the trees – the palms o'ertopping all –
Looked like a Paradise in miniature.

Green foliage on every side appeared,
Bright flowers bloomed in many a gay parterre;
The tufted palm its lofty head upreared,
High above cypress and the azure fir.

The playful beams, e'en though their lord had gone,
Still danced and flickered midst the topmost boughs;
Toying with every leaf they glanced upon,
Kissing at last the tall palm's stately brows.

On air and sky their impress next they showed;
Sunward their course they dancingly pursued,
Purpling and goldening the air, which glowed,
Becoming, through their influence, rosy-hued.

Embosomed in the midst of this fair scene,
Lay, mirror-like, a lakelet calm and clear,
Reflecting back its bordering of green,
The fleecy clouds, the glowing atmosphere.

High overhead, far in the vault of blue,
Rode the pale moon amidst the ambient air;
Her modest glances in the lakelet threw,
Seeing her own fair face reflected there.

Charmed by the beauty of the scenery –
The placid stillness of the lakelet's breast, –
She gazed upon it long and dreamily,
At length she thought she'd seek the bower and rest.

Each step she mounted, backward looks she cast
From thence, another point of view to take;
When suddenly a gust of wind swept past,
Caught up her fan, and hurled it in the lake.

Loudly she called her maid, but no one came.
Finding at length she could not make her hear,
She thought, "Why need I feel false pride or shame?
I'll fetch the fan myself; there's no one near."

No sooner had the girl the thought expressed,
Than down the steps again she lightly ran;
Looked coyly round, then hastily undressed,
Bent on obtaining back the truant fan.

She paused awhile, then, slowly turning round,
Her face and form became suffused with red;
Her eyes in modesty, had sought the ground,
But rested on the lake's clear face instead.

And there she saw – as if ''twere sculpt' of stone –
An unclothed form, a living statuette;
A fair young face – she recognised her own,
And blushed a crimson when her own eyes met.

She gazed admiringly, yet bashfully,
As if she felt an innate sense of shame;
She knew she blushed, for she could plainly see
The rosy blood rush mantling through her frame.

As thus she stood, she chanced to raise her eyes,
    'Ere stepping in the lake to get the fan;
But who can paint her horror and surprise,
    When her eyes met the dark eyes of a man?

Yes, there, beneath the lofty palm-tree's shade,
    There stood a lad, good-looking, tall and slim,
        Intently gazing on the beauteous maid.
    Her gaze in turn became transfixed on him.

The girl, with mingled modesty and fear,
    Arrayed herself in haste as best she could;
She dared not look, she felt him drawing near.
    'Ere she was clothed, the young man by her stood.

A man to see her thus, she was dismayed,
And could have sunk into the ground with fright;
Abashed, confused, perplexed, she yet displayed
    Some anger too, as well indeed she might.

Yet, strange to say, there mingled with all this,
    A pleasant feeling, hitherto unknown;
Making her bosom swell and glow with bliss;
Her bright eyes 'neath its influence brighter shone.

"I bless the chance," the smiling youth began,
    "That led me here – a fugitive – to take
        Shelter awhile; but, oh! I bless the fan,
    Blown by the gust of wind into the lake!

"Ah! but for that, my eyes had ne'er been blest
    With such a vision as I've just surveyed;
The sunset scene, the lakelet's placid breast,
    And its presiding queen, a very naiad."

"Who are you? Whence came you? What is your name?"
Cried the girl, as she reddened with anger and shame;
"Who are your parents? Where do you dwell?
"How came you hither? – the truth at once tell."

Without hesitation, the lad told her all;
How he was wanted to help build the Wall;
The grief of his parents for whose sake he fled,
The placards announcing a price for his head.

How, wearied and footsore, impelled by kind fate,
He saw the flower-garden, and entered the gate,
Intending to rest 'neath the trees for a night,
And early next morning continue his flight.

He continued, "While resting my limbs in the shade,
I heard a sweet voice calling out for her maid;
I looked whence it came and my glad eyes were blest
With a vision of beauty, and – you know the rest.

"You have heard my sad tale, I a fugitive stand;
My liberty, life, all, are now in your hand;
May I crave your permission one night here to stay?
And tomorrow, at dawn, I'll proceed on my way."

The girl had alternately flushed and turned pale,
As the young lad related his pitiful tale;
Then exclaimed, "You must never again quit this spot,
But share, with my parents and me, our poor lot.

"Who sees my fair form, as you did but just now,
Must make me his wife; for I solemnly vow,
All the troubles and griefs he may yet have to bear,
As a true, loving wife I will faithfully share.

On my unclothed form your eyes just now gazed;"
She here dropped her eyes, which before had been raised;
"And I love you far dearer, far better than life;
You must be my husband, I must be your wife."

On the banks of the lake then they sat side by side,
In fancy already a bridegroom and bride;
They lingered awhile in the deepening shade,
And many a vow to each other they made.

Filled with visions of brightness they both prattled on,
Till growing night forced them at last to be gone;
They arose from the ground and ingeniously planned
To enter the house, as they stood, hand in hand.

Thus hand in hand and full of confidence,
Engendered by their youth and innocence;
They gained the house, and now with love grown bold,
The artless girl the whole adventure told.

His own heart warming to the handsome youth,
The father listened, seeing nought but truth
In their ingenuous faces, smiling said,
"So you are Wan-hsi-liang, and you have fled
"From those you hold most dear, from home and friends?
Stay with us here; we'll try to make amends
For all the wrong the Emperor has done;
Be my child's husband; be to me a son.

"Take her, she's all that I love here on earth;
Like me, you'll soon appreciate her worth.
I'm rich, on you my riches I bestow;
My greatest recompense will be to know
Two loving hearts will prop my failing age
Be near me, when I close life's pilgrimage."

"What," cried the lad, "would you your riches give,
Your daughter too, to me, a fugitive?
Your only child on my acceptance press
Cause her to share my suffering and distress?
Much as I love her, I could never dare
To blight the happiness of one so fair,
By linking my unhappy fate to hers,
Bethink you well, if such a thing occurs,
Would not the news on all sides quickly spread,
And soon bring dire misfortune on your head?"

The old man cried, "Your safety I'll ensure
Stay in the inner rooms, there rest secure
Till this unfortunate affair's blown o'er,
And you can safely show yourself once more."
Convinced at last, he'd nought to apprehend,
Loving the girl, and fearing to offend,
The youth no farther opposition showed,
But thankfully confessing all he owed
For the unbounded kindness they had shown
To him, a wanderer, homeless and unknown,
Agreed to everything; – what next befel,
Time, and the following rhymes will clearly tell.

This very night shall the wedding be kept,
Of Wan-hsi-liang with the fair Meng Cheng;
Let the great hall be properly swept,
Garnished, festooned, and the flower-lamps hung.

Hurry and bustle both old and young –
Let the tapers be of the brightest red;
Emblems of joy for the fair Meng Cheng,
And the youthful lover tonight she'll wed.

Alas, how often in worldly things,
Just when our prospects appear most bright,
An apparent trifle misfortune brings,
And our sunny morning is turned to night.

As nothing is hidden under the sun,
The news spread quickly far and wide;
The ceremony was scarcely done,
When clamouring voices were heard outside.

"Open the door! We'll burst it in!
Where is the youth who hither fled?"
Hoarse cries are heard 'mid the uproar and din,
"We'll have the bridegroom, living or dead."

The noise is increasing more and more;
"Hark to the angry voices without!
Hear, how our enemies batter the door,
Raising, at every blow, a wild shout."

"Hide, oh! hide, for your young wife's sake!
Hark, the rude voices are drawing near!
Here, in this store-room, shelter take –
They'll never think of finding you here."

The feeble door, alas, cannot stay
The efforts of those for blood athirst;
'Neath continued blows it at length gives way,
Everyone striving to enter first.

Search was made for him here and there,
Search was made for him high and low –
Kitchen and closet everywhere
Wherever a human form could go.

In every room of the house they sought;
At length in the store-room he was found;
Into the hall the youth was brought,
His legs and arms being tightly bound.

Into his shoulder a spike was thrust,
Causing the lad to writhe with pain;
Like a joint of meat the poor lad was trussed;
His neck was bound with a heavy chain.

In this pitiful plight he stood in the hall;
The old man cried, while the rest looked on,
"What shall I do when you go to the Wall?
Who will console me when you are gone?"

Cried the youth, "When I to the Wall am borne,
I shall die, and my bride will again be free;
She is young – let her not for my sad fate mourn,
She must strive to forget such a wretch as me.

"I carry misfortune wherever I go;
Better by far that I should die;
On some other lover her hand bestow,
And may he be happier far than I."

"Listen to me," was the girl's reply,
"You are my husband, I am your wife;
Death cannot sever that sacred tie, –
A true woman weds but once in her life.

"The good horse is chary of turning his head
To graze off the ground he has just passed o'er;
A faithful wife when her lord is dead,
Is true to him still; she weds no more."

At length the time came to separate,
The bride from her husband's side was torn;
He, to be dragged to a wretched fate,
She, his absence or death to mourn.

Even the bystanders felt for the pair,
And openly murmured their sympathy
For the new married couple so young and fair
Thus torn asunder through tyranny.

The road to the Wall was long and drear,
Day by day the lad weaker grew;
The end of his journey and life drew near,
When at length the Great Wall appeared in view.

Three days after the youth arrived,
He died, and the Great Wall became his tomb:
Flung in by those who yet survived,
Daily expecting a similar doom.

Months passed, the maiden daily grew more pale,
Her parents did the best they could to cheer her;
Their well-meant kindness was of no avail,
Dear were they to her, yet her lord was dearer.

She must go to him – was she not his bride?
And was it not her duty to be near him?
In life or death her place was by his side:
If sick or dying, who but she could cheer him?

Her parents tried this strong desire to check;
Alternately they threatened and persuaded;
How could she travel that long dreary track?
What could she do, a girl, alone, unaided?

Firmly resolved on going to the Wall,
She left her parents almost broken-hearted;
She was his wife – to find him she'd brave all:
So on her long, long journey she departed.

Her dress was plain – no ornaments she wore,
Save a gold ring to show that she was married;
She'd have to beg her way from door to door –
For not a single cash the young girl carried.

On through alley and lane and street,
She tottered along on her tiny feet;
Meeting many a well-known face
As she was leaving her native place:
Hearing many a kind regret
That she was going, from those she met;
Hastily through Soochow she proceeded,
Turning neither to left nor right,
Noise and bustle the girl ne'er heeded,
Till the gate of the city appeared in sight
Many a wondering look was cast
On the lonely girl as she hurried past,
Till she cleared the streets of the city at last.

Through the gate of the city she pressed,
Pausing neither for food nor rest;
Over the dreary road she sped,
Heedless of what the wayfarer said,
Village and town the girl passed through,
Till at dusk she reached the pass of Hsu-shu.
Seeing the girl the guards demanded,
"Why are you out so late, my lass?
You can't have travelled here empty-handed,
So you'll treat us and then we'll let you pass.
You'd no business out on the road so late;

47

If you have no money you'll have to wait,
For we cannot allow you to pass the gate."

She turned to the guards with a bitter smile
"I have travelled today," said she, "many a mile;
Alas! had I money, I'd cheerfully give—"
Here, seeing no other alternative –
She tore off her skirt, which she gave to the man,
"Take it, and pawn it for drink, if you can."
The person in charge of the barrier hearing
Some voices apparently wrangling, came out,
To allay all the hubbub; – on his appearing,
He demanded to know what the noise was about.
Bidding the maiden at once relate
Why she was out on the road so late,
And her motive for wanting to pass the gate.

The trembling girl told the officer all,
How Wan-hsi-liang had been dragged to the Wall –
That she'd scarcely a moment become a bride,
When her husband was ruthlessly torn from her side;
Home, parents, and friends, she had given up all
To follow her husband alone to the Wall
The officer said, when the tale was related,
The truth of your story time only will show;
He then bade the girl, who impatiently waited,
First sing 'Names of Flowers', and then she should go.
A moment's pause, and the night air rung
With the mellow voice of the fair Meng Cheng,
The guards clustered round her, as thus the girl sung: –

Song
1.
"'Tis the first moon – 'tis Spring: the red lamps are lighted:
To hail the New Year, guests now a meet in the hall;

Other husbands and wives in their homes are united,
My husband is taken to build the Great Wall.

2.

The second moon's come, and the swallows are pairing;
How they twitter and chirp, as if proud and elate;
'Neath the eaves their old nests they are busy repairing,
They all have their homes, and each has its mate.

3.

'Tis the 3rd of the 3rd, the peach trees are blending,
Their rose-tinted hues with the willows so green;
Old and young to the tombs, to burn paper, are wending,
But none at the tombs of my people are seen.

4.

'Tis the fourth moon – 'tis genial and mild sunny weather:
This is the time when the silkworms are bred;
Maids and matrons the mulberry leaves go to gather:
They can't pluck them faster than my tears are shed.

5.

'Tis the fifth moon – rice-planting – wife, widow and maiden,
Every one, old and young, busy appears;
The hot air with dampness and mildew is laden. –
My face is mildewed and moistened with tears.

6.

'Tis now the sixth moon – the heat is increasing,
The gold-speckled pailing's too listless to sing;
The hum of mosquitoes at night is unceasing,
My blood they may drink, so he feels not their sting.

7.

'Tis the seventh moon – autumn's cool breezes are blowing;

At each open window and doorway are seen
The matrons aud maidens all busily sewing
Their bright coloured garments of red, blue, and green.

8.

'Tis the eighth moon – the wild geese are overhead winging
Their way to the west; in old time it is said,
One, a token of love to a husband was bringing, –
But the bird at the feet of the husband fell dead.

9.

'Tis the ninth moon – husbands and wives are united;
On the ninth day each pledges the other in wine;
To view the chrysanthemums guests are invited; –
Shall I ever drink out of one cup with mine?

10.

'Tis the tenth moon – the farmers their rich crops in-gather;
The rustics are busy in every field;
They sing as they work in the bright golden weather,
And rejoice o'er their task in the bounteous yield.

11.

'Tis the eleventh moon – the snow-flakes around me are falling;
The snow and the cold do not my heart appal;
At night, in my dreams, I hear his voice calling,
He bids me, his wife, seek for him at the Wall.

12.

'Tis the twelfth moon – each household is busy preparing
To keep the New Year, – pigs and sheep are now slain;
While I, to the far distant Wall am repairing,
Broken-hearted and sad till I see him again."

* * *

While the girl sung,
There was many an eye
That had long been dry
Moistened by tears,
Which, perhaps for long years,
Had never from one of those eyes been wrung.

Yes, those guards, unfeeling and rough,
For once in their lives made good use of a cuff;
Who knows but that two or three tears such as theirs
Were just as efficient as long-winded prayers.
Her right to pass through they owned she had earned;
And even her petticoat they returned.
The officer then bade them open the gate,
And let her pass even though it was late.
Bidding the barrier guards adieu,
In the darkness she shortly was lost to view.

On her journey the young girl sped,
With tottering limbs and feet that bled;
Still she travelled on, day by day,
Having no money, she begged her way.
The poor girl's story like wildfire flew,
Every village she journeyed through,
People came thronging forth to meet her,
Women and children, old and young;
Many a kindly word would greet her –
All would have willingly helped Meng Cheng –
She appeared in truth like the fair Kuan yin,
The vilest man would have scorned the sin
Of insulting so faithful a heroine.

Travelling many a weary mile, –
Sometimes pausing to rest awhile, –
Crossing many a river wide, –

Climbing many a mountain side,
Only to feel as she gazed below,
What a long long distance she'd yet to go.
Will this weary journeying never be ended!
She shades her eyes from the rays of the sun;
She can see where earth and sky appear blended,
And, purpled by space, seem to melt in one.
Still the girl continued her way,
Drawing nearer every day,
She'll see him yet – Heaven grant that she may!

With beating heart and aching head,
Footsore and weary on she sped,
Crossing a river, breasting a hill,
Day after day found her travelling still;
Turning neither to left nor right,
Till at last the 'Great Wall' came into sight.
With tottering steps and limbs that trembled,
On she went till she reached the Wall;
A glance at the faces of those assembled,
Better than words, told the poor girl all.
In every pitying face she read,
Plainer than if the words had been said,
She had reached the Wall but to find him dead.

Thrice she screamed and over the Wall
The black clouds hung like a ghostly pall;
As if they were sent but to point the way
To the place where the corse of her husband lay.
Thrice on her husband's name she called,
The awe-struck labourers stood appalled,
As they gazed they saw with fear and wonder,
A tower that stood on the top of the Wall,
With a roar like thunder, rend asunder,
Sway for a moment, then topple and fall;

Disclosing, when dust and smoke had done,
The clothing worn by her husband Wan
Containing his ghastly skeleton!

The girl knelt down at the skeleton's side,
And, taking its hand, she the 'blood test' applied,
This at once would determine and palpably show
If 'twere really the corse of her husband or no.
Then she pierced her own hand and let the blood drop
On that of the skeleton, where, should it stop,
And congeal, or at once be absorbed in the bone,
That the corse was her husband's would plainly be shown,
If the blood from the hand of the skeleton ran,
Then the corse was not his but of some other man;
The true or false only the 'blood test' could tell,
'Twould be his if congealed, not his, if it fell.

The workmen thronged round her, awe filled every breast,
At seeing the maiden apply the blood test;
A dead silence reigns on them all as they stand,
And watch her blood drop on the skeleton's hand,
That the bones are her husband's the test soon reveals,
For as fast as the blood drops, so fast it congeals.
Then she pulled off her skirt which she over it spread,
And mournfully sat herself down by the dead;
And rocking herself to and fro by its side,
She bewailed his sad fate as she bitterly cried; –

"Oh, my husband! and was it for this that we wed?
Have I travelled this distance to find you here dead?
Ah! why were you dragged here to build the Great Wall?
May he who destroyed you in like manner fall!
Accursed be the monarch by whom it was done!
May the tyrant's unburied bones bleach in the sun!"

A magistrate chancing to pass at this time,
Heard the Emperor cursed; – 'twas so awful a crime
That he instantly went and made out a report
Of the case, which he took with his own hand to court.
The Emperor's 'dragon eye' glanced o'er the page,
Till he'd read its contents, then he trembled with rage;
"What! one of my subjects to dare to asperse
Her sovereign's own acts, and her sovereign curse!
Bring the culprit before me, this case I will try,
And decide, when I've heard it, what death she shall die.
On her and her kindrèd my vengeance I'll launch, –
I'll exterminate all: – cut them up, root and branch!"

In a short time the girl to the palace was led,
And the crime she was charged with before her was read.
Meng Cheng then knelt down in the great hall of gold,
And the whole of her tale to the Emperor told.
As she told her sad story the 'dragon eye' shone
With a lustre surpassing the gems on his throne;
He had ne'er before seen such a beautiful face –
So sylph-like a form – such symmetrical grace.
Then addressing the courtiers, who stood at each side,
"Her beauty would ruin a city," he cried;
"In truth she is lovely and wondrously fair!
And, if she is willing, I solemnly swear,
That she, by whom I but just now was accursed,
Shall, of all my imperial brides, rank the first!"

In a moment a plan in her mind she revolved: –
For the tyrant she never would wed she resolved, –
Concealing her feelings, she hastily cried,
"Since your majesty wishes to make me your bride,
First grant me three things; their fulfilment ensures
My heart's dearest wish – after that, I am yours."
The Emperor felt very pleased and elate,

And bade the young girl at once fearlessly state
These three things; she had only to say what they were
'Twould gratify him, could he gratify her.

The maiden, emboldened, arose from her knees,
And exclaimed, "The three things that I wish for are these; –
First build me a bridge over which I may ride,
From hence to the Wall, ten li long, ten li wide;
Next build for my husband a tomb ten li square;
And lastly your highness must sacrifice there,
In mourning robes clad; – thus my mind will be eased
And, buried with honour, his manes appeased,
If your majesty grant these three things you will earn
My life-long devotion and love in return.

The Emperor smiled, and his breast glowed with pride;
"Your wishes," cried he, "shall be soon gratified
Such trifles as these, they are nothing at all;
What is building a tomb, or a bridge, to the Wall?"
The imperial mandate soon spread far and wide,
And workmen assembled from every side;
They worked with such diligence, history says,
That the bridge and the tomb were complete in three days.

This diligence made the imperial heart glad,
And he instantly ordered the court to be clad
In white mourning robes; and he next orders gave
To march in procession to Wan-hsi-liang's grave;
He, placing himself, with Meng Cheng, at its head,
In a chariot of gold forth the long cortège led,
When they came to the tomb, the Emperor bade
Them all kneel, while himself the due sacrifice made.
All obeyed his commands; next the Emperor flung
Himself on his knees by the side of Meng Cheng.

While prostrated thus, the Emperor thought,
"'Tis her beautiful face all this magic has wrought;
She is fair, but till now it has never been said,
In history either I never have read,
Of a monarch's e'er paying so heavy a price
As I have for Meng Cheng in this sacrifice,
I, an Emperor, worship the ghost of a slave,
And pour an oblation of wine on his grave!"

All present in silence the spirit adored;
The monarch then rose and an offering poured
On the grave – three full cups of imperial wine;
This done, "Now," thought he, "the fair Meng Cheng is mine.
"Her grace, on my reign will increased lustre shed."
On reaching the bridge, when returning, he said,
"Fair maiden, my promise at length is fulfilled,
I now await yours; and tonight I have willed,
In the palace our nuptials shall be solemnized
With due pomp and show. I've already apprised
My ladies and eunuchs, and bade them prepare
Apartments befitting my queen of the fair."

"What!" cried the girl, "think you that I
Could ever with a tyrant wed?
Think you that rank and power could buy
My love from him who now lies dead?
By your harsh orders torn from me,
Slain by your cursed tyranny.

"No! I but fooled you to obtain
A worthy burial for him!
You thought by that my love to gain,
And gratify your latest whim.
Stuffed with conceit you dared presume
To think of conquest at his tomb!

"Your rank and wealth I utterly despise!
Your presence fills my heart with fear and dread!
Your face and form are hateful to my eyes!
I loathe the very ground on which you tread!
The air I breathe near you is odious!
I leave you now to join my husband – thus!"

As she spoke, the brave girl from the chariot stept,
With a loud cry of triumph the parapet cleared,
Plunging into the river as onward it swept,
And her corse 'neath an arch of the bridge disappeared.

'Twas so sudden, it seemed like a horrible dream;
Both monarch and courtiers stood looking aghast,
Gazing helplessly in to the broad flowing stream,
As its deep turgid waters rushed mournfully past.

Thus the faithful Meng Cheng, maiden, widow, and wife,
To prove her devotion e'en death did not dread;
For the sake of her first love she gave up her life;
She was true to him living, she joined him when dead.

The song of Meng Cheng and her journey is finished;
Since she sought her husband long ages have passed,
Yet the halo around her shines on undiminished,
And will shine so long as this empire shall last.

And so long as our race love to hear tales of glory,
And the bosom throbs high when a brave deed is sung,
So long will the breast swell at hearing her story,
And the tear fall in pity for faithful Meng Cheng.

Note: Many have it that the girl collected the bones of her husband together, and, with them in her arms, plunged into the river. She was canonized as the

'River Goddess', and a temple is dedicated to her at a place called Kou-hsi. The tower which fell, revealing the bones of her husband, has repeatedly been rebuilt, but has invariably fallen again. The story goes that it never can be built without toppling down again as soon as it is finished.

Sam-Chung and the Water Demon

SAM-CHUNG WAS ONE of the most famous men in the history of the Buddhist Church, and had distinguished himself by the earnestness and self-denial with which he had entered on the pursuit of eternal life. His mind had been greatly exercised and distressed at the pains and sorrows which mankind were apparently doomed to endure. Even those, however, terrible as they were, he could have managed to tolerate had they not ended, in the case of every human being, in the crowning calamity which comes upon all at the close of life.

Death was the great mystery which cast its shadow on every human being. It invaded every home. The sage whose virtues and teachings were the means of uplifting countless generations of men came under its great law. Men of infamous and abandoned character seemed often to outlive the more virtuous of their fellow-beings; but they too, when the gods saw fit, were hurried off without any ceremony. Even the little ones, who had never violated any of the laws of Heaven, came under this universal scourge; and many of them, who had only just commenced to live were driven out into the Land of Shadows by this mysterious force which dominates all human life.

Accordingly Sam-Chung wanted to be freed from the power of death, so that its shadow should never darken his life in the years to come.

After careful enquiry, and through friendly hints from men who, he had reason to believe, were fairies in disguise and had been sent by the Goddess of Mercy to help those who aspired after a higher life, he learned that it was possible by the constant pursuit of virtue to arrive at that stage of existence in which death would lose all its power to injure, and men should become immortal. This boon of eternal life could be won by every man or woman who was willing to pay the price for so precious a gift. It could be gained by great self-denial, by willingness to suffer, and especially by the exhibition of profound love and sympathy for those who were in sorrow of any kind. It appeared, indeed, that the one thing most imperatively demanded by the gods from those who aspired to enter their ranks was that they should be possessed of a divine compassion, and that their supreme object should be the succouring of distressed humanity. Without this compassion any personal sacrifice that might be made in the search for immortality would be absolutely useless.

Sam-Chung was already conscious that he was a favourite of the gods, for they had given him two companions, both with supernatural powers, to enable him to contend against the cunning schemes of the evil spirits, who are ever planning how to thwart and destroy those whose hearts are set upon higher things.

One day, accompanied by Chiau and Chu, the two attendants commissioned by the Goddess of Mercy to attend upon him, Sam-Chung started on his long journey for the famous Tien-ho river, to cross which is the ambition of every pilgrim on his way to the land of the Immortals. They endured many weeks of painful travelling over high mountains and through deep valleys which lay in constant shadow, and across sandy deserts where men perished of thirst or were struck down by the scorching heat of the sun, before they met any of the infernal foes that they expected to be lying in wait for them.

Weary and footsore, they at last arrived one evening on the shores of the mighty Tien-ho, just as the sun was setting. The glory of the clouds in the west streamed on to the waters of the river, and made them sparkle with a beauty which seemed to our wearied travellers to transform them into something more than earthly. The river here was so wide that it looked like an inland sea. There was no sign of land on the distant horizon, nothing but one interminable vista of waters, stretching away as far as the eye could reach.

One thing, however, greatly disappointed Sam-Chung and his companions, and that was the absence of boats. They had planned to engage one, and by travelling across the river during the night, they hoped to hurry on their way and at the same time to rest and refresh themselves after the fatigues they had been compelled to endure on their long land journey.

It now became a very serious question with them where they were to spend the night. There was no sign of any human habitation round about. There was the sandy beach along which they were walking, and there was the wide expanse of the river, on which the evening mists were slowly gathering; but no appearance of life. Just as they were wondering what course they should pursue, the faint sound of some musical instruments came floating on the air and caught their ear. Hastening forward in the direction from which the music came, they ascended a piece of rising ground, from the top of which they were delighted to see a village nestling on the hillside, and a small temple standing on the very margin of the river.

With hearts overjoyed at the prospect of gaining some place where they could lodge for the night, they hurried forward to the hamlet in front of them. As they drew nearer, the sounds of music became louder and more distinct. They concluded that some festival was being observed, or that some happy gathering amongst the people had thrown them all into a holiday mood. Entering the village, they made their way to a house which stood out prominently from the rest, and which was better built than any others they could see. Besides, it was the one from which the music issued, and around its doors was gathered a number of people who had evidently been attending some feast inside.

As the three travellers came up to the door, a venerable-looking old man came out to meet them. Seeing that they were strangers, he courteously invited them to enter; and on Sam-Chung asking whether they could be entertained for the night, he assured them that there was ample room for them in the house, and that he gladly welcomed them to be his guests for as long as it was their pleasure to remain.

"In the meanwhile you must come in," he said, "and have some food, for you must be tired and hungry after travelling so far, and the tables are still covered with the good things which were prepared for the feast to-day."

After they had finished their meal, they began to talk to the old gentleman who was so kindly entertaining them. They were greatly pleased with his courtesy and with the hearty hospitality which he had pressed upon them.

They noticed, however, that he was very absent-minded, and looked as if some unpleasant thought lay heavy on his heart.

"May I ask," said Sam-Chung, "what was the reason for the great gathering here to-day? There is no festival in the Chinese calendar falling on this date, so I thought I would take the liberty of enquiring what occasion you were really commemorating."

"We were not commemorating anything," the old man replied with a grave face. "It was really a funeral service for two of my grand-children, who, though they are not yet dead, will certainly disappear out of this life before many hours have passed."

"But how can such a ceremony be performed over persons who are still alive?" asked Sam-Chung with a look of wonder in his face.

"When I have explained the circumstances to you, you will then be no longer surprised at this unusual service," replied the old man.

"You must know," he continued, "that this region is under the control of a Demon of a most cruel and bloodthirsty disposition. He is not like the ordinary spirits, whose images are enshrined in our temples, and whose main aim is to protect and guard their worshippers. This one has no love for mankind, but on the contrary the bitterest hatred, and his whole life seems to be occupied in scheming how he may inflict sorrow and disaster on them. His greatest cruelty is to insist that every year just about this time two children, one a boy and the other a girl, shall be conveyed to his temple by the river side to be devoured by him. Many attempts have been made to resist this barbarous demand, but they have only resulted in increased suffering to those who have dared to oppose him. The consequence is that the people submit to this cruel murder of their children, though many a heart is broken at the loss of those dearest to them."

"But is there any system by which the unfortunate people may get to know when this terrible sacrifice is going to be demanded from them?" asked Sam-Chung.

"Oh yes," replied the man. "The families are taken in rotation, and when each one's turn comes round, their children are prepared for the sacrifice. Moreover, that there may be no mistake, the Demon himself appears in the home a few days before, and gives a threatening command to have the victims ready on such a date. Only the day before yesterday, this summons came to us to have our children ready by tomorrow morning at break of day. That is why we had a feast to-day, and performed the funeral rites for the dead, so that their spirits may not be held under the control of this merciless Damon, but may in time be permitted to issue from the Land of Shadows, and be born again under happier circumstances into this world, which they are leaving under such tragic circumstances."

"But what is the Demon like?" enquired Sam-Chung.

"Oh, no one can ever tell what he is like," said the man. "He has no bodily form that one can look upon. His presence is known by a strong blast of wind which fills the place with a peculiar odour, and with an influence so subtle that you feel yourself within the grip of a powerful force, and instinctively bow your head as though you were in the presence of a being who could destroy you in a moment were he so disposed."

"One more question and I have finished," said Sam-Chung. "Where did this Demon come from, and how is it that he has acquired such an overmastering supremacy over the lives of men, that he seems able to defy even Heaven itself, and all the great hosts of kindly gods who are working for the salvation of mankind?"

"This Demon," the man replied, "was once an inhabitant of the Western Heaven, and under the direct control of the Goddess of Mercy. He must, however, have been filled with evil devices and fiendish instincts from the very beginning, for he seized the first opportunity to escape to earth, and to take up his residence in the grottoes and caverns that lie deep down beneath the waters of the Tien-ho. Other spirits almost as bad as himself have also taken up their abode there, and they combine their forces to bring calamity and disaster upon the people of this region."

Sam-Chung, whose heart was filled with the tenderest feelings of compassion for all living things, so much so that his name was a familiar one even amongst the Immortals in the far-off Western Heaven, felt himself stirred by a mighty indignation when he thought of how innocent childhood had been sacrificed to minister to the unnatural passion of this depraved Demon. Chiau and Chu were as profoundly indignant as he, and a serious consultation ensued as to the best methods to be adopted to save the little ones who were doomed to destruction on the morrow, and at the same time to break the monster's rule so that it should cease for ever.

Chiau, who was the more daring of the two whom I the goddess had deputed to protect Sam-Chung, at length cried out with flashing eyes, "I will personate the boy, Chu shall act the girl, and together we will fight the Demon and overthrow and kill him, and so deliver the people from his dreadful tyranny."

Turning to the old man, he said, "Bring the children here so that we may see them, and make our plans so perfect that the Demon with all his cunning will not be able to detect or frustrate them."

In a few moments the little ones were led in by their grandfather. The boy was seven and the girl was one year older. They were both of them nervous and shy, and clung timidly to the old man as if for protection.

They were very interesting-looking children. The boy was a proud, brave-spirited little fellow, as one could see by the poise of his head as he gazed at the strangers. If anything could be predicted from his looks, he would one day turn out to be a man of great power, for he had in his youthful face all the signs which promise a life out of the common. The girl was a shy little thing, with her hair done up in a childlike fashion that well became her. She was a dainty little mortal. Her eyes were almond-shaped, and with the coyness of her sex she kept shooting out glances from the corners of them at the three men who were looking at her. Her cheeks were pale, with just a suspicion of colour painted into them by the deft hand of nature; whilst her lips had been touched with the faintest dash of carmine, evidently just a moment ago, before she left her mother's side.

"Now, my boy," said Chiau to the little fellow, "keep your eyes fixed on me, and never take them from me for a moment; and you, little sister," addressing the girl, "do the same to the man next to me, and you will see something that will make you both laugh."

The eyes of them both were at once riveted on the two men, and a look of amazement slowly crept into their faces. And no wonder, for as they gazed they saw the two men rapidly changing, and becoming smaller and smaller, until they were the exact size and image of themselves. In their features and dress, and in every minute detail they were the precise pattern of the children, who with staring eyes were held spellbound by the magic change which had taken place in front of them.

"Now," said Chiau to the old gentleman, "the transformation is complete. Take the children away and hide them in the remotest and most inaccessible room that you have in your house. Let them be seen by no chattering woman or servant who might divulge our secret, so that in some way or other it might reach the ears of the Demon, and put him on his guard. Remember that from this moment these little ones are not supposed to exist, but that we are your grand-children who are to be taken to the temple tomorrow morning at break of day."

Just as the eastern sky showed the first touch of colour, two sedan-chairs were brought up to the door to carry the two victims away to be devoured by the Demon. A few frightened-looking neighbours peered through the gloom to catch a last glimpse of the children, but not one of them had the least suspicion that the boy and girl were really fairies who were about to wage a deadly battle with the Demon in order to deliver them from the curse under which they lived.

No sooner had the children been put into the temple, where a dim rush-light did but serve to disclose the gloom, and the doors had been closed with a bang, than the chair-bearers rushed away in fear for their very lives.

An instant afterwards a hideous, gigantic form emerged from an inner room and advanced towards the children. The Demon was surprised, however, to find that on this occasion the little victims did not exhibit any signs of alarm, as had always been the case hitherto, but seemed to be calmly awaiting his approach. There was no symptom of fear about them, and not a cry of terror broke from their lips; but with a fearless and composed mien they gazed upon him as he advanced.

Hesitating for a moment, as if to measure the foe which he began to fear might lie concealed beneath the figures of the boy and girl before him, the Demon's great fiery eyes began to flash with deadly passion as he saw the two little ones gradually expand in size, until they were transformed into beings as powerful and as mighty as himself. He knew at once that he had been outwitted, and that he must now battle for his very life; so, drawing a sword which had always stood him in good stead, he rushed upon the two who faced him so calmly and with such apparent confidence in themselves.

Chiau and Chu were all ready for the fray, and with weapons firmly gripped and with hearts made strong by the consciousness of the justice of their cause, they awaited the onslaught of the Demon.

And what a battle it was that then ensued in the dim and shadowy temple! It was a conflict of great and deadly significance, waged on one side for the deliverance of helpless childhood, and on the other for the basest schemes that the spirits of evil could devise. It was a battle royal, in which no quarter was either asked or given. The clash of weapons, and sounds unfamiliar to the human ear, and groans and cries which seemed to come from a lost soul, filled the temple with their hideous uproar.

At last the Demon, who seemed to have been grievously wounded, though by his magic art he had caused his wounds to be instantly healed, began to see that the day was going against him. One more mighty lunge with his broadsword, and one more furious onset, and his craven heart failed him. With a cry of despair he fled from the temple, and plunged headlong into the river flowing by its walls.

Great were the rejoicings when Chiau and Chu returned to report to Sam-Chung the glorious victory they had gained over the Demon. Laughter and rejoicing were heard in every home, and men and women assembled in front of their doors and at the corners of the narrow alley-ways to congratulate each other on the great deliverance which that day had come to them and to their children. The dread of the Demon had already vanished, and a feeling of freedom so inspired the men of the village that as if by a common impulse, they rushed impetuously down to where the temple stood, and in the course of a few hours every vestige of it had disappeared beneath the waters into which the Demon had plunged.

After his great defeat the baffled spirit made his way to the grotto beneath the waters, where he and the other demons had taken up their abode. A general council was called to devise plans to wipe out the disgrace which had been sustained, and to regain the power that had slipped from the Demon's grasp. They wished also to visit Sam-Chung with condign punishment which would render him helpless for the future.

"We must capture him," said one wicked-looking imp, who always acted as counsellor to the rest. "I have been told that to devour some of his flesh would ensure the prolongation of life for more than a thousand years."

The suggestion to seize Sam-Chung was unanimously accepted as a very inspiration of genius, and the precise measures which were to be adopted in order to capture him were agreed to after a long discussion.

On the very next morning, a most violent snowstorm set in, so that the face of the river and the hills all round about, and the very heavens themselves were lost in the blinding snow-drifts that flew before the gale. Gradually the cold became so intense that the Ice King laid his grip upon the waters of the Tien-ho, and turned the flowing stream into a crystal highway, along which men might travel with ease and safety. Such a sight had never been seen before by any of the people who lived upon its banks, and many were the speculations as to what such a phenomenon might mean to the welfare of the people of the region. It never occurred to any one that this great snow-storm which had turned into ice a river that had never been known to freeze before, was all the work of demons determined on the destruction of Sam-Chung.

Next day the storm had passed, but the river was one mass of ice which gleamed and glistened in the morning rays. Much to the astonishment of Sam-Chung and his two companions, they caught sight of a number of people, who appeared to be merchants, moving about on the bank of the river, together with several mules laden with merchandise. The whole party seemed intent on their preparations for crossing the river, which they were observed to test in various places to make sure that it was strong enough to bear their weight. This they seemed satisfied about, for in a short time the men and animals set forward on their journey across the ice.

Sam-Chung immediately insisted upon following their example, though the plan was vigorously opposed by the villagers, who predicted all kinds of dangers if he entered on such an uncertain and hazardous enterprise. Being exceedingly anxious to proceed on his journey, however, and seeing no prospect of doing so if he did not take advantage of the present remarkable condition of the river, he hastened to follow in the footsteps of the merchants, who by this time had already advanced some distance on the ice.

He would have been less anxious to enter on this perilous course, had he known that the innocent-looking traders who preceded him were every one of them demons who had changed themselves into the semblance of men in order to lure him to his destruction.

Sam-Chung and his companions had not proceeded more than five or six miles, when ominous symptoms of coming disaster began to manifest themselves. The extreme cold in the air suddenly ceased, and a warm south wind began to blow. The surface of the ice lost its hardness. Streamlets of water trickled here and there, forming great pools which made walking exceedingly difficult.

Chiau, whose mind was a very acute and intelligent one, became terrified at these alarming symptoms of danger, especially as the ice began to crack, and loud and prolonged reports reached them from every direction. Another most suspicious thing was the sudden disappearance of the company of merchants, whom they had all along kept well in sight. There was something wrong, he was fully convinced, and so with all his wits about him, he kept himself alert for any contingency. It was well that he did this, for before they had proceeded another mile, the ice began to grow thinner, and before they could retreat there was a sudden crash and all three were precipitated into the water.

Hardly had Chiau's feet touched the river, than with a superhuman effort he made a spring into the air, and was soon flying with incredible speed in the direction of the Western Heaven, to invoke the aid of the Goddess of Mercy to deliver Sam-Chung from the hands of an enemy who would show him no quarter.

In the meanwhile Sam-Chung and Chu were borne swiftly by the demons, who were eagerly awaiting their immersion in the water, to the great cave that lay deep down at the bottom of the mighty river. Chu, being an immortal and a special messenger of the Goddess, defied all the arts of the evil spirits to injure him, so that all they could do was to imprison him in one of the inner grottoes and station a guard over him to prevent his escape. Sam-Chung, however, was doomed to death, and the Demon, in revenge for the disgrace he had brought upon him, and in the hope of prolonging his own life by a thousand years, decided that on the morrow he would feast upon his flesh. But he made his plans without taking into consideration the fact that Sam-Chung was an especial favourite with the Goddess.

During the night a tremendous commotion occurred. The waters of the river fled in every direction as before the blast of a hurricane, and the caverns where the demons were assembled were illuminated with a light so brilliant that their eyes became dazzled, and for a time were blinded by the sudden blaze that flashed from every corner. Screaming with terror, they fled in all directions. Only one remained, and that was the fierce spirit who had wrought such sorrow amongst the people of the land near by. He too would have disappeared with the rest, had not some supernatural power chained him to the spot where he stood.

Soon the noble figure of the Goddess of Mercy appeared, accompanied by a splendid train of Fairies who hovered round her to do her bidding. Her first act was to release Sam-Chung, who lay bound ready for his death, which but for her interposition would have taken place within a few hours. He and his two companions were entrusted to the care of a chosen number of her followers, and conveyed with all speed across the river.

The Goddess then gave a command to some who stood near her person, and in a moment, as if by a flash of lightning, the cowering, terrified Demon had vanished, carried away to be confined in one of the dungeons where persistent haters of mankind are kept imprisoned, until their hearts are changed by some noble sentiment of compassion and the Goddess sees that they are once more fit for liberty.

And then the lights died out, and the sounds of fairy voices ceased. The waters of the river, which had been under a divine spell, returned to their course, and the Goddess with her magnificent train of beneficent spirits departed to her kingdom in the far-off Western Heaven.

Sky O'Dawn

ONCE UPON A TIME there was a man who took a child to a woman in a certain village, and told her to take care of him. Then he disappeared. And because the dawn was just breaking in the sky when the woman took the child into her home, she called him Sky O'Dawn. When the child was three years old, he would often look up to the heavens and talk with the stars. One day he ran away and many months passed before he came home again. The woman gave him a whipping. But he ran away again, and did not return for a year. His foster-mother was frightened, and asked: "Where have you been all year long?" The boy answered: "I only made a quick trip to the Purple Sea. There the water stained my clothes red. So I went to the spring at which the sun turns in,

and washed them. I went away in the morning and I came back at noon. Why do you speak about my having been gone a year?"

Then the woman asked: "And where did you pass on your way?"

The boy answered: "When I had washed my clothes, I rested for a while in the City of the Dead and fell asleep. And the King-Father of the East gave me red chestnuts and rosy dawn-juice to eat, and my hunger was stilled. Then I went to the dark skies and drank the yellow dew, and my thirst was quenched. And I met a black tiger and wanted to ride home on his back. But I whipped him too hard, and he bit me in the leg. And so I came back to tell you about it."

Once more the boy ran away from home, thousands of miles, until he came to the swamp where dwelt the Primal Mist. There he met an old man with yellow eyebrows and asked him how old he might be. The old man said: "I have given up the habit of eating, and live on air. The pupils of my eyes have gradually acquired a green glow, which enables me to see all hidden things. Whenever a thousand years have passed I turn around my bones and wash the marrow. And every two thousand years I scrape my skin to get rid of the hair. I have already washed my bones thrice and scraped my skin five times."

Afterward Sky O'Dawn served the Emperor Wu of the Han dynasty. The Emperor, who was fond of the magic arts, was much attached to him. One day he said to him: "I wish that the empress might not grow old. Can you prevent it?"

Sky O'Dawn answered: "I know of only one means to keep from growing old."

The Emperor asked what herbs one had to eat. Sky O'Dawn replied: "In the North-East grow the mushrooms of life. There is a three-legged crow in the sun who always wants to get down and eat them. But the Sun-God holds his eyes shut and does not let him get away. If human beings eat them they become immortal, when animals eat them they grow stupefied."

"And how do you know this?" asked the Emperor.

"When I was a boy I once fell into a deep well, from which I could not get out for many decades. And down there was an immortal who led me to this herb. But one has to pass through a red river whose water is so light that not even a feather can swim on it. Everything that touches its surface sinks to the depths. But the man pulled off one of his shoes and gave it to me. And I crossed the water on the shoe, picked the herb and ate it. Those who dwell in that place weave mats of pearls and precious stones. They led me to a spot before which hung a curtain of delicate, colored skin. And they gave me a pillow carved of black jade, on which were graven sun and moon, clouds and thunder. They covered me with a dainty coverlet spun of the hair of a hundred gnats. A cover of that kind is very cool and refreshing in summer. I felt of it with my hands, and it seemed to be formed of water; but when I looked at it more closely, it was pure light."

Once the Emperor called together all his magicians in order to talk with them about the fields of the blessed spirits. Sky O'Dawn was there, too, and said: "Once I was wandering about the North Pole and I came to the Fire-Mirror Mountain. There neither sun nor moon shines. But there is a dragon who holds a fiery mirror in his jaws in order to light up the darkness. On the mountain is a park, and in the park is a lake. By the lake grows the glimmer-stalk grass, which shines like a lamp of gold. If you pluck it and use it for a candle, you can see all things visible, and the shapes of the spirits as well. It even illuminates the interior of a human being."

Once Sky O'Dawn went to the East, into the country of the fortunate clouds. And he brought back with him from that land a steed of the gods, nine feet high. The Emperor asked him how he had come to find it.

So he told him: "The Queen-Mother of the West had him harnessed to her wagon when she went to visit the King-Father of the East. The steed was staked out in the field of the mushrooms of life. But he trampled down several hundred of them. This made the King-Father angry, and he drove the steed away to the heavenly river. There I found him and rode him home. I rode three times around the sun, because I had fallen asleep on the steed's back. And then, before I knew it, I was here. This steed can catch up with the sun's shadow. When I found him he was quite thin and as sad as an aged donkey. So I mowed the grass of the country of the fortunate clouds, which grows once every two-thousand years on the Mountain of the Nine Springs and fed it to the horse; and that made him lively again."

The Emperor asked what sort of a place the country of the fortunate clouds might be. Sky O'Dawn answered: "There is a great swamp there. The people prophesy fortune and misfortune by the air and the clouds. If good fortune is to befall a house, clouds of five colors form in the rooms, which alight on the grass and trees and turn into a colored dew. This dew tastes as sweet as cider."

The Emperor asked whether he could obtain any of this dew. Sky O'Dawn replied: "My steed could take me to the place where it falls four times in the course of a single day!"

And sure enough he came back by evening, and brought along dew of every color in a crystal flask. The Emperor drank it and his hair grew black again. He gave it to his highest officials to drink, and the old grew young again and the sick became well.

Once, when a comet appeared in the heavens, Sky O'Dawn gave the Emperor the astrologer's wand. The Emperor pointed it at the comet and the comet was quenched.

Sky O'Dawn was an excellent whistler. And whenever he whistled in full tones, long drawn out, the motes in the sunbeams danced to his music.

Once he said to a friend: "There is not a soul on earth who knows who I am with the exception of the astrologer!"

When Sky O'Dawn had died, the Emperor called the astrologer to him and asked: "Did you know Sky O'Dawn?"

He replied: "No!"

The Emperor said: "What do you know?"

The astrologer answered: "I know how to gaze on the stars."

"Are all the stars in their places?" asked the Emperor.

"Yes, but for eighteen years I have not seen the Star of the Great Year. Now it is visible once more."

Then the Emperor looked up towards the skies and sighed: "For eighteen years Sky O'Dawn kept me company, and I did not know that he was the Star of the Great Year!"

The Ballad of Mulan

"JI JI," AND "JI JI," Mulan weaves in front of the door.
"Now we don't hear the loom shuttle; we only hear our daughter sighing.
Daughter, what are you thinking about? What are you nostalgic over?"
"I am not thinking about anything, and I am not nostalgic.

Last night I saw the conscription notice; it's the Khan's Great Callup.

There are twelve scrolls of army rolls, and every scroll has Father's name.

Father has no elder son; I have no big brother.

Let me buy saddle and horse, and go to war in Father's place."

In the east market a fine horse is bought; in the west market, a saddle and its skirt;

In the south market, a bridle; in the north market, a long whip.

In the morning she says good-bye to her parents; in the evening she sleeps at the side of the Yellow River.

She doesn't hear the sound of parents calling her,

But hears the sound of the Yellow River's water going "jian, jian."

In the morning she says good-bye to the Yellow River; in the evening she sleeps on the Black Mountain.

She doesn't hear the sound of parents calling her,

But hears the sound of the Yan Mountains' barbarian horsemen going "jiu, jiu."

For thousands of miles, she goes wherever the battle takes her, crossing passes and mountains as if she flew.

Frigid air transmits the night watch claps; frosty light illumes the iron armor.

Generals die after a hundred battles; heroes return after ten years' time.

They return to see the Son of Heaven, sitting in the Bright Hall.

The merit scrolls confer twelve promotions, awarded to thousands of strong men.

The Khan asks what she wants. "Mulan doesn't need to be an Imperial Cabinet Official,

I'd like a good camel's thousand-mile hooves, to carry me back home."

Hearing that Daughter is coming, the parents come outside the city walls, supporting each other.

Hearing that Little Sister is coming, Big Sister puts on her makeup in front of the door.

Hearing that Big Sister is coming, Little Brother sharpens the knife, eyeing the pig and goat.

"I open up my east bedroom door; I sit on my west bedroom bed.
I take off my wartime clothes; I put on my old times dress."
At the window she arranges cloud-like hair; facing the mirror she
    pastes on her yellow forehead ornaments.
She comes out to see her comrades; her comrades are all shocked.
"We march together for twelve years, and we don't know that Mulan
    is a lady!"
"The male rabbit hops from the beginning; the female rabbit's eyes
    are misty;
Both rabbits are running along the ground; how can you tell whether
    I am male or female?"

The Dragon Princess

IN THE SEA OF DUNGTING there is a hill, and in that hill there
is a hole, and this hole is so deep that it has no bottom. Once
a fisherman was passing there who slipped and fell into the
hole. He came to a country full of winding ways which led over
hill and dale for several miles.

Finally he reached a dragon-castle lying in a great plain. There grew a green
slime which reached to his knees. He went to the gate of the castle. It was
guarded by a dragon who spouted water which dispersed in a fine mist.
Within the gate lay a small hornless dragon who raised his head, showed
his claws, and would not let him in.

The fisherman spent several days in the cave, satisfying his hunger with
the green slime, which he found edible and which tasted like rice-mush. At
last he found a way out again. He told the district mandarin what had
happened to him, and the latter reported the matter to the emperor. The
emperor sent for a wise man and questioned him concerning it.

The wise man said: "There are four paths in this cave. One path leads
to the south-west shore of the Sea of Dungting, the second path leads to

a valley in the land of the four rivers, the third path ends in a cave on the mountain of Lo-Fu and the fourth in an island of the Eastern Sea. In this cave dwells the seventh daughter of the Dragon-King of the Eastern Sea, who guards his pearls and his treasure. It happened once in the ancient days, that a fisherboy dived into the water and brought up a pearl from beneath the chin of a black dragon. The dragon was asleep, which was the reason the fisherboy brought the pearl to the surface without being harmed. The treasure which the daughter of the Dragon-King has in charge is made up of thousands and millions of such jewels. Several thousands of small dragons watch over them in her service. Dragons have the peculiarity of fighting shy of wax. But they are fond of beautiful jade-stones, and of kung-tsing, the hollowgreen wood, and like to eat swallows. If one were to send a messenger with a letter, it would be possible to obtain precious pearls."

The emperor was greatly pleased, and announced a large reward for the man who was competent to go to the dragon-castle as his messenger.

The first man to come forward was named So Pi-Lo. But the wise man said: "A great-great-great-great-grandfather of yours once slew more than a hundred of the dragons of the Eastern Sea, and was finally himself slain by the dragons. The dragons are the enemies of your family and you cannot go."

Then came a man from Canton, Lo-Dsi-Tschun, with his two brothers, who said that his ancestors had been related to the Dragon-King. Hence they were well liked by the dragons and well known to them. They begged to be entrusted with the message.

The wise man asked: "And have you still in your possession the stone which compels the dragons to do your will?"

"Yes," said they, "we have brought it along with us."

The wise man had them show him the stone; then he spoke: "This stone is only obeyed by the dragons who make clouds and send down the rain. It will not do for the dragons who guard the pearls of the sea-king." Then he questioned them further: "Have you the dragon-brain vapor?"

When they admitted that they had not, the wise man said: "How then will you compel the dragons to yield their treasure?"

And the emperor said: "What shall we do?"

The wise man replied: "On the Western Ocean sail foreign merchants who deal in dragon-brain vapor. Someone must go to them and seek it from them. I also know a holy man who is an adept in the art of taming dragons, and who has prepared ten pounds of the dragon-stone. Someone should be sent for that as well."

The emperor sent out his messengers. They met one of the holy man's disciples and obtained two fragments of dragon-stone from him.

Said the wise man: "That is what we want!"

Several more months went by, and at last a pill of dragon-brain vapor had also been secured. The emperor felt much pleased and had his jewelers carve two little boxes of the finest jade. These were polished with the ashes of the Wutung-tree. And he had an essence prepared of the very best hollowgreen wood, pasted with sea-fish lime, and hardened in the fire. Of this two vases were made. Then the bodies and the clothing of the messengers were rubbed with tree-wax, and they were given five hundred roasted swallows to take along with them.

They went into the cave. When they reached the dragon-castle, the little dragon who guarded the gate smelled the tree-wax, so he crouched down and did them no harm. They gave him a hundred roasted swallows as a bribe to announce them to the daughter of the Dragon-King. They were admitted to her presence and offered her the jade caskets, the vases and the four hundred roasted swallows as gifts. The dragon's daughter received them graciously, and they unfolded the emperor's letter.

In the castle there was a dragon who was over a thousand years old. He could turn himself into a human being, and could interpret the language of human beings. Through him the dragon's daughter learned that the emperor was sending her the gifts, and she returned them with a gift of three great pearls, seven smaller pearls and a whole bushel of ordinary pearls. The messengers took leave, rode off with their pearls on a dragon's back, and in a moment they had reached the banks of the Yangtze-kiang. They made their way to Nanking, the imperial capital, and there handed over their treasure of gems.

The emperor was much pleased and showed them to the wise man. He said: "Of the three great pearls one is a divine wishing-pearl of the third class, and two are black dragon-pearls of medium quality. Of the seven smaller pearls two are serpent-pearls, and five are mussel-pearls. The remaining pearls are in part sea-crane pearls, in part snail and oyster-pearls.

They do not approach the great pearls in value, and yet few will be found to equal them on earth."

The emperor also showed them to all his servants. They, however, thought the wise man's words all talk, and did not believe what he said.

Then the wise man said: "The radiance of wishing-pearls of the first class is visible for forty miles, that of the second class for twenty miles, and that of the third for ten miles. As far as their radiance carries, neither wind nor rain, thunder nor lightning, water, fire nor weapons may reach. The pearls of the black dragon are nine-colored and glow by night. Within the circle of their light the poison of serpents and worms is powerless. The serpent-pearls are seven-colored, the mussel-pearls five-colored. Both shine by night. Those most free from spots are the best. They grow within the mussel, and increase and decrease in size as the moon waxes and wanes."

Someone asked how the serpent and sea-crane pearls could be told apart, and the wise man answered: "The animals themselves recognize them."

Then the emperor selected a serpent-pearl and a sea-crane pearl, put them together with a whole bushel of ordinary pearls, and poured the lot out in the courtyard. Then a large yellow serpent and a black crane were fetched and placed among the pearls. At once the crane took up a sea-crane pearl in his bill and began to dance and sing and flutter around. But the serpent snatched at the serpent-pearl, and wound himself about it in many coils. And when the people saw this they acknowledged the truth of the wise man's words. As regards the radiance of the larger and smaller pearls it turned out, too, just as the wise man had said.

In the dragon-castle the messengers had enjoyed dainty fare, which tasted like flowers, herbs, ointment and sugar. They had brought a remnant of it with them to the capital; yet exposed to the air it had become as hard as stone. The emperor commanded that these fragments be preserved in the treasury. Then he bestowed high rank and titles on the three brothers, and made each one of them a present of a thousand rolls of fine silk stuff. He also had investigated why it was that the fisherman, when he chanced upon the cave, had not been destroyed by the dragons. And it turned out that his fishing clothes had been soaked in oil and tree-wax. The dragons had dreaded the odor.

The Girl with the Horse's Head, or The Silkworm Goddess

IN THE DIM AGES of the past there once was an old man who went on a journey. No one remained at home save his only daughter and a white stallion. The daughter fed the horse day by day, but she was lonely and yearned for her father.

So it happened that one day she said in jest to the horse: "If you will bring back my father to me then I will marry you!"

No sooner had the horse heard her say this, than he broke loose and ran away. He ran until he came to the place where her father was. When her father saw the horse, he was pleasantly surprised, caught him and seated himself on his back. And the horse turned back the way he had come, neighing without a pause.

"What can be the matter with the horse?" thought the father. "Something must have surely gone wrong at home!" So he dropped the reins and rode back. And he fed the horse liberally because he had been so intelligent; but the horse ate nothing, and when he saw the girl, he struck out at her with his hoofs and tried to bite her. This surprised the father; he questioned his daughter, and she told him the truth, just as it had occurred.

"You must not say a word about it to any one," spoke her father, "or else people will talk about us."

And he took down his crossbow, shot the horse, and hung up his skin in the yard to dry. Then he went on his travels again.

One day his daughter went out walking with the daughter of a neighbor. When they entered the yard, she pushed the horse-hide with her foot and said: "What an unreasonable animal you were – wanting to marry a human being! What happened to you served you right!"

But before she had finished her speech, the horse-hide moved, rose up, wrapped itself about the girl and ran off.

Horrified, her companion ran home to her father and told him what had happened. The neighbors looked for the girl everywhere, but she could not be found.

At last, some days afterward, they saw the girl hanging from the branches of a tree, still wrapped in the horse-hide; and gradually she turned into a silkworm and wove a cocoon. And the threads which she spun were strong and thick. Her girl friend then took down the cocoon and let her slip out of it; and then she spun the silk and sold it at a large profit.

But the girl's relatives longed for her greatly. So one day the girl appeared riding in the clouds on her horse, followed by a great company and said: "In heaven I have been assigned to the task of watching over the growing of silkworms. You must yearn for me no longer!" And thereupon they built temples to her in her native land, and every year, at the silkworm season, sacrifices are offered to her and her protection is implored. And the Silkworm Goddess is also known as the girl with the Horse's Head.

The Herd Boy and the Weaving Maiden

THE HERD BOY was the child of poor people. When he was twelve years old, he took service with a farmer to herd his cow. After a few years the cow had grown large and fat, and her hair shone like yellow gold. She must have been a cow of the gods.

One day while he had her out at pasture in the mountains, she suddenly began to speak to the Herd Boy in a human voice, as follows: "This is the Seventh Day. Now the White Jade Ruler has nine daughters, who bathe this day in the Sea of Heaven. The seventh daughter is beautiful and wise beyond all measure. She spins the cloud-silk for the King and Queen of Heaven, and presides over the weaving which maidens do on earth. It is for this reason she is called the Weaving Maiden. And if you go and take away her clothes while she bathes, you may become her husband and gain immortality."

"But she is up in Heaven," said the Herd Boy, "and how can I get there?"

"I will carry you there," answered the yellow cow.

So the Herd Boy climbed on the cow's back. In a moment clouds began to stream out of her hoofs, and she rose into the air. About his ears there was a whistling like the sound of the wind, and they flew along as swiftly as lightning. Suddenly the cow stopped.

"Now we are here," said she.

Then round about him the Herd Boy saw forests of chrysophrase and trees of jade. The grass was of jasper and the flowers of coral. In the midst of all this splendor lay a great, four-square sea, covering some five-hundred acres. Its green waves rose and fell, and fishes with golden scales were swimming about in it. In addition there were countless magic birds who winged above it and sang. Even in the distance the Herd Boy could see the nine maidens in the water. They had all laid down their clothes on the shore.

"Take the red clothes, quickly," said the cow, "and hide away with them in the forest, and though she ask you for them never so sweetly do not give them back to her until she has promised to become your wife."

Then the Herd Boy hastily got down from the cow's back, seized the red clothes and ran away. At the same moment the nine maidens noticed him and were much frightened.

"O youth, whence do you come, that you dare to take our clothes?" they cried. "Put them down again quickly!"

But the Herd Boy did not let what they said trouble him; but crouched down behind one of the jade trees. Then eight of the maidens hastily came ashore and drew on their clothes.

"Our seventh sister," said they, "whom Heaven has destined to be yours, has come to you. We will leave her alone with you."

The Weaving Maiden was still crouching in the water.

But the Herd Boy stood before her and laughed.

"If you will promise to be my wife," said he, "then I will give you your clothes."

But this did not suit the Weaving Maiden.

"I am a daughter of the Ruler of the Gods," said she, "and may not marry without his command. Give back my clothes to me quickly, or else my father will punish you!"

Then the yellow cow said: "You have been destined for each other by fate, and I will be glad to arrange your marriage, and your father, the Ruler of the Gods, will make no objection. Of that I am sure."

The Weaving Maiden replied: "You are an unreasoning animal! How could you arrange our marriage?"

The cow said: "Do you see that old willow-tree there on the shore? Just give it a trial and ask it. If the willow tree speaks, then Heaven wishes your union."

And the Weaving Maiden asked the willow.

The willow replied in a human voice:

> *"This is the Seventh day,*
> *The Herd Boy his court to the Weaver doth pay!"*

and the Weaving Maiden was satisfied with the verdict. The Herd Boy laid down her clothes, and went on ahead. The Weaving Maiden drew them on and followed him. And thus they became man and wife.

But after seven days she took leave of him.

"The Ruler of Heaven has ordered me to look after my weaving," said she. "If I delay too long I fear that he will punish me. Yet, although we have to part now, we will meet again in spite of it."

When she had said these words she really went away. The Herd Boy ran after her. But when he was quite near she took one of the long needles from her hair and drew a line with it right across the sky, and this line turned into the Silver River. And thus they now stand, separated by the River, and watch for one another.

And since that time they meet once every year, on the eve of the Seventh Day. When that time comes, then all the crows in the world of men come flying and form a bridge over which the Weaving Maiden crosses the Silver River. And on that day you will not see a single crow in the trees, from morning to night, no doubt because of the reason I have mentioned. And besides, a fine rain often falls on the evening of the Seventh Day. Then the women and old grandmothers say to one another: "Those are the tears which the Herd Boy and the Weaving Maiden shed at parting!" And for this reason the Seventh Day is a rain festival.

To the west of the Silver River is the constellation of the Weaving Maiden, consisting of three stars. And directly in front of it are three other stars in the form of a triangle. It is said that once the Herd Boy was angry because the Weaving Maiden had not wished to cross the Silver River, and had thrown his yoke at her, which fell down just in front of her feet. East of the Silver River is the Herd Boy's constellation, consisting of six stars. To one side of it are countless little stars which form a constellation pointed at both ends and somewhat broader in the middle. It is said that the Weaving Maiden in turn threw her spindle at the Herd Boy; but that she did not hit him, the spindle falling down to one side of him.

Note: "The Herd Boy and the Weaving Maiden" is retold after an oral source. The Herd Boy is a constellation in Aquila, the Weaving Maiden one in Lyra. The Silver River which separates them is the Milky Way. The Seventh Day of the seventh month is the festival of their reunion. The Ruler of the Heavens has nine daughters in all, who dwell in the nine heavens. The oldest married Li Dsing; the second is the mother of Yang Oerlang; the third is the mother of the planet Jupiter; and the fourth dwelt with a pious and industrious scholar, by name of Dung Yung, whom she aided to win riches and honor. The seventh is the Spinner, and the ninth had to dwell on earth as a slave because of some transgression of which she had been guilty. Of the fifth, the sixth and the eighth daughters nothing further is known.

The Lady of the Moon

I N THE DAYS of the Emperor Yau lived a prince by the name of Hou I, who was a mighty hero and a good archer. Once ten suns rose together in the sky, and shone so brightly and burned so fiercely that the people on earth could not endure them. So the Emperor ordered Hou I to shoot at them. And Hou I shot nine of them down from the sky. Besides his bow, Hou I also had a horse which ran so swiftly that even the wind could not catch up with it. He mounted it to go a-hunting, and the horse ran away and could not be stopped. So Hou I came to Kunlun Mountain and met the Queen-Mother of the Jasper Sea. And she gave him the herb of immortality. He took it home with him and hid it in his room. But his wife who was named Tschang O, once ate some of it on the sly when he was not at home, and she immediately floated up to the clouds. When she reached the moon, she ran into the castle there, and has lived there ever since as the Lady of the Moon.

On a night in mid-autumn, an emperor of the Tang dynasty once sat at wine with two sorcerers. And one of them took his bamboo staff and cast it into the air, where it turned into a heavenly bridge, on which the three climbed up to the moon together. There they saw a great castle on which was inscribed: "The Spreading Halls of Crystal Cold." Beside it stood a cassia tree which blossomed and gave forth a fragrance filling all the air. And in the tree sat a man who was chopping off the smaller boughs with an ax. One of the sorcerers said: "That is the man in the moon. The cassia tree grows so luxuriantly that in the course of time it would overshadow all the moon's radiance. Therefore it has to be cut down once in every thousand years." Then they entered the spreading halls. The silver stories of the castle towered one above the other, and its walls and columns were all formed of liquid crystal. In the walls were cages and ponds, where fishes and birds moved as though alive. The whole moon-world seemed made of glass. While they were still looking about them on all sides the Lady of the Moon stepped up to them, clad in a white mantle and a rainbow-colored gown. She smiled and said to the emperor: "You are a prince of the mundane world of dust. Great is your fortune, since you have been able to find your way here!" And she called for her attendants, who came flying up on white birds, and sang and danced beneath the cassia tree. A pure clear music floated through the air. Beside the tree stood a mortar made of white marble, in which a jasper rabbit ground up herbs. That was the dark half of the moon. When the dance had ended, the emperor returned to earth again with the sorcerers. And he had the songs which he had heard on the moon written down and sung to the accompaniment of flutes of jasper in his pear-tree garden.

The Legend of Tchi-Niu

IN THE QUAINT COMMENTARY accompanying the text of that holy book of Lao-tseu called Kan-ing-p'ien may be found a little story so old that the name of the one who first told it has been forgotten for a thousand years, yet so beautiful that it lives still in the memory of four hundred millions of people, like a prayer that, once learned, is forever remembered. The Chinese writer makes no mention of any city nor of any province, although even in the relation of the most ancient traditions such an omission is rare; we are only told that the name of the hero of the legend was Tong-yong, and that he lived in the years of the great dynasty of Han, some twenty centuries ago.

* * *

Tong-Yong's mother had died while he was yet an infant; and when he became a youth of nineteen years his father also passed away, leaving him utterly alone in the world, and without resources of any sort; for, being a very poor man, Tong's father had put himself to great straits to educate the lad, and had not been able to lay by even one copper coin of his earnings. And Tong lamented greatly to find himself so destitute that he could not honor the memory of that good father by having the customary rites of burial performed, and a carven tomb erected upon a propitious site. The poor only are friends of the poor; and among all those whom Tong knew; there was no one able to assist him in defraying the expenses of the funeral. In one way only could the youth obtain money – by selling himself as a slave to some rich cultivator; and this he at last decided to do. In vain his friends did their utmost to dissuade him; and to no purpose did they attempt to delay the accomplishment of his sacrifice by beguiling promises of future aid. Tong only replied that he would sell his freedom a hundred times, if it were possible, rather than suffer his father's memory to remain unhonored even for a brief season. And furthermore, confiding in his youth and strength, he determined to put a high price upon his servitude – a price which would enable him to build a handsome tomb, but which it would be well-nigh impossible for him ever to repay.

* * *

Accordingly he repaired to the broad public place where slaves and debtors were exposed for sale, and seated himself upon a bench of stone, having affixed to his shoulders a placard inscribed with the terms of his servitude and the list of his qualifications as a laborer. Many who read the characters upon the placard smiled disdainfully at the price asked, and passed on without a word; others lingered only to question him out of simple curiosity; some commended him with hollow praise; some openly mocked his unselfishness, and laughed at his childish piety. Thus many hours wearily passed, and Tong had almost despaired of finding a master, when there rode up a high official of the province – a grave and handsome man, lord of a thousand slaves, and owner of vast estates. Reining in his Tartar horse, the official halted to read the placard and to consider the value of the slave. He did not smile, or advise, or ask any questions; but having observed the price asked, and the fine strong limbs of the youth, purchased him without further ado, merely ordering his attendant to pay the sum and to see that the necessary papers were made out.

* * *

Thus Tong found himself enabled to fulfil the wish of his heart, and to have a monument built which, although of small size, was destined to delight the eyes of all who beheld it, being designed by cunning artists and executed by skilful sculptors. And while it was yet designed only, the pious rites were performed, the silver coin was placed in the mouth of the dead, the white lanterns were hung at the door, the holy prayers were recited, and paper shapes of all things the departed might need in the land of the Genii were consumed in consecrated fire. And after the geomancers and the necromancers had chosen a burial-spot which no unlucky star could shine upon, a place of rest which no demon or dragon might ever disturb, the beautiful chih was built. Then was the phantom money strewn along the way; the funeral procession departed from the dwelling of the dead, and with prayers and lamentation the mortal remains of Tong's good father were borne to the tomb.

Then Tong entered as a slave into the service of his purchaser, who allotted him a little hut to dwell in; and thither Tong carried with him those wooden tablets, bearing the ancestral names, before which filial piety must daily burn the incense of prayer, and perform the tender duties of family worship.

* * *

Thrice had spring perfumed the breast of the land with flowers, and thrice had been celebrated that festival of the dead which is called Siu-fan-ti, and thrice had Tong swept and garnished his father's tomb and presented his fivefold offering of fruits and meats. The period of mourning had passed, yet he had not ceased to mourn for his parent. The years revolved with their moons, bringing him no hour of joy, no day of happy rest; yet he never lamented his servitude, or failed to perform the rites of ancestral worship – until at last the fever of the rice-fields laid strong hold upon him, and he could not arise from his couch; and his fellow-laborers thought him destined to die. There was no one to wait upon him, no one to care for his needs, inasmuch as slaves and servants were wholly busied with the duties of the household or the labor of the fields – all departing to toil at sunrise and returning weary only after the sundown.

Now, while the sick youth slumbered the fitful slumber of exhaustion one sultry noon, he dreamed that a strange and beautiful woman stood by him, and bent above him and touched his forehead with the long, fine fingers of her shapely hand. And at her cool touch a weird sweet shock passed through him, and all his veins tingled as if thrilled by new life. Opening his eyes in wonder, he saw verily bending over him the charming being of whom he had dreamed, and he knew that her lithe hand really caressed his throbbing forehead. But the flame of the fever was gone, a delicious coolness now penetrated every fibre of his body, and the thrill of which he had dreamed still tingled in his blood like a great joy. Even at the same moment the eyes of the gentle visitor met his own, and he saw they were singularly beautiful, and shone like splendid black jewels under brows curved like the wings of the swallow. Yet their calm gaze seemed to pass through him as light through crystal; and a vague awe came upon him, so that the question which had risen to his lips found no utterance. Then she, still caressing him, smiled and said: "I have come to restore thy strength and to be thy wife. Arise and worship with me."

Her clear voice had tones melodious as a bird's song; but in her gaze there was an imperious power which Tong felt he dare not resist. Rising from his couch, he was astounded to find his strength wholly restored; but the cool, slender hand which held his own led him away so swiftly that he had little time for amazement. He would have given years of existence for courage to speak of his misery, to declare his utter inability to maintain a wife; but something irresistible in the long dark eyes of his companion forbade him to speak; and as though his inmost thought had been discerned by that wondrous gaze, she said to him, in the same clear voice, "I will provide." Then shame made him blush at the thought of his wretched aspect and tattered apparel; but he observed that she also was poorly attired, like a woman of the people – wearing no ornament of any sort, nor even shoes upon her feet. And before he had yet spoken to her, they came before the ancestral tablets; and there she knelt with him and prayed, and pledged him in a cup of wine – brought he knew not from whence – and together they worshipped Heaven and Earth. Thus she became his wife.

* * *

A mysterious marriage it seemed, for neither on that day nor at any future time could Tong venture to ask his wife the name of her family, or of the place whence she came, and he could not answer any of the curious questions which his fellow-laborers put to him concerning her; and she, moreover, never uttered a word about herself, except to say that her name was Tchi. But although Tong had such awe of her that while her eyes were upon him he was as one having no will of his own, he loved her unspeakably; and the thought of his serfdom ceased to weigh upon him from the hour of his marriage. As through magic the little dwelling had become transformed: its misery was masked with charming paper devices – with dainty decorations created out of nothing by that pretty jugglery of which woman only knows the secret.

Each morning at dawn the young husband found a well-prepared and ample repast awaiting him, and each evening also upon his return; but the wife all day sat at her loom, weaving silk after a fashion unlike anything which had ever been seen before in that province. For as she wove, the silk flowed from the loom like a slow current of glossy gold, bearing upon its undulations strange forms of violet and crimson and jewel-green: shapes of ghostly horsemen riding upon horses, and of phantom chariots dragon-drawn, and of standards of trailing cloud. In every dragon's beard glimmered the mystic pearl; in every rider's helmet sparkled the gem of rank. And each day Tchi would weave a great piece of such figured silk; and the fame of her weaving spread abroad. From far and near people thronged to see the marvellous work; and the silk-merchants of great cities heard of it, and they sent messengers to Tchi, asking her that she should weave for them and teach them her secret. Then she wove for them, as they desired, in return for the silver cubes which they brought her; but when they prayed her to teach them, she laughed and said, "Assuredly I could never teach you, for no one among you has fingers like mine." And indeed no man could discern her fingers when she wove, any more than he might behold the wings of a bee vibrating in swift flight.

* * *

The seasons passed, and Tong never knew want, so well did his beautiful wife fulfil her promise – "I will provide"; and the cubes of bright silver brought by the silk-merchants were piled up higher and higher in the great carven chest which Tchi had bought for the storage of the household goods.

One morning, at last, when Tong, having finished his repast, was about to depart to the fields, Tchi unexpectedly bade him remain; and opening the great chest, she took out of it and gave him a document written in the official characters called li-shu. And Tong, looking at it, cried out and leaped in his joy, for it was the certificate of his manumission. Tchi had secretly purchased her husband's freedom with the price of her wondrous silks!

"Thou shalt labor no more for any master," she said, "but for thine own sake only. And I have also bought this dwelling, with all which is therein, and the tea-fields to the south, and the mulberry groves hard by, all of which are thine."

Then Tong, beside himself for gratefulness, would have prostrated himself in worship before her, but that she would not suffer it.

* * *

Thus he was made free; and prosperity came to him with his freedom; and whatsoever he gave to the sacred earth was returned to him centupled; and his servants loved him and blessed the beautiful Tchi, so silent and yet so kindly to all about her. But the silk-loom soon remained untouched, for Tchi gave birth to a son, a boy so beautiful that Tong wept with delight when he looked upon him. And thereafter the wife devoted herself wholly to the care of the child.

Now it soon became manifest that the boy was not less wonderful than his wonderful mother. In the third month of his age he could speak; in the seventh month he could repeat by heart the proverbs of the sages, and recite the holy prayers; before the eleventh month he could use the writing-brush with skill, and copy in shapely characters the precepts of Lao-tseu. And the priests of the temples came to behold him and to converse with him, and they marvelled at the charm of the child and the wisdom of what he said; and they blessed Tong, saying: "Surely this son of thine is a gift from the Master of Heaven, a sign that the immortals love thee. May thine eyes behold a hundred happy summers!"

* * *

It was in the Period of the Eleventh Moon: the flowers had passed away, the perfume of the summer had flown, the winds were growing chill, and in Tong's home the evening fires were lighted. Long the husband and wife sat in the mellow glow – he speaking much of his hopes and joys, and of his son that was to be so grand a man, and of many paternal projects; while she, speaking little, listened to his words, and

88

often turned her wonderful eyes upon him with an answering smile. Never had she seemed so beautiful before; and Tong, watching her face, marked not how the night waned, nor how the fire sank low, nor how the wind sang in the leafless trees without.

All suddenly Tchi arose without speaking, and took his hand in hers and led him, gently as on that strange wedding-morning, to the cradle where their boy slumbered, faintly smiling in his dreams. And in that moment there came upon Tong the same strange fear that he knew when Tchi's eyes had first met his own – the vague fear that love and trust had calmed, but never wholly cast out, like unto the fear of the gods. And all unknowingly, like one yielding to the pressure of mighty invisible hands, he bowed himself low before her, kneeling as to a divinity. Now, when he lifted his eyes again to her face, he closed them forthwith in awe; for she towered before him taller than any mortal woman, and there was a glow about her as of sunbeams, and the light of her limbs shone through her garments. But her sweet voice came to him with all the tenderness of other hours, saying: "Lo! my beloved, the moment has come in which I must forsake thee; for I was never of mortal born, and the Invisible may incarnate themselves for a time only. Yet I leave with thee the pledge of our love – this fair son, who shall ever be to thee as faithful and as fond as thou thyself hast been. Know, my beloved, that I was sent to thee even by the Master of Heaven, in reward of thy filial piety, and that I must now return to the glory of His house: I AM THE GODDESS XXHI-NIU."

Even as she ceased to speak, the great glow faded; and Tong, re-opening his eyes, knew that she had passed away forever – mysteriously as pass the winds of heaven, irrevocably as the light of a flame blown out. Yet all the doors were barred, all the windows unopened. Still the child slept, smiling in his sleep. Outside, the darkness was breaking; the sky was brightening swiftly; the night was past. With splendid majesty the East threw open high gates of gold for the coming of the sun; and, illuminated by the glory of his coming, the vapors of morning wrought themselves into marvellous shapes of shifting color – into forms weirdly beautiful as the silken dreams woven in the loom of Tchi-Niu.

The Princess Kwan-Yin

ONCE UPON A TIME in China there lived a certain king who had three daughters. The fairest and best of these was Kwan-yin, the youngest. The old king was justly proud of this daughter, for of all the women who had ever lived in the palace she was by far the most attractive. It did not take him long, therefore, to decide that she should be the heir to his throne, and her husband ruler of his kingdom. But, strange to say, Kwan-yin was not pleased at this good fortune. She cared little for the pomp and splendour of court life. She foresaw no pleasure for herself in ruling as a queen, but even feared that in so high a station she might feel out of place and unhappy.

Every day she went to her room to read and study. As a result of this daily labour she soon went far beyond her sisters along the paths of knowledge, and her name was known in the farthest corner of the kingdom as "Kwan-yin, the wise princess." Besides being very fond of books, Kwan-yin was thoughtful of her friends. She was careful about her behaviour both in public and in private. Her warm heart was open at all times to the cries of those in trouble. She was kind to the poor and suffering. She won the love of the lower classes, and was to them a sort of goddess to whom they could appeal whenever they were hungry and in need. Some people even believed that she was a fairy who had come to earth from her home within the Western Heaven, while others said that once, long years before, she had lived in the world as a prince instead of a princess. However this may be, one thing is certain – Kwan-yin was pure and good, and well deserved the praises that were showered upon her.

One day the king called this favourite daughter to the royal bedside, for he felt that the hour of death was drawing near. Kwan-yin kowtowed before her royal father, kneeling and touching her forehead on the floor in sign of deepest reverence. The old man bade her rise and come closer. Taking her hand tenderly in his own, he said, "Daughter, you know well how I love you.

Your modesty and virtue, your talent and your love of knowledge, have made you first in my heart. As you know already, I chose you as heir to my kingdom long ago. I promised that your husband should be made ruler in my stead. The time is almost ripe for me to ascend upon the dragon and become a guest on high. It is necessary that you be given at once in marriage."

"But, most exalted father," faltered the princess, "I am not ready to be married."

"Not ready, child! Why, are you not eighteen? Are not the daughters of our nation often wedded long before they reach that age? Because of your desire for learning I have spared you thus far from any thought of a husband, but now we can wait no longer."

"Royal father, hear your child, and do not compel her to give up her dearest pleasures. Let her go into a quiet convent where she may lead a life of study!"

The king sighed deeply at hearing these words. He loved his daughter and did not wish to wound her. "Kwan-yin," he continued, "do you wish to pass by the green spring of youth, to give up this mighty kingdom? Do you wish to enter the doors of a convent where women say farewell to life and all its pleasures? No! your father will not permit this. It grieves me sorely to disappoint you, but one month from this very day you shall be married. I have chosen for your royal partner a man of many noble parts. You know him by name already, although you have not seen him. Remember that, of the hundred virtues filial conduct is the chief, and that you owe more to me than to all else on earth."

Kwan-yin turned pale. Trembling, she would have sunk to the floor, but her mother and sisters supported her, and by their tender care brought her back to consciousness.

Every day of the month that followed, Kwan-yin's relatives begged her to give up what they called her foolish notion. Her sisters had long since given up hope of becoming queen. They were amazed at her stupidity. The very thought of any one's choosing a convent instead of a throne was to them a sure sign of madness. Over and over again they asked her reason for making so strange a choice. To every question, she shook her head, replying, "A voice from the heavens speaks to me, and I must obey it."

On the eve of the wedding day Kwan-yin slipped out of the palace, and, after a weary journey, arrived at a convent called, "The Cloister of the White

Sparrow." She was dressed as a poor maiden. She said she wished to become a nun. The abbess, not knowing who she was, did not receive her kindly. Indeed, she told Kwan-yin that they could not receive her into the sisterhood, that the building was full. Finally, after Kwan-yin had shed many tears, the abbess let her enter, but only as a sort of servant, who might be cast out for the slightest fault.

Now that Kwan-yin found herself in the life which she had long dreamt of leading, she tried to be satisfied. But the nuns seemed to wish to make her stay among them most miserable. They gave her the hardest tasks to do, and it was seldom that she had a minute to rest. All day long she was busy, carrying water from a well at the foot of the convent hill or gathering wood from a neighbouring forest. At night when her back was almost breaking, she was given many extra tasks, enough to have crushed the spirit of any other woman than this brave daughter of a king. Forgetting her grief, and trying to hide the lines of pain that sometimes wrinkled her fair forehead, she tried to make these hard-hearted women love her. In return for their rough words, she spoke to them kindly, and never did she give way to anger.

One day while poor Kwan-yin was picking up brushwood in the forest she heard a tiger making his way through the bushes. Having no means of defending herself, she breathed a silent prayer to the gods for help, and calmly awaited the coming of the great beast. To her surprise, when the bloodthirsty animal appeared, instead of bounding up to tear her in pieces, he began to make a soft purring noise. He did not try to hurt Kwan-yin, but rubbed against her in a friendly manner, and let her pat him on the head.

The next day the princess went back to the same spot. There she found no fewer than a dozen savage beasts working under the command of the friendly tiger, gathering wood for her. In a short time enough brush and firewood had been piled up to last the convent for six months. Thus, even the wild animals of the forest were better able to judge of her goodness than the women of the sisterhood.

At another time when Kwan-yin was toiling up the hill for the twentieth time, carrying two great pails of water on a pole, an enormous dragon faced her in the road. Now, in China, the dragon is sacred, and Kwan-yin was not at all frightened, for she knew that she had done no wrong.

The animal looked at her for a moment, switched its horrid tail, and shot out fire from its nostrils. Then, dashing the burden from the startled maiden's shoulder, it vanished. Full of fear, Kwan-yin hurried up the hill to the nunnery. As she drew near the inner court, she was amazed to see in the centre of the open space a new building of solid stone. It had sprung up by magic since her last journey down the hill. On going forward, she saw that there were four arched doorways to the fairy house. Above the door facing west was a tablet with these words written on it: "In honour of Kwan-yin, the faithful princess." Inside was a well of the purest water, while, for drawing this water, there a strange machine, the like of which neither Kwan-yin nor the nuns had ever seen.

The sisters knew that this magic well was a monument to Kwan-yin's goodness. For a few days they treated her much better. "Since the gods have dug a well at our very gate," they said, "this girl will no longer need to bear water from the foot of the hill. For what strange reason, however, did the gods write this beggar's name on the stone?"

Kwan-yin heard their unkind remarks in silence. She could have explained the meaning of the dragon's gift, but she chose to let her companions remain in ignorance. At last the selfish nuns began to grow careless again, and treated her even worse than before. They could not bear to see the poor girl enjoy a moment's idleness.

"This is a place for work," they told her. "All of us have laboured hard to win our present station. You must do likewise." So they robbed her of every chance for study and prayer, and gave her no credit for the magic well.

One night the sisters were awakened from their sleep by strange noises, and soon they heard outside the walls of the compound the blare of a trumpet. A great army had been sent by Kwan-yin's father to attack the convent, for his spies had at last been able to trace the runaway princess to this holy retreat.

"Oh, who has brought this woe upon us?" exclaimed all the women, looking at each other in great fear. "Who has done this great evil? There is one among us who has sinned most terribly, and now the gods are about to destroy us." They gazed at one another, but no one thought of Kwan-yin, for they did not believe her of enough importance to attract the anger of heaven, even though she might have done the most shocking of deeds. Then, too, she had been so meek and lowly while in their holy order that they did not once dream of charging her with any crime.

The threatening sounds outside grew louder and louder. All at once a fearful cry arose among the women: "They are about to burn our sacred dwelling." Smoke was rising just beyond the enclosure where the soldiers were kindling a great fire, the heat of which would soon be great enough to make the convent walls crumble into dust.

Suddenly a voice was heard above the tumult of the weeping sisters: "Alas! I am the cause of all this trouble."

The nuns, turning in amazement, saw that it was Kwan-yin who was speaking. "You?" they exclaimed, astounded.

"Yes, I, for I am indeed the daughter of a king. My father did not wish me to take the vows of this holy order. I fled from the palace. He has sent his army here to burn these buildings and to drag me back a prisoner."

"Then, see what you have brought upon us, miserable girl!" exclaimed the abbess. "See how you have repaid our kindness! Our buildings will be burned above our heads! How wretched you have made us! May heaven's curses rest upon you!"

"No, no!" exclaimed Kwan-yin, springing up, and trying to keep the abbess from speaking these frightful words. "You have no right to say that, for I am innocent of evil. But, wait! You shall soon see whose prayers the gods will answer, yours or mine!" So saying, she pressed her forehead to the floor, praying the almighty powers to save the convent and the sisters.

Outside the crackling of the greedy flames could already be heard. The fire king would soon destroy every building on that hill-top. Mad with terror, the sisters prepared to leave the compound and give up all their belongings to the cruel flames and still more cruel soldiers. Kwan-yin alone remained in the room, praying earnestly for help.

Suddenly a soft breeze sprang up from the neighbouring forest, dark clouds gathered overhead, and, although it was the dry season a drenching shower descended on the flames. Within five minutes the fire was put out and the convent was saved. Just as the shivering nuns were thanking Kwan-yin for the divine help she had brought them, two soldiers who had scaled the outer wall of the compound came in and roughly asked for the princess.

The trembling girl, knowing that these men were obeying her father's orders, poured out a prayer to the gods, and straightway made herself known.

They dragged her from the presence of the nuns who had just begun to love her. Thus disgraced before her father's army, she was taken to the capital.

On the morrow, she was led before the old king. The father gazed sadly at his daughter, and then the stern look of a judge hardened his face as he beckoned the guards to bring her forward.

From a neighbouring room came the sounds of sweet music. A feast was being served there amid great splendour. The loud laughter of the guests reached the ears of the young girl as she bowed in disgrace before her father's throne. She knew that this feast had been prepared for her, and that her father was willing to give her one more chance.

"Girl," said the king, at last regaining his voice, "in leaving the royal palace on the eve of your wedding day, not only did you insult your father, but your king. For this act you deserve to die. However, because of the excellent record you had made for yourself before you ran away, I have decided to give you one more chance to redeem yourself. Refuse me, and the penalty is death: obey me, and all may yet be well – the kingdom that you spurned is still yours for the asking. All that I require is your marriage to the man whom I have chosen."

"And when, most august King, would you have me decide?" asked Kwan-yin earnestly.

"This very day, this very hour, this very moment," he answered sternly. "What! would you hesitate between love upon a throne and death? Speak, my daughter, tell me that you love me and will do my bidding!"

It was now all that Kwan-yin could do to keep from throwing herself at her father's feet and yielding to his wishes, not because he offered her a kingdom, but because she loved him and would gladly have made him happy. But her strong will kept her from relenting. No power on earth could have stayed her from doing what she thought her duty.

"Beloved father," she answered sadly, and her voice was full of tenderness, "it is not a question of my love for you – of that there is no question, for all my life I have shown it in every action. Believe me, if I were free to do your bidding, gladly would I make you happy, but a voice from the gods has spoken, has commanded that I remain a virgin, that I devote my life to deeds of mercy. When heaven itself has commanded, what can even a princess do but listen to that power which rules the earth?"

The old king was far from satisfied with Kwan-yin's answer. He grew furious, his thin wrinkled skin turned purple as the hot blood rose to his head. "Then you refuse to do my bidding! Take her, men! Give to her the death that is due to a traitor to the king!" As they bore Kwan-yin away from his presence the white-haired monarch fell, swooning, from his chair.

That night, when Kwan-yin was put to death, she descended into the lower world of torture. No sooner had she set foot in that dark country of the dead than the vast region of endless punishment suddenly blossomed forth and became like the gardens of Paradise. Pure white lilies sprang up on every side, and the odour of a million flowers filled all the rooms and corridors. King Yama, ruler of the dominion, rushed forth to learn the cause of this wonderful change. No sooner did his eyes rest upon the fair young face of Kwan-yin than he saw in her the emblem of a purity which deserved no home but heaven.

"Beautiful virgin, doer of many mercies," he began, after addressing her by her title, "I beg you in the name of justice to depart from this bloody kingdom. It is not right that the fairest flower of heaven should enter and shed her fragrance in these halls. Guilt must suffer here, and sin find no reward. Depart thou, then, from my dominion. The peach of immortal life shall be bestowed upon you, and heaven alone shall be your dwelling place."

Thus Kwan-yin became the Goddess of Mercy; thus she entered into that glad abode, surpassing all earthly kings and queens. And ever since that time, on account of her exceeding goodness, thousands of poor people breathe out to her each year their prayers for mercy. There is no fear in their gaze as they look at her beautiful image, for their eyes are filled with tears of love.

The Spirits of the Yellow River

THE SPIRITS OF the Yellow River are called Dai Wang – Great King. For many hundreds of years past the river inspectors had continued to report that all sorts of monsters show themselves in the waves of the stream, at times in the shape of dragons, at others in that of cattle and horses, and whenever

such a creature makes an appearance a great flood follows. Hence temples are built along the river banks. The higher spirits of the river are honored as kings, the lower ones as captains, and hardly a day goes by without their being honored with sacrifices or theatrical performances. Whenever, after a dam has been broken, the leak is closed again, the emperor sends officials with sacrifices and ten great bars of Tibetan incense. This incense is burned in a great sacrificial censer in the temple court, and the river inspectors and their subordinates all go to the temple to thank the gods for their aid. These river gods, it is said, are good and faithful servants of former rulers, who died in consequence of their toil in keeping the dams unbroken. After they died their spirits became river-kings; in their physical bodies, however, they appear as lizards, snakes and frogs.

The mightiest of all the river-kings is the Golden Dragon-King. He frequently appears in the shape of a small golden snake with a square head, low forehead and four red dots over his eyes. He can make himself large or small at will, and cause the waters to rise and fall. He appears and vanishes unexpectedly, and lives in the mouths of the Yellow River and the Imperial Canal. But in addition to the Golden Dragon-King there are dozens of river-kings and captains, each of whom has his own place. The sailors of the Yellow River all have exact lists in which the lives and deeds of the river-spirits are described in detail.

The river-spirits love to see theatrical performances. Opposite every temple is a stage. In the hall stands the little spirit-tablet of the river-king, and on the altar in front of it a small bowl of golden lacquer filled with clean sand. When a little snake appears in it, the river-king has arrived. Then the priests strike the gong and beat the drum and read from the holy books. The official is at once informed and he sends for a company of actors. Before they begin to perform the actors go up to the temple, kneel, and beg the king to let them know which play they are to give. And the river-god picks one out and points to it with his head; or else he writes signs in the sand with his tail. The actors then at once begin to perform the desired play.

The river-god cares naught for the fortunes or misfortunes of human beings. He appears suddenly and disappears in the same way, as best suits him.

Between the outer and the inner dam of the Yellow River are a number of settlements. Now it often happens that the yellow water moves to the very edge of the inner walls. Rising perpendicularly, like a wall, it gradually advances. When people see it coming they hastily burn incense, bow in prayer before the waters, and promise the river-god a theatrical performance. Then the water retires and the word goes round: "The river-god has asked for a play again!"

In a village in that section there once dwelt a wealthy man. He built a stone wall, twenty feet high, around the village, to keep away the water. He did not believe in the spirits of the river, but trusted in his strong wall and was quite unconcerned.

One evening the yellow water suddenly rose and towered in a straight line before the village. The rich man had them shoot cannon at it. Then the water grew stormy, and surrounded the wall to such a height that it reached the openings in the battlements. The water foamed and hissed, and seemed about to pour over the wall. Then everyone in the village was very much frightened. They dragged up the rich man and he had to kneel and beg for pardon. They promised the river-god a theatrical performance, but in vain; but when they promised to build him a temple in the middle of the village and give regular performances, the water sank more and more and gradually returned to its bed. And the village fields suffered no damage, for the earth, fertilized by the yellow slime, yielded a double crop.

Once a scholar was crossing the fields with a friend in order to visit a relative. On their way they passed a temple of the river-god where a new play was just being performed. The friend asked the scholar to go in with him and look on. When they entered the temple court they saw two great snakes upon the front pillars, who had wound themselves about the columns, and were thrusting out their heads as though watching the performance. In the hall of the temple stood the altar with the bowl of sand. In it lay a small snake with a golden body, a green head and red dots above his eyes. His neck was thrust up and his glittering little eyes never left the stage. The friend bowed and the scholar followed his example.

Softly he said to his friend: "What are the three river-gods called?"

"The one in the temple," was the reply, "is the Golden Dragon-King. The two on the columns are two captains. They do not dare to sit in the temple together with the king."

This surprised the scholar, and in his heart he thought: "Such a tiny snake! How can it possess a god's power? It would have to show me its might before I would worship it."

He had not yet expressed these secret thoughts before the little snake suddenly stretched forth his head from the bowl, above the altar. Before the altar burned two enormous candles. They weighed more than ten pounds and were as thick as small trees. Their flame burned like the flare of a torch. The snake now thrust his head into the middle of the candle-flame. The flame must have been at least an inch broad, and was burning red. Suddenly its radiance turned blue, and was split into two tongues. The candle was so enormous and its fire so hot that even copper and iron would have melted in it; but it did not harm the snake.

Then the snake crawled into the censer. The censer was made of iron, and was so large one could not clasp it with both arms. Its cover showed a dragon design in open-work. The snake crawled in and out of the holes in this cover, and wound his way through all of them, so that he looked like an embroidery in threads of gold. Finally all the openings of the cover, large and small, were filled by the snake. In order to do so, he must have made himself several dozen feet long. Then he stretched out his head at the top of the censer and once more watched the play.

Thereupon the scholar was frightened, he bowed twice, and prayed: "Great King, you have taken this trouble on my account! I honor you from my heart!"

No sooner had he spoken these words than, in a moment, the little snake was back in his bowl, and just as small as he had been before.

In Dsiningdschou they were celebrating the river god's birthday in his temple. They were giving him a theatrical performance for a birthday present. The spectators crowded around as thick as a wall, when who should pass but a simple peasant from the country, who said in a loud voice: "Why, that is nothing but a tiny worm! It is a great piece of folly to honor it like a king!"

Before ever he had finished speaking the snake flew out of the temple. He grew and grew, and wound himself three times around the stage. He became as thick around as a small pail, and his head seemed like that of a dragon. His eyes sparkled like golden lamps, and he spat out red flame with his tongue. When he coiled and uncoiled the whole stage trembled and it seemed as though it would break down. The actors stopped their music and fell down on the stage in prayer. The whole multitude was seized with terror and bowed to the ground. Then some of the old men came along, cast the peasant on the ground, and gave him a good thrashing. So he had to cast himself on his knees before the snake and worship him. Then all heard a noise as though a great many firecrackers were being shot off. This lasted for some time, and then the snake disappeared.

East of Shantung lies the city of Dongschou. There rises an observation-tower with a great temple. At its feet lies the water-city, with a sea-gate at the North, through which the flood-tide rises up to the city. A camp of the boundary guard is established at this gate.

Once upon a time there was an officer who had been transferred to this camp as captain. He had formerly belonged to the land forces, and had not yet been long at his new post. He gave some friends of his a banquet, and before the pavilion in which they feasted lay a great stone shaped somewhat like a table. Suddenly a little snake was seen crawling on this stone. It was spotted with green, and had red dots on its square head. The soldiers were about to kill the little creature, when the captain went out to look into the matter. When he had looked he laughed and said: "You must not harm him! He is the river-king of Dsiningdschou. When I was stationed in Dsiningdschou he sometimes visited me, and then I always gave sacrifices and performances in his honor. Now he has come here expressly in order to wish his old friend luck, and to see him once more."

There was a band in camp; the bandsmen could dance and play like a real theatrical troupe. The captain quickly had them begin a performance, had another banquet with wine and delicate foods prepared, and invited the river-god to sit down to the table.

Gradually evening came and yet the river-god made no move to go.

So the captain stepped up to him with a bow and said: "Here we are far removed from the Yellow River, and these people have never yet heard your name spoken. Your visit has been a great honor for me. But the women and fools who have crowded together chattering outside, are afraid of hearing about you. Now you have visited your old friend, and I am sure you wish to get back home again."

With these words he had a litter brought up; cymbals were beaten and fire-works set off, and finally a salute of nine guns was fired to escort him on his way. Then the little snake crawled into the litter, and the captain followed after. In this order they reached the port, and just when it was about time to say farewell, the snake was already swimming in the water. He had grown much larger, nodded to the captain with his head, and disappeared.

Then there were doubts and questionings: "But the river-god lives a thousand miles away from here, how does he get to this place?"

Said the captain: "He is so powerful that he can get to any place, and besides, from where he dwells a waterway leads to the sea. To come down that way and swim to sea is something he can do in a moment's time!"

Spirits &
The Supernatural World

T HE BIRD FENG explains, 'I can make myself large enough to carry the largest town upon my back, or small enough to pass through the smallest keyhole...' Extraordinary as her powers may be, she is pretty much typical of the spirit-animals, ghosts and mythical creatures of every kind who crowd the folktales of the Chinese.

Frequently, like Feng, they come to the assistance of mortal men and women in love, removing obstacles; invariably they add vividness and colour to the narratives in which they feature. And complexity, for in a great many cases, Chinese spirits are ambivalent in their significance – a fact underlined by their ability to change their form. Shapeshifting fox spirits abound, for example, but while they are often mischievous, malevolent (or disguised young women, 'foxy' in seductiveness), in other cases they can be benign. Many of these creatures featured in the tales collected by Pu Songling (1640–1715), the premier storyteller of the Qing Dynasty era. A celebrated selection of his work (translated here by Herbert A. Giles) was collected as *Strange Tales from a Chinese Studio* (1766).

Miss Chiao-No

K'UNG HSÜEH-LI was a descendant of Confucius. He was a man of considerable ability, and an excellent poet. A fellow-student, to whom he was much attached, became magistrate at T'ien-t'ai, and sent for K'ung to join him. Unfortunately, just before K'ung arrived his friend died, and he found himself without the means of returning home; so he took up his abode in a Buddhist monastery, where he was employed in transcribing for the priests. Several hundred paces to the west of this monastery there was a house belonging to a Mr. Shan, a gentleman who had known better days, but who had spent all his money in a heavy law-suit; and then, as his family was a small one, had gone away to live in the country and left his house vacant.

One day there was a heavy fall of snow which kept visitors away from the monastery; and K'ung, finding it dull, went out. As he was passing by the door of the house above-mentioned, a young man of very elegant appearance came forth, who, the moment he saw K'ung, ran up to him, and with a bow, entered into conversation, asking him to be pleased to walk in. K'ung was much taken with the young man, and followed him inside. The rooms were not particularly large, but adorned throughout with embroidered curtains, and from the walls hung scrolls and drawings by celebrated masters. On the table lay a book, the title of which was, "Jottings from Paradise;" and turning over its leaves, K'ung found therein many strange things. He did not ask the young man his name, presuming that as he lived in the Shan family mansion, he was necessarily the owner of the place. The young man, however, inquired what he was doing in that part of the country, and expressed great sympathy with his misfortunes, recommending him to set about taking pupils. "Alas!" said K'ung, "who will play the Mæcenas to a distressed wayfarer like myself?" "If," replied the young man, "you would condescend so far, I for my part would gladly seek instruction at your hands." K'ung was much gratified at this, but said he dared not arrogate to himself the position of teacher, and begged merely to be considered as the young man's friend. He then asked him why the house had been shut up for so long; to which the young man replied, "This is the Shan family mansion. It has been closed all this time because of the owner's removal into the country. My surname is Huang-fu, and my home is in Shen-si; but as our house has been burnt down in a great fire, we have put up here for a while." Thus Mr. K'ung found out that his name was not Shan. That evening they spent in laughing and talking together, and K'ung remained there for the night. In the morning a lad came in to light the fire; and the young man, rising first, went into the private part of the house. Mr. K'ung was sitting up with the bed-clothes still huddled round him, when the lad looked in and said, "Master's coming!" So he jumped up with a start, and in came an old man with a silvery beard, who began to thank him, saying, "I am very much obliged to you for your condescension in becoming my son's tutor. At present he writes a villainous hand; and I can only hope you will not allow the ties of friendship to interfere with discipline." Thereupon, he presented Mr. K'ung with an embroidered suit of clothes, a sable hat, and a set of shoes and stockings; and when the latter had washed and dressed himself he called for wine and food. K'ung could not make out what the valances of the chairs and tables were made of: they were so very bright-coloured and dazzling. By-and-by, when the wine had circulated several times, the old gentleman picked up his walking-stick and took his leave. After breakfast, the young man handed in his theme, which turned out to be written in an archaic style, and not at all after the modern fashion of essay-writing. K'ung asked him why he had done this, to which the young man replied that he did not contemplate competing at the public examinations. In the evening they had another drinking-bout, but it was agreed that there should be no more of it after that night. The young man then called the boy and told him to see if his father was asleep or not; adding, that if he was, he might quietly summon Miss Perfume. The boy went off, first taking a guitar out of a very pretty case; and in a few minutes in came a very nice-looking young girl. The young man bade her play the Death of Shun; and seizing an ivory plectrum she swept the chords, pouring forth a vocal melody of exquisite sweetness and pathos. He then gave her a goblet of wine to drink, and it was midnight before they parted. Next morning they got up early and settled down to work. The young man proved an apt scholar; he could remember what he had once read, and at the end of two or three months had made astonishing progress. Then they agreed that every five days they would indulge in a symposium, and that Miss Perfume should always be of the party. One night when the wine had gone into K'ung's head, he seemed to be lost in a reverie; whereupon his young friend, who knew what was the matter with him, said, "This girl was brought up by my father. I know you find it lonely, and I have long been looking out for a nice wife for you." "Let her only resemble Miss Perfume," said K'ung, "and she will do." "Your experience," said the young man, laughing, "is but limited, and, consequently, anything is a surprise to you. If Miss Perfume is your beau ideal, why it will not be difficult to satisfy you."

Some six months had passed away, when one day Mr. K'ung took it into his head that he would like to go out for a stroll in the country. The entrance, however, was carefully closed; and on asking the reason, the young man told him that his father wished to receive no guests for fear of causing interruption to his studies. So K'ung thought no more about it; and by-and-by, when the heat of summer came on, they moved their study to a pavilion in the garden. At this time Mr. K'ung had a swelling on the chest about as big as a peach, which, in a single night, increased to the size of a bowl. There he lay groaning with the pain, while his pupil waited upon him day and night. He slept badly and took hardly any food; and in a few days the place got so much worse that he could neither eat nor drink. The old gentleman also came in, and he and his son lamented over him together. Then the young man said, "I was thinking last night that my sister, Chiao-no, would be able to cure Mr. K'ung, and accordingly I sent over to my grandmother's asking her to come. She ought to be here by now." At that moment a servant entered and announced Miss Chiao-no, who had come with her cousin, having been at her aunt's house. Her father and brother ran out to meet her, and then brought her in to see Mr. K'ung. She was between thirteen and fourteen years old, and had beautiful eyes with a very intelligent expression in them, and a most graceful figure besides. No sooner had Mr. K'ung beheld this lovely creature than he quite forgot to groan, and began to brighten up. Meanwhile the young man was saying, "This respected friend of mine is the same to me as a brother. Try, sister, to cure him." Miss Chiao-no immediately dismissed her blushes, and rolling up her long sleeves approached the bed to feel his pulse. As she was grasping his wrist, K'ung became conscious of a perfume more delicate than that of the epidendrum; and then she laughed, saying, "This illness was to be expected; for the heart is touched. Though it is severe, a cure can be effected; but, as there is already a swelling, not without using the knife." Then she drew from her arm a gold bracelet which she pressed down upon the suffering spot, until by degrees the swelling rose within the bracelet and overtopped it by an inch and more, the outlying parts that were inflamed also passing under, and thus very considerably reducing the extent of the tumour. With one hand she opened her robe and took out a knife with an edge as keen as paper, and pressing the bracelet down all the time with the other, proceeded to cut lightly round near the root of the swelling. The dark blood gushed forth, and stained the bed and the mat; but Mr. K'ung was delighted to be near such a beauty, – not only felt no pain, but would willingly have continued the operation that she might sit by him a little longer. In a few moments the whole thing was removed, and the place looked like the knot on a tree where a branch has been cut away. Here Miss Chiao-no called for water to wash the wound, and from between her lips she took a red pill as big as a bullet, which she laid upon the flesh, and, after drawing the skin together, passed round and round the place. The first turn felt like the searing of a hot iron; the second like a gentle itching; and at the third he experienced a sensation of lightness and coolness which penetrated into his very bones and marrow. The young lady then returned the pill to her mouth, and said, "He is cured," hurrying away as fast as she could. Mr. K'ung jumped up to thank her, and found that his complaint had quite disappeared. Her beauty, however, had made such an impression on him that his troubles were hardly at an end. From this moment he gave up his books, and took no interest in anything. This state of things was soon noticed by the young man, who said to him, "My brother, I have found a fine match for you." "Who is it to be?" asked K'ung. "Oh, one of the family," replied his friend. Thereupon Mr. K'ung remained some time lost in thought, and at length said, "Please don't!" Then turning his face to the wall, he repeated these lines:

"Speak not of lakes and streams to him who once has seen the sea;
The clouds that circle Wu's peak are the only clouds for me."

The young man guessed to whom he was alluding, and replied, "My father has a very high opinion of your talents, and would gladly receive you into the family, but that he has only one daughter, and she is much too young. My cousin, Ah-sung, however, is seventeen years old, and not at all a bad-looking girl. If you doubt my word, you can wait in the verandah until she takes her daily walk in the garden, and thus judge for yourself." This Mr. K'ung acceded to, and accordingly saw Miss Chiao-no come out with a lovely girl – her black eyebrows beautifully arched, and her tiny feet encased in phœnix-shaped shoes – as like one another as they well could be. He was of course delighted, and begged the young man to arrange all preliminaries; and the very next day his friend came to tell him that the affair was finally settled. A portion of the house was given up to the bride and bridegroom, and the marriage was celebrated with plenty of music and hosts of guests, more like a fairy wedding than anything else. Mr. K'ung was very happy, and began to think that the position of Paradise had been wrongly laid down, until one day the young man came to him and said, "For the trouble you have been at in teaching me, I shall ever remain your debtor. At the present moment, the Shan family law-suit has been brought to a termination, and they wish to resume possession of their house immediately. We therefore propose returning to Shen-si, and as it is unlikely that you and I will ever meet again, I feel very sorrowful at the prospect of parting." Mr. K'ung replied that he would go too, but the young man advised him to return to his old home. This, he observed, was no easy matter; upon which the young man said, "Don't let that trouble you: I will see you safe there." By-and-by his father came in with Mr. K'ung's wife, and presented Mr. K'ung with one hundred ounces of gold; and then the young man gave the husband and wife each one of his hands to grasp, bidding them shut their eyes. The next instant they were floating away in the air, with the wind whizzing in their ears. In a little while he said, "You have arrived," and opening his eyes, K'ung beheld his former home. Then he knew that the young man was not a human being. Joyfully he knocked at the old door, and his mother was astonished to see him arrive with such a nice wife. They were all rejoicing together, when he turned round and found that his friend had disappeared. His wife attended on her mother-in-law with great devotion, and acquired a reputation both for virtue and beauty, which was spread round far and near. Some time passed away, and then Mr. K'ung took his doctor's degree, and was appointed Governor of the Gaol in Yen-ngan. He proceeded to his post with his wife only, the journey being too long for his mother, and by-and-by a son was born. Then he got into trouble by being too honest an official, and threw up his appointment; but had not the wherewithal to get home again. One day when out hunting he met a handsome young man riding on a nice horse, and seeing that he was staring very hard looked closely at him. It was young Huang-fu. So they drew bridle, and fell to laughing and crying by turns, – the young man then inviting K'ung to go along with him. They rode on together until they had reached a village thickly shaded with trees, so that the sun and sky were invisible overhead, and entered into a most elaborately-decorated mansion, such as might belong to an old-established family. K'ung asked after Miss Chiao-no, and heard that she was married; also that his own mother-in-law was dead, at which tidings he was greatly moved. Next day he went back and returned again with his wife. Chiao-no also joined them, and taking up K'ung's child played with it, saying, "Your mother played us truant." Mr. K'ung did not forget to thank her for her former kindness to him, to which she replied, "You're a great man now. Though the wound has healed, haven't you forgotten the pain yet?" Her husband, too, came to pay his respects, returning with her on the following morning. One day the young Huang-fu seemed troubled in spirit, and said to Mr. K'ung, "A great calamity is impending. Can you help us?" Mr. K'ung did not know what he was alluding to, but readily promised his assistance. The young man then ran out and summoned the whole family to worship in the ancestral hall, at which Mr. K'ung was alarmed, and asked what it all meant. "You know," answered the young man, "I am not a man but a fox. To-day we shall be attacked by thunder; and if only you will aid us in our trouble, we may still hope to escape. If you are unwilling, take your child and go, that you may not be involved with us." Mr. K'ung protested he would live or die with them, and so the young man placed him with a sword at the door, bidding him remain quiet there in spite of all the thunder. He did as he was told, and soon saw black clouds obscuring the light until it was all as dark as pitch. Looking round, he could see that the house had disappeared, and that its place was occupied by a huge mound and a bottomless pit. In the midst of his terror, a fearful peal was heard which shook the very hills, accompanied by a violent wind and driving rain. Old trees were torn up, and Mr. K'ung became both dazed and deaf. Yet he stood firm until he saw in a dense black column of smoke a horrid thing with a sharp beak and long claws, with which it snatched some one from the hole, and was disappearing up with the smoke. In an instant K'ung knew by her clothes and shoes that the victim was no other than Chiao-no, and instantly jumping up he struck the devil violently with his sword, and cut it down. Immediately the mountains were riven, and a sharp peal of thunder laid K'ung dead upon the ground. Then the clouds cleared away, and Chiao-no gradually came round, to find K'ung dead at her feet. She burst out crying at the sight, and declared that she would not live since K'ung had died for her. K'ung's wife also came out, and they bore the body inside. Chiao-no then made Ah-sung hold her husband's head, while her brother prised open his teeth with a hair-pin, and she herself arranged his jaw. She next put a red pill into his mouth, and bending down breathed into him. The pill went along with the current of air, and presently there was a gurgle in his throat, and he came round. Seeing all the family about him, he was disturbed as if waking from a dream. However they were all united together, and fear gave place to joy; but Mr. K'ung objected to live in that out-of-the-way place, and proposed that they should return with him to his native village. To this they were only too pleased to assent – all except Chiao-no; and when Mr. K'ung invited her husband, Mr. Wu, as well, she said she feared her father and mother-in-law would not like to lose the children. They had tried all day to persuade her, but without success, when suddenly in rushed one of the Wu family's servants, dripping with perspiration and quite out of breath. They asked what was the matter, and the servant replied that the Wu family had been visited by a calamity on the very same day, and had every one perished. Chiao-no cried very bitterly at this, and could not be comforted; but now there was nothing to prevent them from all returning together. Mr. K'ung went into the city for a few days on business, and then they set to work packing-up night and day. On arriving at their destination, separate apartments were allotted to young Mr. Huang-fu, and these he kept carefully shut up, only opening the door to Mr. K'ung and his wife.

Mr. K'ung amused himself with the young man and his sister Chiao-no, filling up the time with chess, wine, conversation, and good cheer, as if they had been one family. His little boy, Huan, grew up to be a handsome young man, with a fox-like penchant for roaming about; and it was generally known that he was actually the son of a fox.

Miss Lien-Hsiang, The Fox-Girl

THERE WAS a young man named Sang Tzŭ-ming, a native of I-chou, who had been left an orphan when quite young. He lived near the Saffron market, and kept himself very much to himself, only going out twice a day for his meals to a neighbour's close by, and sitting quietly at home all the rest of his time. One day the said neighbour called, and asked him in joke if he wasn't afraid of devil-foxes, so much alone as he was.

"Oh," replied Sang, laughing, "what has the superior man to fear from devil-foxes. If they come as men, I have here a sharp sword for them; and if as women, why, I shall open the door and ask them to walk in." The neighbour went away, and having arranged with a friend of his, they got a young lady of their acquaintance to climb over Sang's wall with the help of a ladder, and knock at the door. Sang peeped through, and called out, "Who's there?" to which the girl answered, "A devil!" and frightened Sang so dreadfully that his teeth chattered in his head. The girl then ran away, and next morning when his neighbour came to see him, Sang told him what had happened, and said he meant to go back to his native place. The neighbour then clapped his hands, and said to Sang, "Why didn't you ask her in?" Whereupon Sang perceived that he had been tricked, and went on quietly again as before.

Some six months afterwards, a young lady knocked at his door; and Sang, thinking his friends were at their old tricks, opened it at once, and asked her to walk in. She did so; and he beheld to his astonishment a perfect Helen for beauty. Asking her whence she came, she replied that her name was Lien-hsiang, and that she lived not very far off, adding that she had long been anxious to make his acquaintance. After that she used to drop in every now and again for a chat; but one evening when Sang was sitting alone expecting her, another young lady suddenly walked in. Thinking it was Lien-hsiang, Sang got up to meet her, but found that the new-comer was somebody else. She was about fifteen or sixteen years of age, wore very full sleeves, and dressed her hair after the fashion of unmarried girls, being otherwise very stylish-looking and refined, and apparently hesitating whether to go on or go back. Sang, in a great state of alarm, took her for a fox; but the young lady said, "My name is Li, and I am of a respectable family. Hearing of your virtue and talent, I hope to be accorded the honour of your acquaintance." Sang laughed, and took her by the hand, which he found was as cold as ice; and when he asked the reason, she told him that she had always been delicate, and that it was very chilly outside. She then remarked that she intended to visit him pretty frequently, and hoped it would not inconvenience him; so he explained that no one came to see him except another young lady, and that not very often. "When she comes, I'll go," replied the young lady, "and only drop in when she's not here." She then gave him an embroidered slipper, saying that she had worn it, and that whenever he shook it she would know that he wanted to see her, cautioning him at the same time never to shake it before strangers. Taking it in his hand he beheld a very tiny little shoe almost as fine pointed as an awl, with which he was much pleased; and next evening, when nobody was present, he produced the shoe and shook it, whereupon the young lady immediately walked in. Henceforth, whenever he brought it out, the young lady responded to his wishes and appeared before him. This seemed so strange that at last he asked her to give him some explanation; but she only laughed, and said it was mere coincidence. One evening after this Lien-hsiang came, and said in alarm to Sang, "Whatever has made you look so melancholy?" Sang replied that he did not know, and by-and-by she took her leave, saying, they would not meet again for some ten days. During this period Miss Li visited Sang every day, and on one occasion asked him where his other friend was. Sang told her; and then she laughed and said, "What is your opinion of me as compared with Lien-hsiang?" "You are both of you perfection," replied he, "but you are a little *colder* of the two." Miss Li didn't much like this, and cried out, "Both of us perfection is what you say to me. Then she must be a downright Cynthia, and I am no match for her." Somewhat out of temper, she reckoned that Lien-hsiang's ten days had expired, and said she would have a peep at her, making Sang promise to keep it all secret. The next evening Lien-hsiang came, and while they were talking she suddenly exclaimed, "Oh, dear! how much worse you seem to have become in the last ten days. You must have encountered something bad." Sang asked her why so; to which she answered, "First of all your appearance; and then your pulse is very thready. You've got the devil-disease."

The following evening when Miss Li came, Sang asked her what she thought of Lien-hsiang. "Oh," said she, "there's no question about her beauty; but she's a fox. When she went away I followed her to her hole on the hill side." Sang, however, attributed this remark to jealousy, and took no notice of it; but the next evening when Lien-hsiang came, he observed, "I don't believe it myself, but some one has told me you are a fox." Lien-hsiang asked who had said so, to which Sang replied that he was only joking; and then she begged him to explain what difference there was between a fox and an ordinary person. "Well," answered Sang, "foxes frighten people to death, and, therefore, they are very much dreaded." "Don't you believe that!" cried Lien-hsiang; "and now tell me who has been saying this of me." Sang declared at first that it was only a joke of his, but by-and-by yielded to her instances, and let out the whole story. "Of course I saw how changed you were," said Lien-hsiang; "she is surely not a human being to be able to cause such a rapid alteration in you. Say nothing, to-morrow I'll watch her as she watched me." The following evening Miss Li came in; and they had hardly interchanged half-a-dozen sentences when a cough was heard outside the window, and Miss Li ran away. Lien-hsiang then entered and said to Sang, "You are lost! She is a devil, and if you do not at once forbid her coming here, you will soon be on the road to the other world." "All jealousy," thought Sang, saying nothing, as Lien-hsiang continued, "I know that you don't like to be rude to her; but I, for my part, cannot see you sacrificed, and to-morrow I will bring you some medicine to expel the poison from your system. Happily, the disease has not yet taken firm hold of you, and in ten days you will be well again." The next evening she produced a knife and chopped up some medicine for Sang, which made him feel much better; but, although he was very grateful to her, he still persisted in disbelieving that he had the devil-disease. After some days he recovered and Lien-hsiang left him, warning him to have no more to do with Miss Li. Sang pretended that he would follow her advice, and closed the door and trimmed his lamp. He then took out the slipper, and on shaking it Miss Li appeared, somewhat cross at having been kept away for several days. "She merely attended on me these few nights while I was ill," said Sang; "don't be angry." At this Miss Li brightened up a little; but by-and-by Sang told her that people said she was a devil. "It's that nasty fox," cried Miss Li, after a pause, "putting these things into your head. If you don't break with her, I won't come here again." She then began to sob and cry, and Sang had some trouble in pacifying her. Next evening Lien-hsiang came and found out that Miss Li had been there again; whereupon she was very angry with Sang, and told him he would certainly die. "Why need you be so jealous?" said Sang, laughing; at which she only got more enraged, and replied, "When you were nearly dying the other day and I saved you, if I had not been jealous, where would you have been now?" Sang pretended he was only joking, and said that Miss Li had told him his recent illness was entirely owing to the machinations of a fox; to which she replied, "It's true enough what you say, only you don't see whose machinations. However, if any thing happens to you, I should never clear myself even had I a hundred mouths; we will, therefore, part. A hundred days hence I shall see you on your bed." Sang could not persuade her to stay, and away she went; and from that time Miss Li became a regular visitor.

Two months passed away, and Sang began to experience a feeling of great lassitude, which he tried at first to shake off, but by-and-by he became very thin, and could only take thick gruel. He then thought about going back to his native place; however, he could not bear to leave Miss Li, and in a few more days he was so weak that he was unable to get up. His friend next door, seeing how ill he was, daily sent in his boy with food and drink; and now Sang began for the first time to suspect Miss Li. So he said to her,

"I am sorry I didn't listen to Lien-hsiang before I got as bad as this." He then closed his eyes and kept them shut for some time; and when he opened them again Miss Li had disappeared. Their acquaintanceship was thus at an end, and Sang lay all emaciated as he was upon his bed in his solitary room longing for the return of Lien-hsiang. One day, while he was still thinking about her, some one drew aside the screen and walked in. It was Lien-hsiang; and approaching the bed she said with a smile, "Was I then talking such nonsense?" Sang struggled a long time to speak; and, at length, confessing he had been wrong, implored her to save him. "When the disease has reached such a pitch as this," replied Lien-hsiang, "there is very little to be done. I merely came to bid you farewell, and to clear up your doubts about my jealousy." In great tribulation, Sang asked her to take something she would find under his pillow and destroy it; and she accordingly drew forth the slipper, which she proceeded to examine by the light of the lamp, turning it over and over. All at once Miss Li walked in, but when she saw Lien-hsiang she turned back as though she would run away, which Lien-hsiang instantly prevented by placing herself in the doorway. Sang then began to reproach her, and Miss Li could make no reply; whereupon Lien-hsiang said, "At last we meet. Formerly you attributed this gentleman's illness to me; what have you to say now?" Miss Li bent her head in acknowledgment of her guilt, and Lien-hsiang continued, "How is it that a nice girl like you can thus turn love into hate?" Here Miss Li threw herself on the ground in a flood of tears and begged for mercy; and Lien-hsiang, raising her up, inquired of her as to her past life. "I am a daughter of a petty official named Li, and I died young, leaving the web of my destiny incomplete, like the silkworm that perishes in the spring. To be the partner of this gentleman was my ardent wish; but I had never any intention of causing his death." "I have heard," remarked Lien-hsiang, "that the advantage devils obtain by killing people is that their victims are ever with them after death. Is this so?" "It is not," replied Miss Li; "the companionship of two devils gives no pleasure to either. Were it otherwise, I should not have wanted for friends in the realms below. But tell me, how do foxes manage not to kill people?" "You allude to such foxes as suck the breath out of people?" replied Lien-hsiang; "I am not of that class. Some foxes are harmless; no devils are, because of the dominance of the yin in their compositions." Sang now knew that these two girls were really a fox and a devil; however, from being long accustomed to their society, he was not in the least alarmed. His breathing had dwindled to a mere thread, and at length he uttered a cry of pain. Lien-hsiang looked round and said, "How shall we cure him?" upon which Miss Li blushed deeply and drew back; and then Lien-hsiang added, "If he does get well, I'm afraid you will be dreadfully jealous." Miss Li drew herself up, and replied, "Could a physician be found to wipe away the wrong I have done to this gentleman, I would bury my head in the ground. How should I look the world in the face?" Lien-hsiang here opened a bag and drew forth some drugs, saying, "I have been looking forward to this day. When I left this gentleman I proceeded to gather my simples, as it would take three months for the medicine to be got ready; but then, should the poison have brought anyone even to death's door, this medicine is able to call him back. The only condition is that it be administered by the very hand which wrought the ill." Miss Li did as she was told and put the pills Lien-hsiang gave her one after another into Sang's mouth. They burnt his inside like fire; but soon vitality began to return, and Lien-hsiang cried out, "He is cured!" Just at this moment Miss Li heard the cock crow and vanished, Lien-hsiang remaining behind in attendance on the invalid, who was unable to feed himself. She bolted the outside door and pretended that Sang had returned to his native place, so as to prevent visitors from calling. Day and night she took care of him, and every evening Miss Li came in to render assistance, regarding Lien-hsiang as an elder sister, and being treated by her with great consideration and kindness. Three months afterwards Sang was as strong and well as ever he had been, and then for several evenings Miss Li ceased to visit them, only staying a few moments when she did come, and seeming very uneasy in her mind. One evening Sang ran after her and carried her back in his arms, finding her no heavier than so much straw; and then, being obliged to stay, she curled herself up and lay down, to all appearance in a state of unconsciousness, and by-and-by she was gone. For many days they heard nothing of her, and Sang was so anxious that she should come back that he often took out her slipper and shook it. "I don't wonder at your missing her," said Lien-hsiang, "I do myself very much indeed." "Formerly," observed Sang, "when I shook the slipper she invariably came. I thought it very strange, but I never suspected her of being a devil. And now, alas! all I can do is to sit and think about her with this slipper in my hand." He then burst into a flood of tears.

Now a young lady named Yen-êrh, belonging to the wealthy Chang family, and about fifteen years of age, had died suddenly, without any apparent cause, and had come to life again in the night, when she got up and wished to go out. They barred the door and would not hear of her doing so; upon which she said, "I am the spirit daughter of a petty magistrate. A Mr. Sang has been very kind to me, and I have left my slipper at his house. I am really a spirit; what is the use of keeping me in?" There being some reason for what she said, they asked her why she had come there; but she only looked up and down without being able to give any explanation. Some one here observed, that Mr. Sang had already gone home, but the young lady utterly refused to believe them. The family was much disturbed at all this; and when Sang's neighbour heard the story, he jumped over the wall, and peeping through beheld Sang sitting there chatting with a pretty-looking girl. As he went in, there was some commotion, during which Sang's visitor had disappeared, and when his neighbour asked the meaning of it all, Sang replied, laughing, "Why, I told you if any ladies came I should ask them in." His friend then repeated what Miss Yen-êrh had said; and Sang, unbolting his door, was about to go and have a peep at her, but unfortunately had no means of so doing. Meanwhile Mrs. Chang, hearing that he had not gone away, was more lost in astonishment than ever, and sent an old woman-servant to get back the slipper. Sang immediately gave it to her, and Miss Yen-êrh was delighted to recover it, though when she came to try it on it was too small for her by a good inch. In considerable alarm, she seized a mirror to look at herself; and suddenly became aware that she had come to life again in some one else's body. She therefore told all to her mother, and finally succeeded in convincing her, crying all the time because she was so changed for the worse as regarded personal appearance from what she had been before. And whenever she happened to see Lien-hsiang, she was very much disconcerted, declaring that she had been much better off as a devil than now as a human being. She would sit and weep over the slipper, no one being able to comfort her; and finally, covering herself up with bed-clothes, she lay all stark and stiff, positively refusing to take any nourishment. Her body swelled up, and for seven days she refused all food, but did not die; and then the swelling began to subside, and an intense hunger to come upon her which made her once more think about eating. Then she was troubled with a severe irritation, and her skin peeled entirely away; and when she got up in the morning, she found that the shoes had fallen off. On trying to put them on again, she discovered that they did not fit her any longer; and then she went back to her former pair which were now exactly of the right size and shape. In an ecstasy of joy, she grasped her mirror, and saw that her features had also changed back to what they had formerly been; so she washed and dressed herself and went in to visit her mother. Every one who met her was much astonished; and when Lien-hsiang heard the strange story, she tried to persuade Mr. Sang to make her an offer of marriage. But the young lady was rich and Sang was poor, and he did not see his way clearly. However, on Mrs. Chang's birthday, when she completed her cycle of sixty-one years, Sang went along with the others to wish her many happy returns of the day; and when the old lady knew who was coming, she bade Yen-êrh take a peep at him from behind the curtain. Sang arrived last of all; and immediately out rushed Miss Yen-êrh and seized his sleeve, and said she would go back with him. Her mother scolded her well for this, and she ran in abashed; but Sang, who had looked at her closely, began to weep, and threw himself at the feet of Mrs. Chang who raised him up without saying anything unkind. Sang then took his leave, and got his uncle to act as medium between them; the result being that an auspicious day was fixed upon for the wedding. At the appointed time Sang proceeded to the house to fetch her; and when he returned he found that, instead of his former poor-looking furniture, beautiful carpets were laid down from the very door, and thousands of coloured lanterns were hung about in elegant designs. Lien-hsiang assisted the bride to enter, and took off her veil, finding her the same bright girl as ever. She also joined them while drinking the wedding cup, and inquired of her friend as to her recent transmigration; and Yen-êrh related as follows:—"Overwhelmed with grief, I began to shrink from myself as some unclean thing; and, after separating from you that day, I would not return any more to my grave. So I wandered about at random, and whenever I saw a living being, I envied its happy state. By day I remained among trees and shrubs, but at night I used to roam about anywhere. And once I came to the house of the Chang family, where, seeing a young girl lying upon the bed, I took possession of her mortal coil, unknowing that she would be restored to life again." When Lien-hsiang heard this she was for some time lost in thought; and a month or two afterwards became very ill. She refused all medical aid and gradually got worse and worse, to the great grief of Mr. Sang and his wife, who stood weeping at her bedside. Suddenly she opened her eyes, and said, "You wish to live; I am willing to die. If fate so ordains it, we shall meet again ten years hence." As she uttered these words, her spirit passed away, and all that remained was the dead body of a fox. Sang, however, insisted on burying it with all the proper ceremonies.

Now his wife had no children; but one day a servant came in and said, "There is an old woman outside who has got a little girl for sale." Sang's wife gave orders that she should be shown in; and no sooner had she set eyes on the girl than she cried out, "Why, she's the image of Lien-hsiang!" Sang then looked at her, and found to his astonishment that she was really very like his old friend. The old woman said she was fourteen years old; and when asked what her price was, declared that her only wish was to get the girl comfortably settled, and enough to keep herself alive, and ensure not being thrown out into the kennel at death. So Sang gave a good price for her; and his wife, taking the girl's hand, led her into a room by themselves. Then, chucking her under the chin, she asked her, smiling, "Do you know me?" The girl said she did not; after which she told Mrs. Sang that her name was Wei, and that her father, who had been a pickle-merchant at Hsü-ch'êng, had died three years before. Mrs. Sang then calculated that Lien-hsiang had been dead just ten years; and, looking at the girl, who resembled her so exactly in every trait, at length patted her on the head, saying, "Ah, my sister, you promised to visit us again in ten years, and you have not played us false." The girl here seemed to wake up as if from a dream, and, uttering an exclamation of surprise, fixed a steady gaze upon Sang's wife. Sang himself laughed, and said, "Just like the return of an old familiar swallow." "Now I understand," cried the girl, in tears; "I recollect my mother saying that when I was born I was able to speak; and that, thinking it an inauspicious manifestation, they gave me dog's blood to drink, so that I should forget all about my previous state of existence. Is it all a dream, or are you not the Miss Li who was so ashamed of being a devil?" Thus they chatted of their existence in a former life, with alternate tears and smiles; but when it came to the day for worshipping at the tombs, Yen-êrh explained that she and her husband were in the habit of annually visiting and mourning over her grave. The girl replied that she would accompany them; and when they got there they found the whole place in disorder, and the coffin wood all warped. "Lien-hsiang and I," said Yen-êrh to her husband, "have been attached to each other in two states of existence. Let us not be separated, but bury my bones here with hers." Sang consented, and opening Miss Li's tomb, took out the bones and buried them with those of Lien-hsiang, while friends and relatives, who had heard the strange story, gathered round the grave in gala dress to the number of many hundreds.

I learnt the above when travelling through I-chou, where I was detained at an inn by rain, and read a biography of Mr. Sang written by a comrade of his named Wang Tzŭ-chang. It was lent me by a Mr. Liu Tzŭ-ching, a relative of Sang's, and was quite a long account. This is merely an outline of it.

Miss Ying-Ning; or, The Laughing Girl

AT LO-TIEN, in the province of Shantung, there lived a youth named Wang Tzŭ-fu, who had been left an orphan when quite young. He was a clever boy, and took his bachelor's degree at the age of fourteen, being quite his mother's pet, and not allowed by her to stray far away from home. One young lady to whom he had been betrothed having unhappily died, he was still in search of a wife when, on the occasion of the Feast of Lanterns, his cousin Wu asked him to come along for a stroll. But they had hardly got beyond the village before one of his uncle's servants caught them up and told Wu he was wanted.

The latter accordingly went back; but Wang, seeing plenty of nice girls about and being in high spirits himself, proceeded on alone. Amongst others, he noticed a young lady with her maid. She had just picked a sprig of plum-blossom, and was the prettiest girl he had ever heard of – a perfect bunch of smiles. He stared and stared at her quite regardless of appearances; and when she had passed by, she said to her maid, "That young fellow has a wicked look in his eyes."

As she was walking away, laughing and talking, the flower dropped out of her hand; and Wang, picking it up, stood there disconsolate as if he had lost his wits. He then went home in a very melancholy mood; and, putting the flower under his pillow, lay down to sleep. He would neither talk nor eat; and his mother became very anxious about him, and called in the aid of the priests. By degrees, he fell off in flesh and got very thin; and the doctor felt his pulse and gave him medicines to bring out the disease. Occasionally, he seemed bewildered in his mind, but in spite of all his mother's inquiries would give no clue as to the cause of his malady. One day when his cousin Wu came to the house, Wang's mother told him to try and find out what was the matter; and the former, approaching the bed, gradually and quietly led up to the point in question. Wang, who had wept bitterly at the sight of his cousin, now repeated to him the whole story, begging him to lend some assistance in the matter. "How foolish you are, cousin," cried Wu; "there will be no difficulty at all, I'll make inquiries for you. The girl herself can't belong to a very aristocratic family to be walking alone in the country. If she's not already engaged, I have no doubt we can arrange the affair; and even if she is unwilling, an extra outlay will easily bring her round. You make haste and get well: I'll see to it all." Wang's features relaxed when he heard these words; and Wu left him to tell his mother how the case stood, immediately setting on foot inquiries as to the whereabouts of the girl. All his efforts, however, proved fruitless, to the great disappointment of Wang's mother; for since his cousin's visit Wang's colour and appetite had returned. In a few days Wu called again, and in answer to Wang's questions falsely told him that the affair was settled. "Who do you think the young lady is?" said he. "Why, a cousin of ours, who is only waiting to be betrothed; and though you two are a little near, I daresay the circumstances of the case will be allowed to overrule this objection." Wang was overjoyed, and asked where she lived; so Wu had to tell another lie, and say, "On the south-west hills, about ten miles from here." Wang begged him again and again to do his best for him, and Wu undertook to get the betrothal satisfactorily arranged. He then took leave of his cousin, who from this moment was rapidly restored to health. Wang drew the flower from underneath his pillow, and found that, though dried up, the leaves had not fallen away. He often sat playing with this flower and thinking of the young lady; but by-and-by, as Wu did not reappear, he wrote a letter and asked him to come. Wu pleaded other engagements, being unwilling to go; at which Wang got in a rage and quite lost his good spirits; so that his mother, fearing a relapse, proposed to him a speedy betrothal in another quarter. Wang shook his head at this, and sat day after day waiting for Wu, until his patience was thoroughly exhausted. He then reflected that ten miles was no great distance, and that there was no particular reason for asking anybody's aid; so, concealing the flower in his sleeve, he went off in a huff by himself without letting it be known. Having no opportunity of asking the way, he made straight for the hills; and after about ten miles walking found himself right in the midst of them, enjoying their exquisite verdure, but meeting no one, and with nothing better than mountain paths to guide him. Away down in the valley below, almost buried under a densely luxuriant growth of trees and flowers, he espied a small hamlet, and began to descend the hill and make his way thither. He found very few houses, and all built of rushes, but otherwise pleasant enough to look at. Before the door of one, which stood at the northern end of the village, were a number of graceful willow trees, and inside the wall plenty of peach and apricot trees, with tufts of bamboo between them, and birds chirping on the branches. As it was a private house he did not venture to go in, but sat down to rest himself on a huge smooth stone opposite the front door. By-and-by he heard a girl's voice from within calling out Hsiao-jung; and, noticing that it was a sweet-toned voice, set himself to listen, when a young lady passed with a bunch of apricot-flowers in her hand, and occupied in putting hair-pins into her downcast head. As soon as she raised her face she saw Wang, and stopped putting in hair-pins; then, smothering a laugh, picked a few flowers and ran in. Wang perceived to his intense delight that she was none other than his heroine of the Feast of Lanterns; but recollecting that he had no right to follow her in, was on the point of calling after her as his cousin. There was no one, however, in the street, and he was afraid lest he might have made a mistake; neither was there anybody at the door of whom he could make inquiries. So he remained there in a very restless state till the sun was well down in the west, and his hopes were almost at an end, forgetting all about food and drink. He then saw the young lady peep through the door, apparently very much astonished to find him still there; and in a few minutes out came an old woman leaning on a stick, who said to him, "Whence do you come, Sir? I hear you have been here ever since morning. What is it you want? Aren't you hungry?" Wang got up, and making a bow, replied that he was in search of some relatives of his; but the old woman was deaf and didn't catch what he said, so he had to shout it out again at the top of his voice. She asked him what their names were, but he was unable to tell her; at which she laughed and said, "It is a funny thing to look for people when you don't know their names. I am afraid you are an unpractical gentleman. You had better come in and have something to eat; we'll give you a bed and you can go back to-morrow and find out the names of the people you are in quest of." Now Wang was just beginning to get hungry, and, besides, this would bring him nearer to the young lady; so he readily accepted and followed the old woman in. They walked along a paved path banked on both sides with hibiscus, the leaves of which were scattered about on the ground; and passing through another door, entered a court-yard full of trained creepers and other flowers. The old woman showed Wang into a small room with beautifully white walls and a branch of a crab-apple tree coming through the window, the furniture being also nice and clean. They had hardly sat down when it was clear that some one was taking a peep through the window; whereupon the old woman cried out, "Hsiao-jung! make haste and get dinner," and a maid from outside immediately answered "Yes, ma'am." Meanwhile, Wang had been explaining who he was; and then the old lady said, "Was your maternal grandfather named Wu?" "He was," replied Wang. "Well, I never!" cried the old woman, "he was my uncle, and your mother and I are cousins. But in consequence of our poverty, and having no sons, we have kept quite to ourselves, and you have grown to be a man without my knowing you." "I came here," said Wang, "about my cousin, but in the hurry I forgot your name." "My name is Ch'in," replied the old lady; "I have no son: only a girl, the child of a concubine, who, after my husband's death, married again and left her daughter with me. She's a clever girl, but has had very little education; full of fun and ignorant of the sorrows of life. I'll send for her by-and-by to make your acquaintance." The maid then brought in the dinner – a large dish full of choice morsels of fowl – and the old woman pressed him to eat. When they had finished, and the things were taken away, the old woman said, "Call Miss Ning," and the maid went off to do so. After some time there was a giggling at the door, and the old woman cried out, "Ying-ning! your cousin is here." There was then a great tittering as the maid pushed her in, stopping her mouth all the time to try and keep from laughing. "Don't you know better than to behave like that?" asked the old woman, "and before a stranger, too." So Ying-ning controlled her feelings, and Wang made her a bow, the old woman saying, "Mr. Wang is your cousin: you have never seen him before. Isn't that funny?" Wang asked how old his cousin was, but the old woman didn't hear him, and he had to say it again, which sent Ying-ning off into another fit of laughter. "I told you," observed the old woman, "she hadn't much education; now you see it. She is sixteen years old, and as foolish as a baby." "One year younger than I am," remarked Wang. "Oh, you're seventeen are you? Then you were born in the year ——, under the sign of the horse." Wang nodded assent, and then the old woman asked who his wife was, to which Wang replied that he had none. "What! a clever, handsome young fellow of seventeen not yet engaged? Ying-ning is not engaged either: you two would make a nice pair if it wasn't for the relationship." Wang said nothing, but looked hard at his cousin; and just then the maid whispered to her, "It is the fellow with the wicked eyes! He's at his old game." Ying-ning laughed, and proposed to the maid that they should go and see if the peaches were in blossom or not; and off they went together, the former with her sleeve stuffed into her mouth until she got outside, where she burst into a hearty fit of laughing. The old woman gave orders for a bed to be got ready for Wang, saying to him, "It's not often we meet: you must spend a few days with us now you are here, and then we'll send you home. If you are at all dull, there's a garden behind where you can amuse yourself, and books for you to read." So next day Wang strolled into the garden, which was of moderate size, with a well-kept lawn and plenty of trees and flowers. There was also an arbour consisting of three posts with a thatched roof, quite shut in on all sides by the luxurious vegetation. Pushing his way among the flowers, Wang heard a noise from one of the trees, and looking up saw Ying-ning, who at once burst out laughing and nearly fell down. "Don't! don't!" cried Wang, "you'll fall!" Then Ying-ning came down, giggling all the time, until, when she was near the ground, she missed her hold, and tumbled down with a run. This stopped her merriment, and Wang picked her up, gently squeezing her hand as he did so. Ying-ning began laughing again, and was obliged to lean against a tree for support, it being some time before she was able to stop. Wang waited till she had finished, and then drew the flower out of his sleeve and handed it to her. "It's dead," said she; "why do you keep it?" "You dropped it, cousin, at the Feast of Lanterns," replied Wang, "and so I kept it." She then asked him what was his object in keeping it, to which he answered, "To show my love, and that I have not forgotten you. Since that day when we met, I have been very ill from thinking so much of you, and am quite changed from what I was. But now that it is my unexpected good fortune to meet you, I pray you have pity on me." "You needn't make such a fuss about a trifle," replied she, "and with your own relatives, too. I'll give orders to supply you with a whole basketful of flowers when you go away." Wang told her she did not understand, and when she asked what it was she didn't understand, he said, "I didn't care for the flower itself; it was the person who picked the flower." "Of course," answered she, "everybody cares for their relations; you needn't have told me that." "I wasn't talking about ordinary relations," said Wang, "but about husbands and wives." "What's the difference?" asked Ying-ning. "Why," replied Wang, "husband and wife are always together." "Just what I shouldn't like," cried she, "to be always with anybody." At this juncture up came the maid, and Wang slipped quietly away. By-and-by they all met again in the house, and the old woman asked Ying-ning where they had been; whereupon she said they had been talking in the garden. "Dinner has been ready a long time. I can't think what you have had to say all this while," grumbled the old woman. "My cousin," answered Ying-ning, "has been talking to me about husbands and wives." Wang was much disconcerted, and made a sign to her to be quiet, so she smiled and said no more; and the old woman luckily did not catch her words, and asked her to repeat them. Wang immediately put her off with something else, and whispered to Ying-ning that she had done very wrong. The latter did not see that; and when Wang told her that what he had said was private, answered him that she had no secrets from her old mother. "Besides," added she, "what harm can there be in talking on such a common topic as husbands and wives?" Wang was angry with her for being so dull, but there was no help for it; and by the time dinner was over he found some of his mother's servants had come in search of him, bringing a couple of donkeys with them. It appeared that his mother, alarmed at his non-appearance, had made strict search for him in the village; and when unable to discover any traces of him, had gone off to the Wu family to consult. There her nephew, who recollected what he had previously said to young Wang, advised that a search should be instituted in the direction of the hills; and accordingly the servants had been to all the villages on the way until they had at length recognised him as he was coming out of the door. Wang went in and told the old woman, begging that he might be allowed to take Ying-ning with him. "I have had the idea in my head for several days," replied the old woman, overjoyed; "but I am a feeble old thing myself, and couldn't travel so far. If, however, you will take charge of my girl and introduce her to her aunt, I shall be very pleased." So she called Ying-ning, who came up laughing as usual; whereupon the old woman rebuked her, saying, "What makes you always laugh so? You would be a very good girl but for that silly habit. Now, here's your cousin, who wants to take you away with him. Make haste and pack up." The servants who had come for Wang were then provided with refreshment, and the old woman bade them both farewell, telling Ying-ning that her aunt was quite well enough off to maintain her, and that she had better not come back. She also advised her not to neglect her studies, and to be very attentive to her elders, adding that she might ask her aunt to provide her with a good husband. Wang and Ying-ning then took their leave; and when they reached the brow of the hill, they looked back and could just discern the old woman leaning against the door and gazing towards the north. On arriving at Wang's home, his mother, seeing a nice-looking young girl with him, asked in astonishment who she might be; and Wang at once told her the whole story. "But that was all an invention of your cousin Wu's," cried his mother; "I haven't got a sister, and consequently I can't have such a niece." Ying-ning here observed, "I am not the daughter of the old woman; my father was named Ch'in and died when I was a little baby, so that I can't remember anything." "I had a sister," said Wang's mother, "who actually did marry a Mr. Ch'in, but she died many years ago, and can't be still living, of course."

However, on inquiring as to facial appearance and characteristic marks, Wang's mother was obliged to acknowledge the identity, wondering at the same time how her sister could be alive when she had died many years before. Just then in came Wu, and Ying-ning retired within; and when he heard the story, remained some time lost in astonishment, and then said, "Is this young lady's name Ying-ning?" Wang replied that it was, and asked Wu how he came to know it. "Mr. Ch'in," answered he, "after his wife's death was bewitched by a fox, and subsequently died. The fox had a daughter named Ying-ning, as was well known to all the family; and when Mr. Ch'in died, as the fox still frequented the place, the Taoist Pope was called in to exorcise it. The fox then went away, taking Ying-ning with it, and now here she is." While they were thus discussing, peals of laughter were heard coming from within, and Mrs. Wang took occasion to remark what a foolish girl she was. Wu begged to be introduced, and Mrs. Wang went in to fetch her, finding her in an uncontrollable fit of laughter, which she subdued only with great difficulty, and by turning her face to the wall. By-and-by she went out; but, after making a bow, ran back and burst out laughing again to the great discomfiture of all the ladies. Wang then said he would go and find out for them all about Ying-ning and her queer story, so as to be able to arrange the marriage; but when he reached the spot indicated, village and houses had all vanished, and nothing was to be seen except hill-flowers scattered about here and there. Wu recollected that Mrs. Ch'in had been buried at no great distance from that spot; he found, however, that the grave had disappeared, and he was no longer able to determine its position. Not knowing what to make of it all, he returned home, and then Mrs. Wang told him she thought the girl must be a disembodied spirit. Ying-ning shewed no signs of alarm at this remark; neither did she cry at all when Mrs. Wang began to condole with her on no longer having a home. She only laughed in her usual silly way, and fairly puzzled them all. Sharing Miss Wang's room, she now began to take her part in the duties of a daughter of the family; and as for needlework, they had rarely seen anything like hers for fineness. But she could not get over that trick of laughing, which, by the way, never interfered with her good looks, and consequently rather amused people than otherwise, amongst others a young married lady who lived next door. Wang's mother fixed an auspicious day for the wedding, but still feeling suspicious about Ying-ning, was always secretly watching her. Finding, however, that she had a proper shadow, and that there was nothing extraordinary in her behaviour, she had her dressed up when the day came, in all the finery of a bride; and would have made her perform the usual ceremonies, only Ying-ning laughed so much she was unable to kneel down. They were accordingly obliged to excuse her, but Wang began to fear that such a foolish girl would never be able to keep the family counsel. Luckily, she was very reticent and did not indulge in gossip; and moreover, when Mrs. Wang was in trouble or out of temper, Ying-ning could always bring her round with a laugh. The maid-servants, too, if they expected a whipping for anything, would always ask her to be present when they appeared before their mistress, and thus they often escaped punishment. Ying-ning had a perfect passion for flowers. She got all she could out of her relations, and even secretly pawned her jewels to buy rare specimens; and by the end of a few months the whole place was one mass of flowers. Behind the house there was one especial tree which belonged to the neighbours on that side; but Ying-ning was always climbing up and picking the flowers, for which Mrs. Wang rebuked her severely, though without any result. One day the owner saw her, and gazed at her some time in rapt astonishment; however, she didn't move, deigning only to laugh. The gentleman was much smitten with her; and when she smilingly descended the wall on her own side, pointing all the time with her finger to a spot hard by, he thought she was making an assignation. So he presented himself at nightfall at the same place, and sure enough Ying-ning was there. Seizing her hand, to tell his passion, he found that he was grasping only a log of wood which stood against the wall; and the next thing he knew was that a scorpion had stung him violently on the finger. There was an end of his romance, except that he died of the wound during the night, and his family at once commenced an action against Wang for having a witch-wife. The magistrate happened to be a great admirer of Wang's talent, and knew him to be an accomplished scholar; he therefore refused to grant the summons, and ordered the prosecutor to be bambooed for false accusation. Wang interposed and got him off this punishment, and returned home himself. His mother then scolded Ying-ning well, saying, "I knew your too playful disposition would some day bring sorrow upon you. But for our intelligent magistrate we should have been in a nice mess. Any ordinary hawk-like official would have had you publicly interrogated in court; and then how could your husband ever have held up his head again?" Ying-ning looked grave and did not laugh this time; and Mrs. Wang continued, "There's no harm in laughing as long as it is seasonable laughter;" but from that moment Ying-ning laughed no more, no matter what people did to make her, though at the same time her expression was by no means gloomy. One evening she went in tears to her husband, who wanted to know what was the matter. "I couldn't tell you before," said she, sobbing; "we had known each other such a short time. But now that you and your mother have been so kind to me, I will keep nothing from you, but tell you all. I am the daughter of a fox. When my mother went away she put me in the charge of the disembodied spirit of an old woman, with whom I remained for a period of over ten years. I have no brothers: only you to whom I can look. And now my foster-mother is lying on the hill-side with no one to bury her and appease her discontented shade. If not too much, I would ask you to do this, that her spirit may be at rest, and know that it was not neglected by her whom she brought up." Wang consented, but said he feared they would not be able to find her grave; on which Ying-ning said there was no danger of that, and accordingly they set forth together. When they arrived, Ying-ning pointed out the tomb in a lonely spot amidst a thicket of brambles, and there they found the old woman's bones. Ying-ning wept bitterly, and then they proceeded to carry her remains home with them, subsequently interring them in the Ch'in family vault. That night Wang dreamt that the old woman came to thank him, and when he waked he told Ying-ning, who said that she had seen her also, and had been warned by her not to frighten Mr. Wang. Her husband asked why she had not detained the old lady; but Ying-ning replied, "She is a disembodied spirit, and would be ill at ease for any time surrounded by so much life." Wang then enquired after Hsiao-jung, and his wife said, "She was a fox too, and a very clever one. My foster-mother kept her to wait on me, and she was always getting fruit and cakes for me, so that I have a friendship for her and shall never forget her. My foster-mother told me yesterday she was married."

After this, whenever the great fast-day came round, husband and wife went off without fail to worship at the Ch'in family tomb; and by the time a year had passed she gave birth to a son, who wasn't a bit afraid of strangers, but laughed at everybody, and in fact took very much after his mother.

Old Dschang

ONCE UPON A TIME there was a man who went by the name of Old Dschang. He lived in the country, near Yangdschou, as a gardener. His neighbor, named Sir We, held an official position in Yangdschou. Sir We had decided that it was time for his daughter to marry, so he sent for a match-maker and commissioned her to find a suitable husband. Old Dschang heard this, and was pleased. He prepared food and drink, entertained the match-maker, and told her to recommend him as a husband. But the old match-maker went off scolding.

The next day he invited her to dinner again and gave her money. Then the old match-maker said: "You do not know what you wish! Why should a gentleman's beautiful daughter condescend to marry a poor old gardener like yourself? Even though you had money to burn, your white hair would not match her black locks. Such a marriage is out of the question!"

But Old Dschang did not cease to entreat her: "Make an attempt, just one attempt, to mention me! If they will not listen to you, then I must resign myself to my fate!"

The old match-maker had taken his money, so she could not well refuse, and though she feared being scolded, she mentioned him to Sir We. He grew angry and wanted to throw her out of the house.

"I knew you would not thank me," said she, "but the old man urged it so that I could not refuse to mention his intention."

"Tell the old man that if this very day he brings me two white jade-stones, and four hundred ounces of yellow gold, then I will give him my daughter's hand in marriage."

But he only wished to mock the old man's folly, for he knew that the latter could not give him anything of the kind. The match-maker went to Old Dschang and delivered the message. And he made no objection; but at once brought the exact quantity of gold and jewels to Sir We's house. The latter was very much frightened and when his wife heard of it, she began to weep and wail loudly. But the girl encouraged her mother: "My father has given his word now and cannot break it. I will know how to bear my fate."

So Sir We's daughter was married to Old Dschang. But even after the wedding the latter did not give up his work as a gardener. He spaded the field and sold vegetables as usual, and his wife had to fetch water and build the kitchen fire herself. But she did her work without false shame and, though her relatives reproached her, she continued to do so.

Once an aristocratic relative visited Sir We and said: "If you had really been poor, were there not enough young gentlemen in the neighborhood for your daughter? Why did you have to marry her to such a wrinkled old gardener? Now that you have thrown her away, so to speak, it would be better if both of them left this part of the country."

Then Sir We prepared a banquet and invited his daughter and Old Dschang to visit him. When they had had sufficient to eat and drink he allowed them to get an inkling of what was in his mind.

Said Old Dschang: "I have only remained here because I thought you would long for your daughter. But since you are tired of us, I will be glad to go. I have a little country house back in the hills, and we will set out for it early tomorrow morning."

The following morning, at break of dawn, Old Dschang came with his wife to say farewell. Sir We said: "Should we long to see you at some later time, my son can make inquiries." Old Dschang placed his wife on a donkey and gave her a straw hat to wear. He himself took his staff and walked after.

A few years passed without any news from either of them. Then Sir We and his wife felt quite a longing to see their daughter and sent their son to make inquiries. When the latter got back in the hills he met a plow-boy who was plowing with two yellow steers. He asked him: "Where is Old Dschang's country house?" The plow-boy left the plow in the harrow, bowed and answered: "You have been a long time coming, sir! The village is not far from here: I will show you the way."

They crossed a hill. At the foot of the hill flowed a brook, and when they had crossed the brook they had to climb another hill. Gradually the landscape changed. From the top of the hill could be seen a valley, level in the middle, surrounded by abrupt crags and shaded by green trees, among which houses and towers peeped forth. This was the country house of Old Dschang. Before the village flowed a deep brook full of clear, blue water. They passed over a stone bridge and reached the gate. Here flowers and trees grew in luxurious profusion, and peacocks and cranes flew about. From the distance could be heard the sound of flutes and of stringed instruments. Crystal-clear tones rose to the clouds. A messenger in a purple robe received the guest at the gate and led him into a hall of surpassing splendor. Strange fragrances filled the air, and there was a ringing of little bells of pearl. Two maid-servants came forth to greet him, followed by two rows of beautiful girls in a long processional. After them a man in a flowing turban, clad in scarlet silk, with red slippers, came floating along. The guest saluted him. He was serious and dignified, and at the same time seemed youthfully fresh. At first We's son did not recognize him, but when he looked more closely, why it was Old Dschang! The latter said with a smile: "I am pleased that the long road to travel has not prevented your coming. Your sister is just combing her hair. She will welcome you in a moment." Then he had him sit down and drink tea.

After a short time a maid-servant came and led him to the inner rooms, to his sister. The beams of her room were of sandalwood, the doors of tortoise-shell and the windows inlaid with blue jade; her curtains were formed of strings of pearls and the steps leading into the room of green nephrite. His sister was magnificently gowned, and far more beautiful than before. She asked him carelessly how he was getting along, and what her parents were doing; but was not very cordial. After a splendid meal she had an apartment prepared for him.

"My sister wishes to make an excursion to the Mountain of the Fairies," said Old Dschang to him. "We will be back about sunset, and you can rest until we return."

Then many-colored clouds rose in the courtyard, and dulcet music sounded on the air. Old Dschang mounted a dragon, while his wife and sister rode on phenixes and their attendants on cranes. So they rose into the air and disappeared in an easterly direction. They did not return until after sunset.

Old Dschang and his wife then said to him: "This is an abode of the blessed. You cannot remain here overlong. Tomorrow we will escort you back."

On the following day, when taking leave, Old Dschang gave him eighty ounces of gold and an old straw hat. "Should you need money," said he, "you can go to Yangdschou and inquire in the northern suburb for old Wang's drug-shop. There you can collect ten million pieces of copper. This hat is the order for them." Then he ordered his plow-boy to take him home again.

Quite a few of the folks at home, to whom he described his adventures, thought that Old Dschang must be a holy man, while others regarded the whole thing a magic vision.

After five or six years Sir We's money came to an end. So his son took the straw hat to Yangdschou and there asked for old Wang. The latter just happened to be standing in his drug-shop, mixing herbs. When the son explained his errand he said: "The money is ready. But is your hat genuine?" And he took the hat and examined it. A young girl came from an inner room and said: "I wove the hat for Old Dschang myself. There must be a red thread in it." And sure enough, there was. Then old Wang gave young We the ten million pieces of copper, and the latter now believed that Old Dschang was really a saint. So he once more went over the hills to look for him. He asked the forest-keepers, but they could tell him naught. Sadly he retraced his steps and decided to inquire of old Wang, but he had also disappeared.

When several years had passed he once more came to Yangdschou, and was walking in the meadow before the city gate. There he met Old Dschang's plow-boy. The latter cried out: "How are you? How are you?" and drew out ten pounds of gold, which he gave to him, saying: "My mistress told me to give you this. My master is this very moment drinking tea with old Wang in the inn." Young We followed the plow-boy, intending to greet his brother-in-law. But when he reached the inn there was no one in sight. And when he turned around the plow-boy had disappeared as well. And since that time no one ever heard from Old Dschang again.

Rose of Evening

ON THE FIFTH DAY of the fifth month the festival of the Dragon Junk is held along the Yangtze-kiang. A dragon is hollowed out of wood, painted with an armor of scales, and adorned with gold and bright colors. A carved red railing surrounds this ship, and its sails and flags are made of silks and brocade. The after part of the vessel is called the dragon's tail. It rises ten feet above the water, and a board which floats in the water is tied to it by means of a cloth. Upon this board sit boys who turn somersaults, stand on their heads, and perform all sorts of tricks. Yet, being so close to the water their danger is very great. It is the custom, therefore, when a boy is hired for this purpose, to give his parents money before he is trained. Then, if he falls into the water and is drowned, no one has him on their conscience. Farther South the custom differs in so much that instead of boys, beautiful girls are chosen for this purpose.

In Dschen-Giang there once lived a widow named Dsiang, who had a son called Aduan. When he was no more than seven years of age he was extraordinarily skilful, and no other boy could equal him. And his reputation increasing as he grew, he earned more and more money. So it happened that he was still called upon at the Dragon Junk Festival when he was already sixteen.

But one day he fell into the water below the Gold Island and was drowned. He was the only son of his mother, and she sorrowed over him, and that was the end of it.

Yet Aduan did not know that he had been drowned. He met two men who took him along with them, and he saw a new world in the midst of the waters of the Yellow River. When he looked around, the waves of the river towered steeply about him like walls, and a palace was visible, in which sat a man wearing armor and a helmet. His two companions said to him: "That is the Prince of the Dragon's Cave!" and bade him kneel.

The Prince of the Dragon's Cave seemed to be of a mild and kindly disposition and said: "We can make use of such a skilful lad. He may take part in the dance of the willow branches!"

So he was brought to a spot surrounded by extensive buildings. He entered, and was greeted by a crowd of boys who were all about fourteen years of age.

An old woman came in and they all called out: "This is Mother Hia!" And she sat down and had Aduan show his tricks. Then she taught him the dance of the flying thunders of Tsian-Tang River, and the music that calms the winds on the sea of Dung-Ting. When the cymbals and kettledrums reechoed through all the courts, they deafened the ear. Then, again, all the courts would fall silent. Mother Hia thought that Aduan would not be able to grasp everything the very first time; so she taught him with great patience. But Aduan had understood everything from the first, and that pleased old Mother Hia. "This boy," said she, "equals our own Rose of Evening!"

The following day the Prince of the Dragon's Cave held a review of his dancers. When all the dancers had assembled, the dance of the Ogres was danced first. Those who performed it all wore devil-masks and garments of scales. They beat upon enormous cymbals, and their kettledrums were so large that four men could just about span them. Their sound was like the sound of a mighty thunder, and the noise was so great that nothing else could be heard. When the dance began, tremendous waves spouted up to the very skies, and then fell down again like star-glimmer which scatters in the air.

The Prince of the Dragon Cave hastily bade the dance cease, and had the dancers of the nightingale round step forth. These were all lovely young girls of sixteen. They made a delicate music with flutes, so that the breeze blew and the roaring of the waves was stilled in a moment. The water gradually became as quiet as a crystal world, transparent to its lowest depths. When the nightingale dancers had finished, they withdrew and posted themselves in the western courtyard.

Then came the turn of the swallow dancers. These were all little girls. One among them, who was about fifteen years of age, danced the dance of the giving of flowers with flying sleeves and waving locks. And as their garments fluttered, many-colored flowers dropped from their folds, and were caught up by the wind and whirled about the whole courtyard. When the dance had ended, this dancer also went off with the rest of the girls to the western courtyard. Aduan looked at her from out the corner of his eye, and fell deeply in love with her. He asked his comrades who she might be and they told him she was named "Rose of Evening."

But the willow-spray dancers were now called out. The Prince of the Dragon Cave was especially desirous of testing Aduan. So Aduan danced alone, and he danced with joy or defiance according to the music. When he looked up and when he looked down his glances held the beat of the measure. The Dragon Prince, enchanted with his skill, presented him with a garment of five colors, and gave him a carbuncle set in golden threads of fish-beard for a hair-jewel. Aduan bowed his thanks for the gift, and then also hastened to the western courtyard. There all the dancers stood in rank and file. Aduan could only look at Rose of Evening from a distance, but still Rose of Evening returned his glances.

After a time Aduan gradually slipped to the end of his file and Rose of Evening also drew near to him, so that they stood only a few feet away from each other. But the strict rules allowed no confusion in the ranks, so they could only gaze and let their souls go out to each other.

Now the butterfly dance followed the others. This was danced by the boys and girls together, and the pairs were equal in size, age and the color of their garments. When all the dances had ended, the dancers marched out with the goose-step. The willow-spray dancers followed the swallow dancers, and Aduan hastened in advance of his company, while Rose of Evening lingered along after hers. She turned her head, and when she spied Aduan she purposely let a coral pin fall from her hair. Aduan hastily hid it in his sleeve.

When he had returned, he was sick with longing, and could neither eat nor sleep. Mother Hia brought him all sorts of dainties, looked after him three or four times a day, and stroked his forehead with loving care. But his illness did not yield in the least. Mother Hia was unhappy, and yet helpless.

"The birthday of the King of the Wu River is at hand," said she. "What is to be done?"

In the twilight there came a boy, who sat down on the edge of Aduan's bed and chatted with him. He belonged to the butterfly dancers, said he, and asked casually: "Are you sick because of Rose of Evening?" Aduan, frightened, asked him how he came to guess it. The other boy said, with a smile: "Well, because Rose of Evening is in the same case as yourself."

Disconcerted, Aduan sat up and begged the boy to advise him. "Are you able to walk?" asked the latter. "If I exert myself," said Aduan, "I think I could manage it."

So the boy led him to the South. There he opened a gate and they turned the corner, to the West. Once more the doors of the gate flew open, and now Aduan saw a lotus field about twenty acres in size. The lotus flowers were all growing on level earth, and their leaves were as large as mats and their flowers like umbrellas. The fallen blossoms covered the ground beneath the stalks to the depth of a foot or more. The boy led Aduan in and said, "Now first of all sit down for a little while!" Then he went away.

After a time a beautiful girl thrust aside the lotus flowers and came into the open. It was Rose of Evening. They looked at each other with happy timidity, and each told how each had longed for the other. And they also told each other of their former life. Then they weighted the lotus-leaves with stones so that they made a cozy retreat, in which they could be together, and promised to meet each other there every evening. And then they parted.

Aduan came back and his illness left him. From that time on he met Rose of Evening every day in the lotus field.

After a few days had passed they had to accompany the Prince of the Dragon Cave to the birthday festival of the King of the Wu River. The festival came to an end, and all the dancers returned home. Only, the King had kept back Rose of Evening and one of the nightingale dancers to teach the girls in his castle.

Months passed and no news came from Rose of Evening, so that Aduan went about full of longing and despair. Now Mother Hia went every day to the castle of the god of the Wu River. So Aduan told her that Rose of Evening was his cousin, and entreated her to take him along with her so that he could at least see her a single time. So she took him along, and let him stay at the lodge-house of the river-god for a few days. But the indwellers of the castle were so strictly watched that he could not see Rose of Evening even a single time. Sadly Aduan went back again.

Another month passed and Aduan, filled with gloomy thoughts, wished that death might be his portion.

One day Mother Hia came to him full of pity, and began to sympathize with him. "What a shame," said she, "that Rose of Evening has cast herself into the river!"

Aduan was extremely frightened, and his tears flowed resistlessly. He tore his beautiful garments, took his gold and his pearls, and went out with the sole idea of following his beloved in death. Yet the waters of the river stood up before him like walls, and no matter how often he ran against them, head down, they always flung him back.

He did not dare return, since he feared he might be questioned about his festival garments, and severely punished because he had ruined them. So he stood there and knew not what to do, while the perspiration ran down to his ankles. Suddenly, at the foot of the water-wall he saw a tall tree. Like a monkey he climbed up to its very top, and then, with all his might, he shot into the waves.

And then, without being wet, he found himself suddenly swimming on the surface of the river. Unexpectedly the world of men rose up once more before his dazzled eyes. He swam to the shore, and as he walked along the river-bank, his thoughts went back to his old mother. He took a ship and traveled home.

When he reached the village, it seemed to him as though all the houses in it belonged to another world. The following morning he entered his mother's house, and as he did so, heard a girl's voice beneath the window saying: "Your son has come back again!" The voice sounded like the voice of Rose of Evening, and when she came to greet him at his mother's side, sure enough, it was Rose of Evening herself.

And in that hour the joy of these two who were so fond of each other overcame all their sorrow. But in the mother's mind sorrow and doubt, terror and joy mingled in constant succession in a thousand different ways.

When Rose of Evening had been in the palace of the river-king, and had come to realize that she would never see Aduan again, she determined to die, and flung herself into the waters of the stream. But she was carried to the surface, and the waves carried and cradled her till a ship came by and took her aboard. They asked whence she came. Now Rose of Evening had originally been a celebrated singing girl of Wu, who had fallen into the river and whose body had never been found. So she thought to herself that, after all, she could not return to her old life again. So she answered: "Madame Dsiang, in Dschen-Giang is my mother-in-law." Then the travelers took passage for her in a ship which brought her to the place she had mentioned. The widow Dsiang first said she must be mistaken, but the girl insisted that there was no mistake, and told Aduan's mother her whole story. Yet, though the latter was charmed by her surpassing loveliness, she feared that Rose of Evening was too young to live a widow's life. But the girl was respectful and industrious, and when she saw that poverty ruled in her new home, she took her pearls and sold them for a high price. Aduan's old mother was greatly pleased to see how seriously the girl took her duties.

Now that Aduan had returned again Rose of Evening could not control her joy. And even Aduan's old mother cherished the hope that, after all, perhaps her son had not died. She secretly dug up her son's grave, yet all his bones were still lying in it. So she questioned Aduan. And then, for the first time, the latter realized that he was a departed spirit. Then he feared that Rose of Evening might regard him with disgust because he was no longer a human being. So he ordered his mother on no account to speak of it, and this his mother promised. Then she spread the report in the village that the body which had been found in the river had not been that of her son at all. Yet she could not rid herself of the fear that, since Aduan was a departed spirit, heaven might refuse to send him a child.

In spite of her fear, however, she was able to hold a grandson in her arms in course of time. When she looked at him, he was no different from other children, and then her cup of joy was filled to overflowing.

Rose of Evening gradually became aware of the fact that Aduan was not really a human being. "Why did you not tell me at once?" said she. "Departed spirits who wear the garments of the dragon castle, surround themselves with a soul-casing so heavy in texture that they can no longer be distinguished from the living. And if one can obtain the lime made of dragon-horn which is in the castle, then the bones may be glued together in such wise that flesh and blood will grow over them again. What a pity that we could not obtain the lime while we were there!"

Aduan sold his pearl, for which a merchant from foreign parts gave him an enormous sum. Thus his family grew very wealthy. Once, on his mother's birthday, he danced with his wife and sang, in order to please her. The news reached the castle of the Dragon Prince and he thought to carry off Rose of Evening by force. But Aduan, alarmed, went to the Prince, and declared that both he and his wife were departed spirits. They examined him and since he cast no shadow, his word was taken, and he was not robbed of Rose of Evening.

The Disembodied Friend

MR. CH'EN, M.A., of Shun-t'ien Fu, when a boy of sixteen, went to school at a Buddhist temple. There were a great many scholars besides himself, and, among others, one named Ch'u, who said he came from Shantung. This Ch'u was a very hard-working fellow; he never seemed to be idle, and actually slept in the school-room, not going home at all. Ch'en became much attached to him, and one day asked him why he never went away. "Well, you see," replied Ch'u, "my people are very poor, and can hardly afford to pay for my schooling; but, by dint of working half the night, two of my days are equal to three of anybody else's." Thereupon Ch'en said he would bring his own bed to the school, and that they would sleep there together; to which Ch'u replied that the teaching they got wasn't worth much, and that they would do better by putting themselves under a certain old scholar named Lu. This they were easily able to do, as the arrangement at the temple was monthly, and at the end of each month anyone was free to go or to come.

So off they went to this Mr. Lu, a man of considerable literary attainments, who had found himself in Shun-t'ien Fu without a cash in his pocket, and was accordingly obliged to take pupils. He was delighted at getting two additions to his number and, Ch'u showing himself an apt scholar, the two soon became very great friends, sleeping in the same room and eating at the same table.

At the end of the month Ch'u asked for leave of absence, and, to the astonishment of all, ten days elapsed without anything being heard of him. It then chanced that Ch'en went to the T'ien-ning temple, and there he saw Ch'u under one of the verandahs, occupied in cutting wood for lucifer-matches. The latter was much disconcerted by the arrival of Ch'en, who asked him why he had given up his studies; so the latter took him aside, and explained that he was so poor as to be obliged to work half a month to scrape together funds enough for his next month's schooling. "You come along back with me," cried Ch'en, on hearing this, "I will arrange for the payment," which Ch'u immediately consented to do on condition that Ch'en would keep the whole thing a profound secret.

Now Ch'en's father was a wealthy tradesman, and from his till Ch'en abstracted money wherewith to pay for Ch'u; and by-and-by, when his father found him out, he confessed why he had done so. Thereupon Ch'en's father called him a fool, and would not let him resume his studies; at which Ch'u was much hurt, and would have left the school too, but that old Mr. Lu discovered what had taken place, and gave him the money to return to Ch'en's father, keeping him still at the school, and treating him quite like his own son. So Ch'en studied no more, but whenever he met Ch'u he always asked him to join in some refreshment at a restaurant, Ch'u invariably refusing, but yielding at length to his entreaties, being himself loth to break off their old acquaintanceship.

Thus two years passed away, when Ch'en's father died, and Ch'en went back to his books under the guidance of old Mr. Lu, who was very glad to see such determination. Of course Ch'en was now far behind Ch'u; and in about six months Lu's son arrived, having begged his way in search of his father, so Mr. Lu gave up his school and returned home with a purse which his pupils had made up for him, Ch'u adding nothing thereto but his tears. At parting, Mr. Lu advised Ch'en to take Ch'u as his tutor, and this he did, establishing him comfortably in the house with him. The examination was very shortly to commence, and Ch'en felt convinced that he should not get through; but Ch'u said he thought he should be able to manage the matter for him. On the appointed day he introduced Ch'en to a gentleman who he said was a cousin of his, named Liu, and asked Ch'en to accompany this cousin, which Ch'en was just proceeding to do when Ch'u pulled him back from behind, and he would have fallen down but that the cousin pulled him up again, and then, after having scrutinized his appearance, carried him off to his own house. There being no ladies there, Ch'en was put into the inner apartments; and a few days afterwards Liu said to him, "A great many people will be at the gardens to-day; let us go and amuse ourselves awhile, and afterwards I will send you home again." He then gave orders that a servant should proceed on ahead with tea and wine, and by-and-by they themselves went, and were soon in the thick of the fete. Crossing over a bridge, they saw beneath an old willow tree a little painted skiff, and were soon on board, engaged in freely passing round the wine. However, finding this a little dull, Liu bade his servant go and see if Miss Li, the famous singing-girl, was at home; and in a few minutes the servant returned bringing Miss Li with him. Ch'en had met her before, and so they at once exchanged greetings, while Liu begged her to be good enough to favour them with a song. Miss Li, who seemed labouring under a fit of melancholy, forthwith began a funeral dirge; at which Ch'en was not much pleased, and observed that such a theme was hardly suitable to the occasion. With a forced smile, Miss Li changed her key, and gave them a love-song; whereupon Ch'en seized her hand, and said, "There's that song of the Huan-sha river, which you sang once before; I have read it over several times, but have quite forgotten the words." Then Miss Li began:

"Eyes overflowing with tears, she sits gazing into her glass,
Lifting the bamboo screen, one of her comrades approaches;
She bends her head and seems intent on her bow-like slippers,
And forces her eyebrows to arch themselves into a smile.
With her scarlet sleeve she wipes the tears from her perfumed cheek,
In fear and trembling lest they should guess
the thoughts that o'erwhelm her."

Ch'en repeated this over several times, until at length the skiff stopped, and they passed through a long verandah, where a great many verses had been inscribed on the walls, to which Ch'en at once proceeded to add a stanza of his own. Evening was now coming on, and Liu remarked that the candidates would be just about leaving the examination-hall; so he escorted him back to his own home, and there left him. The room was dark, and there was no one with him; but by-and-by the servants ushered in someone whom at first he took to be Ch'u. However, he soon saw that it was not Ch'u, and in another moment the stranger had fallen against him and knocked him down. "Master's fainted!" cried the servants, as they ran to pick him up; and then Ch'en discovered that the one who had fallen down was really no other than himself.

On getting up, he saw Ch'u standing by his side; and when they had sent away the servants the latter said, "Don't be alarmed: I am nothing more than a disembodied spirit. My time for re-appearing on earth is long overdue, but I could not forget your great kindness to me, and accordingly I have remained under this form in order to assist in the accomplishment of your wishes. The three bouts are over, and your ambition will be gratified." Ch'en then inquired if Ch'u could assist him in like manner for his doctor's degree; to which the latter replied, "Alas! the luck descending to you from your ancestors is not equal to that. They were a niggardly lot, and unfit for the posthumous honours you would thus confer on them." Ch'en next asked him whither he was going; and Ch'u replied that he hoped, through the agency of his cousin, who was a clerk in Purgatory, to be born again in old Mr. Lu's family.

They then bade each other adieu; and, when morning came, Ch'en set off to call on Miss Li, the singing-girl; but on reaching her house he found that she had been dead some days. He walked on to the gardens, and there he saw traces of verses that had been written on the walls, and evidently rubbed out, so as to be hardly decipherable. In a moment it flashed across him that the verses and their composers belonged to the other world. Towards evening Ch'u re-appeared in high spirits, saying that he had succeeded in his design, and had come to wish Ch'en a long farewell. Holding out his open palms, he requested Ch'en to write the word Ch'u on each; and then, after refusing to take a parting cup, he went away, telling

Ch'en that the examination-list would soon be out, and that they would meet again before long. Ch'en brushed away his tears and escorted him to the door, where a man, who had been waiting for him, laid his hand on Ch'u's head and pressed it downwards until Ch'u was perfectly flat. The man then put him in a sack and carried him off on his back.

A few days afterwards the list came out, and, to his great joy, Ch'en found his name among the successful candidates; whereupon he immediately started off to visit his old tutor, Mr. Lu. Now Mr. Lu's wife had had no children for ten years, being about fifty years of age, when suddenly she gave birth to a son, who was born with both fists doubled up so that no one could open them. On his arrival Ch'en begged to see the child, and declared that inside its hands would be found written the word Ch'u. Old Mr. Lu laughed at this; but no sooner had the child set eyes on Ch'en than both its fists opened spontaneously, and there was the word as Ch'en had said. The story was soon told, and Ch'en went home, after making a handsome present to the family; and later on, when Mr. Lu went up for his doctor's degree and stayed at Ch'en's house, his son was thirteen years old, and had already matriculated as a candidate for literary honours.

The Ghost Who Was Foiled

THERE ARE GHOSTS of many kinds, but the ghosts of those who have hung themselves are the worst. Such ghosts are always coaxing other living people to hang themselves from the beams of the roof. If they succeed in persuading someone to hang himself, then the road to the Nether World is open to them, and they can once more enter into the wheel of transformation. The following story of such a ghost is told by persons worthy of belief.

Once upon a time there lived a man in Tsing Tschoufu who had passed his military examination, and had been ordered to Tsinanfu to report for duty.

It was at the season of rains. So it happened that evening came on before he could reach the town-inn where he had expected to pass the night. Just as the sun was setting he reached a small village and asked for a night's lodging. But there were only poor families in the village who had no room for him in their huts. So they directed him to an old temple which stood outside the village, and said he could spend the night there.

The images of the gods in the temple were all decayed, so that one could not distinguish one from the other. Thick spider-webs covered the entrance, and the dust lay inches high everywhere. So the soldier went out into the open, where he found an old flight of steps. He spread out his knapsack on a stone step, tied his horse to an old tree, took his flask from his pocket and drank – for it had been a hot day. There had been a heavy rain, but it had just cleared again. The new moon was on the decline. The soldier closed his eyes and tried to sleep.

Suddenly he heard a rustling sound in the temple, and a cool wind passed over his face and made him shudder. And he saw a woman come out of the temple, dressed in an old dirty red gown, and with a face as white as a chalk wall. She stole past quietly as though she were afraid of being seen. The soldier knew no fear. So he pretended to be asleep and did not move, but watched her with half-shut eyes. And he saw her draw a rope from her sleeve and disappear. Then he knew that she was the ghost of one who had hung herself. He got up softly and followed her, and, sure enough, she went into the village.

When she came to a certain house she slipped into the court through a crack in the door. The soldier leaped over the wall after her. It was a house with three rooms. In the rear room a lamp was burning dimly. The soldier looked through the window into the room, and there was a young woman of about twenty sitting on the bed, sighing deeply, and her kerchief was wet through with tears. Beside her lay a little child, asleep. The woman looked up toward the beam of the ceiling. One moment she would weep and the next she would stroke the child. When the soldier looked more closely, there was the ghost sitting up on the beam. She had passed the rope around her neck and was hanging herself in dumb show. And whenever she beckoned with her hand the woman looked up toward her. This went on for some time.

Finally the woman said: "You say it would be best for me to die. Very well, then, I will die; but I cannot part from my child!"

And once more she burst into tears. But the ghost merely laughed and coaxed her again.

So the woman said determinedly: "It is enough. I will die!"

With these words she opened her chest of clothes, put on new garments, and painted her face before the mirror. Then she drew up a bench and climbed up on it. She undid her girdle and knotted it to the beam. She had already stretched forth her neck and was about to leap from the bench, when the child suddenly awoke and began to cry. The woman climbed down again and soothed and quieted her child, and while she was petting it she wept, so that the tears fell from her eyes like a string of pearls. The ghost frowned and hissed, for it feared to lose its prey. In a short time the child had fallen asleep again, and the woman once more began to look aloft. Then she rose, again climbed on the bench, and was about to lay the noose about her neck when the soldier began to call out loudly and drum on the window-pane. Then he broke it and climbed into the room. The woman fell to the ground and the ghost disappeared. The soldier recalled the woman to consciousness, and then he saw something hanging down from the beam, like a cord without an end. Knowing that it belonged to the ghost of the hanged woman he took and kept it.

Then he said to the woman: "Take good care of your child! You have but one life to lose in this world!"

And with that he went out.

Then it occurred to him that his horse and his baggage were still in the temple. And he went there to get them. When he came out of the village there was the ghost, waiting for him in the road.

The ghost bowed and said: "I have been looking for a substitute for many years, and to-day, when it seemed as though I should really get one, you came along and spoiled my chances. So there is nothing more for me to do. Yet there is something which I left behind me in my hurry. You surely must have found it, and I will ask you to return it to me. If I only have this one thing, my not having found a substitute will not worry me."

Then the soldier showed her the rope and said with a laugh: "Is this the thing you mean? Why, if I were to give it back to you then someone is sure to hang themselves. And that I could not allow."

With these words he wound the rope around his arm, drove her off and said: "Now be off with you!"

But then the ghost grew angry. Her face turned greenish-black, her hair fell in wild disorder down her neck, her eyes grew bloodshot, and her tongue hung far out of her mouth. She stretched forth both hands and tried to seize the soldier, but he struck out at her with his clenched fist. By mistake he hit himself in the nose and it began to bleed. Then he sprinkled a few drops of blood in her direction and, since the ghosts cannot endure human blood, she ceased her attack, moved off a few paces and began to abuse him. This she did for some time, until the cock in the village began to crow. Then the ghost disappeared.

In the meantime the farmer-folk of the village had come to thank the soldier. It seems that after he had left the woman her husband had come home, and asked his wife what had happened. And then for the first time he had learned what had occurred. So they all set out together along the road in order to look for the soldier outside the village. When they found him he was still beating the air with his fists and talking wildly. So they called out to him and he told them what had taken place. The rope could still be seen on his bare arm; yet it had grown fast to it, and surrounded it in the shape of a red ring of flesh.

The day was just dawning, so the soldier swung himself into his saddle and rode away.

The Night on the Battlefield

ONCE UPON A TIME there was a merchant, who was wandering toward Shantung with his wares, along the road from the South. At about the second watch of the night, a heavy storm blew up from the North. And he chanced to see an inn at one side of the road, whose lights were just being lit. He went in to get something to drink and order lodgings for the night, but the folk at the inn raised objections. Yet an old man among them took

pity on his unhappy situation and said: "We have just prepared a meal for warriors who have come a long distance, and we have no wine left to serve you. But there is a little side room here which is still free, and there you may stay overnight." With these words he led him into it. But the merchant could not sleep because of his hunger and thirst. Outside he could hear the noise of men and horses. And since all these proceedings did not seem quite natural to him, he got up and looked through a crack in the door. And he saw that the whole inn was filled with soldiers, who were sitting on the ground, eating and drinking, and talking about campaigns of which he had never heard. After a time they began calling to each other: "The general is coming!" And far off in the distance could be heard the cries of his bodyguard. All the soldiers hurried out to receive him. Then the merchant saw a procession with many paper lanterns, and riding in their midst a man of martial appearance with a long beard. He dismounted, entered the inn, and took his place at the head of the board. The soldiers mounted guard at the door, awaiting his commands, and the inn-keeper served food and drink, to which the general did full justice.

When he had finished his officers entered, and he said to them: "You have now been underway for some time. Go back to your men. I shall rest a little myself. It will be time enough to beat the assembly when the order to advance is given."

The officers received his commands and withdrew. Then the general called out: "Send Asti in!" and a young officer entered from the left side of the house. The people of the inn locked the gates and withdrew for the night, while Asti conducted the long-haired general to a door at the left, through a crack of which shone the light of a lamp. The merchant stole from his room and looked through the crack in the door. Within the room was a bed of bamboo, without covers or pillows. The lamp stood on the ground. The long-bearded general took hold of his head. It came off and he placed it on the bed. Then Asti took hold of his arms. These also came off and were carefully placed beside the head. Then the old general threw himself down on the bed crosswise, and Asti took hold of his body, which came apart below the thighs, and the two legs fell to the ground. Then the lamp went out. Overcome by terror the merchant hurried back to his room as fast as he could, holding his sleeves before his eyes, and laid down on his bed, where he tossed about sleepless all night.

At last he heard a cock crow in the distance. He was shivering. He took his sleeves from his face and saw that dawn was stealing along the sky. And when he looked about him, there he was lying in the middle of a thick clump of brush. Round about him was a wilderness, not a house, not even a grave was to be seen anywhere. In spite of being chilled, he ran about three miles till he came to the nearest inn. The inn-keeper opened the door and asked him with astonishment where he came from at that early hour. So the merchant told him his experiences and inquired as to the sort of place at which he had spent the night. The inn-keeper shook his head: "The whole neighborhood is covered with old battlefields," was his reply, "and all sorts of supernatural things take place on them after dark."

The Phantom Vessel

ONCE A SHIP LOADED with pleasure-seekers was sailing from North China to Shanghai. High winds and stormy weather had delayed her, and she was still one week from port when a great plague broke out on board. This plague was of the worst kind. It attacked passengers and sailors alike until there were so few left to sail the vessel that it seemed as if she would soon be left to the mercy of winds and waves.

On all sides lay the dead, and the groans of the dying were most terrible to hear. Of that great company of travellers only one, a little boy named Ying-lo, had escaped. At last the few sailors, who had been trying hard to save their ship, were obliged to lie down upon the deck, a prey to the dreadful sickness, and soon they too were dead.

Ying-lo now found himself alone on the sea. For some reason – he did not know why – the gods or the sea fairies had spared him, but as he looked about in terror at the friends and loved ones who had died, he almost wished that he might join them.

The sails flapped about like great broken wings, while the giant waves dashed higher above the deck, washing many of the bodies overboard and wetting the little boy to the skin. Shivering with cold, he gave himself up for lost and prayed to the gods, whom his mother had often told him about, to take him from this dreadful ship and let him escape the fatal illness.

As he lay there praying he heard a slight noise in the rigging just above his head. Looking up, he saw a ball of fire running along a yardarm near the top of the mast. The sight was so strange that he forgot his prayer and stared with open-mouthed wonder. To his astonishment, the ball grew brighter and brighter, and then suddenly began slipping down the mast, all the time increasing in size. The poor boy did not know what to do or to think. Were the gods, in answer to his prayer, sending fire to burn the vessel? If so, he would soon escape. Anything would be better than to be alone upon the sea.

Nearer and nearer came the fireball. At last, when it reached the deck, to Ying-lo's surprise, something very, very strange happened. Before he had time to feel alarmed, the light vanished, and a funny little man stood in front of him peering anxiously into the child's frightened face.

"Yes, you are the lad I'm looking for," he said at last, speaking in a piping voice that almost made Ying-lo smile. "You are Ying-lo, and you are the only one left of this wretched company." This he said, pointing towards the bodies lying here and there about the deck.

Although he saw that the old man meant him no harm, the child could say nothing, but waited in silence, wondering what would happen next.

By this time the vessel was tossing and pitching so violently that it seemed every minute as if it would upset and go down beneath the foaming waves, never to rise again. Not many miles distant on the right, some jagged rocks stuck out of the water, lifting their cruel heads as if waiting for the helpless ship.

The newcomer walked slowly towards the mast and tapped on it three times with an iron staff he had been using as a cane. Immediately the sails spread, the vessel righted itself and began to glide over the sea so fast that the gulls were soon left far behind, while the threatening rocks upon which the ship had been so nearly dashed seemed like specks in the distance.

"Do you remember me?" said the stranger, suddenly turning and coming up to Ying-lo, but his voice was lost in the whistling of the wind, and the boy knew only by the moving of his lips that the old man was talking. The greybeard bent over until his mouth was at Ying-lo's ear: "Did you ever see me before?"

With a puzzled look, at first the child shook his head. Then as he gazed more closely there seemed to be something that he recognized about the wrinkled face. "Yes, I think so, but I don't know when."

With a tap of his staff the fairy stopped the blowing of the wind, and then spoke once more to his small companion: "One year ago I passed through your village. I was dressed in rags, and was begging my way along the street, trying to find someone who would feel sorry for me. Alas! no one answered my cry for mercy. Not a crust was thrown into my bowl. All the people were deaf, and fierce dogs drove me from door to door. Finally when I was almost dying of hunger, I began to feel that here was a village without one good person in it. Just then you saw my suffering, ran into the house, and brought me out food. Your heartless mother saw you doing this and beat you cruelly. Do you remember now, my child?"

"Yes, I remember," he answered sadly, "and that mother is now lying dead. Alas! all, all are dead, my father and my brothers also. Not one is left of my family."

"Little did you know, my boy, to whom you were giving food that day. You took me for a lowly beggar, but, behold, it was not a poor man that you fed, for I am Iron Staff. You must have heard of me when they were telling of the fairies in the Western Heaven, and of their adventures here on earth."

"Yes, yes," answered Ying-lo, trembling half with fear and half with joy, "indeed I have heard of you many, many times, and all the people love you for your kind deeds of mercy."

"Alas! they did not show their love, my little one. Surely you know that if any one wishes to reward the fairies for their mercies, he must begin to do deeds of the same kind himself. No one but you in all your village had pity on me in my rags. If they had known that I was Iron Staff, everything would have been different; they would have given me a feast and begged for my protection.

> *"The only love that loves aright*
> *Is that which loves in every plight.*
> *The beggar in his sad array*
> *Is moulded of the selfsame clay.*
>
> *"Who knows a man by what he wears,*
> *By what he says or by his prayers?*
> *Hidden beneath that wrinkled skin*
> *A fairy may reside within.*
>
> *"Then treat with kindness and with love*
> *The lowly man, the god above;*
> *A friendly nod, a welcome smile –*
> *For love is ever worth the while."*

Ying-lo listened in wonder to Iron Staff's little poem, and when he had finished, the boy's face was glowing with the love of which the fairy had spoken. "My poor, poor father and mother!" he cried; "they knew nothing of these beautiful things you are telling me. They were brought up in poverty. As they were knocked about in childhood by those around them, so they learned to beat others who begged them for help. Is it strange that they did not have hearts full of pity for you when you looked like a beggar?"

"But what about you, my boy? You were not deaf when I asked you. Have you not been whipped and punished all your life? How then did you learn to look with love at those in tears?"

The child could not answer these questions, but only looked sorrowfully at Iron Staff. "Oh, can you not, good fairy, will you not restore my parents and brothers, and give them another chance to be good and useful people?"

"Listen, Ying-lo; it is impossible – unless you do two things first," he answered, stroking his beard gravely and leaning heavily upon his staff.

"What are they? What must I do to save my family? Anything you ask of me will not be too much to pay for your kindness."

"First you must tell me of some good deed done by these people for whose lives you are asking. Name only one, for that will be enough; but it is against our rules to help those who have done nothing."

Ying-lo was silent, and for a moment his face was clouded. "Yes, I know," he said finally, brightening. "They burned incense once at the temple. That was certainly a deed of virtue."

"But when was it, little one, that they did this?"

"When my big brother was sick, and they were praying for him to get well. The doctors could not save him with boiled turnip juice or with any other of the medicines they used, so my parents begged the gods."

"Selfish, selfish!" muttered Iron Staff. "If their eldest son had not been dying they would have spent no money at the temple. They tried in this way to buy back his health, for they were expecting him to support them in their old age."

Ying-lo's face fell. "You are right," he answered.

"Can you think of nothing else?"

"Yes, oh, yes, last year when the foreigner rode through our village and fell sick in front of our house, they took him in and cared for him."

"How long?" asked the other sharply.

"Until he died the next week."

"And what did they do with the mule he was riding, his bed, and the money in his bag? Did they try to restore them to his people?"

"No, they said they'd keep them to pay for the trouble." Ying-lo's face turned scarlet.

"But try again, dear boy! Is there not one little deed of goodness that was not selfish? Think once more."

For a long time Ying-lo did not reply. At length he spoke in a low voice; "I think of one, but I fear it amounts to nothing."

"No good, my child, is too small to be counted when the gods are weighing a man's heart."

"Last spring the birds were eating in my father's garden. My mother wanted to buy poison from the shop to destroy them, but my father said no, that the little things must live, and he for one was not in favour of killing them."

"At last, Ying-lo, you have named a real deed of mercy, and as he spared the tiny birds from poison, so shall his life and the lives of your mother and brothers be restored from the deadly plague.

"But remember there is one other thing that depends on you."

Ying-lo's eyes glistened gratefully. "Then if it rests with me, and I can do it, you have my promise. No sacrifice should be too great for a son to make for his loved ones even though his life itself is asked in payment."

"Very well, Ying-lo. What I require is that you carry out to the letter my instructions. Now it is time for me to keep my promise to you."

So saying, Iron Staff called on Ying-lo to point out the members of his family, and, approaching them one by one, with the end of his iron stick he touched their foreheads. In an instant each, without a word, arose. Looking round and recognising Ying-lo, they stood back, frightened at seeing him with the fairy. When the last had risen to his feet, Iron Staff beckoned all of them to listen. This they did willingly, too much terrified to speak, for they saw on all sides signs of the plague that had swept over the vessel, and they remembered the frightful agony they had suffered in dying. Each knew that he had been lifted by some magic power from darkness into light.

"My friends," began the fairy, "little did you think when less than a year ago you drove me from your door that soon you yourselves would be in need of mercy. To-day you have had a peep into the awful land of Yama. You have seen the horror of his tortures, have heard the screams of his slaves, and by another night you would have been carried before him to be judged. What power is it that has saved you from his clutches? As you look back through your wicked lives can you think of any reason why you deserved this rescue? No, there is no memory of goodness in your black hearts. Well, I shall tell you: it is this little boy, this Ying-lo, who many times has felt the weight of your wicked hands and has hidden in terror at your coming. To him alone you owe my help."

Father, mother, and brothers all gazed in turn, first at the fairy and then at the timid child whose eyes fell before their looks of gratitude.

"By reason of his goodness this child whom you have scorned is worthy of a place within the Western Heaven. In truth, I came this very day to lead him to that fairyland. For you, however, he wishes to make a sacrifice. With sorrow I am yielding to his wishes. His sacrifice will be that of giving up a place among the fairies and of continuing to live here on this earth with you. He will try to make a change within your household. If at any time you treat him badly and do not heed his wishes – mark you well my words – by the power of this magic staff which I shall place in his hands, he may enter at once into the land of the fairies, leaving you to die in your wickedness. This I command him to do, and he has promised to obey my slightest wish.

"This plague took you off suddenly and ended your wicked lives. Ying-lo has raised you from its grasp and his power can lift you from the bed of sin. No other hand than his can bear the rod which I am leaving. If one of you but touch it, instantly he will fall dead upon the ground.

"And now, my child, the time has come for me to leave you. First, however, I must show you what you are now able to do. Around you lie the corpses of sailors and passengers. Tap three times upon the mast and wish that they shall come to life." So saying he handed Ying-lo the iron staff.

Although the magic rod was heavy, the child lifted it as if it were a fairy's wand. Then, stepping forward to the mast, he rapped three times as he had been commanded. Immediately on all sides arose the bodies, once more full of life and strength.

"Now command the ship to take you back to your home port, for such sinful creatures as these are in no way fit to make a journey among strangers. They must first return and free their homes of sin."

Again rapping on the mast, the child willed the great vessel to take its homeward course. No sooner had he moved the staff than, like a bird wheeling in the heavens, the bark swung round and started on the return journey. Swifter than a flash of lightning flew the boat, for it was now become a fairy vessel. Before the sailors and the travellers could recover from their surprise, land was sighted and they saw that they were indeed entering the harbour.

Just as the ship was darting toward the shore the fairy suddenly, with a parting word to Ying-lo, changed into a flaming ball of fire which rolled along the deck and ascended the spars. Then, as it reached the top of the rigging, it floated off into the blue sky, and all on board, speechless with surprise, watched it until it vanished.

With a cry of thanksgiving, Ying-lo flung his arms about his parents and descended with them to the shore.

The Story of Ming-Y

DO YOU ASK me who she was, the beautiful Sie-Thao? For a thousand years and more the trees have been whispering above her bed of stone. And the syllables of her name come to the listener with the lisping of the leaves; with the quivering of many-fingered boughs; with the fluttering of lights and shadows; with the breath, sweet as a woman's presence, of numberless savage flowers – Sie-Thao. But, saving the whispering of her name, what the trees say cannot be understood; and they alone remember the years of Sie-Thao. Something about her you might, nevertheless, learn from any of those Kiang-kou-jin – those famous Chinese story-tellers, who nightly narrate to listening crowds, in consideration of a few tsien, the legends of the past. Something concerning her you may also find in the book entitled "Kin-Kou-Ki-Koan," which signifies in our tongue: "The Marvellous Happenings of Ancient and of Recent Times." And perhaps of all things therein written, the most marvellous is this memory of Sie-Thao:

Five hundred years ago, in the reign of the Emperor Houng-Wou, whose dynasty was Ming, there lived in the City of Genii, the city of Kwang-tchau-fu, a man celebrated for his learning and for his piety, named Tien-Pelou. This Tien-Pelou had one son, a beautiful boy, who for scholarship and for bodily grace and for polite accomplishments had no superior among the youths of his age. And his name was Ming-Y.

Now when the lad was in his eighteenth summer, it came to pass that Pelou, his father, was appointed Inspector of Public Instruction at the city of Tching-tou; and Ming-Y accompanied his parents thither. Near the city of Tching-tou lived a rich man of rank, a high commissioner of the government, whose name was Tchang, and who wanted to find a worthy teacher for his children. On hearing of the arrival of the new Inspector of Public Instruction, the noble Tchang visited him to obtain advice in this matter; and happening to meet and converse with Pelou's accomplished son, immediately engaged Ming-Y as a private tutor for his family.

Now as the house of this Lord Tchang was situated several miles from town, it was deemed best that Ming-Y should abide in the house of his employer. Accordingly the youth made ready all things necessary for his new sojourn; and his parents, bidding him farewell, counselled him wisely, and cited to him the words of Lao-tseu and of the ancient sages:

"By a beautiful face the world is filled with love; but Heaven may never be deceived thereby. Shouldst thou behold a woman coming from the East, look thou to the West; shouldst thou perceive a maiden approaching from the West, turn thine eyes to the East."

If Ming-Y did not heed this counsel in after days, it was only because of his youth and the thoughtlessness of a naturally joyous heart.

And he departed to abide in the house of Lord Tchang, while the autumn passed, and the winter also.

* * *

When the time of the second moon of spring was drawing near, and that happy day which the Chinese call Hoa-tchao, or, "The Birthday of a Hundred Flowers," a longing came upon Ming-Y to see his parents; and he opened his heart to the good Tchang, who not only gave him the permission he desired, but also pressed into his hand a silver gift of two ounces, thinking that the lad might wish to bring some little memento to his father and mother. For it is the Chinese custom, on the feast of Hoa-tchao, to make presents to friends and relations.

That day all the air was drowsy with blossom perfume, and vibrant with the droning of bees. It seemed to Ming-Y that the path he followed had not been trodden by any other for many long years; the grass was tall upon it; vast trees on either side interlocked their mighty and moss-grown arms above him, beshadowing the way; but the leafy obscurities quivered with bird-song, and the deep vistas of the wood were glorified by vapors of gold, and odorous with flower-breathings as a temple with incense. The dreamy joy of the day entered into the heart of Ming-Y; and he sat him down among the young blossoms, under the branches swaying against the violet sky, to drink in the perfume and the light, and to enjoy the great sweet silence. Even while thus reposing, a sound caused him to turn his eyes toward a shady place where wild peach-trees were in bloom; and he beheld a young woman, beautiful as the pinkening blossoms themselves, trying to hide among them. Though he looked for a moment only, Ming-Y could not avoid discerning the loveliness of her face, the golden purity of her complexion, and the brightness of her long eyes, that sparkled under a pair of brows as daintily curved as the wings of the silkworm butterfly outspread. Ming-Y at once turned his gaze away, and, rising quickly, proceeded on his journey. But so much embarrassed did he feel at the idea of those charming eyes peeping at him through the leaves, that he suffered the money he had been carrying in his sleeve to fall, without being aware of it. A few moments later he heard the patter of light feet running behind him, and a woman's voice calling him by name. Turning his face in great surprise, he saw a comely servant-maid, who said to him, "Sir, my mistress bade me pick up and return you this silver which you dropped upon the road." Ming-Y thanked the girl gracefully, and requested her to convey his compliments to her mistress. Then he proceeded on his way through the perfumed silence, athwart the shadows that dreamed along the forgotten path, dreaming himself also, and feeling his heart beating with strange quickness at the thought of the beautiful being that he had seen.

* * *

It was just such another day when Ming-Y, returning by the same path, paused once more at the spot where the gracious figure had momentarily appeared before him. But this time he was surprised to perceive, through a long vista of immense trees, a dwelling that had previously escaped his notice – a country residence, not large, yet elegant to an unusual degree. The bright blue tiles of its curved and serrated double roof, rising above the foliage, seemed to blend their color with the luminous azure of the day; the green-and-gold designs of its carven porticos were exquisite artistic mockeries of leaves and flowers bathed in sunshine. And at the summit of terrace-steps before it, guarded by great porcelain tortoises, Ming-Y saw standing the mistress of the mansion – the idol of his passionate fancy – accompanied by the same waiting-maid who had borne to her his message of gratitude. While Ming-Y looked, he perceived that their eyes were upon him; they smiled and conversed together as if speaking about him; and, shy though he was, the youth found courage to salute the fair one from a distance. To his astonishment, the young servant beckoned him to approach; and opening a rustic gate half veiled by trailing plants bearing crimson flowers, Ming-Y advanced along the verdant alley leading to the terrace, with mingled feelings of surprise and timid joy. As he drew near, the beautiful lady withdrew from sight; but the maid waited at the broad steps to receive him, and said as he ascended:

"Sir, my mistress understands you wish to thank her for the trifling service she recently bade me do you, and requests that you will enter the house, as she knows you already by repute, and desires to have the pleasure of bidding you good-day."

Ming-Y entered bashfully, his feet making no sound upon a matting elastically soft as forest moss, and found himself in a reception-chamber vast, cool, and fragrant with scent of blossoms freshly gathered. A delicious quiet pervaded the mansion; shadows of flying birds passed over the bands of light that fell through the half-blinds of bamboo; great butterflies, with pinions of fiery color, found their way in, to hover a moment about the painted vases, and pass out again into the mysterious woods. And noiselessly as they, the young mistress of the mansion entered by another door, and kindly greeted the boy, who lifted his hands to his breast and bowed low in salutation. She was taller than he had deemed her, and supply-slender as a beauteous lily; her black hair was interwoven with the creamy blossoms of the chu-sha-kih; her robes of pale silk took shifting tints when she moved, as vapors change hue with the changing of the light.

"If I be not mistaken," she said, when both had seated themselves after having exchanged the customary formalities of politeness, "my honored visitor is none other than Tien-chou, surnamed Ming-Y, educator of the children of my respected relative, the High Commissioner Tchang. As the family of Lord Tchang is my family also, I cannot but consider the teacher of his children as one of my own kin."

"Lady," replied Ming-Y, not a little astonished, "may I dare to inquire the name of your honored family, and to ask the relation which you hold to my noble patron?"

"The name of my poor family," responded the comely lady, "is Ping – an ancient family of the city of Tching-tou. I am the daughter of a certain Sie of Moun-hao; Sie is my name, likewise; and I was married to a young man of the Ping family, whose name was Khang. By this marriage I became related to your excellent patron; but my husband died soon after our wedding, and I have chosen this solitary place to reside in during the period of my widowhood."

There was a drowsy music in her voice, as of the melody of brooks, the murmurings of spring; and such a strange grace in the manner of her speech as Ming-Y had never heard before. Yet, on learning that she was a widow, the youth would not have presumed to remain long in her presence without a formal invitation; and after having sipped the cup of rich tea presented to him, he arose to depart. Sie would not suffer him to go so quickly.

"Nay, friend," she said; "stay yet a little while in my house, I pray you; for, should your honored patron ever learn that you had been here, and that I had not treated you as a respected guest, and regaled you even as I would him, I know that he would be greatly angered. Remain at least to supper."

So Ming-Y remained, rejoicing secretly in his heart, for Sie seemed to him the fairest and sweetest being he had ever known, and he felt that he loved her even more than his father and his mother. And while they talked the long shadows of the evening slowly blended into one violet darkness; the great citron-light of the sunset faded out; and those starry beings that are called the Three Councillors, who preside over life and death and the destinies of men, opened their cold bright eyes in the northern sky. Within the mansion of Sie the painted lanterns were lighted; the table was laid for the evening repast; and Ming-Y took his place at it, feeling little inclination to eat, and thinking only of the charming face before him. Observing that he scarcely tasted the dainties laid upon his plate, Sie pressed her young guest to partake of wine; and they drank several cups together. It was a purple wine, so cool that the cup into which it was poured became covered with vapory dew; yet it seemed to warm the veins with strange fire. To Ming-Y, as he drank, all things became more luminous as by enchantment; the walls of the chamber appeared to recede, and the roof to heighten;

the lamps glowed like stars in their chains, and the voice of Sie floated to the boy's ears like some far melody heard through the spaces of a drowsy night. His heart swelled; his tongue loosened; and words flitted from his lips that he had fancied he could never dare to utter. Yet Sie sought not to restrain him; her lips gave no smile; but her long bright eyes seemed to laugh with pleasure at his words of praise, and to return his gaze of passionate admiration with affectionate interest.

"I have heard," she said, "of your rare talent, and of your many elegant accomplishments. I know how to sing a little, although I cannot claim to possess any musical learning; and now that I have the honor of finding myself in the society of a musical professor, I will venture to lay modesty aside, and beg you to sing a few songs with me. I should deem it no small gratification if you would condescend to examine my musical compositions."

"The honor and the gratification, dear lady," replied Ming-Y, "will be mine; and I feel helpless to express the gratitude which the offer of so rare a favor deserves."

The serving-maid, obedient to the summons of a little silver gong, brought in the music and retired. Ming-Y took the manuscripts, and began to examine them with eager delight. The paper upon which they were written had a pale yellow tint, and was light as a fabric of gossamer; but the characters were antiquely beautiful, as though they had been traced by the brush of Hei-song Che-Tchoo himself – that divine Genius of Ink, who is no bigger than a fly; and the signatures attached to the compositions were the signatures of Youen-tchin, Kao-pien, and Thou-mou – mighty poets and musicians of the dynasty of Thang! Ming-Y could not repress a scream of delight at the sight of treasures so inestimable and so unique; scarcely could he summon resolution enough to permit them to leave his hands even for a moment. "O Lady!" he cried, "these are veritably priceless things, surpassing in worth the treasures of all kings. This indeed is the handwriting of those great masters who sang five hundred years before our birth. How marvellously it has been preserved! Is not this the wondrous ink of which it was written: Po-nien-jou-chi, i-tien-jou-ki: 'After centuries I remain firm as stone, and the letters that I make like lacquer'? And how divine the charm of this composition! The song of Kao-pien, prince of poets, and Governor of Sze-tchouen five hundred years ago!"

"Kao-pien! darling Kao-pien!" murmured Sie, with a singular light in her eyes. "Kao-pien is also my favorite. Dear Ming-Y, let us chant his verses together, to the melody of old, the music of those grand years when men were nobler and wiser than to-day."

And their voices rose through the perfumed night like the voices of the wonder-birds – of the Fung-hoang – blending together in liquid sweetness. Yet a moment, and Ming-Y, overcome by the witchery of his companion's voice, could only listen in speechless ecstasy, while the lights of the chamber swam dim before his sight, and tears of pleasure trickled down his cheeks.

So the ninth hour passed; and they continued to converse, and to drink the cool purple wine, and to sing the songs of the years of Thang, until far into the night. More than once Ming-Y thought of departing; but each time Sie would begin, in that silver-sweet voice of hers, so wondrous a story of the great poets of the past, and of the women whom they loved, that he became as one entranced; or she would sing for him a song so strange that all his senses seemed to die except that of hearing. And at last, as she paused to pledge him in a cup of wine, Ming-Y could not restrain himself from putting his arm about her round neck and drawing her dainty head closer to him, and kissing the lips that were so much ruddier and sweeter than the wine. Then their lips separated no more; – the night grew old, and they knew it not.

* * *

The birds awakened, the flowers opened their eyes to the rising sun, and Ming-Y found himself at last compelled to bid his lovely enchantress farewell. Sie, accompanying him to the terrace, kissed him fondly and said, "Dear boy, come hither as often as you are able – as often as your heart whispers you to come. I know that you are not of those without faith and truth, who betray secrets; yet, being so young, you might also be sometimes thoughtless; and I pray you never to forget that only the stars have been the witnesses of our love. Speak of it to no living person, dearest; and take with you this little souvenir of our happy night."

And she presented him with an exquisite and curious little thing – a paper-weight in likeness of a couchant lion, wrought from a jade-stone yellow as that created by a rainbow in honor of Kong-fu-tze. Tenderly the boy kissed the gift and the beautiful hand that gave it. "May the Spirits punish me," he vowed, "if ever I knowingly give you cause to reproach me, sweetheart!" And they separated with mutual vows.

That morning, on returning to the house of Lord Tchang, Ming-Y told the first falsehood which had ever passed his lips. He averred that his mother had requested him thenceforward to pass his nights at home, now that the weather had become so pleasant; for, though the way was somewhat long, he was strong and active, and needed both air and healthy exercise. Tchang believed all Ming-Y said, and offered no objection. Accordingly the lad found himself enabled to pass all his evenings at the house of the beautiful Sie. Each night they devoted to the same pleasures which had made their first acquaintance so charming: they sang and conversed by turns; they played at chess – the learned game invented by Wu-Wang, which is an imitation of war; they composed pieces of eighty rhymes upon the flowers, the trees, the clouds, the streams, the birds, the bees. But in all accomplishments Sie far excelled her young sweetheart. Whenever they played at chess, it was always Ming-Y's general, Ming-Y's tsiang, who was surrounded and vanquished; when they composed verses, Sie's poems were ever superior to his in harmony of word-coloring, in elegance of form, in classic loftiness of thought. And the themes they selected were always the most difficult – those of the poets of the Thang dynasty; the songs they sang were also the songs of five hundred years before – the songs of Youen-tchin, of Thou-mou, of Kao-pien above all, high poet and ruler of the province of Sze-tchouen.

So the summer waxed and waned upon their love, and the luminous autumn came, with its vapors of phantom gold, its shadows of magical purple.

* * *

Then it unexpectedly happened that the father of Ming-Y, meeting his son's employer at Tching-tou, was asked by him: "Why must your boy continue to travel every evening to the city, now that the winter is approaching? The way is long, and when he returns in the morning he looks fordone with weariness. Why not permit him to slumber in my house during the season of snow?" And the father of Ming-Y, greatly astonished, responded: "Sir, my son has not visited the city, nor has he been to our house all this summer. I fear that he must have acquired wicked habits, and that he passes his nights in evil company – perhaps in gaming, or in drinking with the women of the flower-boats." But the High Commissioner returned: "Nay! that is not to be thought of. I have never found any evil in the boy, and there are no taverns nor flower-boats nor any places of dissipation in our neighborhood. No doubt Ming-Y has found some amiable youth of his own age with whom to spend his evenings, and only told me an untruth for fear that I would not otherwise permit him to leave my residence. I beg that you will say nothing to him until I shall have sought to discover this mystery; and this very evening I shall send my servant to follow after him, and to watch whither he goes."

Pelou readily assented to this proposal, and promising to visit Tchang the following morning, returned to his home. In the evening, when Ming-Y left the house of Tchang, a servant followed him unobserved at a distance. But on reaching the most obscure portion of the road, the boy disappeared from sight as suddenly as though the earth had swallowed him. After having long sought after him in vain, the domestic returned in great bewilderment to the house, and related what had taken place. Tchang immediately sent a messenger to Pelou.

In the mean time Ming-Y, entering the chamber of his beloved, was surprised and deeply pained to find her in tears. "Sweetheart," she sobbed, wreathing her arms around his neck, "we are about to be separated forever, because of reasons which I cannot tell you. From the very first I knew this must come to pass; and nevertheless it seemed to me for the moment so cruelly sudden a loss, so unexpected a misfortune, that I could not prevent myself from weeping! After this night we shall never see each other again, beloved, and I know that you will not be able to forget me while you live; but I know also that you will become a great scholar, and that honors and riches will be showered upon you, and that some beautiful and loving woman will console you for my loss. And now let us speak no more of grief; but let us pass this last evening joyously, so that your recollection of me may not be a painful one, and that you may remember my laughter rather than my tears."

She brushed the bright drops away, and brought wine and music and the melodious kin of seven silken strings, and would not suffer Ming-Y to speak for one moment of the coming separation. And she sang him an ancient song about the calmness of summer lakes reflecting the blue of heaven only, and the calmness of the heart also, before the clouds of care and of grief and of weariness darken its little world. Soon they forgot their sorrow in the joy of song and wine; and those last hours seemed to Ming-Y more celestial than even the hours of their first bliss.

But when the yellow beauty of morning came their sadness returned, and they wept. Once more Sie accompanied her lover to the terrace-steps; and as she kissed him farewell, she pressed into his hand a parting gift – a little brush-case of agate, wonderfully chiselled, and worthy the table of a great poet. And they separated forever, shedding many tears.

* * *

Still Ming-Y could not believe it was an eternal parting. "No!" he thought, "I shall visit her tomorrow; for I cannot now live without her, and I feel assured that she cannot refuse to receive me." Such were the thoughts that filled his mind as he reached the house of Tchang, to find his father and his patron standing on the porch awaiting him. Ere he could speak a word, Pelou demanded: "Son, in what place have you been passing your nights?"

Seeing that his falsehood had been discovered, Ming-Y dared not make any reply, and remained abashed and silent, with bowed head, in the presence of his father. Then Pelou, striking the boy violently with his staff, commanded him to divulge the secret; and at last, partly through fear of his parent, and partly through fear of the law which ordains that "the son refusing to obey his father shall be punished with one hundred blows of the bamboo," Ming-Y faltered out the history of his love.

Tchang changed color at the boy's tale. "Child," exclaimed the High Commissioner, "I have no relative of the name of Ping; I have never heard of the woman you describe; I have never heard even of the house which you speak of. But I know also that you cannot dare to lie to Pelou, your honored father; there is some strange delusion in all this affair."

Then Ming-Y produced the gifts that Sie had given him – the lion of yellow jade, the brush-case of carven agate, also some original compositions made by the beautiful lady herself. The astonishment of Tchang was now shared by Pelou. Both observed that the brush-case of agate and the lion of jade bore the appearance of objects that had lain buried in the earth for centuries, and were of a workmanship beyond the power of living man to imitate; while the compositions proved to be veritable master-pieces of poetry, written in the style of the poets of the dynasty of Thang.

"Friend Pelou," cried the High Commissioner, "let us immediately accompany the boy to the place where he obtained these miraculous things, and apply the testimony of our senses to this mystery. The boy is no doubt telling the truth; yet his story passes my understanding." And all three proceeded toward the place of the habitation of Sie.

* * *

But when they had arrived at the shadiest part of the road, where the perfumes were most sweet and the mosses were greenest, and the fruits of the wild peach flushed most pinkly, Ming-Y, gazing through the groves, uttered a cry of dismay. Where the azure-tiled roof had risen against the sky, there was now only the blue emptiness of air; where the green-and-gold facade had been, there was visible only the flickering of leaves under the aureate autumn light; and where the broad terrace had extended, could be discerned only a ruin – a tomb so ancient, so deeply gnawed by moss, that the name graven upon it was no longer decipherable. The home of Sie had disappeared!

All suddenly the High Commissioner smote his forehead with his hand, and turning to Pelou, recited the well-known verse of the ancient poet Tching-Kou:

"Surely the peach-flowers blossom over the tomb of SIE-THAO."

"Friend Pelou," continued Tchang, "the beauty who bewitched your son was no other than she whose tomb stands there in ruin before us! Did she not say she was wedded to Ping-Khang? There is no family of that name, but Ping-Khang is indeed the name of a broad alley in the city near. There was a dark riddle in all that she said. She called herself Sie of Moun-Hiao: there is no person of that name; there is no street of that name; but the Chinese characters Moun and hiao, placed together, form the character 'Kiao'. Listen! The alley Ping-Khang, situated in the street Kiao, was the place where dwelt the great courtesans of the dynasty of Thang! Did she not sing the songs of Kao-pien? And upon the brush-case and the paper-weight she gave your son, are there not characters which read, 'Pure object of art belonging to Kao, of the city of Pho-hai'? That city no longer exists; but the memory of Kao-pien remains, for he was governor of the province of Sze-tchouen, and a mighty poet. And when he dwelt in the land of Chou, was not his favorite the beautiful wanton Sie – Sie-Thao, unmatched for grace among all the women of her day? It was he who made her a gift of those manuscripts of song; it was he who gave her those objects of rare art. Sie-Thao died not as other women die. Her limbs may have crumbled to dust; yet something of her still lives in this deep wood – her Shadow still haunts this shadowy place."

Tchang ceased to speak. A vague fear fell upon the three. The thin mists of the morning made dim the distances of green, and deepened the ghostly beauty of the woods. A faint breeze passed by, leaving a trail of blossom-scent – a last odor of dying flowers – thin as that which clings to the silk of a forgotten robe; and, as it passed, the trees seemed to whisper across the silence, "Sie-Thao."

* * *

Fearing greatly for his son, Pelou sent the lad away at once to the city of Kwang-tchau-fu. And there, in after years, Ming-Y obtained high dignities and honors by reason of his talents and his learning; and he married the daughter of an illustrious house, by whom he became the father of sons and daughters famous for their virtues and their accomplishments. Never could he forget Sie-Thao; and yet it is said that he never spoke of her – not even when his children begged him to tell them the story of two beautiful objects that always lay upon his writing-table: a lion of yellow jade, and a brush-case of carven agate.

The Story of the Bird Feng

IN THE BOOK of the Ten Thousand Wonders there are three hundred and thirty-three stories about the bird called Feng, and this is one of them.

Ta-Khai, Prince of Tartary, dreamt one night that he saw in a place where he had never been before an enchantingly beautiful young maiden who could only be a princess. He fell desperately in love with her, but before he could either move or speak, she had vanished. When he awoke he called for his ink and brushes, and, in the most accomplished willow-leaf style, he drew her image on a piece of precious silk, and in one corner he wrote these lines:

> *The flowers of the pæony*
> *Will they ever bloom?*
> *A day without her*
> *Is like a hundred years.*

He then summoned his ministers, and, showing them the portrait, asked if any one could tell him the name of the beautiful maiden; but they all shook their heads and stroked their beards They knew not who she was.

So displeased was the prince that he sent them away in disgrace to the most remote provinces of his kingdom. All the courtiers, the generals, the officers, and every man and woman, high and low, who lived in the palace came in turn to look at the picture. But they all had to confess their ignorance. Ta-Khai then called upon the magicians of the kingdom to find out by their art the name of the princess of his dreams, but their answers were so widely different that the prince, suspecting their ability, condemned them all to have their noses cut off. The portrait was shown in the outer court of the palace from sunrise till sunset, and exalted travellers came in every day, gazed upon the beautiful face, and came out again. None could tell who she was.

Meanwhile the days were weighing heavily upon the shoulders of Ta-Khai, and his sufferings cannot be described; he ate no more, he drank no more, and ended by forgetting which was day and which was night, what was in and what was out, what was left and what was right. He spent his time roaming over the mountains and through the woods crying aloud to the gods to end his life and his sorrow.

It was thus, one day, that he came to the edge of a precipice. The valley below was strewn with rocks, and the thought came to his mind that he had been led to this place to put a term to his misery. He was about to throw himself into the depths below when suddenly the bird Feng flew across the valley and appeared before him, saying:

"Why is Ta-Khai, the mighty Prince of Tartary, standing in this place of desolation with a shadow on his brow?"

Ta-Khai replied: "The pine tree finds its nourishment where it stands, the tiger can run after the deer in the forests, the eagle can fly over the mountains and the plains, but how can I find the one for whom my heart is thirsting?"

And he told the bird his story.

The Feng, which in reality was a Feng-Hwang, that is, a female Feng, rejoined:

"Without the help of Supreme Heaven it is not easy to acquire wisdom, but it is a sign of the benevolence of the spiritual beings that I should have come between you and destruction. I can make myself large enough to carry the largest town upon my back, or small enough to pass through the smallest keyhole, and I know all the princesses in all the palaces of the earth. I have taught them the six intonations of my voice, and I am their friend. Therefore show me the picture, O Ta-Khai, and I will tell you the name of her whom you saw in your dream."

They went to the palace, and, when the portrait was shown, the bird became as large as an elephant, and exclaimed, "Sit on my back, O Ta-Khai, and I will carry you to the place of your dream. There you will find her of the transparent face with the drooping eyelids under the crown of dark hair such as you have depicted, for these are the features of Sai-Jen, the daughter of the King of China, and alone can be likened to the full moon rising under a black cloud."

At nightfall they were flying over the palace of the king just above a magnificent garden. And in the garden sat Sai-Jen, singing and playing upon the lute. The Feng-Hwang deposited the prince outside the wall near a place where bamboos were growing and showed him how to cut twelve bamboos between the knots to make the flute which is called Pai-Siao and has a sound sweeter than the evening breeze on the forest stream.

And as he blew gently across the pipes, they echoed the sound of the princess's voice so harmoniously that she cried:

"I hear the distant notes of the song that comes from my own lips, and I can see nothing but the flowers and the trees; it is the melody the heart alone can sing that has suffered sorrow on sorrow, and to which alone the heart can listen that is full of longing."

At that moment the wonderful bird, like a fire of many colours come down from heaven, alighted before the princess, dropping at her feet the portrait. She opened her eyes in utter astonishment at the sight of her own image. And when she had read the lines inscribed in the corner, she asked, trembling:

"Tell me, O Feng-Hwang, who is he, so near, but whom I cannot see, that knows the sound of my voice and has never heard me, and can remember my face and has never seen me?"

Then the bird spoke and told her the story of Ta-Khai's dream, adding:

"I come from him with this message; I brought him here on my wings. For many days he has longed for this hour, let him now behold the image of his dream and heal the wound in his heart."

Swift and overpowering is the rush of the waves on the pebbles of the shore, and like a little pebble felt Sai-Jen when Ta-Khai stood before her...

The Feng-Hwang illuminated the garden sumptuously, and a breath of love was stirring the flowers under the stars.

It was in the palace of the King of China that were celebrated in the most ancient and magnificent style the nuptials of Sai-Jen and Ta-Khai, Prince of Tartary.

And this is one of the three hundred and thirty-three stories about the bird Feng as it is told in the Book of the Ten Thousand Wonders.

The Talking Silver Foxes

THE SILVER FOXES resemble other foxes, but are yellow, fire-red or white in color. They know how to influence human beings, too. There is a kind of silver fox which can learn to speak like a man in a year's time. These foxes are called "Talking Foxes".

South-west of the bay of Kaiutschou there is a mountain by the edge of the sea, shaped like a tower, and hence known as Tower Mountain. On the mountain there is an old temple with the image of a goddess, who is known as the Old Mother of Tower Mountain. When children fall ill in the surrounding villages, the magicians often give orders that paper figures of them be burned at her altar, or little lime images of them be placed around it. And for this reason the altar and its surroundings are covered with hundreds of figures of children made in lime. Paper flowers, shoes and clothing are also brought to the Old Mother, and lie in a confusion of colors. The pilgrimage festivals take place on the third day of the third month, and the ninth day of the ninth month, and then there are theatrical performances, and the holy writings are read. And there is also an annual fair. The girls and women of the neighborhood burn incense and pray to the goddess. Parents who have no children go there and pick out one of the little children made of lime, and tie a red thread around its neck, or even secretly break off a small bit of its body, dissolve it in water and drink it. Then they pray quietly that a child may be sent them.

Behind the temple is a great cave where, in former times, some talking foxes used to live. They would even come out and seat themselves on the point of a steep rock by the wayside. When a wanderer came by they would begin to talk to him in this fashion: "Wait a bit, neighbor; first smoke a pipe!" The traveler would look around in astonishment, to see where the voice came from, and would become very much frightened. If he did not happen to be exceptionally brave, he would begin to perspire with terror, and run away. Then the fox would laugh: "Hi hi!"

Once a farmer was plowing on the side of the mountain. When he looked up he saw a man with a straw hat, wearing a mantle of woven grass and carrying a pick across his shoulder coming along the way.

"Neighbor Wang," said he, "first smoke a pipeful and take a little rest! Then I will help you plow."

Then he called out "Hu!" the way farmers do when they talk to their cattle.

The farmer looked at him more closely and saw then that he was a talking fox. He waited for a favorable opportunity, and when it came gave him a lusty blow with his ox-whip. He struck home, for the fox screamed, leaped into the air and ran away. His straw hat, his mantle of woven grass and the rest he left lying on the ground. Then the farmer saw that the straw hat was just woven out of potato-leaves; he had cut it in two with his whip. The mantle was made of oak-leaves, tied together with little blades of grass. And the pick was only the stem of a kau-ling plant, to which a bit of brick had been fastened.

Not long after, a woman in a neighboring village became possessed. A picture of the head priest of the Taoists was hung up in her room, but the evil spirit did not depart. Since there were none who could exorcise devils in the neighborhood, and the trouble she gave was unendurable, the woman's relatives decided to send to the temple of the God of War and beg for aid.

But when the fox heard of it he said: "I am not afraid of your Taoist high-priest nor of your God of War; the only person I fear is your neighbor Wang in the Eastern village, who once struck me cruelly with his whip."

This suited the people to a T. They sent to the Eastern village, and found out who Wang was. And Wang took his ox-whip and entered the house of the possessed woman.

Then he said in a deep voice: "Where are you? Where are you? I have been on your trail for a long time. And now, at last, I have caught you!"

With that he snapped his whip.

The fox hissed and spat and flew out of the window.

They had been telling stories about the talking fox of Tower Mountain for more than a hundred years when one fine day, a skilful archer came to that part of the country who saw a creature like a fox, with a fiery-red pelt, whose back was striped with gray. It was lying under a tree. The archer aimed and shot off its hind foot.

At once it said in a human voice: "I brought myself into this danger because of my love for sleep; but none may escape their fate! If you capture me you will get at the most no more than five thousand pieces of copper for my pelt. Why not let me go instead? I will reward you richly, so that all your poverty will come to an end."

But the archer would not listen to him. He killed him, skinned him and sold his pelt; and, sure enough, he received five thousand pieces of copper for it.

From that time on the fox-spirit ceased to show itself.

Tales of Magic & Transformation

WANG CHIH'S DAUGHTER warns, 'Remember, it is the Feast of Lanterns tonight... Don't fall asleep upon the mountain.' That he wanders off, finds a secret cave, meets two mysterious sages, journeys several centuries into the future, flies to the moon and *still* gets home in time to see the lanterns lit typifies the extravagance of so much Chinese mythology.

Life for millions, for millennia, may have been an endless round of unremitting toil but the imagination of the people was always free. Magic broke the bounds of reality, making the impossible easy, the outrageous the norm. (It of course underpinned the achievements of many of the heroes and the spirits in other sections of this book.) Fun as it is to find in folktale, enchantment is essential to literature, to poetry – what else is a metaphor than the transformation of one thing into another? It is really no surprise that the great Argentinean writer Jorge Luis Borges (1899–1986) should have loved the Chinese story of 'The Tiger Guest' so much.

The Feast of the Lanterns

WANG CHIH was only a poor man, but he had a wife and children to love, and they made him so happy that he would not have changed places with the Emperor himself.

He worked in the fields all day, and at night his wife always had a bowl of rice ready for his supper. And sometimes, for a treat, she made him some bean soup, or gave him a little dish of fried pork.

But they could not afford pork very often; he generally had to be content with rice.

One morning, as he was setting off to his work, his wife sent Han Chung, his son, running after him to ask him to bring home some firewood.

"I shall have to go up into the mountain for it at noon," he said. "Go and bring me my axe, Han Chung."

Han Chung ran for his father's axe, and Ho-Seen-Ko, his little sister, came out of the cottage with him.

"Remember, it is the Feast of Lanterns to-night, father," she said. "Don't fall asleep upon the mountain; we want you to come back and light them for us."

She had a lantern in the shape of a fish, painted red and black and yellow, and Han Chung had got a big round one, all bright crimson, to carry in the procession; and, besides that, there were two large lanterns to be hung outside the cottage door as soon as it grew dark.

Wang Chih was not likely to forget the Feast of Lanterns, for the children had talked of nothing else for a month, and he promised to come home as early as he could.

At noontide, when his fellow-laborers gave up working, and sat down to rest and eat, Wang Chih took his axe and went up the mountain slope to find a small tree he might cut down for fuel.

He walked a long way, and at last saw one growing at the mouth of a cave.

"This will be just the thing," he said to himself. But, before striking the first blow, he peeped into the cave to see if it were empty.

To his surprise, two old men, with long, white beards, were sitting inside playing chess, as quietly as mice, with their eyes fixed on the chessboard.

Wang Chih knew something of chess, and he stepped in and watched them for a few minutes.

"As soon as they look up I can ask them if I may chop down a tree," he said to himself. But they did not look up, and by and by Wang Chih got so interested in the game that he put down his axe, and sat on the floor to watch it better.

The two old men sat cross-legged on the ground, and the chessboard rested on a slab, like a stone table, between them.

On one corner of the slab lay a heap of small brown objects which Wang Chih took at first to be date stones; but after a time the chess-players ate one each, and put one in Wang Chih's mouth, and he found it was not a date stone at all.

It was a delicious kind of sweetmeat, the like of which he had never tasted before; and the strangest thing about it was that it took his hunger and thirst away.

He had been both hungry and thirsty when he came into the cave, as he had not waited to have his mid-day meal with the other field-workers; but now he felt quite comforted and refreshed.

He sat there some time longer, and noticed that as the old men frowned over the chessboard, their beards grew longer and longer, until they swept the floor of the cave, and even found their way out of the door.

"I hope my beard will never grow as quickly," said Wang Chih, as he rose and took up his axe again.

Then one of the old men spoke, for the first time. "Our beards have not grown quickly, young man. How long is it since you came here?"

"About half an hour, I dare say," replied Wang Chih. But as he spoke, the axe crumbled to dust beneath his fingers, and the second chess-player laughed, and pointed to the little brown sweetmeats on the table.

"Half an hour, or half a century – aye, half a thousand years are all alike to him who tastes of these. Go down into your village and see what has happened since you left it."

So Wang Chih went down as quickly as he could from the mountain, and found the fields where he had worked covered with houses, and a busy town where his own little village had been. In vain he looked for his house, his wife, and his children.

There were strange faces everywhere; and although when evening came the Feast of Lanterns was being held once more, there was no Ho-Seen-Ko carrying her red and yellow fish, or Han Chung with his flaming red ball.

At last he found a woman, a very, very old woman, who told him that when she was a tiny girl she remembered her grand-mother saying how, when she was a tiny girl, a poor young man had been spirited away by the Genii of the mountains on the day of the Feast of Lanterns, leaving his wife and little children with only a few handfuls of rice in the house.

"Moreover, if you wait while the procession passes, you will see two children dressed to represent Han Chung and Ho-Seen-Ko, and their mother carrying the empty rice-bowl between them; for this is done every year to remind people to take care of the widow and fatherless," she said. So Wang Chih waited in the street; and in a little while the procession came to an end, and the last three figures in it were a boy and girl, dressed like his own two children, walking on either side of a young woman carrying a rice-bowl. But she was not like his wife in anything but her dress, and the children were not at all like Han Chung and Ho-Seen-Ko; and poor Wang Chih's heart was very heavy as he walked out of the town.

He slept out on the mountain, and early in the morning found his way back to the cave where the two old men were playing chess.

At first they said they could do nothing for him and told him to go away and not disturb them; but Wang Chih would not go, and they found the only way to get rid of him was to give him some really good advice.

"You must go to the White Hare of the Moon, and ask him for a bottle of the elixir of life. If you drink that you will live forever," said one of them.

"But I don't want to live forever," objected Wang Chih. "I wish to go back and live in the days when my wife and children were here."

"Ah, well! For that you must mix the elixir of life with some water out of the sky-dragon's mouth."

"And where is the sky-dragon to be found?" inquired Wang Chih.

"In the sky, of course. You really ask very stupid questions. He lives in a cloud-cave. And when he comes out of it he breathes fire, and sometimes water. If he is breathing fire you will be burned up, but if it is only water, you will easily be able to catch some in a little bottle. What else do you want?"

For Wang Chih still lingered at the mouth of the cave.

"I want a pair of wings to fly with, and a bottle to catch the water in," he replied boldly.

So they gave him a little bottle and before he had time to say "Thank you!" a white crane came sailing past and lighted on the ground close to the cave.

"The crane will take you wherever you like," said the old men. "Go now, and leave us in peace."

So Wang Chih sat on the white crane's back, and was taken up and up through the sky to the cloud-cave where the sky-dragon lived. And the dragon had the head of a camel, the horns of a deer, the eyes of a rabbit, the ears of a cow, and the claws of a hawk.

Besides this, he had whiskers and a beard, and in his beard was a bright pearl.

All these things show that he was a real, genuine dragon, and if you ever meet a dragon who is not exactly like this, you will know he is only a make-believe one.

Wang Chih felt rather frightened when he perceived the cave in the distance, and if it had not been for the thought of seeing his wife again, and his little boy and girl, he would have been glad to turn back.

While he was far away the cloud-cave looked like a dark hole in the midst of a soft woolly mass, such as one sees in the sky on an April day; but as he came nearer he found the cloud was as hard as a rock, and covered with a kind of dry, white grass.

When he got there, he sat down on a tuft of grass near the cave, and considered what he should do next.

The first thing was, of course, to bring the dragon out, and the next to make him breathe water instead of fire.

"I have it!" cried Wang Chih at last; and he nodded his head so many times that the little white crane expected to see it fall off.

He struck a light, and set the grass on fire, and it was so dry that the flames spread all around the entrance to the cave, and made such a smoke and crackling that the sky-dragon put his head out to see what was the matter.

"Ho! Ho!" cried the dragon, when he saw what Wang Chih had done, "I can soon put this to rights." And he breathed once, and the water came out of his nose and mouth in three streams.

But this was not enough to put the fire out. Then he breathed twice, and the water came out in three mighty rivers, and Wang Chih, who had taken care to fill his bottle when the first stream began to flow, sailed away on the white crane's back as fast as he could go, to escape being drowned.

The rivers poured over the cloud rock, until there was not a spark left alight, and rushed down through the sky into the sea below.

Fortunately, the sea lay right underneath the dragon's cave, or he would have done some nice mischief. As it was, the people on the coast looked out across the water toward Japan, and saw three inky-black clouds stretching from the sky into the sea.

"My word! There is a fine rain-storm out at sea!" they said to each other.

But, of course, it was nothing of the kind; it was only the sky-dragon putting out the fire Wang Chih had kindled.

Meanwhile, Wang Chih was on his way to the moon, and when he got there he went straight to the hut where the Hare of the Moon lived, and knocked at the door.

The Hare was busy pounding the drugs which make up the elixir of life; but he left his work, opened the door, and invited Wang Chih to come in.

He was not ugly, like the dragon; his fur was quite white and soft and glossy, and he had lovely, gentle brown eyes.

The Hare of the Moon lives a thousand years, as you know, and when he is five hundred years old he changes his color from brown to white, and becomes, if possible, better tempered and nicer than he was before.

As soon as he heard what Wang Chih wanted, he opened two windows at the back of the hut, and told him to look through each of them in turn.

"Tell me what you see," said the Hare, going back to the table where he was pounding the drugs.

"I can see a great many houses and people," said Wang Chih, "and streets – why, this is the town I was in yesterday, the one which has taken the place of my old village."

Wang Chih stared, and grew more and more puzzled. Here he was up in the moon, and yet he could have thrown a stone into the busy street of the Chinese town below his window.

"How does it come here," he stammered, at last.

"Oh, that is my secret," replied the wise old Hare. "I know how to do a great many things which would surprise you. But the question is, do you want to go back there?"

Wang Chih shook his head.

"Then close the window. It is the window of the Present. And look through the other, which is the window of the Past."

Wang Chih obeyed, and through this window he saw his own dear little village, and his wife, and Han Chung and Ho-Seen-Ko jumping about her as she hung up the colored lanterns outside the door.

"Father won't be in time to light them for us, after all," Han Chung was saying.

Wang Chih turned, and looked eagerly at the White Hare.

"Let me go to them," he said. "I have got a bottle of water from the sky-dragon's mouth, and—"

"That's all right," said the White Hare. "Give it to me."

He opened the bottle, and mixed the contents carefully with a few drops of the elixir of life, which was clear as crystal, and of which each drop shone like a diamond as he poured it in.

"Now, drink this," he said to Wang Chih, "and it will give you the power of living once more in the past, as you desire."

Wang Chih held out his hand, and drank every drop.

The moment he had done so the window grew larger, and he saw some steps leading from it down into the village street.

Thanking the Hare, he rushed through it, and ran toward his own house, arriving in time to take from his wife's hand the taper with which she was about to light the red and yellow lanterns which swung over the door.

"What has kept you so long, father? Where have you been?" asked Han Chung, while little Ho-Seen-Ko wondered why he kissed and embraced them all so eagerly.

But Wang Chih did not tell them his adventures just then; only when darkness fell, and the Feast of Lanterns began, he took his part in it with a merry heart.

The Fighting Cricket

DURING THE REIGN of Hsüan Tê, cricket fighting was very much in vogue at court, levies of crickets being exacted from the people as a tax. On one occasion the magistrate of Hua-yin, wishing to make friends with the Governor, presented him with a cricket which, on being set to fight, displayed very remarkable powers; so much so that the Governor commanded the magistrate to supply him regularly with these insects. The latter, in his turn, ordered the beadles of his district to provide him with crickets; and then it became a practice for people who had nothing else to do to catch and rear them for this purpose. Thus the price of crickets rose very high; and when the beadle's runners came to exact even a single one, it was enough to ruin several families.

Now in the village of which we are speaking there lived a man named Ch'êng, a student who had often failed for his bachelor's degree; and, being a stupid sort of fellow, his name was sent in for the post of beadle. He did all he could to get out of it, but without success; and by the end of the year his small patrimony was gone. Just then came a call for crickets, and Ch'êng, not daring to make a like call upon his neighbours, was at his wits' end, and in his distress determined to commit suicide. "What's the use of that?" cried his wife. "You'd do better to go out and try to find some." So off went Ch'êng in the early morning, with a bamboo tube and a silk net, not returning till late at night; and he searched about in tumble-down walls, in bushes, under stones, and in holes, but without catching more than two or three, do what he would. Even those he did catch were weak creatures, and of no use at all, which made the magistrate fix a limit of time, the result of which was that in a few days Ch'êng got one hundred blows with the bamboo. This made him so sore that he was quite unable to go after the crickets any more, and, as he lay tossing and turning on the bed, he determined once again to put an end to his life.

About that time a hump-backed fortune-teller of great skill arrived at the village, and Ch'êng's wife, putting together a trifle of money, went off to seek his assistance. The door was literally blocked up – fair young girls and white-headed dames crowding in from all quarters. A room was darkened, and a bamboo screen hung at the door, an altar being arranged outside at which the fortune-seekers burnt incense in a brazier, and prostrated themselves twice, while the soothsayer stood by the side, and, looking up into vacancy, prayed for a response. His lips opened and shut, but nobody heard what he said, all standing there in awe waiting for the answer. In a few moments a piece of paper was thrown from behind the screen, and the soothsayer said that the petitioner's desire would be accomplished in the way he wished. Ch'êng's wife now advanced, and, placing some money on the altar, burnt her incense and prostrated herself in a similar manner. In a few moments the screen began to move, and a piece of paper was thrown down, on which there were no words, but only a picture. In the middle was a building like a temple, and behind this a small hill, at the foot of which were a number of curious stones, with the long, spiky feelers of innumerable crickets appearing from behind. Hard by was a frog, which seemed to be engaged in putting itself into various kinds of attitudes. The good woman had no idea what it all meant; but she noticed the crickets, and accordingly went off home to tell her husband. "Ah," said he, "this is to shew me where to hunt for crickets;" and, on looking closely at the picture, he saw that the building very much resembled a temple to the east of their village. So he forced himself to get up, and, leaning on a stick, went out to seek crickets behind the temple. Rounding an old grave, he came upon a place where stones were lying scattered about as in the picture, and then he set himself to watch attentively. He might as well have been looking for a needle or a grain of mustard-seed; and by degrees he became quite exhausted, without finding anything, when suddenly an old frog jumped out. Ch'êng was a little startled, but immediately pursued the frog, which retreated into the bushes. He then saw one of the insects he wanted sitting at the root of a bramble; but on making a grab at it, the cricket ran into a hole, from which he was unable to move it until he poured in some water, when out the little creature came. It was a magnificent specimen, strong and handsome, with a fine tail, green neck, and golden wings; and, putting it in his basket, he returned home in high glee to receive the congratulations of his family. He would not have taken anything for this cricket, and proceeded to feed it up carefully in a bowl. Its belly was the colour of a crab's, its back that of a sweet chestnut; and Ch'êng tended it most lovingly, waiting for the time when the magistrate should call upon him for a cricket.

Meanwhile, a son of Ch'êng's, aged nine, one day took the opportunity of his father being out to open the bowl. Instantaneously the cricket made a spring forward and was gone; and all efforts to catch it again were unavailing. At length the boy made a grab at it with his hand, but only succeeded in seizing one of its legs, which thereupon broke, and the little creature soon afterwards died. Ch'êng's wife turned deadly pale when her son, with tears in his eyes, told her what had happened. "Oh! won't you catch it when your father comes home," said she; at which the boy ran away, crying bitterly. Soon after Ch'êng arrived, and when he heard his wife's story he felt as if he had been turned to ice, and went in search of his son, who, however, was nowhere to be found, until at length they discovered his body lying at the bottom of a well. Their anger was thus turned to grief, and death seemed as though it would be a pleasant relief to them as they sat facing each other in silence in their thatched and smokeless hut. At evening they prepared to bury the boy; but, on touching the body, lo! he was still breathing. Overjoyed, they placed him upon the bed, and towards the middle of the night he came round; but a drop of bitterness was mingled in his parents' cup when they found that his reason had fled. His father, however, caught sight of the empty bowl in which he had kept the cricket, and ceased to think any more about his son, never once closing his eyes all night; and as day gradually broke, there he lay stiff and stark, until suddenly he heard the chirping of a cricket outside the house door. Jumping up in a great hurry to see, there was his lost insect; but, on trying to catch it, away it hopped directly. At last he got it under his hand, though, when he came to close his fingers on it, there was nothing in them. So he went on, chasing it up and down, until finally it hopped into a corner of the wall; and then, looking carefully about, he espied it once more, no longer the same in appearance, but small, and of a dark red colour. Ch'êng stood looking at it, without trying to catch such a worthless specimen, when all of a sudden the little creature hopped into his sleeve; and, on examining it more nearly, he saw that it really was a handsome insect, with well-formed head and neck, and forthwith took it indoors. He was now anxious to try its prowess; and it so happened that a young fellow of the village, who had a fine cricket which used to win every bout it fought, and was so valuable to him that he wanted a high price for it, called on Ch'êng that very day. He laughed heartily at Ch'êng's champion, and, producing his own, placed it side by side, to the great disadvantage of the former. Ch'êng's countenance fell, and he no longer wished to back his cricket; however, the young fellow urged him, and he thought that there was no use in rearing a feeble insect, and that he had better sacrifice it for a laugh; so they put them together in a bowl. The little cricket lay quite still like a piece of wood, at which the young fellow roared again, and louder than ever when it did not move even though tickled with a pig's bristle. By dint of tickling it was roused at last, and then it fell upon its adversary with such fury, that in a moment the young fellow's cricket would have been killed outright had not its master interfered and stopped the fight. The little cricket then stood up and chirped to Ch'êng as a sign of victory; and Ch'êng, overjoyed, was just talking over the battle with the young fellow, when a cock caught sight of the insect, and ran up to eat it. Ch'êng was in a great state of alarm; but the cock luckily missed its aim, and the cricket hopped away, its enemy pursuing at full speed. In another moment it would have been snapped up, when, lo! to his great astonishment, Ch'êng saw his cricket seated on the cock's head, holding firmly on to its comb. He then put it into a cage, and by-and-by sent it to the magistrate, who, seeing what a small one he had provided, was very angry indeed. Ch'êng told the story of the cock, which the magistrate refused to believe, and set it to fight with other crickets, all of which it vanquished without exception. He then tried it with a cock, and as all turned out as Ch'êng had said, he gave him a present, and sent the cricket in to the Governor. The Governor put it into a golden cage, and forwarded it to the palace, accompanied by some remarks on its performances; and when there, it was found that of all the splendid collection of His Imperial Majesty, not one was worthy to be placed alongside of this one. It would dance in time to music, and thus became a great favourite, the Emperor in return bestowing magnificent gifts of horses and silks upon the Governor. The Governor did not forget whence he had obtained the cricket, and the magistrate also well rewarded Ch'êng by excusing him from the duties of beadle, and by instructing the Literary Chancellor to pass him for the first degree. A few months afterwards Ch'êng's son recovered his intellect, and said that he had been a cricket, and had proved himself a very skilful fighter. The Governor, too, rewarded Ch'êng handsomely, and in a few years he was a rich man, with flocks, and herds, and houses, and acres, quite one of the wealthiest of mankind.

The Kindly Magician

ONCE UPON A TIME there was a man named Du Dsi Tschun. In his youth he was a spendthrift and paid no heed to his property. He was given to drink and idling. When he had run through all his money, his relatives cast him out. One winter day he was walking barefoot about the city, with an empty stomach and torn clothes. Evening came on and still he had not found any food. Without end or aim he wandered about the market place. He was hungry, and the cold seemed well nigh unendurable. So he turned his eyes upward and began to lament aloud.

Suddenly an ancient man stood before him, leaning on a staff, who said: "What do you lack since you complain so?"

"I am dying of hunger," replied Du Dsi Tschun, "and not a soul will take pity on me!"

The ancient man said: "How much money would you need in order to live in all comfort?"

"If I had fifty thousand pieces of copper it would answer my purpose," replied Du Dsi Tschun.

The ancient said: "That would not answer."

"Well, then, a million!"

"That is still too little!"

"Well, then, three million!"

The ancient man said: "That is well spoken!" He fetched a thousand pieces of copper out of his sleeve and said: "That is for this evening. Expect me tomorrow by noon, at the Persian Bazaar!"

At the time set Du Dsi Tschun went there, and, sure enough, there was the ancient, who gave him three million pieces of copper. Then he disappeared, without giving his name.

When Du Dsi Tschun held the money in his hand, his love for prodigality once more awoke. He rode pampered steeds, clothed himself in the finest furs, went back to his wine, and led such an extravagant life that the money gradually came to an end. Instead of wearing brocade he had to wear cotton, and instead of riding horseback he went to the dogs. Finally he was again running about barefoot and in rags as before, and did not know how to satisfy his hunger. Once more he stood in the market-place and sighed. But the ancient was already there, took him by the hand and said: "Are you back already to where you were? That is strange! However, I will aid you once more!"

But Du Dsi Tschun was ashamed and did not want to accept his help. Yet the ancient insisted, and led him along to the Persian Bazaar. This time he gave him ten million pieces of copper, and Du Dsi Tschun thanked him with shame in his heart.

With money in hand, he tried to give time to adding to it, and saving in order to gain great wealth. But, as is always the case, it is hard to overcome ingrown faults. Gradually he began to fling his money away again, and gave free rein to all his desires. And once more his purse grew empty. In a couple of years he was as poor as ever he had been.

Then he met the ancient the third time, but was so ashamed of himself that he hid his face when he passed him.

The ancient seized his arm and said: "Where are you going? I will help you once more. I will give you thirty million. But if then you do not improve you are past all aid!"

Full of gratitude, Du Dsi Tschun bowed before him and said: "In the days of my poverty my wealthy relatives did not seek me out. You alone have thrice aided me. The money you give me to-day shall not be squandered, that I swear; but I will devote it to good works in order to repay your great kindness. And when I have done this I will follow you, if needs be through fire and through water."

The ancient replied: "That is right! When you have ordered these things ask for me in the temple of Laotsze beneath the two mulberry trees!"

Du Dsi Tschun took the money and went to Yangdschou. There he bought a hundred acres of the best land, and built a lofty house with many hundreds of rooms on the highway. And there he allowed widows and orphans to live. Then he bought a burial-place for his ancestors, and supported his needy relations. Countless people were indebted to him for their livelihood.

When all was finished, he went to inquire after the ancient in the temple of Laotsze. The ancient was sitting in the shade of the mulberry trees blowing the flute. He took Du Dsi Tschun along with him to the cloudy peaks of the holy mountains of the West. When they had gone some forty miles into the mountains, he saw a dwelling, fair and clean. It was surrounded by many-colored clouds, and peacocks and cranes were flying about it. Within the house was a herb-oven nine feet high. The fire burned with a purple flame, and its glow leaped along the walls. Nine fairies stood at the oven, and a green dragon and a white tiger crouched beside it. Evening came. The ancient was no longer clad like an ordinary man; but wore a yellow cap and wide, flowing garments. He took three pellets of the White Stone, put them into a flagon of wine, and gave them to Du Dsi Tschun to drink. He spread out a tiger-skin against the western wall of the inner chamber, and bade Du Dsi Tschun sit down on it, with his face turned toward the East. Then he said to him: "Now beware of speaking a single word – no matter what happens to you, whether you encounter powerful gods or terrible demons, wild beasts or ogres, or all the tortures of the nether world, or even if you see your own relatives suffer – for all these things are only deceitful images! They cannot harm you. Think only of what I have said, and let your soul be at rest!" And when he had said this the ancient disappeared.

Then Du Dsi Tschun saw only a large stone jug full of clear water standing before him. Fairies, dragon and tiger had all vanished. Suddenly he heard a tremendous crash, which made heaven and earth tremble. A man towering more than ten feet in height appeared. He called himself the great captain, and he and his horse were covered with golden armor. He was surrounded by more than a hundred soldiers, who drew their bows and swung their swords, and halted in the courtyard.

The giant called out harshly: "Who are you? Get out of my way!"

Du Dsi Tschun did not move. And he returned no answer to his questions.

Then the giant flew into a passion and cried with a thundering voice: "Chop off his head!"

But Du Dsi Tschun remained unmoved, so the giant went off raging.

Then a furious tiger and a poisonous serpent came up roaring and hissing. They made as though to bite him and leaped over him. But Du Dsi Tschun remained unperturbed in spirit, and after a time they dissolved and vanished.

Suddenly a great rain began to fall in streams. It thundered and lightninged incessantly, so that his ears rang and his eyes were blinded. It seemed as though the house would fall. The water rose to a flood in a few moments' time, and streamed up to the place where he was sitting. But Du Dsi Tschun remained motionless and paid no attention to it. And after a time the water receded.

Then came a great demon with the head of an ox. He set up a kettle in the middle of the courtyard, in which bubbled boiling oil. He caught Du Dsi Tschun by the neck with an iron fork and said: "If you will tell me who you are I will let you go!"

Du Dsi Tschun shut his eyes and kept silent. Then the demon picked him up with the fork and flung him into the kettle. He withstood the pain, and the boiling oil did not harm him. Finally the demon dragged him out again, and drew him down the steps of the house before a man with red hair and a blue face, who looked like the prince of the nether world. The latter cried: "Drag in his wife!"

After a time Du Dsi Tschun's wife was brought on in chains. Her hair was torn and she wept bitterly.

The demon pointed to Du Dsi Tschun and said: "If you will speak your name we will let her go!"

But he answered not a word.

Then the prince of evil had the woman tormented in all sorts of ways. And she pleaded with Du Dsi Tschun: "I have been your wife now for ten years. Will you not speak one little word to save me? I can endure no more!" And the tears ran in streams from her eyes. She screamed and scolded. Yet he spoke not a word.

Thereupon the prince of evil shouted: "Chop her into bits!" And there, before his eyes, it seemed as though she were really being chopped to pieces. But Du Dsi Tschun did not move.

"The scoundrel's measure is full!" cried the prince of evil. "He shall dwell no longer among the living! Off with his head!" And so they killed him, and it seemed to him that his soul fled his body. The ox-headed demon dragged him down into the nether regions, where he tasted all the tortures in turn. But Du Dsi Tschun remembered the words of the ancient. And the tortures, too, seemed bearable. So he did not scream and said not a word.

Now he was once more dragged before the prince of evil. The latter said: "As punishment for his obstinacy this man shall come to earth again in the shape of a woman!"

The demon dragged him to the wheel of life and he returned to earth in the shape of a girl. He was often ill, had to take medicine continually, and was pricked and burned with hot needles. Yet he never uttered a sound. Gradually he grew into a beautiful maiden. But since he never spoke, he was known as the dumb maid. A scholar finally took him for his bride, and they lived in peace and good fellowship. And a son came to them who, in the course of two years was already beyond measure wise and intelligent. One day the father was carrying the son on his arm. He spoke jestingly to his wife and said: "When I look at you it seems to me that you are not really dumb. Won't you say one little word to me? How delightful it would be if you were to become my speaking rose!"

The woman remained silent. No matter how he might coax and try to make her smile, she would return no answer.

Then his features changed: "If you will not speak to me, it is a sign that you scorn me; and in that case your son is nothing to me, either!" And with that he seized the boy and flung him against the wall.

But since Du Dsi Tschun loved this little boy so dearly, he forgot the ancient's warning, and cried out: "Oh, oh!"

And before the cry had died away Du Dsi Tschun awoke as though from a dream and found himself seated in his former place. The ancient was there as well. It must have been about the fifth hour of the night. Purple flames rose wildly from the oven, and flared up to the sky. The whole house caught fire and burned like a torch.

"You have deceived me!" cried the ancient. Then he seized him by the hair and thrust him into the jug of water. And in a minute the fire went out. The ancient spoke: "You overcame joy and rage, grief and fear, hate and desire, it is true; but love you had not driven from your soul. Had you not cried out when the child was flung against the wall, then my elixir would have taken shape and you would have attained immortality. But in the last moment you failed me. Now it is too late. Now I can begin brewing my elixir of life once more from the beginning and you will remain a mere mortal man!"

Du Dsi Tschun saw that the oven had burst, and that instead of the philosopher's stone it held only a lump of iron. The ancient man cast aside his garments and chopped it up with a magic knife. Du Dsi Tschun took leave of him and returned to Yangdschou, where he lived in great affluence. In his old age he regretted that he had not completed his task. He once more went to the mountain to look for the ancient. But the ancient had vanished without leaving a trace.

The Painted Skin

A T T'AI-YUAN THERE lived a man named Wang. One morning he was out walking when he met a young lady carrying a bundle and hurrying along by herself. As she moved along with some difficulty, Wang quickened his pace and caught her up, and found she was a pretty girl of about sixteen. Much smitten he inquired whither she was going so early, and no one with her.

"A traveller like you," replied the girl, "cannot alleviate my distress; why trouble yourself to ask?" "What distress is it?" said Wang; "I'm sure I'll do anything I can for you." "My parents," answered she, "loved money, and they sold me as concubine into a rich family, where the wife was very jealous, and beat and abused me morning and night. It was more than I could stand, so I have run away." Wang asked her where she was going; to which she replied that a runaway had no fixed place of abode. "My house," said Wang, "is at no great distance; what do you say to coming there?"

She joyfully acquiesced; and Wang, taking up her bundle, led the way to his house. Finding no one there, she asked Wang where his family were; to which he replied that that was only the library. "And a very nice place, too," said she; "but if you are kind enough to wish to save my life, you mustn't let it be known that I am here." Wang promised he would not divulge her secret, and so she remained there for some days without anyone knowing anything about it. He then told his wife, and she, fearing the girl might belong to some influential family, advised him to send her away. This, however, he would not consent to do; when one day, going into the town, he met a Taoist priest, who looked at him in astonishment, and asked him what he had met. "I have met nothing," replied Wang. "Why," said the priest, "you are bewitched; what do you mean by not having met anything?" But Wang insisted that it was so, and the priest walked away, saying, "The fool! Some people don't seem to know when death is at hand." This startled Wang, who at first thought of the girl; but then he reflected that a pretty young thing as she was couldn't well be a witch, and began to suspect that the priest merely wanted to do a stroke of business. When he returned, the library door was shut, and he couldn't get in, which made him suspect that something was wrong; and so he climbed over the wall, where he found the door of the inner room shut too. Softly creeping up, he looked through the window and saw a hideous devil, with a green face and jagged teeth like a saw, spreading a human skin upon the bed and painting it with a paint-brush. The devil then threw aside the brush, and giving the skin a shake out, just as you would a coat, threw it over its shoulders, when, lo! it was the girl. Terrified at this, Wang hurried away with his head down in search of the priest who had gone he knew not whither; subsequently finding him in the fields, where he threw himself on his knees and begged the priest to save him. "As to driving her away," said the priest, "the creature must be in great distress to be seeking a substitute for herself; besides, I could hardly endure to injure a living thing." However, he gave Wang a fly-brush, and bade him hang it at the door of the bedroom, agreeing to meet again at the Ch'ing-ti temple. Wang went home, but did not dare enter the library; so he hung up the brush at the bedroom door, and before long heard a sound of footsteps outside. Not daring to move, he made his wife peep out; and she saw the girl standing looking at the brush, afraid to pass it. She then ground her teeth and went away; but in a little while came back, and began cursing, saying, "You priest, you won't frighten me. Do you think I am going to give up what is already in my grasp?" Thereupon, she tore the brush to pieces, and bursting open the door, walked straight up to the bed, where she ripped open Wang and tore out his heart, with which she went away. Wang's wife screamed out, and the servant came in with a light; but Wang was already dead and presented a most miserable spectacle. His wife, who was in an agony of fright, hardly dared cry for fear of making a noise; and next day she sent Wang's brother to see the priest. The latter got into a great rage, and cried out, "Was it for this that I had compassion on you, devil that you are?" proceeding at once with Wang's brother to the house, from which the girl had disappeared without anyone knowing whither she had gone. But the priest, raising his head, looked all round, and said, "Luckily she's not far off." He then asked who lived in the apartments on the south side, to which Wang's brother replied that he did; whereupon the priest declared that there she would be found. Wang's brother was horribly frightened and said he did not think so; and then the priest asked him if any stranger had been to the house. To this he answered that he had been out to the Ch'ing-ti temple and couldn't possibly say; but he went off to inquire, and in a little while came back and reported that an old woman had sought service with them as a maid-of-all-work, and had been engaged by his wife. "That is she," said the priest, as Wang's brother added she was still there; and they all set out to go to the house together. Then the priest took his wooden sword, and standing in the middle of the court-yard, shouted out, "Base-born fiend, give me back my fly-brush!" Meanwhile the new maid-of-all-work was in a great state of alarm, and tried to get away by the door; but the priest struck her and down she fell flat, the human skin dropped off, and she became a hideous devil. There she lay grunting like a pig, until the priest grasped his wooden sword and struck off her head. She then became a dense column of smoke curling up from the ground, when the priest took an uncorked gourd and threw it right into the midst of the smoke. A sucking noise was heard, and the whole column was drawn into the gourd; after which the priest corked it up closely and put it in his pouch. The skin, too, which was complete even to the eyebrows, eyes, hands, and feet, he also rolled up as if it had been a scroll, and was on the point of leaving with it, when Wang's wife stopped him, and with tears entreated him to bring her husband to life. The priest said he was unable to do that; but Wang's wife flung herself at his feet, and with loud lamentations implored his assistance. For some time he remained immersed in thought, and then replied, "My power is not equal to what you ask. I myself cannot raise the dead; but I will direct you to someone who can, and if you apply to him properly you will succeed." Wang's wife asked the priest who it was; to which he replied, "There is a maniac in the town who passes his time grovelling in the dirt. Go, prostrate yourself before him, and beg him to help you. If he insults you, shew no sign of anger." Wang's brother knew the man to whom he alluded, and accordingly bade the priest adieu, and proceeded thither with his sister-in-law.

They found the destitute creature raving away by the road side, so filthy that it was all they could do to go near him. Wang's wife approached him on her knees; at which the maniac leered at her, and cried out, "Do you love me, my beauty?" Wang's wife told him what she had come for, but he only laughed and said, "You can get plenty of other husbands. Why raise the dead one to life?" But Wang's wife entreated him to help her; whereupon he observed, "It's very strange: people apply to me to raise their dead as if I was king of the infernal regions." He then gave Wang's wife a thrashing with his staff, which she bore without a murmur, and before a gradually increasing crowd of spectators. After this he produced a loathsome pill which he told her she must swallow, but here she broke down and was quite unable to do so. However, she did manage it at last, and then the maniac crying out, "How you do love me!" got up and went away without taking any more notice of her. They followed him into a temple with loud supplications, but he had disappeared, and every effort to find him was unsuccessful. Overcome with rage and shame, Wang's wife went home, where she mourned bitterly over her dead husband, grievously repenting the steps she had taken, and wishing only to die. She then bethought herself of preparing the corpse, near which none of the servants would venture; and set to work to close up the frightful wound of which he died.

While thus employed, interrupted from time to time by her sobs, she felt a rising lump in her throat, which by-and-by came out with a pop and fell straight into the dead man's wound. Looking closely at it, she saw it was a human heart; and then it began as it were to throb, emitting a warm vapour like smoke. Much excited, she at once closed the flesh over it, and held the sides of the wound together with all her might. Very soon, however, she got tired, and finding the vapour escaping from the crevices, she tore up a piece of silk and bound it round, at the same time bringing back circulation by rubbing the body and covering it up with clothes. In the night, she removed the coverings, and found that breath was coming from the nose; and by next morning her husband was alive again, though disturbed in mind as if awaking from a dream and feeling a pain in his heart. Where he had been wounded, there was a cicatrix about as big as a cash, which soon after disappeared.

The Painted Wall

A KIANG-SI GENTLEMAN, named Mêng Lung-t'an, was lodging at the capital with a Mr. Chu, M.A., when one day chance led them to a certain monastery, within which they found no spacious halls or meditation chambers, but only an old priest in deshabille. On observing the visitors, he arranged his dress and went forward to meet them, leading them round and showing whatever there was to be seen.

In the chapel they saw an image of Chih Kung, and the walls on either side were beautifully painted with life-like representations of men and things. On the east side were pictured a number of fairies, among whom was a young girl whose maiden tresses were not yet confined by the matron's knot. She was picking flowers and gently smiling, while her cherry lips seemed about to move, and the moisture of her eyes to overflow. Mr. Chu gazed at her for a long time without taking his eyes off, until at last he became unconscious of anything but the thoughts that were engrossing him. Then, suddenly, he felt himself floating in the air, as if riding on a cloud, and found himself passing through the wall, where halls and pavilions stretched away one after another, unlike the abodes of mortals. Here an old priest was preaching the Law of Buddha, surrounded by a large crowd of listeners. Mr. Chu mingled with the throng, and after a few moments perceived a gentle tug at his sleeve. Turning round, he saw the young girl above-mentioned, who walked laughing away. Mr. Chu at once followed her, and passing a winding balustrade arrived at a small apartment beyond which he dared not venture further. But the young lady, looking back, waved the flowers she had in her hand as though beckoning him to come on. He accordingly entered and found nobody else within. Then they fell on their knees and worshipped heaven and earth together, and rose up as man and wife, after which the bride went away, bidding Mr. Chu keep quiet until she came back. This went on for a couple of days, when the young lady's companions began to smell a rat and discovered Mr. Chu's hiding-place. Thereupon they all laughed and said, "My dear, you are now a married woman, and should leave off that maidenly coiffure." So they gave her the proper hair-pins and head ornaments, and bade her go bind her hair, at which she blushed very much but said nothing. Then one of them cried out, "My sisters, let us be off. Two's company, more's none." At this they all giggled again and went away.

Mr. Chu found his wife very much improved by the alteration in the style of her hair. The high top-knot and the coronet of pendants were very becoming to her. But suddenly they heard a sound like the tramping of heavy-soled boots, accompanied by the clanking of chains and the noise of angry discussion. The bride jumped up in a fright, and she and Mr. Chu peeped out. They saw a man clad in golden armour, with a face as black as jet, carrying in his hand chains and whips, and surrounded by all the girls. He asked, "Are you all here?" "All," they replied. "If," said he, "any mortal is here concealed amongst you, denounce him at once, and lay not up sorrow for yourselves." Here they all answered as before that there was no one. The man then made a movement as if he would search the place, upon which the bride was dreadfully alarmed, and her face turned the colour of ashes. In her terror she said to Mr. Chu, "Hide yourself under the bed," and opening a small lattice in the wall, disappeared herself. Mr. Chu in his concealment hardly dared to draw his breath; and in a little while he heard the boots tramp into the room and out again, the sound of the voices getting gradually fainter and fainter in the distance. This reassured him, but he still heard the voices of people going backwards and forwards outside; and having been a long time in a cramped position, his ears began to sing as if there was a locust in them, and his eyes to burn like fire. It was almost unbearable; however, he remained quietly awaiting the return of the young lady without giving a thought to the why and wherefore of his present position.

Meanwhile, Mêng Lung-t'an had noticed the sudden disappearance of his friend, and thinking something was wrong, asked the priest where he was. "He has gone to hear the preaching of the Law," replied the priest. "Where?" said Mr. Mêng. "Oh, not very far," was the answer. Then with his finger the old priest tapped the wall and called out, "Friend Chu! what makes you stay away so long?" At this, the likeness of Mr. Chu was figured upon the wall, with his ear inclined in the attitude of one listening. The priest added, "Your friend here has been waiting for you some time;" and immediately Mr. Chu descended from the wall, standing transfixed like a block of wood, with starting eyeballs and trembling legs. Mr. Mêng was much terrified, and asked him quietly what was the matter. Now the matter was that while concealed under the bed he had heard a noise resembling thunder and had rushed out to see what it was.

Here they all noticed that the young lady on the wall with the maiden's tresses had changed the style of her coiffure to that of a married woman. Mr. Chu was greatly astonished at this and asked the old priest the reason.

He replied, "Visions have their origin in those who see them: what explanation can I give?" This answer was very unsatisfactory to Mr. Chu; neither did his friend, who was rather frightened, know what to make of it all; so they descended the temple steps and went away.

The Sorcerer of the White Lotus Lodge

ONCE UPON A TIME there was a sorcerer who belonged to the White Lotus Lodge. He knew how to deceive the multitude with his black arts, and many who wished to learn the secret of his enchantments became his pupils.

One day the sorcerer wished to go out. He placed a bowl which he covered with another bowl in the hall of his house, and ordered his pupils to watch it. But he warned them against uncovering the bowl to see what might be in it.

No sooner had he gone than the pupils uncovered the bowl and saw that it was filled with clear water. And floating on the water was a little ship made of straw, with real masts and sails. They were surprised and pushed it with their fingers till it upset. Then they quickly righted it again and once more covered the bowl. By that time the sorcerer was already standing among them. He was angry and scolded them, saying: "Why did you disobey my command?"

His pupils rose and denied that they had done so.

But the sorcerer answered: "Did not my ship turn turtle at sea, and yet you try to deceive me?"

On another evening he lit a giant candle in his room, and ordered his pupils to watch it lest it be blown out by the wind. It must have been at the second watch of the night and the sorcerer had not yet come back. The pupils grew tired and sleepy, so they went to bed and gradually fell asleep. When they woke up again the candle had gone out. So they rose quickly and re-lit it. But the sorcerer was already in the room, and again he scolded them.

"Truly we did not sleep! How could the light have gone out?"

Angrily the sorcerer replied: "You let me walk fifteen miles in the dark, and still you can talk such nonsense!"

Then his pupils were very much frightened.

In the course of time one of his pupils insulted the sorcerer. The latter made note of the insult, but said nothing. Soon after he told the pupil to feed the swine, and no sooner had he entered the sty than his master turned him into a pig. The sorcerer then at once called in a butcher, sold the pig to the man, and he went the way of all pigs who go to the butcher.

One day this pupil's father turned up to ask after his son, for he had not come back to his home for a long time. The sorcerer told him that his son had left him long ago. The father returned home and inquired everywhere for his son without success. But one of his son's fellow-pupils, who knew of the matter, informed the father. So the father complained to the district mandarin. The latter, however, feared that the sorcerer might make himself invisible. He did not dare to have him arrested, but informed his superior and begged for a thousand well-armed soldiers. These surrounded the sorcerer's home and seized him, together with his wife and child. All three were put into wooden cages to be transported to the capital.

The road wound through the mountains, and in the midst of the hills up came a giant as large as a tree, with eyes like saucers, a mouth like a plate, and teeth a foot long. The soldiers stood there trembling and did not dare to move.

Said the sorcerer: "That is a mountain spirit. My wife will be able to drive him off."

They did as he suggested, unchained the woman, and she took a spear and went to meet the giant. The latter was angered, and he swallowed her, tooth and nail. This frightened the rest all the more.

The sorcerer said: "Well, if he has done away with my wife, then it is my son's turn!"

So they let the son out of his cage. But the giant swallowed him in the same way. The rest all looked on without knowing what to do.

The sorcerer then wept with rage and said: "First he destroys my wife, and then my son. If only he might be punished for it! But I am the only one who can punish him!"

And, sure enough, they took him out of his cage, too, gave him a sword, and sent him out against the giant. The sorcerer and the giant fought with each other for a time, and at last the giant seized the sorcerer, thrust him into his maw, stretched his neck and swallowed him. Then he went his way contentedly.

And now when it was too late, the soldiers realized that the sorcerer had tricked them.

The Talking Fish

L ONG, LONG BEFORE your great-grandfather was born there lived in the village of Everlasting Happiness two men called Li and Sing. Now, these two men were close friends, living together in the same house. Before settling down in the village

of Everlasting Happiness they had ruled as high officials for more than twenty years. They had often treated the people very harshly, so that everybody, old and young, disliked and hated them. And yet, by robbing the wealthy merchants and by cheating the poor, these two evil companions had become rich, and it was in order to spend their ill-gotten gains in idle amusements that they sought out the village of Everlasting Happiness. "For here," said they, "we can surely find that joy which has been denied us in every other place. Here we shall no longer be scorned by men and reviled by women."

Consequently these two men bought for themselves the finest house in the village, furnished it in the most elegant manner, and decorated the walls with scrolls filled with wise sayings and pictures by famous artists. Outside there were lovely gardens filled with flowers and birds, and oh, ever so many trees with queer twisted branches growing in the shape of tigers and other wild animals.

Whenever they felt lonely Li and Sing invited rich people of the neighbourhood to come and dine with them, and after they had eaten, sometimes they would go out upon the little lake in the centre of their estate, rowing in an awkward flat-bottomed boat that had been built by the village carpenter.

One day, on such an occasion, when the sun had been beating down fiercely upon the clean-shaven heads of all those on the little barge, for you must know this was long before the day when hats were worn – at least, in the village of Everlasting Happiness – Mr. Li was suddenly seized with a giddy feeling, which rapidly grew worse and worse until he was in a burning fever.

"Snake's blood mixed with powdered deer-horn is the thing for him," said the wise-looking doctor who was called in, peering at Li carefully through his huge glasses, "Be sure," he continued, addressing Li's personal attendant, and, at the same time, snapping his long finger-nails nervously, "be sure, above all, not to leave him alone, for he is in danger of going raving mad at any moment, and I cannot say what he may do if he is not looked after carefully. A man in his condition has no more sense than a baby."

Now, although these words of the doctor's really made Mr. Li angry, he was too ill to reply, for all this time his head had been growing hotter and hotter, until at last a feverish sleep overtook him. No sooner had he closed his eyes than his faithful servant, half-famished, rushed out of the room to join his fellows at their mid-day meal.

Li awoke with a start. He had slept only ten minutes. "Water, water," he moaned, "bathe my head with cold water. I am half dead with pain!" But there was no reply, for the attendant was dining happily with his fellows.

"Air, air," groaned Mr. Li, tugging at the collar of his silk shirt. "I'm dying for water. I'm starving for air. This blazing heat will kill me. It is hotter than the Fire god himself ever dreamed of making it. Wang, Wang!" clapping his hands feebly and calling to his servant, "air and water, air and water!"

But still no Wang.

At last, with the strength that is said to come from despair, Mr. Li arose from his couch and staggered toward the doorway. Out he went into the paved courtyard, and then, after only a moment's hesitation, made his way across it into a narrow passage that led into the lake garden.

"What do they care for a man when he is sick?" he muttered. "My good friend Sing is doubtless even now enjoying his afternoon nap, with a servant standing by to fan him, and a block of ice near his head to cool the air. What does he care if I die of a raging fever? Doubtless he expects to inherit all my money. And my servants! That rascal Wang has been with me these ten years, living on me and growing lazier every season! What does he care if I pass away? Doubtless he is certain that Sing's servants will think of something for him to do, and he will have even less work than he has now. Water, water! I shall die if I don't soon find a place to soak myself!"

So saying, he arrived at the bank of a little brook that flowed in through a water gate at one side of the garden and emptied itself into the big fish-pond. Flinging himself down by a little stream Li bathed his hands and wrists in the cool water. How delightful! If only it were deep enough to cover his whole body, how gladly would he cast himself in and enjoy the bliss of its refreshing embrace!

For a long time he lay on the ground, rejoicing at his escape from the doctor's clutches. Then, as the fever began to rise again, he sprang up with a determined cry, "What am I waiting for? I will do it. There's no one to prevent me, and it will do me a world of good. I will cast myself head first into the fish-pond. It is not deep enough near the shore to drown me if I should be too weak to swim, and I am sure it will restore me to strength and health."

He hastened along the little stream, almost running in his eagerness to reach the deeper water of the pond. He was like some small Tom Brown who had escaped from the watchful eye of the master and run out to play in a forbidden spot.

Hark! Was that a servant calling? Had Wang discovered the absence of his employer? Would he sound the alarm, and would the whole place soon be alive with men searching for the fever-stricken patient?

With one last sigh of satisfaction Li flung himself, clothes and all, into the quiet waters of the fish-pond. Now Li had been brought up in Fukien province on the seashore, and was a skilful swimmer. He dived and splashed to his heart's content, then floated on the surface. "It takes me back to my boyhood," he cried, "why, oh why, is it not the fashion to swim? I'd love to live in the water all the time and yet some of my countrymen are even more afraid than a cat of getting their feet wet. As for me, I'd give anything to stay here for ever."

"You would, eh?" chuckled a hoarse voice just under him, and then there was a sort of wheezing sound, followed by a loud burst of laughter. Mr. Li jumped as if an arrow had struck him, but when he noticed the fat, ugly monster below, his fear turned into anger. "Look here, what do you mean by giving a fellow such a start! Don't you know what the Classics say about such rudeness?"

The giant fish laughed all the louder. "What time do you suppose I have for Classics? You make me laugh till I cry!"

"But you must answer my question," cried Mr. Li, more and more persistently, forgetting for the moment that he was not trying some poor culprit for a petty crime. "Why did you laugh? Speak out at once, fellow!"

"Well, since you are such a saucy piece," roared the other, "I will tell you. It was because you awkward creatures, who call yourselves men, the most highly civilized beings in the world, always think you understand a thing fully when you have only just found out how to do it."

"You are talking about the island dwarfs, the Japanese," interrupted Mr. Li, "We Chinese seldom undertake to do anything new."

"Just hear the man!" chuckled the fish. "Now, fancy your wishing to stay in the water for ever! What do you know about water? Why you're not even provided with the proper equipment for swimming. What would you do if you really lived here always?"

"What am I doing now?" spluttered Mr. Li, so angry that he sucked in a mouthful of water before he knew it.

"Floundering," retorted the other.

"Don't you see me swimming? Are those big eyes of yours made of glass?"

"Yes, I see you all right," guffawed the fish, "that's just it! I see you too well. Why you tumble about as awkwardly as a water buffalo wallowing in a mud puddle!"

Now, as Mr. Li had always considered himself an expert in water sports, he was, by this time, speechless with rage, and all he could do was to paddle feebly round and round with strokes just strong enough to keep himself from sinking.

"Then, too," continued the fish, more and more calm as the other lost his temper, "you have a very poor arrangement for breathing. If I am not mistaken, at the bottom of this pond you would find yourself worse off than I should be at the top of a palm tree. What would you do to keep yourself from starving? Do you think it would be convenient if you had to flop yourself out on to the land every time you wanted a bite to eat? And yet, being a man, I doubt seriously if you would be content to take the proper food for fishes. You have hardly a single feature that would make you contented if you were to join an under-water school. Look at your clothes, too, water-soaked and heavy. Do you think them suitable to protect you from cold and sickness? Nature forgot to give you any scales. Now I'm going to tell you a joke, so you must be sure to laugh. Fishes are like grocery shops – always judged by their scales. As you haven't a sign of a scale, how will people judge you? See the point, eh? Nature gave you a skin, but forgot the outer covering, except, perhaps at the ends of your fingers and your toes You surely see by this time why I consider your idea ridiculous?"

Sure enough, in spite of his recent severe attack of fever, Mr. Li had really cooled completely off. He had never understood before what great disadvantages there were connected with being a man. Why not make use of this chance acquaintance, find out from him how to get rid of that miserable possession he had called his manhood, and gain the delights that only a fish can have? "Then, are you indeed contented with your lot?" he asked finally. "Are there not moments when you would prefer to be a man?"

"I, a man!" thundered the other, lashing the water with his tail. "How dare you suggest such a disgraceful change! Can it be that you do not know my rank? Why, my fellow, you behold in me a favourite nephew of the king!"

"Then, may it please your lordship," said Mr. Li, softly, "I should be exceedingly grateful if you would speak a kind word for me to your master. Do you think it possible that he could change me in some manner into a fish and accept me as a subject?"

"Of course!" replied the other, "all things are possible to the king. Know you not that my sovereign is a loyal descendant of the great water dragon, and, as such, can never die, but lives on and on and on, for ever and ever and ever, like the ruling house of Japan?"

"Oh, oh!" gasped Mr. Li, "even the Son of Heaven, our most worshipful emperor, cannot boast of such long years. Yes, I would give my fortune to be a follower of your imperial master."

"Then follow me," laughed the other, starting off at a rate that made the water hiss and boil for ten feet around him.

Mr. Li struggled vainly to keep up. If he had thought himself a good swimmer, he now saw his mistake and every bit of remaining pride was torn to tatters. "Please wait a moment," he cried out politely, "I beg of you to remember that I am only a man!"

"Pardon me," replied the other, "it was stupid of me to forget, especially as I had just been talking about it."

Soon they reached a sheltered inlet at the farther side of the pond. There Mr. Li saw a gigantic carp idly floating about in a shallow pool, and then lazily flirting his huge tail or fluttering his fins proudly from side to side. Attendant courtiers darted hither and thither, ready to do the master's slightest bidding. One of them, splendidly attired in royal scarlet, announced, with a downward flip of the head, the approach of the King's nephew who was leading Mr. Li to an audience with his Majesty.

"Whom have you here, my lad?" began the ruler, as his nephew, hesitating for words to explain his strange request, moved his fins nervously backwards and forwards. "Strange company, it seems to me, you are keeping these days."

"Only a poor man, most royal sir," replied the other, "who beseeches your Highness to grant him your gracious favour."

> *"When man asks favour of a fish,*
> *'Tis hard to penetrate his wish –*
> *He often seeks a lordly dish*
> *To serve upon his table,"*

repeated the king, smiling. "And yet, nephew, you think this fellow is really peaceably inclined and is not coming among us as a spy?"

Before his friend could answer, Mr. Li had cast himself upon his knees in the shallow water, before the noble carp, and bowed thrice, until his face was daubed with mud from the bottom of the pool. "Indeed, your Majesty, I am only a poor mortal who seeks your kindly grace. If you would but consent to receive me into your school of fishes. I would for ever be your ardent admirer and your lowly slave."

"In sooth, the fellow talks as if in earnest," remarked the king, after a moment's reflection, "and though the request is, perhaps, the strangest to which I have ever listened, I really see no reason why I should not turn a fishly ear. But, have the goodness first to cease your bowing. You are stirring up enough mud to plaster the royal palace of a shark."

Poor Li, blushing at the monarch's reproof, waited patiently for the answer to his request.

"Very well, so be it," cried the king impulsively, "your wish is granted. Sir Trout," turning to one of his courtiers, "bring hither a fish-skin of proper size for this ambitious fellow."

No sooner said than done. The fish-skin was slipped over Mr. Li's head, and his whole body was soon tucked snugly away in the scaly coat. Only his arms remained uncovered. In the twinkling of an eye Li felt sharp pains shoot through every part of his body. His arms began to shrivel up and his hands changed little by little until they made an excellent pair of fins, just as good as those of the king himself. As for his legs and feet, they suddenly began to stick together until, wriggle as he would, Li could not separate them. "Ah, ha!" thought he, "my kicking days are over, for my toes are now turned into a first-class tail."

"Not so fast," laughed the king, as Li, after thanking the royal personage profusely, started out to try his new fins; "not so fast, my friend. Before you depart, perhaps I'd better give you a little friendly advice, else your new powers are likely to land you on the hook of some lucky fisherman, and you will find yourself served up as a prize of the pond."

"I will gladly listen to your lordly counsel, for the words of the Most High to his lowly slave are like pearls before sea slugs. However, as I was once a man myself I think I understand the simple tricks they use to catch us fish, and I am therefore in position to avoid trouble."

"Don't be so sure about it. 'A hungry carp often falls into danger,' as one of our sages so wisely remarked. There are two cautions I would impress upon you. One is, never, never, eat a dangling worm; no matter how tempting it looks there are sure to be horrible hooks inside. Secondly, always swim like lightning if you see a net, but in the opposite direction. Now, I will have you served your first meal out of the royal pantry, but after that, you must hunt for yourself, like every other self-respecting citizen of the watery world."

After Li had been fed with several slugs, followed by a juicy worm for dessert, and after again thanking the king and the king's nephew for their kindness, he started forth to test his tail and fins. It was no easy matter, at first, to move them properly. A single flirt of the tail, no more vigorous than those he had been used to giving with his legs, would send him whirling round and round in the water, for all the world like a living top; and when he wriggled his fins, ever so slightly, as he thought, he found himself sprawling on his back in a most ridiculous fashion for a dignified member of fishkind. It took several hours of constant practice to get the proper stroke, and then he found he could move about without being conscious of any effort. It was the easiest thing he had ever done in his life; and oh! the water was so cool and delightful! "Would that I might enjoy that endless life the poets write of!" he murmured blissfully.

Many hours passed by until at last Li was compelled to admit that, although he was not tired, he was certainly hungry. How to get something to eat? Oh! why had he not asked the friendly nephew a few simple questions? How easily his lordship might have told him the way to get a good breakfast! But alas! without such advice, it would be a whale's task to accomplish it. Hither and thither he swam, into the deep still water, and along the muddy shore; down, down to the pebbly bottom – always looking, looking for a tempting worm. He dived into the weeds and rushes, poked his nose among the lily pads. All for nothing! No fly or worm of any kind to gladden his eager eyes! Another hour passed slowly away, and all the time his hunger was growing greater and greater. Would the fish god, the mighty dragon, not grant him even one little morsel to satisfy his aching stomach, especially since, now that he was a fish, he had no way of tightening up his belt, as hungry soldiers do when they are on a forced march?

Just as Li was beginning to think he could not wriggle his tail an instant longer, and that soon, very soon, he would feel himself slipping, slipping, slipping down to the bottom of the pond to die – at that very moment, chancing to look up, he saw, oh joy! a delicious red worm dangling a few inches above his nose. The sight gave new strength to his weary fins and tail. Another minute, and he would have had the delicate morsel in his mouth, when alas! he chanced to recall the advice given him the day before by great King Carp. "No matter how tempting it looks, there are sure to be horrible hooks inside." For an instant Li hesitated. The worm floated a trifle nearer to his half-open mouth. How tempting! After all, what was a hook to a fish when he was dying? Why be a coward? Perhaps this worm was an exception to the rule, or perhaps, perhaps any thing – really a fish in such a plight as Mr. Li could not be expected to follow advice – even the advice of a real KING.

Pop! He had it in his mouth. Oh, soft morsel, worthy of a king's desire! Now he could laugh at words of wisdom, and eat whatever came before his eye. But ugh! What was that strange feeling that – Ouch! it was the fatal hook!

With one frantic jerk, and a hundred twists and turns, poor Li sought to pull away from the cruel barb that stuck so fast in the roof of his mouth. It was now too late to wish he had kept away from temptation. Better far to have starved at the bottom of the cool pond than to be jerked out by some miserable fisherman to the light and sunshine of the busy world. Nearer and nearer he approached the surface. The more he struggled the sharper grew the cruel barb. Then, with one final splash, he found himself dangling in mid-air, swinging helplessly at the end of a long line. With a chunk he fell into a flat-bottomed boat, directly on top of several smaller fish.

"Ah, a carp!" shouted a well-known voice gleefully; "the biggest fish I've caught these three moons. What good luck!"

It was the voice of old Chang, the fisherman, who had been supplying Mr. Li's table ever since that official's arrival in the village of Everlasting Happiness. Only a word of explanation, and he, Li, would be free once more to swim about where he willed. And then there should be no more barbs for him. An escaped fish fears the hook.

"I say, Chang," he began, gasping for breath, "really now, you must chuck me overboard at once, for, don't you see, I am Mr. Li, your old master. Come, hurry up about it. I'll excuse you this time for your mistake, for, of course, you had no way of knowing. Quick!"

But Chang, with a savage jerk, pulled the hook from Li's mouth, and looked idly towards the pile of glistening fish, gloating over his catch, and wondering how much money he could demand for it. He had heard nothing of Mr. Li's remarks, for Chang had been deaf since childhood.

"Quick, quick, I am dying for air," moaned poor Li, and then, with a groan, he remembered the fisherman's affliction.

By this time they had arrived at the shore, and Li, in company with his fellow victims, found himself suddenly thrown into a wicker basket. Oh, the horrors of that journey on land! Only a tiny bit of water remained in the closely-woven thing. It was all he could do to breathe.

Joy of joys! At the door of his own house he saw his good friend Sing just coming out. "Hey, Sing," he shouted, at the top of his voice, "help, help! This son of a turtle wants to murder me. He has me in here with these fish, and doesn't seem to know that I am Li, his master. Kindly order him to take me to the lake and throw me in, for it's cool there and I like the water life much better than that on land."

Li paused to hear Sing's reply, but there came not a single word.

"I beg your honour to have a look at my catch," said old Chang to Sing. "Here is the finest fish of the season. I have brought him here so that you and my honoured master, Mr. Li, may have a treat. Carp is his favourite delicacy."

"Very kind of you, my good Chang, I'm sure, but I fear poor Mr. Li will not eat fish for some time. He has a bad attack of fever."

"There's where you're wrong," shouted Li, from his basket, flopping about with all his might, to attract attention, "I'm going to die of a chill. Can't you recognise your old friend? Help me out of this trouble and you may have all my money for your pains."

"Hey, what's that!" questioned Sing, attracted, as usual, by the word money. "Shades of Confucius! It sounds as if the carp were talking."

"What, a talking fish," laughed Chang. "Why, master, I've lived nigh on to sixty year, and such a fish has never come under my sight. There are talking birds and talking beasts for that matter; but talking fish, who ever heard of such a wonder? No, I think your ears must have deceived you, but this carp will surely cause talk when I get him into the kitchen. I'm sure the cook has never seen his like. Oh, master! I hope you will be hungry when you sit down to this fish. What a pity Mr. Li couldn't help you to devour it!"

"Help to devour myself, eh?" grumbled poor Li, now almost dead for lack of water. "You must take me for a cannibal, or some other sort of savage."

Old Chang had now gone round the house to the servants' quarters, and, after calling out the cook, held up poor Li by the tail for the chef to inspect.

With a mighty jerk Li tore himself away and fell at the feet of his faithful cook. "Save me, save me!" he cried out in despair; "this miserable Chang is deaf and doesn't know that I am Mr. Li, his master. My fish voice is not strong enough for his hearing. Only take me back to the pond and set me free. You shall have a pension for life, wear good clothes and eat good food, all the rest of your days. Only hear me and obey! Listen, my dear cook, listen!"

"The thing seems to be talking," muttered the cook, "but such wonders cannot be. Only ignorant old women or foreigners would believe that a fish could talk." And seizing his former master by the tail, he swung him on to a table, picked up a knife, and began to whet it on a stone.

"Oh, oh!" screamed Li, "you will stick a knife into me! You will scrape off my beautiful shiny scales! You will whack off my lovely new fins! You will murder your old master!"

"Well, you won't talk much longer," growled the cook, "I'll show you a trick or two with the blade."

So saying, with a gigantic thrust, he plunged the knife deep into the body of the trembling victim.

With a shrill cry of horror and despair, Mr. Li awoke from the deep sleep into which he had fallen. His fever was gone, but he found himself trembling with fear at thought of the terrible death that had come to him in dreamland.

"Thanks be to Buddha, I am not a fish!" he cried out joyfully; "and now I shall be well enough to enjoy the feast to which Mr. Sing has bidden guests for tomorrow. But alas, now that I can eat the old fisherman's prize carp, it has changed back into myself.

"If only the good of our dreams came true,
I shouldn't mind dreaming the whole day through."

The Tiger Guest

A YOUNG MAN named Kung, a native of Min-chou, on his way to the examination at Hsi-ngan, rested awhile in an inn, and ordered some wine to drink. Just then a very tall and noble-looking stranger walked in, and, seating himself by the side of Kung, entered into conversation with him.

Kung offered him a cup of wine, which the stranger did not refuse; saying, at the same time, that his name was Miao. But he was a rough, coarse fellow; and Kung, therefore, when the wine was finished, did not call for any more. Miao then rose, and observing that Kung did not appreciate a man of his capacity, went out into the market to buy some, returning shortly with a huge bowl full. Kung declined the proffered wine; but Miao, seizing his arm to persuade him, gripped it so painfully that Kung was forced to drink a few more cups, Miao himself swilling away as hard as he could go out of a soup-plate. "I am not good at entertaining people," cried Miao, at length; "pray go on or stop just as you please." Kung accordingly put together his things and went off; but he had not gone more than a few miles when his horse was taken ill, and lay down in the road. While he was waiting there with all his heavy baggage, revolving in his mind what he should do, up came Mr. Miao; who, when he heard what was the matter, took off his coat and handed it to the servant, and lifting up the horse, carried it off on his back to the nearest inn, which was about six or seven miles distant. Arriving there he put the animal in the stable, and before long Kung and his servants arrived too. Kung was much astonished at Mr. Miao's feat; and, believing him to be superhuman, began to treat him with the utmost deference, ordering both wine and food to be procured for their refreshment. "My appetite," remarked Miao, "is one that you could not easily satisfy. Let us stick to wine." So they finished another stoup together, and then Miao got up and took his leave, saying, "It will be some time before your horse is well; I cannot wait for you." He then went away.

After the examination several friends of Kung's invited him to join them in a picnic to the Flowery Hill; and just as they were all feasting and laughing together, lo! Mr. Miao walked up. In one hand he held a large flagon, and in the other a ham, both of which he laid down on the ground before them. "Hearing," said he, "that you gentlemen were coming here, I have tacked myself on to you, like a fly to a horse's tail." Kung and his friends then rose and received him with the usual ceremonies, after which they all sat down promiscuously. By-and-by, when the wine had gone round pretty freely, some one proposed capping verses; whereupon Miao cried out, "Oh, we're very jolly drinking like this; what's the use of making oneself uncomfortable?" The others, however, would not listen to him, and agreed that as a forfeit a huge goblet of wine should be drunk by any defaulter. "Let us rather make death the penalty," said Miao; to which they replied, laughing, that such a punishment was a trifle too severe; and then Miao retorted that if it was not to be death, even a rough fellow like himself might be able to join. A Mr. Chin, who was sitting at the top of the line, then began:—

"From the hill-top high, wide extends the gaze—"

upon which Miao immediately carried on with

"Redly gleams the sword o'er the shattered vase."

The next gentleman thought for a long time, during which Miao was helping himself to wine; and by-and-by they had all capped the verse, but so wretchedly that Miao called out, "Oh, come! if we aren't to be fined for these, we had better abstain from making any more." As none of them would agree to this, Miao could stand it no longer, and roared like a dragon till the hills and valleys echoed again. He then went down on his hands and knees, and jumped about like a lion, which utterly confused the poets, and put an end to their lucubrations. The wine had now been round a good many times, and being half tipsy each began to repeat to the other the verses he had handed in at the recent examination, all at the same time indulging in any amount of mutual flattery. This so disgusted Miao that he drew Kung aside to have a game at "guess-fingers;" but as they went on droning away all the same, he at length cried out, "Do stop your rubbish, fit only for your own wives, and not for general company." The others were much abashed at this, and so angry were they at Miao's rudeness that they went on repeating all the louder. Miao then threw himself on the ground in a passion, and with a roar changed into a tiger, immediately springing upon the company, and killing them all except Kung and Mr. Chin. He then ran off roaring loudly. Now this Mr. Chin succeeded in taking his master's degree; and three years afterwards, happening to revisit the Flowery Hill, he beheld a Mr. Chi, one of those very gentlemen who had previously been killed by the tiger. In great alarm he was making off, when Chi seized his bridle and would not let him proceed. So he got down from his horse, and inquired what was the matter; to which Chi replied, "I am now the slave of Miao, and have to endure bitter toil for him. He must kill some one else before I can be set free. Three days hence a man, arrayed in the robes and cap of a scholar, should be eaten by the tiger at the foot of the Ts'ang-lung Hill. Do you on that day take some gentleman thither, and thus help your old friend." Chin was too frightened to say much, but promising that he would do so, rode away home. He then began to consider the matter over with himself, and, regarding it as a plot, he determined to break his engagement, and let his friend remain the tiger's devil. He chanced, however, to repeat the story to a Mr. Chiang who was a relative of his, and one of the local scholars; and as this gentleman had a grudge against another scholar, named Yu, who had come out equal with him at the examination, he made up his mind to destroy him. So he invited Yu to accompany him on that day to the place in question, mentioning that he himself should appear in undress only. Yu could not make out the reason for this; but when he reached the spot there he found all kinds of wine and food ready for his entertainment. Now that very day the Prefect had come to the hill; and being a friend of the Chiang family, and hearing that Chiang was below, sent for him to come up. Chiang did not dare to appear before him in undress, and borrowed Yu's clothes and hat; but he had no sooner got them on than out rushed the tiger and carried him away in its mouth.

The Two Jugglers

ONE BEAUTIFUL SPRING DAY two men strolled into the public square of a well-known Chinese city. They were plainly dressed and looked like ordinary countrymen who had come in to see the sights. Judging by their faces, they were father and son. The elder, a wrinkled man of perhaps fifty, wore a scant grey beard. The younger had a small box on his shoulder.

At the hour when these strangers entered the public square, a large crowd had gathered, for it was a feast day, and everyone was bent on having a good time. All the people seemed very happy. Some, seated in little open-air booths, were eating, drinking, and smoking. Others were buying odds and ends from the street-vendors, tossing coins, and playing various games of chance.

The two men walked about aimlessly. They seemed to have no friends among the pleasure-seekers. At last, however, as they stood reading a public notice posted at the entrance of the town-hall or yamen, a bystander asked them who they were.

"Oh, we are jugglers from a distant province," said the elder, smiling and pointing towards the box. "We can do many tricks for the amusement of the people."

Soon it was spread about among the crowd that two famous jugglers had just arrived from the capital, and that they were able to perform many wonderful deeds. Now it happened that the mandarin or mayor of the city, at that very moment was entertaining a number of guests in the yamen. They had just finished eating, and the host was wondering what he should do to amuse his friends, when a servant told him of the jugglers.

"Ask them what they can do," said the mandarin eagerly. "I will pay them well if they can really amuse us, but I want something more than the old tricks of knife-throwing and balancing. They must show us something new."

The servant went outside and spoke to the jugglers: "The great man bids you tell him what you can do. If you can amuse his visitors he will bring them out to the private grand stand, and let you perform before them and the people who are gathered together."

"Tell your honourable master," said the elder, whom we shall call Chang, "that, try us as he will, he will not be disappointed. Tell him that we come from the unknown land of dreams and visions, that we can turn rocks into mountains, rivers into oceans, mice into elephants, in short, that there is nothing in magic too difficult for us to do."

The official was delighted when he heard the report of his servant. "Now we may have a little fun," he said to his guests, "for there are jugglers outside who will perform their wonderful tricks before us."

The guests filed out on to the grand stand at one side of the public square. The mandarin commanded that a rope should be stretched across so as to leave an open space in full view of the crowd, where the two Changs might give their exhibition.

For a time the two strangers entertained the people with some of the simpler tricks, such as spinning plates in the air, tossing bowls up and catching them on chopsticks, making flowers grow from empty pots, and transforming one object into another. At last, however, the mandarin cried out: "These tricks are very good of their kind, but how about those idle boasts of changing rivers into oceans and mice into elephants? Did you not say that you came from the land of dreams? These tricks you have done are stale and shopworn. Have you nothing new with which to regale my guests on this holiday?"

"Most certainly, your excellency. But surely you would not have a labourer do more than his employer requires? Would that not be quite contrary to the teachings of our fathers? Be assured, sir, anything that you demand I can do for you. Only say the word."

The mandarin laughed outright at this boasting language. "Take care, my man! Do not go too far with your promises. There are too many impostors around for me to believe every stranger. Hark you! no lying, for if you lie in the presence of my guests, I shall take great pleasure in having you beaten."

"My words are quite true, your excellency," repeated Chang earnestly. "What have we to gain by deceit, we who have performed our miracles before the countless hosts of yonder Western Heaven?"

"Ha, ha! hear the braggarts!" shouted the guests. "What shall we command them to do?"

For a moment they consulted together, whispering and laughing.

"I have it," cried the host finally. "Our feast was short of fruit, since this is the off season. Suppose we let this fellow supply us. Here, fellow, produce us a peach, and be quick about it. We have no time for fooling."

"What, masters, a peach?" exclaimed the elder Chang in mock dismay. "Surely at this season you do not expect a peach."

"Caught at his own game," laughed the guests, and the people began to hoot derisively.

"But, father, you promised to do anything he required," urged the son. "If he asks even a peach, how can you refuse and at the same time save your face?"

"Hear the boy talk," mumbled the father, "and yet, perhaps he's right. Very well, masters," turning to the crowd, "if it's a peach you want, why, a peach you shall have, even though I must send into the garden of the Western Heaven for the fruit."

The people became silent and the mandarin's guests forgot to laugh. The old man, still muttering, opened the box from which he had been taking the magic bowls, plates, and other articles. "To think of people wanting peaches at this season! What is the world coming to?"

After fumbling in the box for some moments he drew out a skein of golden thread, fine spun and as light as gossamer. No sooner had he unwound a portion of this thread than a sudden gust of wind carried it up into the air above the heads of the onlookers. Faster and faster the old man paid out the magic coil, higher and higher the free end rose into the heavens, until, strain his eyes as he would, no one present could see into what far-region it had vanished.

"Wonderful, wonderful!" shouted the people with one voice, "the old man is a fairy."

For a moment they forgot all about the mandarin, the jugglers, and the peach, so amazed were they at beholding the flight of the magic thread.

At last the old man seemed satisfied with the distance to which his cord had sailed, and, with a bow to the spectators, he tied the end to a large wooden pillar which helped to support the roof of the grand stand. For a moment the structure trembled and swayed as if it too would be carried off into the blue ether, the guests turned pale and clutched their chairs for support, but not even the mandarin dared to speak, so sure were they now that they were in the presence of fairies.

"Everything is ready for the journey," said old Chang calmly.

"What! shall you leave us?" asked the mayor, finding his voice again.

"I? Oh, no, my old bones are not spry enough for quick climbing. My son here will bring us the magic peach. He is handsome and active enough to enter that heavenly garden. Graceful, oh graceful is that peach tree – of course, you remember the line from the poem – and a graceful man must pluck the fruit."

The mandarin was still more surprised at the juggler's knowledge of a famous poem from the classics. It made him and his friends all the more certain that the newcomers were indeed fairies.

The young man at a sign from his father tightened his belt and the bands about his ankles, and then, with a graceful gesture to the astonished people, sprang upon the magic string, balanced himself for a moment on the steep incline, and then ran as nimbly up as a sailor would have mounted a rope ladder. Higher and higher he climbed till he seemed no bigger than a lark ascending into the blue sky, and then, like some tiny speck, far, far away, on the western horizon.

The people gazed in open-mouthed wonder. They were struck dumb and filled with some nameless fear; they hardly dared to look at the enchanter who stood calmly in their midst, smoking his long-stemmed pipe.

The mandarin, ashamed of having laughed at and threatened this man who was clearly a fairy, did not know what to say. He snapped his long finger nails and looked at his guests in mute astonishment. The visitors silently drank their tea, and the crowd of sightseers craned their necks in a vain effort to catch sight of the vanished fairy. Only one in all that assembly, a bright-eyed little boy of eight, dared to break the silence, and he caused a hearty burst of merriment by crying out, "Oh, daddy, will the bad young man fly off into the sky and leave his poor father all alone?"

The greybeard laughed loudly with the others, and tossed the lad a copper. "Ah, the good boy," he said smiling, "he has been well trained to love his father; no fear of foreign ways spoiling his filial piety."

After a few moments of waiting, old Chang laid aside his pipe and fixed his eyes once more on the western sky. "It is coming," he said quietly. "The peach will soon be here."

Suddenly he held out his hand as if to catch some falling object, but, look as they would, the people could see nothing. Swish! thud! it came like a streak of light, and, lo, there in the magician's fingers was a peach, the most beautiful specimen the people had ever seen, large and rosy. "Straight from the garden of the gods," said Chang, handing the fruit to the mandarin, "a peach in the Second Moon, and the snow hardly off the ground."

Trembling with excitement, the official took the peach and cut it open. It was large enough for all his guests to have a taste, and such a taste it was! They smacked their lips and wished for more, secretly thinking that never again would ordinary fruit be worth the eating.

But all this time the old juggler, magician, fairy or whatever you choose to call him, was looking anxiously into the sky. The result of this trick was more than he had bargained for. True, he had been able to produce the magic peach which the mandarin had called for, but his son, where was his son? He shaded his eyes and looked far up into the blue heavens, and so did the people, but no one could catch a glimpse of the departed youth.

"Oh, my son, my son," cried the old man in despair, "how cruel is the fate that has robbed me of you, the only prop of my declining years! Oh, my boy, my boy, would that I had not sent you on so perilous a journey! Who now will look after my grave when I am gone?"

Suddenly the silken cord on which the young man had sped so daringly into the sky, gave a quick jerk which almost toppled over the post to which it was tied, and there, before the very eyes of the people, it fell from the lofty height, a silken pile on the ground in front of them.

The greybeard uttered a loud cry and covered his face with his hands. "Alas! the whole story is plain enough," he sobbed. "My boy was caught in the act of plucking the magic peach from the garden of the gods, and they have thrown him into prison. Woe is me! Ah! woe is me!"

The mandarin and his friends were deeply touched by the old man's grief, and tried in vain to comfort him. "Perhaps he will return," they said. "Have courage!"

"Yes, but in what a shape?" replied the magician. "See! even now they are restoring him to his father."

The people looked, and they saw twirling and twisting through the air the young man's arm. It fell upon the ground in front of them at the fairy's feet. Next came the head, a leg, the body. One by one before the gasping, shuddering people, the parts of the unfortunate young man were restored to his father.

After the first outburst of wild, frantic grief the old man by a great effort gained control of his feelings, and began to gather up these parts, putting them tenderly into the wooden box.

By this time many of the spectators were weeping at the sight of the father's affliction. "Come," said the mandarin at last, deeply moved, "let us present the old man with sufficient money to give his boy a decent burial."

All present agreed willingly, for there is no sight in China that causes greater pity than that of an aged parent robbed by death of an only son. The copper cash fell in a shower at the juggler's feet, and soon tears of gratitude were mingled with those of sorrow. He gathered up the money and tied it in a large black cloth. Then a wonderful change came over his face. He seemed all of a sudden to forget his grief. Turning to the box, he raised the lid. The people heard him say: "Come, my son; the crowd is waiting for you to thank them. Hurry up! They have been very kind to us."

In an instant the box was thrown open with a bang, and before the mandarin and his friends, before the eyes of all the sightseers the young man, strong and whole once more, stepped forth and bowed, clasping his hands and giving the national salute.

For a moment all were silent. Then, as the wonder of the whole thing dawned upon them, the people broke forth into a tumult of shouts, laughter, and compliments. "The fairies have surely come to visit us!" they shouted. "The city will be blessed with good fortune! Perhaps it is Fairy Old Boy himself who is among us!"

The mandarin rose and addressed the jugglers, thanking them in the name of the city for their visit and for the taste they had given to him and his guests of the peach from the heavenly orchard.

Even as he spoke, the magic box opened again; the two fairies disappeared inside, the lid closed, and the chest rose from the ground above the heads of the people. For a moment it floated round in a circle like some homing pigeon trying to find its bearings before starting on a return journey. Then, with a sudden burst of speed, it shot off into the heavens and vanished from the sight of those below, and not a thing remained as proof of the strange visitors except the magic peach seed that lay beside the teacups on the mandarin's table.

According to the most ancient writings there is now nothing left to tell of this story. It has been declared, however, by later scholars that the official and his friends who had eaten the magic peach, at once began to feel a change in their lives. While, before the coming of the fairies, they had lived unfairly, accepting bribes and taking part in many shameful practices, now, after tasting of the heavenly fruit, they began to grow better. The people soon began to honour and love them, saying, "Surely these great men are not like others of their kind, for these men are just and honest in their dealings with us. They seem not to be ruling for their own reward!"

However this may be, we do know that before many years their city became the centre of the greatest peach-growing section of China, and even yet when strangers walk in the orchards and look up admiringly at the beautiful sweet-smelling fruit, the natives sometimes ask proudly, "And have you never heard about the wonderful peach which was the beginning of all our orchards, the magic peach the fairies brought us from the Western Heaven?"

Lessons, Rewards & Justice

THE NIGHTINGALE the Emperor banished eventually came back to save his life with his enchanting song. The Emperor learned the importance of gratitude. Folktales have always been a vehicle for the codification of morality and the teaching of life-lessons, as well as being such entertaining stories!

As remarkable as these stories are, some of their translators are almost as extraordinary. Born in Greece's Ionian Islands, Lafcadio Hearn (1850–1904) was an authority on Japan, a distinguished translator of French writers like Flaubert, Zola and Maupassant and a significant writer in the supernatural. Frederick H. Martens (1874–1932) was a US music journalist with a sideline in translating foreign children's books: he is believed to have taken his *The Chinese Fairy Book* (1921) from the German. Another American, Norman Hinsdale Pitman (1876–1925) had a day job as an English professor in Beijing but explored the folklore of his host country in his spare time. Stories from all of these and more are brought together for this final category of Chinese folktales.

How the Birds Saved the Emperor's Life

THERE WAS ONCE an Emperor of China whose palace was the most wonderful in the world, being built entirely of priceless porcelain. In the garden were the most beautiful flowers, on some of which were little golden bells which tinkled in the wind so that you could not help looking at them.

It was a really wonderful garden, and so large that even the Head Gardener himself did not know where it ended. If you should reach the end of the garden you would come to a magnificent forest in which were great trees and deep lakes. The banks sloped down to the water, which was as clear as crystal. Overhanging the lakes were the boughs of some of the trees, which were so large that ships could sail beneath them. In one of these trees there lived a Nightingale which sang so beautifully that a poor fisherman, who had a great deal to do, even stopped his work to listen to the bird singing. "How beautiful it is!" he said, but he had to attend to his duties and then forgot about the bird. But each night it was the same; the fisherman could not resist the temptation and he left his work to listen to the bird.

The Emperor's palace and garden were so magnificent that many travelers from foreign countries wrote books describing their beauty; but every scholar who wrote said that the finest thing of all was the singing of this Nightingale.

These books were read by many people all over the world, and at last some of them reached the Emperor, who sat in his chair of solid jade and read and read and read. He was very much pleased that so many people who were scholars should write so much about his palace and garden, but he was surprised to find that in each book the Nightingale was spoken of as the finest and most wonderful thing of all.

"It is very strange," said the Emperor, "I've never heard this Nightingale and it does seem unusual that I should know about it for the first time from reading books written by travellers."

He called his First Lord to him and said, "In all of these books there is mention of a very remarkable bird which is called 'The Nightingale.' The writers all say that it is the most glorious thing in my kingdom. How is it that no one has ever told me about it?"

"Why, I don't know anything about it myself," said the First Lord, "but I will go and find it."

The First Lord didn't know where it was, so he ran all over the palace and asked everybody there, but none of them had ever heard of the Nightingale. Then he returned to the Emperor and said it must be an invention of those who had written the books.

"Your Royal Highness must know that not all that is written is true, and that much of it is invented," said he.

"But the last book I read," said the Emperor, "was sent to me by the great ruler of Japan, so that it must be true, and I insist upon your bringing the Nightingale here this evening; if you do not, every one in this palace shall be trampled under foot."

"All right, your Majesty," said the First Lord; and he ran up and down the stairs, through halls and corridors, and as he told the people what would happen to them if the Nightingale were not brought there that evening they all followed him, because they had no wish to be trampled under foot, and all were most curious to know about this wonderful Nightingale which it seemed that everybody in the world knew about except those who lived in the palace.

At last they met a poor little girl in the kitchen who said, "Why, I know the Nightingale, and I have often heard her sing. Every night when I go home to my Mother I am so tired that I sit and rest for a little while in the wood, and then I hear the Nightingale sing, and it is so wonderful that it always brings tears to my eyes."

"Then," said the First Lord, "little kitchen maid, if you can lead us to this Nightingale you shall have leave to see the Emperor at dinner this evening, for she is invited by His Majesty to come and sing to him." Then they all went into the garden where the Nightingale lived, and on the way they heard the mooing of a cow.

"Oh, this must be the Nightingale! How wonderful that such a little bird has such a tremendous voice!" said they.

"That is not a bird singing, that is a cow mooing," said the little kitchen maid. "We have a long way to go yet."

A little farther on they heard some frogs croaking in the marsh. The Chinese Chaplain was with them and he said, "How sublime! That is just like the ringing of a church bell."

"Why," said the little kitchen maid, "those are frogs croaking, but very soon we shall hear her."

Just then the Nightingale began to sing.

"Hark!" cried the little girl. "Listen!" and pointing to a little bird sitting up in the branches, said, "There she is."

"It doesn't seem possible that so very common looking a bird as that can sing," said the First Lord. "It must be that she has lost her brilliant plumage because there are so many distinguished people here."

Then the little kitchen maid called out, "Little Nightingale, our gracious Emperor invites you to sing before him this evening!"

"It will give me great pleasure to do so," said the Nightingale; and then she began to sing so gloriously that they were all entranced. The First Lord said, "I have never heard anything so beautiful before. His Majesty will be delighted."

The Nightingale, thinking the First Lord was the Emperor, said, "Shall I sing again for your Majesty?"

"My dear little bird," said the First Lord, "His Most Gracious Highness has sent me to invite you to his palace this evening so that he may listen to your charming song."

"It's much better out here in the forest," replied the Nightingale, but when she heard that the Emperor wished her to go to the palace, she gladly offered to go with them.

At the palace everything was splendidly prepared. The many lights made the porcelain walls and floors glitter, and the gorgeous tinkling flowers helped to make the place look very beautiful. The people moving back and forth caused the little golden bells to tinkle all the time. In the center of the great hall, in which was the Emperor's throne, was a golden perch, put there for the Nightingale. The whole court was present, and the little kitchen maid, who had shown the First Lord where the bird could be found, was allowed to stand behind the door where she could see and hear everything.

All were dressed in their best clothes and everyone looked toward the little bird, whom the Emperor requested to commence singing.

And how the Nightingale did sing! Very soon the tears came into the Emperor's eyes and ran down his cheeks. At this the Nightingale sang even more beautifully, and the heart of everyone was touched. The Emperor was so delighted that he said she should wear the golden necklace around her neck, but the Nightingale said that she had already received a sufficient reward, for she had brought tears to the eyes of the Emperor.

Even the servants, who were always most difficult to please, said that they were greatly touched. This in itself proved how successful was the Nightingale's concert.

The Emperor requested her to stay at the court, and he gave her a large golden cage and allowed her to go out twice every day. He provided her with twelve servants, each of whom held a silken string which was fastened to her leg, and you may be sure that she found but little pleasure flying about, hampered in this way.

Very soon everyone in the city was talking about the wonderful bird, and even the tradesmen's children were all named after her, although none of them could sing a note.

Some time after this the Emperor received a large parcel on which was written "The Nightingale."

"This must be another book about our famous bird," said the Emperor.

But he was mistaken, for it was a mechanical toy, an artificial Nightingale which looked something like a real bird but was covered with jewels. When it was wound up it could sing the piece the real bird sang, and moved its tail up and down. Around its neck was a collar on which was written: "The Nightingale of the Emperor of Japan cannot be compared with that of the Emperor of China."

"How wonderful!" said everyone, and the man who had brought the clock-work bird was given the title of "Bringer of the Imperial First Nightingale."

They sang together, but it did not sound well, for the real Nightingale sang her own song, and the clock-work bird sang waltzes.

"It isn't its fault!" said the bandmaster. "It keeps very good time and is quite after my style."

Then the artificial bird had to sing alone. It was very pleasant to listen to, and it was also pretty to look at, as the jewels with which it was covered sparkled so. It sang the same piece many times without becoming tired, and then the Emperor thought that the real Nightingale should sing again. But she was not to be found; the window was open and without anybody seeing her go, she had flown away to her beloved forest.

The Emperor was very angry when it was discovered that the real bird had gone away, and everyone agreed that it was a very ungracious thing for her to have done. But they all said that the bird sent by the Japanese ruler was the better of the two, and especially did the bandmaster praise it. He said that one knew just what to expect from the artificial bird, but the real one would sing the most unusual tunes. The bird they had now could be opened, and the inside shown and explained, but if this were done to the other it would die.

Everyone agreed that what the bandmaster said was correct, and the Emperor commanded that all the people of the city should be allowed to listen to the bird's beautiful music on a certain day of the following week.

So on the day appointed the bandmaster showed the jeweled bird to the people, and after they had heard it sing everyone said that its music was wonderful, that is all but the poor fisherman who had heard the real one, and he said: "This one looks very pretty and is quite pleasant to listen to, but its singing does not compare with that of the other."

The Emperor banished the real bird from the kingdom, and the artificial one was put on a golden perch by the side of his bed, and was given the title of Imperial Nightsinger.

Several months passed away when one evening, as the Emperor lay in bed listening to it, something inside snapped, and the music stopped. The Royal Physician was summoned, but could do nothing. Then the Royal Clockmaker was called, and after examining it very carefully he took out the works, which he found to be almost worn out. It took him quite a long time to put these back again, but at last he got it into something like order, although he said it must not be used more than once a year, and then only for a very short time.

Some time after this the Emperor became very ill, and as the physicians said that he could not live for more than a few days, his successor was chosen.

The poor Emperor lay all alone in his great bed, and as everyone believed him to be dead the courtiers left him to pay their respects to the new ruler. But he was only in a trance, and when he came out of this he felt very lonely indeed, for there was no one to speak to him. He turned his head and saw the artificial bird by his bedside. A great longing for music came over him, and he cried: "Sing, golden bird! Please sing!"

But there was no one to wind it up, and he was too weak to do this himself. It was so quiet, and he felt so terribly lonely and sad that he was sure he was going to die.

Suddenly there came through the open window the sound of such beautiful music that new life came to the sick man. He raised his head, and saw, sitting upon the bough of a large tree, the real bird whom he had banished from his kingdom.

"What divine singing!" said the Emperor. "You have given me new life in return for my unkindness in banishing you from my kingdom. What can I do to reward you?"

"I need no more reward than the sight of the tears which came to your eyes when I first sang to you," said the Nightingale. "That is something which I can never forget. But now you must sleep, and to-morrow, when you will feel much stronger, I can promise you such music as you would not believe possible." The Emperor smiled happily, and fell at once into a deep, calm sleep.

He was awakened in the morning by the sun, which was shining brightly. So much better did he feel that he was able to get out of bed and walk to the open window, and there his eyes beheld a wonderful sight.

Upon every bough of the tree in front of him were perched many birds, and in the center of them sat the poor fisherman, who held to his lips a reed instrument. On seeing the Emperor at the window he gave a sign, and there came forth from the throats of the assembled birds such a glorious burst of melody that tears of thankfulness flowed from the Emperor's eyes; he could scarcely believe that such wonderful music was possible.

No longer was he a sick man. The bird chorus had brought back to him the health and strength which all the doctors, with their medicines, had not been able to do. In his gratitude to the birds he gave them the tree for their very own, and the poor fisherman he appointed bandmaster-in-chief.

How Three Heroes Came by their Deaths Because of Two Peaches

AT THE BEGINNING of his reign Duke Ging of Tsi loved to draw heroes about him. Among those whom he attached to him were three of quite extraordinary bravery. The first was named Gung Sun Dsia, the second Tian Kai Giang, the third Gu I Dsi. All three were highly honored by the prince, but the honor paid them made them presumptuous, they kept the court in a turmoil, and overstepped the bounds of respect which lie between a prince and his servants.

At the time Yan Dsi was chancellor of Tsi. The duke consulted him as to what would be best to do. And the chancellor advised him to give a great court banquet and invite all his courtiers. On the table, the choicest dish of all, stood a platter holding four magnificent peaches.

Then, in accordance with his chancellor's advice, the Duke rose and said: "Here are some magnificent peaches, but I cannot give one to each of you. Only those most worthy may eat of them. I myself reign over the land, and am the first among the princes of the empire. I have been successful in holding my possessions and power, and that is my merit. Hence one of the peaches falls to me. Yan Dsi sits here as my chancellor. He regulates communications with foreign lands and keeps the peace among the people. He has made my kingdom powerful among the kingdoms of the earth. That is his merit, and hence the second peach falls to him. Now there are but two peaches left; yet I cannot tell which ones among you are the worthiest. You may rise yourselves and tell us of your merits. But whoever has performed no great deeds, let him hold his tongue!"

Then Gung Sun Dsia beat upon his sword, rose up and said: "I am the prince's captain general. In the South I besieged the kingdom of Lu, in the West I conquered the kingdom of Dsin, in the North I captured the army of Yan. All the princes of the East come to the Duke's court and acknowledge the overlordship of Tsi. That is my merit. I do not know whether it deserves a peach."

The Duke replied: "Great is your merit! A peach is your just due!"

Then Tian Kai Giang rose, beat on the table, and cried: "I have fought a hundred battles in the army of the prince. I have slain the enemy's general-in-chief, and captured the enemy's flag. I have extended the borders of the Duke's land till the size of his realm has been increased by a thousand miles. How is it with my merit?"

The Duke said: "Great is your merit! A peach is your just due!"

Then Gu I Dsi arose; his eyes started from their sockets, and he shouted with a loud voice: "Once, when the Duke was crossing the Yellow River, wind and waters rose. A river-dragon snapped up one of the steeds of the chariot and tore it away. The ferry-boat rocked like a sieve and was about to capsize. Then I took my sword and leaped into the stream. I fought with the dragon in the midst of the foaming waves. And by reason of my strength I managed to kill him, though my eyes stood out of my head with my exertions. Then I came to the surface with the dragon's head in one hand, and holding the rein of the rescued horse in the other, and I had saved my prince from drowning. Whenever our country was at war with neighboring states, I refused no service. I commanded the van, I fought in single combat. Never did I turn my back on the foe. Once the prince's chariot stuck fast in the swamp, and the enemy hurried up on all sides. I pulled the chariot out, and drove off the hostile mercenaries. Since I have been in the prince's service I have saved his life more than once. I grant that my merit is not to be compared with that of the prince and that of the chancellor, yet it is greater than that of my two companions. Both have received peaches, while I must do without. This means that real merit is not rewarded, and that the Duke looks on me with disfavor. And in such case how may I ever show myself at court again!"

With these words he drew his sword and killed himself.

Then Gung Sun Dsia rose, bowed twice, and said with a sigh: "Both my merit and that of Tian Kai Giang does not compare with Gu I Dsi's and yet the peaches were given us. We have been rewarded beyond our deserts, and such reward is shameful. Hence it is better to die than to live dishonored!"

He took his sword and swung it, and his own head rolled on the sand.

Tian Kai Giang looked up and uttered a groan of disgust. He blew the breath from his mouth in front of him like a rainbow, and his hair rose on end with rage. Then he took sword in hand and said: "We three have always served our prince bravely. We were like the same flesh and blood. The others are dead, and it is my duty not to survive them!"

And he thrust his sword into his throat and died.

The Duke sighed incessantly, and commanded that they be given a splendid burial. A brave hero values his honor more than his life. The chancellor knew this, and that was why he purposely arranged to incite the three heroes to kill themselves by means of the two peaches.

Planting a Pear Tree

ACOUNTRYMAN was one day selling his pears in the market. They were unusually sweet and fine flavoured, and the price he asked was high. A Taoist priest in rags and tatters stopped at the barrow and begged one of them. The countryman told him to go away, but as he did not do so he began to curse and swear at him.

The priest said, "You have several hundred pears on your barrow; I ask for a single one, the loss of which, Sir, you would not feel. Why then get angry?" The lookers-on told the countryman to give him an inferior one and let him go, but this he obstinately refused to do. Thereupon the beadle of the place, finding the commotion too great, purchased a pear and handed it to the priest. The latter received it with a bow and turning to the crowd said, "We who have left our homes and given up all that is dear to us are at a loss to understand selfish niggardly conduct in others. Now I have some exquisite pears which I shall do myself the honour to put before you."

Here somebody asked, "Since you have pears yourself, why don't you eat those?" "Because," replied the priest, "I wanted one of these pips to grow them from." So saying, he munched up the pear; and when he had finished took a pip in his hand, unstrapped a pick from his back, and proceeded to make a hole in the ground, several inches deep, wherein he deposited the pip, filling in the earth as before. He then asked the bystanders for a little hot water to water it with, and one among them who loved a joke fetched him some boiling water from a neighbouring shop. The priest poured this over the place where he had made the hole, and every eye was fixed upon him when sprouts were seen shooting up, and gradually growing larger and larger. By-and-by, there was a tree with branches sparsely covered with leaves; then flowers, and last of all fine, large, sweet-smelling pears hanging in great profusion. These the priest picked and handed round to the assembled crowd until all were gone, when he took his pick and hacked away for a long time at the tree, finally cutting it down. This he shouldered, leaves and all, and sauntered quietly away. Now, from the very beginning, our friend the countryman had been amongst the crowd, straining his neck to see what was going on, and forgetting all about his business. At the departure of the priest he turned round and discovered that every one of his pears was gone. He then knew that those the old fellow had been giving away so freely were really his own pears. Looking more closely at the barrow he also found that one of the handles was missing, evidently having been newly cut off. Boiling with rage, he set out in pursuit of the priest, and just as he turned the corner he saw the lost barrow-handle lying under the wall, being in fact the very pear-tree that the priest had cut down. But there were no traces of the priest – much to the amusement of the crowd in the market-place.

Retribution

ONCE UPON A TIME there was a boy named Ma, whose father taught him himself, at home. The window of the upper story looked out on the rear upon a terrace belonging to old Wang, who had a garden of chrysanthemums there. One day Ma rose early, and stood leaning against the window, watching the day

dawn. And out came old Wang from his terrace and watered his chrysanthemums. When he had just finished and was going in again, along came a water-carrier, bearing two pails on his shoulders, who seemed to want to help him. But the old man grew annoyed and motioned him off. Yet the water-carrier insisted on mounting the terrace. So they pulled each other about on the terrace-edge. It had been raining, the terrace was slippery, its border high and narrow, and when the old man thrust back the water-carrier with his hand, the latter lost his balance, slipped and tumbled down the slope. Then the old man hastened down to pick him up; but the two pails had fallen on his chest and he lay there with feet outstretched. The old man was extremely frightened. Without uttering a sound, he took hold of the water-carrier's feet, and dragged him through the back door to the bank of the stream which flowed by the garden. Then he fetched the pails and set them down beside the corpse. After that he went home, locked the door and went to bed again.

Little Ma, in spite of his youth, thought it would be better to say nothing about an affair of this kind, in which a human life was involved. He shut the window and withdrew. The sun rose higher, and soon he heard a clamor without: "A dead man is lying on the river-bank!" The constable gave notice, and in the afternoon the judge came up to the beating of gongs, and the inspector of the dead knelt down and uncovered the corpse; yet the body showed no wound. So it was said: "He slipped and fell to his death!" The judge questioned the neighbors, but the neighbors all insisted that they knew nothing of the matter. Thereupon the judge had the body placed in a coffin, sealed it with his seal, and ordered that the relatives of the deceased be found. And then he went his way.

Nine years passed by, and young Ma had reached the age of twenty-one and become a baccalaureate. His father had died, and the family was poor. So it came about that in the same room in which he had formerly studied his lessons, he now gathered a few pupils about him, to instruct them.

The time for examinations drew near. Ma had risen early, in order to work. He opened the window and there, in the distant alley, he saw a man with two pails gradually drawing nearer. When he looked more closely, it was the water-carrier. Greatly frightened, he thought that he had returned to repay old Wang. Yet he passed the old man's door without entering it. Then he went a few steps further to the house of the Lis; and there went in. The Lis were wealthy people, and since they were near neighbors the Mas and they were on a visiting footing. The matter seemed very questionable to Ma, and he got up and followed the water-carrier.

At the door of Li's house he met an old servant who was just coming out and who said: "Heaven is about to send a child to our mistress! I must go buy incense to burn to the gods in order to show our gratitude!"

Ma asked: "Did not a man with two pails of water on his shoulder just go in?"

The servant said there had not, but before he had finished speaking a maid came from the house and said: "You need not go to buy incense, for I have found some. And, through the favor of heaven, the child has already come to us." Then Ma began to realize that the water-carrier had returned to be born again into the life of earth, and not to exact retribution. He wondered, though, for what merit of his the former water-carrier happened to be re-born into so wealthy a family. So he kept the matter in mind, and from time to time inquired as to the child's well-being.

Seven more years went by, and the boy gradually grew up. He did not show much taste for learning, but he loved to keep birds. Old Wang was still strong and healthy. And though he was by this time more than eighty years old, his love for his chrysanthemums had only increased with age.

One day Ma once more rose early, and stood leaning against his window. And he saw old Wang come out upon his terrace and begin to water his chrysanthemums. Little Li sat in the upper story of his house flying his pigeons. Suddenly some of the pigeons flew down on the railing of the flower-garden. The boy was afraid they might fly off and called them, but the pigeons did not move. The boy did not know what to do: he picked up stones and threw them at the birds. By mistake one of them struck old Wang. The old man started, slipped, and fell down over the terrace. Time passed and he did not rise. He lay there with his feet outstretched. The boy was very much frightened. Without uttering a sound he softly closed his window and went away. The sun gradually rose higher, and the old man's sons and grandsons all came out to look for him. They found him and said: "He slipped and fell to his death!" And they buried him as was the custom.

The Bird with Nine Heads

L ONG, LONG AGO, there once lived a king and a queen who had a daughter. One day, when the daughter went walking in the garden, a tremendous storm suddenly came up and carried her away with it. Now the storm had come from the bird with nine heads, who had robbed the princess, and brought her to his cave. The king did not know whither his daughter had disappeared, so he had proclaimed throughout the land: "Whoever brings back the princess may have her for his bride!"

Now a youth had seen the bird as he was carrying the princess to his cave. This cave, though, was in the middle of a sheer wall of rock. One could not climb up to it from below, nor could one climb down to it from above. And as the youth was walking around the rock, another youth came along and asked him what he was doing there. So the first youth told him that the bird with nine heads had carried off the king's daughter, and had brought her up to his cave. The other chap knew what he had to do. He called together his friends, and they lowered the youth to the cave in a basket. And when he went into the cave, he saw the king's daughter sitting there, and washing the wound of the bird with nine heads; for the hound of heaven had bitten off his tenth head, and his wound was still bleeding. The princess, however, motioned to the youth to hide, and he did so. When the king's daughter had washed his wound and bandaged it, the bird with nine heads felt so comfortable, that one after another, all his nine heads fell asleep. Then the youth stepped forth from his hiding-place, and cut off his nine heads with a sword. But the king's daughter said: "It would be best if you were hauled up first, and I came after."

"No," said the youth. "I will wait below here, until you are in safety." At first the king's daughter was not willing; yet at last she allowed herself to be persuaded, and climbed into the basket. But before she did so, she took a long pin from her hair, broke it into two halves and gave him one and kept the other. She also divided her silken kerchief with him, and told him to take good care of both her gifts. But when the other man had drawn up the king's daughter, he took her along with him, and left the youth in the cave, in spite of all his calling and pleading.

The youth now took a walk about the cave. There he saw a number of maidens, all of whom had been carried off by the bird with nine heads, and who had perished there of hunger. And on the wall hung a fish, nailed against it with four nails. When he touched the fish, the latter turned into a handsome youth, who thanked him for delivering him, and they agreed to regard each other as brothers. Soon the first youth grew very hungry. He stepped out in front of the cave to search for food, but only stones were lying there. Then, suddenly, he saw a great dragon, who was licking a stone. The youth imitated him, and before long his hunger had disappeared. He next asked the dragon how he could get away from the cave, and the dragon nodded his head in the direction of his tail, as much as to say he should seat himself upon it. So he climbed up, and in the twinkling of an eye he was down on the ground, and the dragon had disappeared. He then went on until he found a tortoise-shell full of beautiful pearls. But they were magic pearls, for if you flung them into the fire, the fire ceased to burn and if you flung them into the water, the water divided and you could walk through the midst of it. The youth took the pearls out of the tortoise-shell, and put them in his pocket. Not long after he reached the sea-shore. Here he flung a pearl into the sea, and at once the waters divided and he could see the sea-dragon. The sea-dragon cried: "Who is disturbing me here in my own kingdom?" The youth answered: "I found pearls in a tortoise-shell, and have flung one into the sea, and now the waters have divided for me."

"If that is the case," said the dragon, "then come into the sea with me and we will live there together." Then the youth recognized him for the same dragon whom he had seen in the cave. And with him was the youth with whom he had formed a bond of brotherhood: He was the dragon's son.

"Since you have saved my son and become his brother, I am your father," said the old dragon. And he entertained him hospitably with food and wine.

One day his friend said to him: "My father is sure to want to reward you. But accept no money, nor any jewels from him, but only the little gourd flask over yonder. With it you can conjure up whatever you wish."

And, sure enough, the old dragon asked him what he wanted by way of a reward, and the youth answered: "I want no money, nor any jewels. All I want is the little gourd flask over yonder."

At first the dragon did not wish to give it up, but at last he did let him have it, after all. And then the youth left the dragon's castle.

When he set his foot on dry land again he felt hungry. At once a table stood before him, covered with a fine and plenteous meal. He ate and drank. After he had gone on a while, he felt weary. And there stood an ass, waiting for him, on which he mounted. After he had ridden for a while, the ass's gait seemed too uneven, and along came a wagon, into which he climbed. But the wagon shook him up too, greatly, and he thought: "If I only had a litter! That would suit me better." No more had he thought so, than the litter came along, and he seated himself in it. And the bearers carried him to the city in which dwelt the king, the queen and their daughter.

When the other youth had brought back the king's daughter, it was decided to hold the wedding. But the king's daughter was not willing, and said: "He is not the right man. My deliverer will come and bring with him half of the long pin for my hair, and half my silken kerchief as a token." But when the youth did not appear for so long a time, and the other one pressed the king, the king grew impatient and said: "The wedding shall take place tomorrow!" Then the king's daughter went sadly through the streets of the city, and searched and searched in the hope of finding her deliverer. And this was on the very day that the litter arrived. The king's daughter saw the half of her silken handkerchief in the youth's hand, and filled with joy, she led him to her father. There he had to show his half of the long pin, which fitted the other exactly, and then the king was convinced that he was the right, true deliverer. The false bridegroom was now punished, the wedding celebrated, and they lived in peace and happiness till the end of their days.

The Flower Elves

ONCE UPON A TIME there was a scholar who lived retired from the world in order to gain hidden wisdom. He lived alone and in a secret place. And all about the little house in which he dwelt he had planted every kind of flower, and bamboos and other trees. There it lay, quite concealed in its thick grove of flowers. With him he had only a boy servant, who dwelt in a separate hut, and who carried out his orders. He was not allowed to appear before his master unless summoned. The scholar loved his flowers as he did himself. Never did he set his foot beyond the boundaries of his garden.

It chanced that once there came a lovely spring evening. Flowers and trees stood in full bloom, a fresh breeze was blowing, the moon shone clearly. And the scholar sat over his goblet and was grateful for the gift of life.

Suddenly he saw a maiden in dark garments come tripping up in the moonlight. She made a deep courtesy, greeted him and said: "I am your neighbor. We are a company of young maids who are on our way to visit the eighteen aunts. We should like to rest in this court for awhile, and therefore ask your permission to do so."

The scholar saw that this was something quite out of the common, and gladly gave his consent. The maiden thanked him and went away.

In a short time she brought back a whole crowd of maids carrying flowers and willow branches. All greeted the scholar. They were charming, with delicate features, and slender, graceful figures. When they moved their sleeves, a delightful fragrance was exhaled. There is no fragrance known to the human world which could be compared with it.

The scholar invited them to sit down for a time in his room. Then he asked them: "Whom have I really the honor of entertaining? Have you come from the castle of the Lady in the Moon, or the Jade Spring of the Queen-Mother of the West?"

"How could we claim such high descent?" said a maiden in a green gown, with a smile. "My name is Salix." Then she presented another, clad in white, and said: "This is Mistress Prunophora"; then one in rose, "and this is Persica"; and finally one in a dark-red gown, "and this is Punica. We are all sisters and we want to visit the eighteen zephyr-aunts to-day. The moon shines so beautifully this evening and it is so charming here in the garden. We are most grateful to you for taking pity on us."

"Yes, yes," said the scholar.

Then the sober-clad servant suddenly announced: "The zephyr-aunts have already arrived!"

At once the girls rose and went to the door to meet them.

"We were just about to visit you, aunts," they said, smiling. "This gentleman here had just invited us to sit for a moment. What a pleasant coincidence that you aunts have come here, too. This is such a lovely night that we must drink a goblet of nectar in honor of you aunts!"

Thereon they ordered the servant to bring what was needed.

"May one sit down here?" asked the aunts.

"The master of the house is most kind," replied the maids, "and the spot is quiet and hidden."

And then they presented the aunts to the scholar. He spoke a few kindly words to the eighteen aunts. They had a somewhat irresponsible and airy manner. Their words fairly gushed out, and in their neighborhood one felt a frosty chill.

Meanwhile the servant had already brought in table and chairs. The eighteen aunts sat at the upper end of the board, the maids followed, and the scholar sat down with them at the lowest place. Soon the entire table was covered with the most delicious foods and most magnificent fruits, and the goblets were filled with a fragrant nectar. They were delights such as the world of men does not know! The moon shone brightly and the flowers exhaled intoxicating odors. After they had partaken of food and drink the maids rose, danced and sung. Sweetly the sound of their singing echoed through the falling gloam, and their dance was like that of butterflies fluttering about the flowers. The scholar was so overpowered with delight that he no longer knew whether he were in heaven or on earth.

When the dance had ended, the girls sat down again at the table, and drank the health of the aunts in flowing nectar. The scholar, too, was remembered with a toast, to which he replied with well-turned phrases.

But the eighteen aunts were somewhat irresponsible in their ways. One of them, raising her goblet, by accident poured some nectar on Punica's dress. Punica, who was young and fiery, and very neat, stood up angrily when she saw the spot on her red dress.

"You are really very careless," said she, in her anger. "My other sisters may be afraid of you, but I am not!"

Then the aunts grew angry as well and said: "How dare this young chit insult us in such a manner!"

And with that they gathered up their garments and rose.

All the maids then crowded about them and said: "Punica is so young and inexperienced! You must not bear her any ill-will! Tomorrow she shall go to you switch in hand, and receive her punishment!"

But the eighteen aunts would not listen to them and went off. Thereupon the maids also said farewell, scattered among the flower-beds and disappeared. The scholar sat for a long time lost in dreamy yearning.

On the following evening the maids all came back again.

"We all live in your garden," they told him. "Every year we are tormented by naughty winds, and therefore we have always asked the eighteen aunts to protect us. But yesterday Punica insulted them, and now we fear they will help us no more. But we know that you have always been well disposed toward us, for which we are heartily grateful. And now we have a great favor to ask, that every New Year's day you make a small scarlet flag, paint the sun, moon and five planets on it, and set it up in the eastern part of the garden. Then we sisters will be left in peace and will be protected from all evil. But since New Year's day has passed for this year, we beg that you will set up the flag on the twenty-first of this month. For the East Wind is coming and the flag will protect us against him!"

The scholar readily promised to do as they wished, and the maids all said with a single voice: "We thank you for your great kindness and will repay it!" Then they departed and a sweet fragrance filled the entire garden.

The scholar, however, made a red flag as described, and when early in the morning of the day in question the East Wind really did begin to blow, he quickly set it up in the garden.

Suddenly a wild storm broke out, one that caused the forests to bend, and broke the trees. The flowers in the garden alone did not move.

Then the scholar noticed that Salix was the willow; Prunophora the plum; Persica the peach, and the saucy Punica the Pomegranate, whose powerful blossoms the wind cannot tear. The eighteen zephyr-aunts, however, were the spirits of the winds.

In the evening the flower-elves all came and brought the scholar radiant flowers as a gift of thanks.

"You have saved us," they said, "and we have nothing else we can give you. If you eat these flowers you will live long and avoid old age. And if you, in turn, will protect us every year, then we sisters, too, will live long."

The scholar did as they told him and ate the flowers. And his figure changed and he grew young again like a youth of twenty. And in the course of time he attained the hidden wisdom and was placed among the Immortals.

The Golden Nugget

ONCE UPON A TIME many, many years ago, there lived in China two friends named Ki-wu and Pao-shu. These two young men, like Damon and Pythias, loved each other and were always together. No cross words passed between them; no unkind thoughts marred their friendship. Many an interesting tale might be told of their unselfishness, and of how the good fairies gave them the true reward of virtue. One story alone, however, will be enough to show how strong was their affection and their goodness.

It was a bright beautiful day in early spring when Ki-wu and Pao-shu set out for a stroll together, for they were tired of the city and its noises.

"Let us go into the heart of the pine forest," said Ki-wu lightly. "There we can forget the cares that worry us; there we can breathe the sweetness of the flowers and lie on the moss-covered ground."

"Good!" said Pao-shu, "I, too, am tired. The forest is the place for rest."

Happy as two lovers on a holiday, they passed along the winding road, their eyes turned in longing toward the distant tree-tops. Their hearts beat fast in youthful pleasure as they drew nearer and nearer to the woods.

"For thirty days I have worked over my books," sighed Ki-wu. "For thirty days I have not had a rest. My head is stuffed so full of wisdom, that I am afraid it will burst. Oh, for a breath of the pure air blowing through the greenwood."

"And I," added Pao-shu sadly, "have worked like a slave at my counter and found it just as dull as you have found your books. My master treats me badly. It seems good, indeed, to get beyond his reach."

Now they came to the border of the grove, crossed a little stream, and plunged headlong among the trees and shrubs. For many an hour they rambled on, talking and laughing merrily; when suddenly on passing round a clump of flower-covered bushes, they saw shining in the pathway directly in front of them a lump of gold.

"See!" said both, speaking at the same time, and pointing toward the treasure.

Ki-wu, stooping, picked up the nugget. It was nearly as large as a lemon, and was very pretty. "It is yours, my dear friend," said he, at the same time handing it to Pao-shu; "yours because you saw it first."

"No, no," answered Pao-shu, "you are wrong, my brother, for you were first to speak. Now, you can never say hereafter that the good fairies have not rewarded you for all your faithful hours of study."

"Repaid me for my study! Why, that is impossible. Are not the wise men always saying that study brings its own reward? No, the gold is yours: I insist upon it. Think of your weeks of hard labour – of the masters that have ground you to the bone! Here is something far better. Take it," laughing. "May it be the nest egg by means of which you may hatch out a great fortune."

Thus they joked for some minutes, each refusing to take the treasure for himself; each insisting that it belonged to the other. At last, the chunk of gold was dropped in the very spot where they had first spied it, and the two comrades went away, each happy because he loved his friend better than anything else in the world. Thus they turned their backs on any chance of quarrelling.

"It was not for gold that we left the city," exclaimed Ki-wu warmly.

"No," replied his friend, "One day in this forest is worth a thousand nuggets."

"Let us go to the spring and sit down on the rocks," suggested Ki-wu. "It is the coolest spot in the whole grove."

When they reached the spring they were sorry to find the place already occupied. A countryman was stretched at full length on the ground.

"Wake up, fellow!" cried Pao-shu, "there is money for you near by. Up yonder path a golden apple is waiting for some man to go and pick it up."

Then they described to the unwelcome stranger the exact spot where the treasure was, and were delighted to see him set out in eager search.

For an hour they enjoyed each other's company, talking of all the hopes and ambitions of their future, and listening to the music of the birds that hopped about on the branches overhead.

At last they were startled by the angry voice of the man who had gone after the nugget. "What trick is this you have played on me, masters? Why do you make a poor man like me run his legs off for nothing on a hot day?"

"What do you mean, fellow?" asked Ki-wu, astonished. "Did you not find the fruit we told you about?"

"No," he answered, in a tone of half-hidden rage, "but in its place a monster snake, which I cut in two with my blade. Now, the gods will bring me bad luck for killing something in the woods. If you thought you could drive me from this place by such a trick, you'll soon find you were mistaken, for I was first upon this spot and you have no right to give me orders."

"Stop your chatter, bumpkin, and take this copper for your trouble. We thought we were doing you a favour. If you are blind, there's no one but yourself to blame. Come, Pao-shu, let us go back and have a look at this wonderful snake that has been hiding in a chunk of gold."

Laughing merrily, the two companions left the countryman and turned back in search of the nugget.

"If I am not mistaken," said the student, "the gold lies beyond that fallen tree."

"Quite true; we shall soon see the dead snake."

Quickly they crossed the remaining stretch of pathway, with their eyes fixed intently on the ground. Arriving at the spot where they had left the shining treasure, what was their surprise to see, not the lump of gold, not the dead snake described by the idler, but, instead, two beautiful golden nuggets, each larger than the one they had seen at first.

Each friend picked up one of these treasures and handed it joyfully to his companion.

"At last the fairies have rewarded you for your unselfishness!" said Ki-wu.

"Yes," answered Pao-shu, "by granting me a chance to give you your deserts."

The King of the Ants

ONCE UPON A TIME there was a scholar, who wandered away from his home and went to Emmet village. There stood a house which was said to be haunted. Yet it was beautifully situated and surrounded by a lovely garden. So the scholar hired it. One evening he was sitting over his books, when several hundred knights suddenly came galloping into the room. They were quite tiny, and their horses were about the size of flies. They had hunting falcons and dogs about as large as gnats and fleas.

They came to his bed in the corner of the room, and there they held a great hunt, with bows and arrows: one could see it all quite plainly. They caught a tremendous quantity of birds and game, and all this game was no larger than little grains of rice.

When the hunt was over, in came a long procession with banners and standards. They wore swords at their side and bore spears in their hands, and came to a halt in the north-west corner of the room. They were followed by several hundred serving-men. These brought with them curtains and covers, tents and tent-poles, pots and kettles, cups and plates, tables and chairs. And after them some hundreds of other servants carried in all sorts of fine dishes, the best that land and water had to offer. And several hundred more ran to and fro without stopping, in order to guard the roads and carry messages.

The scholar gradually accustomed himself to the sight. Although the men were so very small he could distinguish everything quite clearly.

Before long, a bright colored banner appeared. Behind it rode a personage wearing a scarlet hat and garments of purple. He was surrounded by an escort of several thousands. Before him went runners with whips and rods to clear the way.

Then a man wearing an iron helmet and with a golden ax in his hand cried out in a loud voice: "His Highness is graciously pleased to look at the fish in the Purple Lake!" Whereupon the one who wore the scarlet hat got down from his horse, and, followed by a retinue of several hundred men, approached the saucer which the scholar used for his writing-ink. Tents were put up on the edge of the saucer and a banquet was prepared. A great number of guests sat down to the table. Musicians and dancers stood ready. There was a bright confusion of mingled garments of purple and scarlet, crimson and green. Pipes and flutes, fiddles and cymbals sounded, and the dancers moved in the dance. The music was very faint, and yet its melodies could be clearly distinguished. All that was said, too, the table-talk and orders, questions and calls, could be quite distinctly heard.

After three courses, he who wore the scarlet hat said: "Quick! Make ready the nets and lines for fishing!"

And at once nets were thrown out into the saucer which held the water in which the scholar dipped his brush. And they caught hundreds of thousands of fishes. The one with the scarlet hat contented himself with casting a line in the shallow waters of the saucer, and caught a baker's dozen of red carp.

Then he ordered the head cook to cook the fish, and the most varied dishes were prepared with them. The odor of roasting fat and spices filled the whole room.

And then the wearer of the scarlet hat in his arrogance, decided to amuse himself at the scholar's expense. So he pointed to him and said: "I know nothing at all about the writings and customs of the saints and wise men, and still I am a king who is highly honored! Yonder scholar spends his whole life toiling over his books and yet he remains poor and gets nowhere. If he could make up his mind to serve me faithfully as one of my officials, I might allow him to partake of our meal."

This angered the scholar, and he took his book and struck at them. And they all scattered, wriggling and crawling out of the door. He followed them and dug up the earth in the place where they had disappeared. And there he found an ants' nest as large as a barrel, in which countless green ants were wriggling around. So he built a large fire and smoked them out.

The Nodding Tiger

JUST OUTSIDE THE WALLS of a Chinese city there lived a young woodcutter named T'ang and his old mother, a woman of seventy. They were very poor and had a tiny one-room shanty, built of mud and grass, which they rented from a neighbour. Every day young T'ang rose bright and early and went up on the mountain near their house. There he spent the day cutting firewood to sell in the city near by. In the evening he would return home, take the wood to market, sell it, and bring back food for his mother and himself. Now, though these two people were poor, they were very happy, for the young man loved his mother dearly, and the old woman thought there was no one like her son in all the world. Their friends, however, felt sorry for them and said, "What a pity we have no grasshoppers here, so that the T'angs could have some food from heaven!"

One day young T'ang got up before daylight and started for the hills, carrying his axe on his shoulder. He bade his mother good-bye, telling her that he would be back early with a heavier load of wood than usual, for the morrow would be a holiday and they must eat good food. All day long Widow T'ang waited patiently, saying to herself over and over as she went about her simple work, "The good boy, the good boy, how he loves his old mother!"

In the afternoon she began watching for his return – but in vain. The sun was sinking lower and lower in the west, but still he did not come. At last the old woman was frightened. "My poor son!" she muttered. "Something has happened to him." Straining her feeble eyes, she looked along the mountain path. Nothing was to be seen there but a flock of sheep following the shepherd. "Woe is me!" moaned the woman. "My boy! my boy!" She took her crutch from its corner and limped off to a neighbour's house to tell him of her trouble and beg him to go and look for the missing boy.

Now this neighbour was kind-hearted, and willing to help old Mother T'ang, for he felt very sorry for her. "There are many wild beasts in the mountains," he said, shaking his head as he walked away with her, thinking to prepare the frightened woman for the worst, "and I fear that your son has been carried off by one of them." Widow T'ang gave a scream of horror and sank upon the ground. Her friend walked slowly up the mountain path, looking carefully for signs of a struggle. At last when he had gone half way up the slope he came to a little pile of torn clothing spattered with blood. The woodman's axe was lying by the side of the path, also his carrying pole and some rope. There could be no mistake: after making a brave fight, the poor youth had been carried off by a tiger.

Gathering up the torn garments, the man went sadly down the hill. He dreaded seeing the poor mother and telling her that her only boy was indeed gone for ever. At the foot of the mountain he found her still lying on the ground. When she looked up and saw what he was carrying, with a cry of despair she fainted away. She did not need to be told what had happened.

Friends bore her into the little house and gave her food, but they could not comfort her. "Alas!" she cried, "of what use is it to live? He was my only boy. Who will take care of me in my old age? Why have the gods treated me in this cruel way?"

She wept, tore her hair, and beat her chest, until people said she had gone mad. The longer she mourned, the more violent she became.

The next day, however, much to the surprise of her neighbours, she set out for the city, making her way along slowly by means of her crutch. It was a pitiful sight to see her, so old, so feeble, and so lonely. Everyone was sorry for her and pointed her out, saying, "See! the poor old soul has no one to help her!"

In the city she asked her way to the public hall. When she found the place she knelt at the front gate, calling out loudly and telling of her ill-fortune. Just at this moment the mandarin, or city judge, walked into the court room to try any cases which might be brought before him. He heard the old woman weeping and wailing outside, and bade one of the servants let her enter and tell him of her wrongs.

Now this was just what the Widow T'ang had come for. Calming herself, she hobbled into the great hall of trial.

"What is the matter, old woman? Why do you raise such an uproar in front of my yamen? Speak up quickly and tell me of your trouble."

"I am old and feeble," she began; "lame and almost blind. I have no money and no way of earning money. I have not one relative now in all the empire. I depended on my only son for a living. Every day he climbed the mountain, for he was a woodcutter, and every evening he came back home, bringing enough money for our food. But yesterday he went and did not return. A mountain tiger carried him off and ate him, and now, alas! there seems to be no help for it – I must die of hunger. My bleeding heart cries out for justice. I have come into this hall to-day, to beg your worship to see that the slayer of my son is punished. Surely the law says that none may shed blood without giving his own blood in payment."

"But, woman, are you mad?" cried the mandarin, laughing loudly. "Did you not say it was a tiger that killed your son? How can a tiger be brought to justice? Of a truth, you must have lost your senses."

The judge's questions were of no avail. The Widow T'ang kept up her clamour. She would not be turned away until she had gained her purpose. The hall echoed with the noise of her howling. The mandarin could stand it no longer. "Hold! woman," he cried, "stop your shrieking. I will do what you ask. Only go home and wait until I summon you to court. The slayer of your son shall be caught and punished."

The judge was, of course, only trying to get rid of the demented mother, thinking that if she were only once out of his sight, he could give orders not to let her into the hall again. The old woman, however, was too sharp for him. She saw through his plan and became more stubborn than ever.

"No, I cannot go," she answered, "until I have seen you sign the order for that tiger to be caught and brought into this judgment hall."

Now, as the judge was not really a bad man, he decided to humour the old woman in her strange plea. Turning to the assistants in the court room he asked which of them would be willing to go in search of the tiger. One of these men, named Li-neng, had been leaning against the wall, half asleep. He had been drinking heavily and so had not heard what had been going on in the room. One of his friends gave him a poke in the ribs just as the judge asked for volunteers.

Thinking the judge had called him by name, he stepped forward, knelt on the floor, saying, "I, Li-neng, can go and do the will of your worship."

"Very well, you will do," answered the judge. "Here is your order. Go forth and do your duty." So saying, he handed the warrant to Li-neng. "Now, old woman, are you satisfied?" he continued.

"Quite satisfied, your worship," she replied.

"Then go home and wait there until I send for you."

Mumbling a few words of thanks, the unhappy mother left the building.

When Li-neng went outside the court room, his friends crowded round him. "Drunken sot!" they laughed; "do you know what you have done?"

Li-neng shook his head. "Just a little business for the mandarin, isn't it? Quite easy."

"Call it easy, if you like. What! man, arrest a tiger, a man-eating tiger and bring him to the city! Better go and say good-bye to your father and mother. They will never see you again."

Li-neng slept off his drunkenness, and then saw that his friends were right. He had been very foolish. But surely the judge had meant the whole thing only as a joke! No such order had ever been written before! It was plain that the judge had hit on this plan simply to get rid of the wailing old woman. Li-neng took the warrant back to the judgment hall and told the mandarin that the tiger could not be found.

But the judge was in no mood for joking. "Can't be found? And why not? You agreed to arrest this tiger. Why is it that to-day you try to get out of your promise? I can by no means permit this, for I have given my word to satisfy the old woman in her cry for justice."

Li-neng knelt and knocked his head on the floor. "I was drunk," he cried, "when I gave my promise. I knew not what you were asking. I can catch a man, but not a tiger. I know nothing of such matters. Still, if you wish it, I can go into the hills and hire hunters to help me."

"Very well, it makes no difference how you catch him, as long as you bring him into court. If you fail in your duty, there is nothing left but to beat you until you succeed. I give you five days."

During the next few days Li-neng left no stone unturned in trying to find the guilty tiger. The best hunters in the country were employed. Night and day they searched the hills, hiding in mountain caves, watching and waiting, but finding nothing. It was all very trying for Li-neng, since he now feared the heavy hands of the judge more than the claws of the tiger. On the fifth day he had to report his failure. He received a thorough beating, fifty blows on the back. But that was not the worst of it. During the next six weeks, try as he would, he could find no traces of the missing animal. At the end of each five days, he got another beating for his pains. The poor fellow was in despair. Another month of such treatment would lay him on his deathbed. This he knew very well, and yet he had little hope. His friends shook their heads when they saw him. "He is drawing near the wood," they said to each other, meaning that he would soon be in his coffin. "Why don't you flee the country?" they asked him. "Follow the tiger's example. You see he has escaped completely. The judge would make no effort to catch you if you should go across the border into the next province."

Li-neng shook his head on hearing this advice. He had no desire to leave his family for ever, and he felt sure of being caught and put to death if he should try to run away.

One day after all the hunters had given up the search in disgust and gone back to their homes in the valley, Li-neng entered a mountain temple to pray. The tears rained down his cheeks as he knelt before the great fierce-looking idol. "Alas! I am a dead man!" he moaned between his prayers; "a dead man, for now there is no hope. Would that I had never touched a drop of wine!"

Just then he heard a slight rustling near by. Looking up, he saw a huge tiger standing at the temple gate. But Li-neng was no longer afraid of tigers.

He knew there was only one way to save himself. "Ah," he said, looking the great cat straight in the eye, "you have come to eat me, have you? Well, I fear you would find my flesh a trifle tough, since I have been beaten with four hundred blows during these six weeks. You are the same fellow that carried off the woodman last month, aren't you? This woodman was an only son, the sole support of an old mother. Now this poor woman has reported you to the mandarin, who, in turn, has had a warrant drawn up for your arrest. I have been sent out to find you and lead you to trial. For some reason or other you have acted the coward, and remained in hiding. This has been the cause of my beating. Now I don't want to suffer any longer as a result of your murder. You must come with me to the city and answer the charge of killing the woodman."

All the time Li-neng was speaking, the tiger listened closely. When the man was silent, the animal made no effort to escape, but, on the contrary, seemed willing and ready to be captured. He bent his head forward and let Li-neng slip a strong chain over it. Then he followed the man quietly down the mountain, through the crowded streets of the city, into the court room. All along the way there was great excitement. "The man-slaying tiger has been caught," shouted the people. "He is being led to trial."

The crowd followed Li-neng into the hall of justice. When the judge walked in, everyone became as quiet as the grave. All were filled with wonder at the strange sight of a tiger being called before a judge.

The great animal did not seem to be afraid of those who were watching so curiously. He sat down in front of the mandarin, for all the world like a huge cat. The judge rapped on the table as a signal that all was ready for the trial.

"Tiger," said he, turning toward the prisoner, "did you eat the woodman whom you are charged with killing?"

The tiger gravely nodded his head.

"Yes, he killed my boy!" screamed the aged mother. "Kill him! Give him the death that he deserves!"

"A life for a life is the law of the land," continued the judge, paying no attention to the forlorn mother, but looking the accused directly in the eye. "Did you not know it? You have robbed a helpless old woman of her only son. There are no relatives to support her. She is crying for vengeance. You must be punished for your crime. The law must be enforced. However, I am not a cruel judge. If you can promise to take the place of this widow's son and support the woman in her old age, I am quite willing to spare you from a disgraceful death. What say you, will you accept my offer?"

The gaping people craned their necks to see what would happen, and once more they were surprised to see the savage beast nod his head in silent agreement.

"Very well, then, you are free to return to your mountain home; only, of course, you must remember your promise."

The chains were taken from the tiger's neck, and the great animal walked silently out of the yamen, down the street, and through the gate opening towards his beloved mountain cave.

Once more the old woman was very angry. As she hobbled from the room, she cast sour glances at the judge, muttering over and over again, "Who ever heard of a tiger taking the place of a son? A pretty game this is, to catch the brute, and then to set him free." There was nothing for her to do, however, but to return home, for the judge had given strict orders that on no account was she to appear before him again.

Almost broken-hearted she entered her desolate hovel at the foot of the mountain. Her neighbours shook their heads as they saw her. "She cannot live long," they said. "She has the look of death on her wrinkled face. Poor soul! she has nothing to live for, nothing to keep her from starving."

But they were mistaken. Next morning when the old woman went outside to get a breath of fresh air she found a newly killed deer in front of her door. Her tiger-son had begun to keep his promise, for she could see the marks of his claws on the dead animal's body. She took the carcass into the house and dressed it for the market. On the city streets next day she had no trouble in selling the flesh and skin for a handsome sum of money. All had heard of the tiger's first gift, and no one was anxious to drive a close bargain.

Laden with food, the happy woman went home rejoicing, with money enough to keep her for many a day. A week later the tiger came to her door with a roll of cloth and some money in his mouth. He dropped these new gifts at her feet and ran away without even waiting for her thank-you. The

Widow T'ang now saw that the judge had acted wisely. She stopped grieving for her dead son and began to love in his stead the handsome animal that had come to take his place so willingly.

The tiger grew much attached to his foster-mother and often purred contentedly outside her door, waiting for her to come and stroke his soft fur. He no longer had the old desire to kill. The sight of blood was not nearly so tempting as it had been in his younger days. Year after year he brought the weekly offerings to his mistress until she was as well provided for as any other widow in the country.

At last in the course of nature the good old soul died. Kind friends laid her away in her last resting place at the foot of the great mountain. There was money enough left out of what she had saved to put up a handsome tombstone, on which this story was written just as you have read it here. The faithful tiger mourned long for his dear mistress. He lay on her grave, wailing like a child that had lost its mother. Long he listened for the voice he had loved so well, long he searched the mountain-slopes, returning each night to the empty cottage, but all in vain. She whom he loved was gone for ever.

One night he vanished from the mountain, and from that day to this no one in that province has ever seen him. Some who know this story say that he died of grief in a secret cave which he had long used as a hiding-place. Others add, with a wise shrug of the shoulders, that, like Shanwang, he was taken to the Western Heaven, there to be rewarded for his deeds of virtue and to live as a fairy for ever afterwards.

The Return of Yen-Tchin-King

IN THE THIRTY-EIGHTH CHAPTER of the holy book, Kan-ing-p'ien, wherein the Recompense of Immortality is considered, may be found the legend of Yen-Tchin-King. A thousand years have passed since the passing of the good Tchin-King; for it was in the period of the greatness of Thang that he lived and died.

Now, in those days when Yen-Tchin-King was Supreme Judge of one of the Six August Tribunals, one Li-hi-lie, a soldier mighty for evil, lifted the black banner of revolt, and drew after him, as a tide of destruction, the millions of the northern provinces. And learning of these things, and knowing also that Hi-lie was the most ferocious of men, who respected nothing on earth save fearlessness, the Son of Heaven commanded Tchin-King that he should visit Hi-lie and strive to recall the rebel to duty, and read unto the people who followed after him in revolt the Emperor's letter of reproof and warning. For Tchin-King was famed throughout the provinces for his wisdom, his rectitude, and his fearlessness; and the Son of Heaven believed that if Hi-lie would listen to the words of any living man steadfast in loyalty and virtue, he would listen to the words of Tchin-King. So Tchin-King arrayed himself in his robes of office, and set his house in order; and, having embraced his wife and his children, mounted his horse and rode away alone to the roaring camp of the rebels, bearing the Emperor's letter in his bosom. "I shall return; fear not!" were his last words to the gray servant who watched him from the terrace as he rode.

* * *

And Tchin-King at last descended from his horse, and entered into the rebel camp, and, passing through that huge gathering of war, stood in the presence of Hi-lie. High sat the rebel among his chiefs, encircled by the wave-lightning of swords and the thunders of ten thousand gongs: above him undulated the silken folds of the Black Dragon, while a vast fire rose bickering before him. Also Tchin-King saw that the tongues of that fire were licking human bones, and that skulls of men lay blackening among the ashes. Yet he was not afraid to look upon the fire, nor into the eyes of Hi-lie; but drawing from his bosom the roll of perfumed yellow silk upon which the words of the Emperor were written, and kissing it, he made ready to read, while the multitude became silent. Then, in a strong, clear voice he began:

"The words of the Celestial and August, the Son of Heaven, the Divine Ko-Tsu-Tchin-Yao-ti, unto the rebel Li-Hi-lie and those that follow him."

And a roar went up like the roar of the sea – a roar of rage, and the hideous battle-moan, like the moan of a forest in storm – "Hoo! hoo-oo-oo-oo!"

– and the sword-lightnings brake loose, and the thunder of the gongs moved the ground beneath the messenger's feet. But Hi-lie waved his gilded wand, and again there was silence. "Nay!" spake the rebel chief; "let the dog bark!" So Tchin-King spake on:

"Knowest thou not, O most rash and foolish of men, that thou leadest the people only into the mouth of the Dragon of Destruction? Knowest thou not, also, that the people of my kingdom are the first-born of the Master of Heaven? So it hath been written that he who doth needlessly subject the people to wounds and death shall not be suffered by Heaven to live! Thou who wouldst subvert those laws founded by the wise – those laws in obedience to which may happiness and prosperity alone be found – thou art committing the greatest of all crimes – the crime that is never forgiven!

"O my people, think not that I your Emperor, I your Father, seek your destruction. I desire only your happiness, your prosperity, your greatness; let not your folly provoke the severity of your Celestial Parent. Follow not after madness and blind rage; hearken rather to the wise words of my messenger."

"Hoo! hoo-oo-oo-oo-oo!" roared the people, gathering fury. "Hoo! hoo-oo-oo-oo!" – till the mountains rolled back the cry like the rolling of a typhoon; and once more the pealing of the gongs paralyzed voice and hearing. Then Tchin-King, looking at Hi-lie, saw that he laughed, and that the words of the letter would not again be listened to. Therefore he read on to the end without looking about him, resolved to perform his mission in so far as lay in his power. And having read all, he would have given the letter to Hi-lie; but Hi-lie would not extend his hand to take it. Therefore Tchin-King replaced it in his bosom, and folding his arms, looked Hi-lie calmly in the face, and waited. Again Hi-lie waved his gilded wand; and the roaring ceased, and the booming of the gongs, until nothing save the fluttering of the Dragon-banner could be heard. Then spake Hi-lie, with an evil smile:

"Tchin-King, O son of a dog! if thou dost not now take the oath of fealty, and bow thyself before me, and salute me with the salutation of Emperors – even with the luh-kao, the triple prostration – into that fire thou shalt be thrown."

But Tchin-King, turning his back upon the usurper, bowed himself a moment in worship to Heaven and Earth; and then rising suddenly, ere any man could lay hand upon him, he leaped into the towering flame, and stood there, with folded arms, like a God.

Then Hi-lie leaped to his feet in amazement, and shouted to his men; and they snatched Tchin-King from the fire, and wrung the flames from his robes with their naked hands, and extolled him, and praised him to his face. And even Hi-lie himself descended from his seat, and spoke fair words to him, saying: "O Tchin-King, I see thou art indeed a brave man and true, and worthy of all honor; be seated among us, I pray thee, and partake of whatever it is in our power to bestow!"

But Tchin-King, looking upon him unswervingly, replied in a voice clear as the voice of a great bell:

"Never, O Hi-lie, shall I accept aught from thy hand, save death, so long as thou shalt continue in the path of wrath and folly. And never shall it be said that Tchin-King sat him down among rebels and traitors, among murderers and robbers."

Then Hi-lie in sudden fury, smote him with his sword; and Tchin-King fell to the earth and died, striving even in his death to bow his head toward the South – toward the place of the Emperor's palace – toward the presence of his beloved Master.

* * *

Even at the same hour the Son of Heaven, alone in the inner chamber of his palace, became aware of a Shape prostrate before his feet; and when he spake, the Shape arose and stood before him, and he saw that it was Tchin-King. And the Emperor would have questioned him; yet ere he could question, the familiar voice spake, saying:

"Son of Heaven, the mission confided to me I have performed; and thy command hath been accomplished to the extent of thy humble servant's feeble power. But even now must I depart, that I may enter the service of another Master."

And looking, the Emperor perceived that the Golden Tigers upon the wall were visible through the form of Tchin-King; and a strange coldness, like a winter wind, passed through the chamber; and the figure faded out. Then the Emperor knew that the Master of whom his faithful servant had spoken was none other than the Master of Heaven.

Also at the same hour the gray servant of Tchin-King's house beheld him passing through the apartments, smiling as he was wont to smile when he saw that all things were as he desired. "Is it well with thee, my lord?" questioned the aged man. And a voice answered him: "It is well"; but the presence of Tchin-King had passed away before the answer came.

* * *

So the armies of the Son of Heaven strove with the rebels. But the land was soaked with blood and blackened with fire; and the corpses of whole populations were carried by the rivers to feed the fishes of the sea; and still the war prevailed through many a long red year. Then came to aid the Son of Heaven the hordes that dwell in the desolations of the West and North – horsemen born, a nation of wild archers, each mighty to bend a two-hundred-pound bow until the ears should meet. And as a whirlwind they came against rebellion, raining raven-feathered arrows in a storm of death; and they prevailed against Hi-lie and his people. Then those that survived destruction and defeat submitted, and promised allegiance; and once more was the law of righteousness restored. But Tchin-King had been dead for many summers.

And the Son of Heaven sent word to his victorious generals that they should bring back with them the bones of his faithful servant, to be laid with honor in a mausoleum erected by imperial decree. So the generals of the Celestial and August sought after the nameless grave and found it, and had the earth taken up, and made ready to remove the coffin.

But the coffin crumbled into dust before their eyes; for the worms had gnawed it, and the hungry earth had devoured its substance, leaving only a phantom shell that vanished at touch of the light. And lo! as it vanished, all beheld lying there the perfect form and features of the good Tchin-King. Corruption had not touched him, nor had the worms disturbed his rest, nor had the bloom of life departed from his face. And he seemed to dream only – comely to see as upon the morning of his bridal, and smiling as the holy images smile, with eyelids closed, in the twilight of the great pagodas.

Then spoke a priest, standing by the grave: "O my children, this is indeed a Sign from the Master of Heaven; in such wise do the Powers Celestial preserve them that are chosen to be numbered with the Immortals. Death may not prevail over them, neither may corruption come nigh them. Verily the blessed Tchin-King hath taken his place among the divinities of Heaven!"

Then they bore Tchin-King back to his native place, and laid him with highest honors in the mausoleum which the Emperor had commanded; and there he sleeps, incorruptible forever, arrayed in his robes of state. Upon his tomb are sculptured the emblems of his greatness and his wisdom and his virtue, and the signs of his office, and the Four Precious Things: and the monsters which are holy symbols mount giant guard in stone about it; and the weird Dogs of Fo keep watch before it, as before the temples of the gods.

FLAME TREE PUBLISHING

In the same series:

MYTH, FOLKLORE AND ANCIENT HISTORY

Alexander the Great
Cyrus the Great
Genghis Khan
Hannibal of Carthage
Achilles the Hero
The Tale of Beowulf
The Four Branches of
the Mabinogi
African Myths
West African Folktales
East African Folktales
Central African Folktales
Southern African Folktales
Irish Fairy Tales
Celtic Myths
Scottish Myths
Arthurian Myths
Korean Folktales

Chinese Myths
Japanese Myths
Greek & Roman Myths
Indian Myths
Polynesian Island Myths
Native American Myths
Aztec Myths
Norse Myths
Viking Folktales
Myths of Babylon
Egyptian Myths
Persian Myths
Turkish Folktales
Slavic Myths
Hungarian Folktales
Czech Folktales
Serbian Folktales
Gawain and the Green Knight

Also available:

EPIC TALES DELUXE EDITIONS

African Myths & Tales
Celtic Myths & Tales
Irish Fairy Tales
Scottish Folk & Fairy Tales
Norse Myths & Tales
Viking Folk & Fairy Tales
Chinese Myths & Tales
Japanese Myths & Tales
Greek Myths & Tales

Egyptian Myths & Tales
Aztec Myths & Tales
Native American Myths & Tales
Persian Myths & Tales
Heroes & Heroines Myths & Tales
Witches, Wizards, Seers &
Healers Myths & Tales
Gods & Monsters Myths & Tales
Beasts & Creatures Myths & Tales

flametreepublishing.com
and all good bookstores